SARAH COOLEY

THE BONE FOREST

Copyright © 2023 by Sarah Cooley

All rights reserved. No part of this publication may be reproduced, stored or transmitted in any form or by any means, electronic, mechanical, photocopying, recording, scanning, or otherwise without written permission from the publisher. It is illegal to copy this book, post it to a website, or distribute it by any other means without permission.

First edition

ISBN: 9798853036987

This book was professionally typeset on Reedsy. Find out more at reedsy.com

Dedicated to my mom and dad, for always encouraging me to chase my dreams.

And to Matt, my love, for your unwavering belief in me.

This book exists thanks to the three of you.

Prologue

The gnarled, bare branches of the ancient oak trees cast shadows across the blanket of snow covering the earth below. Silence loomed and only the faint breeze and rare piping of birdsong broke its reverie.

A sudden crash sent birds fluttering out of the trees, and the sound of snow crunching under someone's boots inched closer and closer. Clara lifted the camera to her eye once more, adjusting the lens to focus on the maze of trees. She took another quick snap before pausing to flip through the photos she'd just captured.

As she stood, silently critiquing her work, her partner, Jason, walked up behind her, huffing, and puffing with each step. Exhausted, he threw his pack to the ground before collapsing on a nearby stump. Jason was tall and in decent shape, but he was no outdoorsman, despite living in a town surrounded entirely by woods.

"Can we take a breather?"

Clara scoffed, not bothering to look up from her camera. They'd been hiking several hours already, rarely stopping to rest. The cutting January wind sliced through their clothes with little effort. Snot mercilessly ran from Jason's nostrils.

"Oh, come on we're almost there! I'd like to make it to the creek before the sun goes down."

Jason rolled his eyes. "You go ahead then; I need a break." He pulled a water bottle from his bag, gulping down its contents.

"We shouldn't separate, especially in this area." The thought of walking through the forest alone made Clara's voice waver.

"It'll be fine," he responded, his sharp tone catching Clara off guard, "it's not that far ahead. I know how to get there. You go on ahead and I'll catch up."

Jason took Clara's hand and raised it gently to his lips. The simple, soothing gesture smoothing the worry from her delicate features.

"I'll be right behind you," he reassured her, "I just need a minute to catch my breath."

Clara squeezed his hand in return, leaning down to plant a quick kiss on his forehead.

"Fine, but don't be long," she shouted over her shoulder as she walked away, "and call if you need me!"

Clara's eyes were bright and alert, her camera at the ready. She was sore from head to toe, and her cheeks burned from the frigid wind. A few more steps and the echo of trickling water grabbed her attention. She steered toward it, nearly slipping on the wet ground. Clara pushed through the brush and into the clearing beyond. A bright smile crossed her face.

Untouched white frost surrounded a steady flowing stream. Clara's first instinct was to call out to Jason so he could share this experience with her. But, in that moment she chose to be greedy—to take in the magic by herself for just a little longer.

She inched closer to the creek; the pads of her boots sinking into the ground. When she reached the edge, she lowered herself to the ground and slid off one of her gloves. She dipped her fingers into the water, sending an icy shiver down her spine.

Glimmering prisms of light filtered down through the clouds, creating a blinding glare as it reflected off the snow. Clara lifted a hand to shield her gaze.

A branch snapped sharply in the distance. Clara went rigid. She sent a frantic glance in the direction of the noise, her heart thundering in her chest.

A massive, majestic buck stood just across the creek, his tall antlers curving toward the sky, its black, shimmering eyes taking her in. The buck's moist snout flared as it sniffed the air, and she quickly adjusted her stance, trying not to move too suddenly. She lifted the camera to her eye, carefully framing the perfect shot in her lens.

Just as she moved to press the shutter release, something rustled in the distance, catching the buck's attention. Its enormous head jerked to the left, his muscular form tight and alert. Sensing that her chance was slipping away, Clara hurriedly snapped the picture, only for the creature to instantly turn and dart back into the cover of the forest.

"Shit!" she growled, jerking the camera away from her face. Clara skimmed through her photos once again, irritated with herself for waiting so long. Her heart sank when she landed on a blurred image of the deer. The form of the animal was recognizable, but the creature's distinct face and features blended into the background.

A string of curses flew from her lips. She kicked her foot into the dirt, resisting the urge to toss her camera into the creek. Focusing her eyes into the woods, Clara tried to see what had caused the buck to run. Ultimately, it didn't matter. The buck was gone, any hope of a photograph swept away with it. It was time for her to focus on the reason they came out here.

"Not far from where her trail went cold," she whispered to herself.

"Clara!"

She flinched and turned toward the sound of Jason's voice echoing through the trees.

"Jesus, what the hell does he want now?" Clara grumbled.

"Clara!" Jason's voice rang out again; a few startled birds clamored out of the trees. Her heart seized with panic. If he continued to yell, he would scare off any animals that might be close. She had lost her chance at the buck; she wouldn't let Jason's stupidity rip away the chance of something else coming along.

"Christ, Jay," Clara hissed through gritted teeth, storming back toward where she left Jason. Once again, her name sounded through the wilderness, closer this time.

"He better have a damn good reason for this shit."

She quickened her pace, beads of sweat formed on her temples as she pushed her aching muscles to keep going.

A smile teased at the corners of her mouth as she shoved her way into the small clearing. She shook the powder out of her hair.

"What is it, Jay? Did you find some…" Clara trailed off.

The clearing was empty. Her smile fell. Her eyes darted to all corners of the clearing as she circled the area.

"Jason?"

Surely, at any moment, he would come popping out of the foliage, a goofy grin on his face. Her skin tingled with anticipation, but the time never came. There was no response.

"Jason! What the hell!? Where are you?"

Clara's eyes traced the wood line, searching for any trace of movement. Her feet wandered slowly as she scanned the distance and she stumbled when her right foot slammed into something bulky. When she caught her balance, Clara looked down and saw Jason's hiking pack. It was turned over, the top left gaping open as the contents spilled out onto the ground. Clara dropped to her knees, her trembling hands hovering over his belongings, not sure what to pick up first. Terror wrapped its icy fingers around her neck.

"Jason!"

Her scream ricocheted between the trees, distorting her voice, making it sound inhuman. Hot tears blurred her vision, and she scrambled to shove Jason's things back into the bag. When she rose to her feet again, what she saw on the dirt ahead of her filled her with absolute horror.

A few feet away from the stump, leading toward another wall of trees, was a haphazard trail carved into the snow. Something large had clearly been dragged through the brush and snow. No footsteps, just one large line, as if someone had yanked something heavy along with about as much grace as one would haul a sack of trash. Clara's feet moved of their own volition. She ignored the nagging voice in her mind telling her that she should turn back.

"J-Jason?" she whimpered.

As she followed the trail, the trees parted, and the drag marks became more chaotic. In her periphery, she saw strange markings carved into the trunk of a tree. The gouges were enormous, slicing clean through bark and nearly cleaving the tree in half. She struggled to raise her camera back to her eyes.

Clara took a picture. It was all she could think to do, the only message her brain was capable of sending.

Bile burned the back of her throat as the acrid smell of blood rose from the ground around her. As she walked, the white flakes at her feet became stained with red. Just off the path, a shred of Jason's blue jacket was matted against the base of a mangled tree trunk. It sat soaking in a pool of blood. The sight wrenched the air from her lungs, the tremors in her hands now flooding to the rest of her body.

As she trudged forward down the blood tainted path, her foot caught in a tangle of tree roots hidden by the snow. Clara tumbled forward and let out a yelp as she collapsed to the ground. Rolling to her back, she pulled her foot free. Glancing upward toward the sky, only meager slices of light were visible through the thick, scraggly canopy that shrouded her in dusky shadow.

The air was thick, the scent of iron overwhelming. Her stomach turned and she rolled to her side, allowing her body to purge itself. Clear vomit spilled from her lips. Her vision slowly cleared; tears streamed down her cheeks Clara forced herself to stand. Her legs were weak and unsteady under her weight.

Everything around her was covered in blood. It streaked across the dead bushes and bare branches, puddling into the dips and crevices of the landscape around her.

"Oh my God... oh my..." The words barely escaped her mouth. Her breaths were short and unfruitful as her senses became frenzied.

Her mind was telling her to run, but her body was still weak and frozen with fear. As she frantically took in her surroundings, her eyes focused in on one of the pools of blood nearest her foot. She choked down another surge of sour bile when she noticed small chunks of white flesh and pink muscle gleaming in the silver light. A few feet away a sharp sliver of ivory bone sat discarded on the ground, stained with blackened innards.

"JASON!" Clara screeched. The sudden sound of her voice was piercing against the stillness that surrounded her.

Clara broke. Her sobs came in a torrent of choked gasps and whimpers. She buried her snot-dampened face in the sleeves of her wet jacket. It was all she could do to muffle the sound of her screams.

A gust of hot air fluttered against the back of her neck, ruffling her hair. She froze, the hairs on her arms and neck standing on end. Clara swallowed her tears and reluctantly opened her eyes. She could feel the presence of someone standing behind her. The few beams of sunlight filtering in through the trees allowed her to see its massive shadow as it creeped up silently behind her.

The silence surrounding her was deafening. She heard her heart pound inside her ears with every beat. Clara could feel the creature's immense and terrifying strength. The air shivered with electricity.

She held her breath until her lungs ached. Millimeter by millimeter she turned toward the sound of its breathing. She forced herself to keep her eyes open. Her chest ached from the pounding in her ribcage.

"Clara." She sucked in an agonizing breath. Tears streamed down her cheeks. It sounded just like Jason. "Help. Me."

The words were quiet and strained, like he was hurt. Clara's mind went blank, and she whipped around.

Its shadow grew, enveloping her in darkness as it rose to its full height. Clara's vision went white, the ringing in her ears increasing to a thunderous peak. She couldn't bear to look upon it directly, seeing it only in flashes. The jagged points of its claws, and its impossibly infinite rows of teeth.

She opened her mouth to scream but her cries would die before they ever hit the air. Her wild eyes bulged in horror as the audible tearing of her flesh from the muscle startled the birds in the trees nearby. They scattered, fluttering off through the branches of the forest canopy. The forest fell quiet once again.

Chapter 1

Alessa couldn't remember the last time she slept through the night. She either tossed and turned until the dark hours of the morning, or drifted into a temporary peace, only for the nightmares to come. She ached for a deep sleep to smother the horrors of her imagination.

She sniffed and rubbed her eyes, straightening herself in the chair that faced her bedroom window. In the early moments of the dew-covered mornings, the sky reminded her of stained glass, a miraculous kaleidoscope of colors reflecting off the snow.

The clock struck 6:30 AM. Alessa's alarm let out a shrill cry, but she was prepared and silenced the machine before it finished its first chime.

Moving on autopilot, Alessa went through the motions of readying herself for another day. She glanced in the mirror by her door and checked her appearance. Her sallow, tired face stared back at her.

"Alessa! Breakfast is ready!" Her mother's comforting voice rang through the house, distracting her from the imposter in the mirror. No point in dwelling on her appearance now. Throwing her backpack over one shoulder, her eyes landed on the pile of papers stacked neatly next to her laptop – as usual, the photo on top sent her thoughts into a chaotic spiral.

CHAPTER 1

"*MISSING*," the giant, bold word stretched across the top of the page. The headline sat atop a professional photograph of a young woman, her scarlet hair over her shoulders in a partial up-do. She had a bright smile on her face and features that closely resembled Alessa's. She picked up the stack of papers and grabbed the staple gun from her drawer, then headed toward the sound of her mother's call.

The smell of eggs and bacon guided Alessa toward the kitchen. The curtains had been opened to let in the morning sun, shining a spotlight upon a pillow and a pile of folded blankets sitting on the couch facing the fireplace; family photographs were displayed with pride on the mantle. Several of the photos had been gently laid face down on the wood. Alessa forced herself to look away when her mother emerged from the kitchen.

Lillian Hale was the picture of perfection. As always, her pristine blonde hair was in a tight bun, not a strand out of place. Lily smiled warmly at her daughter and cupped her chin, giving her face a good once over before pulling away, clicking her tongue.

"You look tired, sweetheart. Have you been sleeping?"

Alessa shrugged and darted away from her prying gaze by dipping into the kitchen. Lily followed; lips pressed into a thin line. Alessa grabbed a few slices of bacon from the plate left out for her.

"Dad gone to work already?"

She didn't need to look at her mother to know she was frowning.

"Yes, he had to go in early again, but he'll be back before dinner."

Alessa hummed in response, not surprised, but a stabbing ache of disappointment still flared in her chest. Her mother seemed to sense it, coming closer to place a delicate palm on her shoulder.

"Work has just been really hard on him recently; it shouldn't go on for much longer." As she attempted to reassure her, Alessa resisted the urge to shrug her mother's hand off, the touch setting her more on edge.

"Sure, Mom," was all she could manage; she popped another piece of bacon into her mouth.

Lily sighed. "Be patient with your father, kiddo. He's doing the best he can, given the circumstances."

A white-hot flush of rage overtook her senses, and Alessa clenched her jaw shut to keep her spiteful thoughts from tumbling out of her mouth. She knew it wasn't her mother's fault, but her defense of his actions lit a vicious flame of resentment inside of her. All Alessa managed was a nod, afraid that if she opened her mouth, she wouldn't be able to control what came out.

Lily planted a brief kiss to her daughter's temple. "I'll see you tonight. Have a good day." Heels clicked rhythmically against the floor as Lily pulled away and walked out.

"Bye, Mom," Alessa mumbled, and ate one last piece.

Alessa took a deep breath as she stood on the front step of their home. The crisp, chilled air cooling the hot rage she felt just moments before. She waved her mother off as she backed out of the driveway and began her journey to school, her posters at the ready in her arms.

Alessa's family lived in a modest, upscale neighborhood, where the homes were scant but remarkable. Each exuded its own unique flair. Most, of them dated back to when the town was first settled in the 1800's and still retained their turn-of-the-century charm. However, pieces of modern flair could be seen here and there. A Tudor style home across the street had solar panels reflecting white sunlight, and a gothic looking Victorian was accentuated with a below ground pool. The forest created a wall around their cul-de-sac, with trees so tightly packed together they seemed impenetrable.

Alessa used to gaze upon the woods with wonder. These days, the sight of them froze the blood in her veins. As she walked along, she stapled a flier to each telephone pole she passed until there were none

CHAPTER 1

left untouched. The deeper into town she went, she found poles and bulletin boards with aging, sun-faded pictures–ones she'd posted weeks before. Alessa tore them down, and replaced them with new ones.

Aria Hale, 17 years old, had been missing since October, or to be more precise, two months and three days. One night she went to sleep, and the next morning she was gone, bed unmade, and belongings untouched.

Alessa remembered waking up that day. She relived the memory every morning. It was strange, she mused, how you can literally feel someone's absence in your bones. It was both agony and numbness, a limbo that left Alessa wondering if she should mourn or continue to hold out hope.

Seeing Aria smile, even though she was frozen in time, was one of her few motivations. She would do anything just to see her smile in person again. Alessa's bottom lip quivered as she stared at another posted sign. The colors molded together, smearing into an indiscernible mass as the tears built up. She squeezed her eyes shut, and choked down her sorrow before it could escape.

People didn't often talk about what it's like being related to a missing person: what it does to you, what it takes from you–being the one left behind. Alessa had never wondered before what it felt like to miss someone for the infinite future.

She focused on her movement, carefully placing one foot in front of the other. The distraction kept the tears at bay. Her sadness haunted her like a restless spirit. It was always there, just under the surface waiting for a moment when there weren't enough distractions to ward off her deepest anxieties. The worst part was feeling like everyone could see it. Every day, she faced looks of pity and embarrassment from people she used to call friends.

Alessa's breath fanned out in puffs of visible mist; she shivered as she approached yet another pole, carefully avoiding the uneven bricks jutting out of the sidewalk. A pair of older women, locked arm in arm, walked behind her and she swiveled on her heels, extending a flier toward them, and nearly smacking them in the face.

"Oh, Alessa, you startled us."

"Sorry Mrs. Anderson, Ms. McIntyre, just doing my usual rounds. Just want to make sure everyone gets one."

Gloria Henderson, their local librarian, nestled into her cozy winter sweater, embroidered with various farm animals in festive garments of their own. The curled ends of her stark white hair danced under a knit beanie. Her friend, Ruth McIntyre, clutched her arm, features pinched as if she smelled something foul.

She offered a couple of fliers to the women. Ruth hesitated, her nose wrinkling at the paper. Alessa did her best to hold her smile and Mrs. Anderson finally took them with a shaky, wrinkled hand, a tenderness in her expression.

"Thank you, dear. I'm sorry to hear that they haven't found her. Every morning and night, I pray for her. I hope she returns home safely soon."

"We appreciate it, Mrs. Anderson. I hope so too."

The librarian cleared her throat, awkwardness filling the space between them. Alessa tended to make people feel awkward these days. She took this as her queue to leave.

"If either of you see or hear anything…"

"Of course, dear. We'll keep our eyes and ears peeled. You just keep doing what you're doing."

Alessa nodded, stepping aside as the two women continued on. She locked eyes with Ruth, her sharp gaze glued to Alessa. She swore she saw the faintest quiver of a snarl on her lips before she spun away.

"You really shouldn't encourage her, Gloria." Alessa paused when she heard Ruth finally speak. "Everyone knows that girl is gone."

CHAPTER 1

Her grip around her fliers tightened. She chanced one more look at them, alarm propelling her forward when Gloria glanced back. Gloria's quiet shushing taunted Alessa as she turned the corner, feet pounding against concrete and eyes set forward.

If she kept going, she wouldn't have time to think about her sister, starved and freezing. She wouldn't have to think about her father, who'd turned over all the photographs of Aria they had on the mantle, unable to stomach seeing them any longer.

The streets soon became flooded with people as she entered the town center. Alessa always found Pine Hollow somewhat underwhelming but its mom-and-pop shops, and the singular, historic inn had a certain bit of charm. Every brick sidewalk coalesced into the town square, where a cobblestone roundabout encircled the town's true center, an ancient but magnificent stone clock tower. Natural ivy crept up the sides of the structure, almost making it look alive.

She offered weak smiles to those she brushed by on the sidewalk, as she purposely made her way from pole to pole. A cinnamon sugar scent traveled from the bakery, famously known for their French toast cupcakes. They were opening their doors for the day, and she gulped down the delicious smell as she drifted past the potted arrangements of yellow and pink tulips outside the similarly colored building.

"Excuse me, miss? Do you have a moment to talk about our Lord and Savior Jesus Christ?"

A genuine warmth filled her chest when she turned and saw Maya, her long-time friend standing behind her attempting to hold a semi-serious face. It wasn't working. Her overly dramatized southern accent made Alessa giggle.

Ever since Aria's disappearance, Maya had been her only real source of comfort and support; the only one who could draw an authentic laugh from her hollow shell. Alessa wondered how she would have survived the last couple of months without her.

The girl made her way toward Maya's car: a beat up but very well-loved Lincoln. It was an old clunker that Maya's parents handed down to her.

"You're the last person who should be preaching about Jesus," Alessa teased, wiggling a finger at her. Maya rolled her eyes in playful response.

"Come on, slowpoke, let's roll."

Alessa always felt a calm settle over her when she was in Maya's car. It was their own little island, away from the adults and the rest of the world. The radio played the typical top 40 playlist, and the air inside had absorbed some of Maya's wildflower perfume.

"How was it this morning?" Maya asked. Alessa shrugged nonchalantly, poking at a hole in the leg of her jeans.

"Same as every day, I suppose. Dad gone before I got up, Mom struggling to make eye contact but still defending Dad."

Alessa had always struggled when it came to untangling the feelings she had about her parents, especially after Aria went missing. She knew that they loved her but sometimes, on the bad days, they acted as if their only daughter had died.

Alessa felt a tickle against the back of her hand. Startled out of her thoughts, she looked up, tears spilling down her cheeks. Maya was holding her hand. The softness of her skin was a comforting anchor bringing her back to the present. Maya slowly intertwined their fingers.

"Is there anything I can do?" Maya asked.

Alessa glanced down at their interlocked hands, the sensation of her gentle touch causing her heart to clamber madly in her chest. Alessa locked in on Maya's gaze, and in those fleeting seconds, a million questions rose to her mind. Maya leaned closer, an intensity in her expression that made Alessa's curiosity spike. It almost seemed like there was something in particular Maya wanted her to say. Alessa's

CHAPTER 1

throat went bone dry.

"This helps," Alessa whispered, her brain short-circuiting with all the possibilities.

Maya leaned away, a frown flashing across her lips so quickly Alessa thought she was seeing things. It was replaced with an easy grin. Maya's eyes drifted to their joined hands and she cleared her throat.

"Well, whatever you need. You know I've got you," she said and turned back toward the wheel. As they made their way toward school, their hands remained clasped and resting on the center console between them.

Alessa's throat tightened as they passed the police station. The mere sight of the building itself made her blood boil. She'd spent weeks being dragged in and out of that place, bombarded with questions but never answers, until one day everything just... stopped. Her parents seemed reluctant to push them for answers for reasons she failed to understand.

Police Chief Gavin Roswell leaned casually against the outside wall of the precinct. Alessa's eyes narrowed as he entered her view. Nursing a thermos of coffee, he watched morning crowds go by. Their eyes met for just a moment. He strained a smile her way and tipped his hat. A wave of irritation rolled over her and she twisted away, unable to stomach holding his gaze for another second.

"My grandfather is holding a special prayer for Aria during this Sunday's service." Maya's voice was a welcome reprieve. "I know it's been hard to go back, but I think it'll be really nice; we'd love to see you there."

Maya fidgeted in her seat. Alessa could tell she was nervous about bringing it up. Her family's church was a huge part of their community, and the Hale family had once attended Sunday service religiously each week. Of course, that was before Aria. However, her mother had somehow managed to hold on to her faith, and still managed to follow the flock to the pew every Sunday.

Regardless of Alessa's jilted relationship with God, this was important to Maya, and it was a kind gesture — no matter how uncomfortable the thought of returning made her.

"Maybe."

She knew she made the right decision when she saw Maya's smile return. "That's all I need to hear."

After whipping her car into the student parking lot, Maya pulled a hiking bag from the back seat and dropped it in Alessa's lap.

"Kay, I put a few extra Cliff bars inside this time, and Mom made some hot chocolate this morning, so I put some in a thermos for you. It's there on the side."

"I don't deserve you."

Maya made a tsking noise and shook her head. "Now, now, I will not have you besmirching my dearest friend."

Alessa burst out laughing, her shoulders trembling with the force of it. When she caught her breath, she noticed Maya's expression. Her lips were tight. She looked like she'd seen a ghost.

"Oh shit, it's Noah," she whispered. Alessa almost strained her neck with how quickly she turned to look at him. Noah Harrison, Aria's boyfriend.

"God, he looks..." Alessa started.

"Awful?"

"I wasn't going to say it. But... yeah."

The boy looked like he hadn't slept in days, if not weeks. His already unkempt hair was tangled into knots, and his shirt looked like it hadn't been washed in days.

"Have you spoken to him since she went missing?" Maya asked, and Alessa shook her head. Alessa tore her eyes away. It was time to go.

"Right, I'll meet you back here after school. If anyone asks, I've got the stomach bug," she said, all business.

"And I'll get all your catch-up work. Yeah, yeah, I know the drill."

Alessa smiled. "Thank you."

Maya held out her hand. "Give me some of those. I want to post them on the bulletin boards."

Alessa swallowed down a knot of emotions and nodded, silently handing over the rest of her fliers.

The two stepped out of the car, Alessa hoisting the bag over her shoulders and securing the buckle across her chest.

"Hey."

Maya hesitated, and then stepped closer, placing a hand on the back of Alessa's head, bringing their foreheads together. The closeness of their faces made Alessa's heart flutter. Through dark lashes, Maya glanced at Alessa's lips, her eyes lingering for just a few seconds too long. Alessa forgot how to breathe.

"Be careful, okay?"

Alessa nodded, a pink flush hot on the apples of her cheeks. "Of course."

As Maya pulled away Alessa swore she saw a flicker of disappointment in her eyes. It was just a flash, and it was gone in an instant.

"Good luck."

Maya gave her a playful nudge as they parted ways. Alessa played along and let out a weak laugh, despite the sinking feeling in her stomach. The further away Maya walked, the worse it felt.

"May the Lord guide my search," Alessa joked. It earned her a wink before Maya turned away. Alessa waited until her friend began to blend in with the rest of the crowd.

Spinning on her heels, Alessa fled away from the school and toward the wooded tree line at the edge of the property. She'd long ago discovered the best route for avoiding the school's security officers, and there was plenty of sports equipment for her to hide behind, just in case. She reached the trees without issue and didn't hesitate before stepping through. Once she was sure she wouldn't be seen, she pulled an old piece of paper from her jacket. Unfolded, it revealed a map of the woods surrounding their town. Large sections of the map were already crossed out in angry, red marker.

Alessa clicked open her marker and circled the section she wanted to cover. Just a few miles away from the church, it would probably take her just over an hour if she hauled ass.

She folded up the map, stuffing it in her back pocket before she could talk herself out of the search. Rolling, gray storm clouds threatened overhead, but Alessa rolled her shoulders and continued into the darkened woods.

Chapter 2

Roswell was no stranger to the ins and outs of Pine Hollow; he was just one of many folks born and raised in the same town he planned to die. It was almost an unspoken tradition here. Those who were born in Pine Hollow rarely left. Nestled in the mountains of Black Hills, South Dakota, Pine Hollow was barely a speck of dust on the map, boasting a measly population that barely breached 150. The closest neighboring town was several miles down the mountain and officially labeled a ghost town after being abandoned in the 1950s.

Unless they were coming up for an express purpose, most did not chance the narrow, winding roads that led there. The surrounding forest was full of towering evergreens, their appearance reminding Roswell of a silent, vigilant army. One step in the wrong direction could get you killed out here, so visitors were few and far between. Roswell compared it to being on their own little island, isolated from the troubles of the rest of the world, and that was exactly how he liked it.

The chief didn't flinch as he gulped a mouthful of steaming coffee. After all these years of guzzling the burnt swill his wife sent for him, the inside of his mouth was mostly numb.

Alessa Hale's face flashed into his mind, in this memory she was pleading with him, eyes red and runny. She was asking where her sister was, and he didn't know how to answer her. He tightened his grip on his thermos and shook his head to hurl the thoughts out.

The chime of the front door opening made him jump. The questioning expression of his Deputy Chief, Shirley Powell, replaced Alessa's face. She held a coffee of her own in one hand while the other fidgeted with the radio clipped to her belt.

"Morning, Shirley."

"Good morning, Boss." Shirley gestured down the road where Alessa was heading. "That the Hale girl?"

Roswell nodded with a grunt. It was his trademark, something Shirley was not unfamiliar with.

She cleared her throat. "We got another message from Father Samuel. A few more of his patrons reported bear activity near the church. He tried not to make a big deal of it, but you know how he is."

Roswell chuckled. "Yes, yes. We should probably make an appearance before the poor man has a coronary."

He pushed himself off the wall and eased by her to get back inside. Shirley glanced back down the road, following the ghost of Alessa's presence. Across the street, a flier with Aria's face on it fluttered in the breeze.

Green needles sprinkled with snow passed by Shirley's eyes in a blur as Roswell drove them to the church. It was about a twenty-minute drive south of the town square. The further they went the sparser the houses became, and the cobblestone roads smoothed out into flat pavement.

"Remind me how many sightings this makes," Roswell said.

"Three in the last month, and one wolf sighting near the town square."

His rough hand massaged his stubbled jaw. It was a peculiar theme, multiple dangerous predators wandering far away from their natural homes and into town. There were no attacks yet, thank God, but the sudden confidence these animals had was a coincidence they couldn't ignore.

What made it even more befuddling was the time of year. This was their typical period of hibernation. From October until around April or May, the bears were mostly dormant, but that didn't mean something couldn't disturb them.

The last thing they needed was a mother bear with her cubs to come strolling through town and have someone get a bit too curious. Granted, it wasn't breeding season either – but the way things were going it seemed better to be safe than sorry. Worry lines carved deep creases into Roswell's forehead.

Shirley peered up at the lone standing church of Pine Hollow, St. Lawrence Catholic Parish. It's peaked roof and tall steeple towered over the landscape around them. The structure itself had been around since the town was founded, but age and weather damage called for regular repairs and upgrades over the years. The entire campus of St. Lawrence was quaint and welcoming. The white paneling had started to fade and show its age, but the tall stained-glass windows were still something to be marveled at. Father Samuel did his best to keep up the grounds, but thankfully, their community was more than willing to lend a hand from time to time.

A huge crow shimmied its midnight feathers, sitting on the cross atop the steeple. Roswell flinched when the crow released a grating cry into the air. He glared at the bird when it took off, watching it become an inky black blur against an ashen sky. The heavy front door creaked open on ancient hinges, and as they reached the top step, Father Samuel had emerged to greet his visitors.

The man shuffled toward them, his body beginning to show the deficits of aging. Despite his weak muscles and aching joints, he was active for a man in his seventies. He moved with purpose.

Black robes billowed around his towering frame. He had a lean build and stood a solid six feet despite having lost a few inches of height in his golden years. What little hair he had left was thin and patchy, but he had the eyes of a much younger man who was still brimming with strength and charisma.

Father Samuel extended his hand to Roswell with a welcoming smile.

"I see you received my message; I wish you both a splendid morning. May the Lord smile upon you both today."

Roswell shook his hand firmly. "Good morning, Father, and thank you for accommodating us on such short notice. We know you likely weren't expecting us so early."

Samuel shushed him with the graceful wave of his pale hand. "Please, think nothing of it. I'm simply thrilled to see it being taken so seriously. I haven't experienced any sightings myself, but many of the Parrish have discussed their concerns with me."

The two nodded and Shirley slid out the small notepad she kept in her back pocket, pen at the ready.

"Then maybe you'll be able to fill in some blanks. The reports have been vaguer than I'd like."

"Absolutely. I'll take you to where they were spotted. It's just around the back."

They broke apart to make way for the pastor to squeeze between them. Roswell jumped forward, offering an arm for Father Samuel to grab in case he lost in balance on the slick, ice covered stairs. He shot the chief a grateful smile. Roswell and Shirley stayed close at his side as he led them around the corner.

Behind the church was a small parking lot, as well as a playground resting on a patch of grass that was half the size of a football field. Beyond the property line loomed the ever-present row of trees separating their town from the forest surrounding them. Here, the only thing that protected Father Samuel's flock against the wandering predators was a picket fence enclosing the play area.

"Mr. Hanson claims to have seen a bear coming through the tree line just over there." Father Samuel pointed to a small opening in the trees past the swing sets.

"Did he provide any details about the bear's appearance? Size, coloring, anything like that?" Roswell inquired.

"He was certain it was a brown bear, said it looked like an adult, maybe a female."

Shirley diligently scribbled down every detail. Roswell pursed his lips.

"Has anyone seen any cubs around here?"

Father Samuel shook his head. "Not that I've been told. It's just so strange. They usually never wander this close to town. If I'm not mistaken, they are usually asleep this time of year."

"You would be correct, Father."

Roswell propped his hands up on his hips. His superhero pose is what Shirley always called it.

"Did anyone else besides Mr. Hanson see the bear?"

"Yes, last week after our Wednesday evening service, Samantha Reid, from the bakery, approached me and claimed to have spotted a bear in the same area. But it was dark, and she wasn't one-hundred percent certain of what she saw. I wanted to wait until we were sure before I called you both down here."

"We appreciate all your help, Father," Shirley said.

Roswell faced Father Samuel. "All right, we'll give the area a good sweep. You hang back and we'll return shortly."

"Wonderful. Please let me know if there is anything you need. Check with Sylvia when you return and there will be fresh coffee waiting for you."

"Thank you, Father, that's very kind," Shirley said.

"You both have more than earned it. Please be safe and may the Lord bless your search."

He bowed his head before heading back to the church, his robes swirling around his feet as if he were gliding.

In a matter of minutes, the pair reached the tree line – the church they left behind was naught but a speck across the wide grassy field. Roswell took the lead as they entered the forest, carving the simplest path he could across the bumpy terrain. Though they said nothing, both officers were on high alert. Shirley's hand hovered over her side-arm, eyes darting from the trees to the ground as she moved, carefully keeping her balance, and remaining wary of potential predators lurking in the shadows. She watched the back of Roswell's head as it jerked to the side.

"There."

As she moved up quietly alongside Roswell, he pointed to the imprint of tracks left behind in the snow. They followed the footprints to a tall patch of gnarled bushes and gridlocked trees. The thick foliage made it impossible to see any further into the woods. Roswell held up a hand, signaling her to wait as he unclipped his gun from his holster and gesturing for her to do the same. Shirley lifted her weapon to eye level in a smooth, practiced motion.

Roswell continued to shove his way through the brush, a few of the branches snapping back and leaving shallow slices in his cheeks. The officer squared his shoulders and continued pushing into the brush until he emerged on the other side. Shirley twisted her way out behind him seconds later.

His gaze fell to the ground, his back muscles visibly tense through his now-tattered uniform shirt. Shirley followed his stare, and a bone-deep shiver froze her in place. Her expression matched Roswell's feeling of confusion, and he swiveled his head around to look at his partner, searching for validation in her eyes and trying to make sense of the madness in front of them.

Much of the grass in the small clearing had been ripped from the ground completely, chunks of earth torn out with it, leaving deep divots engraved in the soil. Shirley slowly approached a nearby evergreen, its thick trunk mangled with deep, claw-like slashes. Roswell's gaze locked in on Shirley – who was doing the same, albeit less calmly. He could see the whites of her eyes, vibrant with fear. Her gun had been placed back in its holster - but she kept a firm grip on the handle, her hand never once shaking. Roswell nodded his head, gesturing toward the direction the markings lead. There was a millisecond of hesitation, but she trusted him. Shirley fell in close behind and the two of them followed the tracks, pushing deeper into the woods. The path of the struggle grew in both intensity and size the longer they followed it. The pair came to a halt in the center of the carnage.

Shirley stopped to examine a set of deep slashes on a broad tree trunk. Noticing that the scratches started at eye level, she let her chin tilt upward, squinting her eyes as she peered up the base of the massive blue spruce. Her jaw dropped in shock when she realized the slashes in the bark rose at least seven feet high, ten in some spots. There was no defined pattern to the blood spatter, the spray could be seen in all directions. But beyond the visceral calamity that was left behind here in the woods – the most disturbing thing they found was, in fact, what they didn't find: a body. There were no victim remains found, no animal carcasses, no bear, no... nothing. At least, nothing whole enough to give them any answers. Overcome by anxiety, Shirley suddenly hunched forward. Hot bile burst from her gullet and into the blood-stained snow near her feet. Roswell shushed her softly as he rubbed the space between her shoulder blades.

"Take a moment, Shirl. Here."

He passed her the water canteen from his belt and watched her take a few careful sips. When she righted herself, she flashed him a weak smile of thanks.

Ribbons of glistening pink intestines festered in the open air; some hanging from low branches and vines while others were strewn across the ground. A gruesome pile of torn flesh squished unexpectedly under Roswell's shoe as he turned to view the scene a full 360 degrees. Tossed haplessly to the side of the path, he saw the remnants of a human hand with bent and broken fingers, bones protruding through the decaying flesh at ugly angles.

"Jesus," Shirley gasped, "what kind of bear does this?"

They had lost the bear tracks a quarter of a mile back, and he certainly did not see any now.

While he desperately tried to remain stoic, the bones in his jaw ached with tension. His teeth were clenched tightly, and his temples pulsed in protest. Decades of living in Pine Hollow, of playing in these woods as a child and hunting in these woods as a man — he'd never seen anything like this.

"I don't think we're dealing with a bear here, Shirl."

Shirley knitted her eyes tightly shut and took one more centering breath before she allowed herself to move. She was careful, training her gaze on the ground directly in front of her, letting her chief take the lead.

Shirley heard a crunch under a thin layer of snow. She squatted, using her gloved hand to gently uncover what would hide beneath. She slowly revealed a couple of sharp-edged, white fragments laying in the dirt near her feet. She snatched up a broken twig from a nearby bush and carefully picked through the shards. A few of the more delicate pieces fell away. Shirley found a larger piece near the bottom of the tiny pile, curved and broken but about the size of her hand.

"Oh, God."

Roswell perked up. "What is it?"

Shirley wordlessly waved him over, and he moved just behind her looking down over her shoulder at the pile, puzzled. As Shirley moved to the side to give him a better view, what he was seeing became a lot clearer. Partly uncovered from the snow was a human jawbone, smeared with blood, cracked, and missing some teeth.

"We're going to have to call in some more guys," Shirley said, out of breath.

"Powell, we're going to have to call in *all* the guys."

"On it."

Roswell discreetly watched Shirley as she grabbed her radio and called their location in to dispatch. He knew she'd only seen a few dead bodies in her career, and of which were mangled and discarded in such a brutal, inhuman way. Crime around Pine Hollow mostly consisted of the occasional misfit teen hanging out in an abandoned building or a drunken brawl in the pub parking lot over the score of a football game. But nothing like this, never like this.

The brush rustled and both of their heads turned in unison toward the direction of the sound. They raised their guns in near perfect tandem, shoulders squared, feet planted. Shirley waited for Roswell's next command.

"This is Chief Gavin Roswell of the Pine Hollow Police Department. If there's someone there, come out now with your arms raised over your head!"

There was another rustle, and then a small, frightened voice.

"I'm sorry, I'm coming out!"

A hand emerged from the undergrowth, followed shortly by another, both of them empty. They lowered their weapons as the petite form revealed itself. Shirley shoved her gun back into the holster.

"Alessa? Jesus!" she groaned.

Alessa steadied herself on quivering knees. Her cheeks were red and wind-burnt, a film of tears glimmered at the corners of her blue eyes. Both of the officers sagged with sighs of relief and Alessa released a choked breath once the chief put his weapon away.

"What in God's name are you doing out here, Alessa? Shouldn't you be in school?"

The powerful rumble of his voice made Alessa wince. Her arms fell limp to her sides and she took a step back, glancing around to reorient herself.

"Wh-What happened? What is this?" Alessa stuttered.

Shirley approached Alessa slowly and outstretched her arms to either side to focus the girl's attention on her. Roswell cursed himself, having momentarily forgotten what they found and what Alessa had unwittingly stumbled into. He stayed back, not wanting to crowd her, but he could see in the young woman's eyes, lost in horror.

"That's blood... oh–oh my..." Alessa's words faded. Shirley moved even closer, careful not to touch her until absolutely necessary. Alessa leaned away, her head darting around frantically.

"Alessa, I need you to breathe, all right? You're hyperventilating."

Alessa heard none of her pleas. The color seeped from her complexion when she noticed the fractured jawbone on the ground. One of her hands lifted to trace the curve of her own jaw.

"Oh my God... oh my God..."

Alessa whirled around, vomiting up her morning bacon and a few splashes of hot cocoa. Shirley reacted swiftly, keeping Alessa's hair out of her face. Tears mingled with the bile and snot and Alessa wiped her face on her coat sleeve. Roswell passed Shirley his canteen, just like before. Alessa trembled as she took it, trying to calm her frantic breathing between small sips of water.

Shirley stood in front of her, gently taking her by the shoulders, so they were eye to eye.

"Ms. Hale, we need to get you home right away. This is a potential crime scene."

She blinked slowly at Shirley. "Do you think it could be her?"

Shirley's lips pressed into a hard line and her eyes shifted to Roswell for an answer. He gave his partner a silent but firm shake of his head. "We don't know anything yet. Come with me and we'll head back to the car." Shirley wrapped an arm around Alessa's shoulders, purposefully steering her away from the massacre they had stumbled upon. "We'll need to alert your parents."

Alessa dug her heels into the ground. "Why," Alessa asked, "you just said you didn't think..."

Shirley didn't speak, but her eyes said it all. Alessa gasped for air.

"Alessa, breathe! You need to breathe!"

Alessa sobbed, the horrible, wrenching wails scraping Roswell's eardrums. Birds went streaking through the sky as her cries hit the air.

"No, no, no, no..." Alessa wept.

Alessa fell into Shirley's arms as she screamed, blinded by her tears. Aria's name became a whimper on her lips as the officer cradled the girl in her arms like a child. Roswell stood over them, frowning worriedly. The wind howled, sounding almost mournful, as the girl cried, and he called for backup.

Chapter 3

Four Months Ago

Alessa groaned and snuggled deeper into the cocoon of blankets she had wrapped herself in. She faced the window, hoping a glimpse of the night sky and its dazzling stars might ease her into a peaceful slumber. Alessa imagined herself among them – a bright and carefree celestial force. The promise of dances along the Milky Way lured her into the beginnings of sleep.

The ever-looming date of Aria's high school graduation had Alessa constantly on edge. She had been warring with herself over it for months. The day used to feel so far away. Whenever it came up in conversation, Alessa would laugh it off and remind herself that she had years to go. Those years quickly fell away.

A muffled thump from the next room shook the wall behind her, jarring her back into the waking world. Anger rose in her chest – but she forcefully pushed it back down. There was whimpering coming from her sister's room. She pressed her ear against the wall, palms, and cheek flush against the cool surface. As she listened, Aria's cries grew louder.

Alessa kicked the blankets out from around her body as she vaulted to her feet and rushed next door. Unfortunately, Alessa was not the only sister who had been having trouble sleeping lately. Neither of

CHAPTER 3

the girls knew why Aria's nightmares suddenly manifested. In fact, her older sister had slept like a rock most of her life – so much so that people made jokes that she would surely miss the apocalypse if it happened after bedtime. During these last few months, however, Alessa was often startled awake by the sounds of soft weeping or wrenching howls on the other side of the wall. Weeks had passed since Aria's last incident, and secretly the two of them had hoped that they were over.

Alessa paused in the hallway. The door to Aria's room was open already. She stopped just outside the doorway and arched her neck to peek inside. She heard sniffling, and then bare feet thumping on the carpeted floor.

"It's all right, sweetheart. Keep taking deep breaths for me, okay?"

It was her mother. Alessa leaned a little closer. She froze when she finally saw Aria. Her sister was sitting on the floor, knees pulled tightly to her chest. Their mother was kneeling before her with her back to the door. Alessa caught only fleeting glimpses her sister's face. Her eyes were red-rimmed and puffy.

Her mother spoke to Aria. Soothing her in hushed tones. Alessa couldn't make out the words, but they sounded strange on her tongue. Lillian's hands were moving. Something shook, like a small rattle, and then came a pop. Aria's head was swaying back and forth, tangled hair tumbling over her shoulders. Her mother leaned in close to Aria, her voice lowering to a whisper once again.

Alessa strained to hear, but it was all for naught. She bit back a sigh and settled for what she could see. Her mother gingerly placed something on the bedside table. In the dim glow of the lamp Alessa could see a bright orange medication bottle. Lily stepped away to fix her sister's bedding. Aria continued to rock herself, sitting quietly on the floor, cradling a small pill in her hand.

She looked like she had been crying and her eyelids hung lazily from exhaustion. Alessa wanted so badly to comfort her. Her mother's presence ultimately kept her away but having to stand there, unable to help was agony.

"Here, down the hatch."

Alessa moved out of sight as her mother stepped back into view and handed Aria a glass of water. Aria gazed up at her, a weak smile danced across her lips. Lillian stood vigilant, a mother bear hovering over her cub. Aria forced the pill down with a few sips of water, handing the glass back to her mother. Alessa leaned in close to the crack in the door, trying to get a better view. She slowed her breathing to avoid making extra noise. While her mother remained oblivious, Aria's small smile widened into a smirk when she detected her sister's presence. She shot a pointed look at their mother and lifted a single finger to her lips in a shushing manner. Alessa choked down a giggle and nodded. She pointed to Aria and proceeded to use her hands to signal out a silent message to her sibling.

'You OK?' she relayed as best she could.

Aria blinked slowly, a dazed and sleepy grin now on her face. Aria eventually managed to nod.

Alessa wasn't sure if she believed her, and in other circumstances she'd try to whittle more information out of her, but what was she to do? She was no longer crying and the shaking in her shoulders finally settled. Alessa watched Lily pull back the blankets on the bed and scanned the bottle on the table once more. Whatever their mother gave her, she hoped it worked.

As their mother lead her eldest daughter toward her bed, Aria looked over her shoulder and winked at Alessa. The knot of tension between Alessa's brows softened when Aria's head hit the pillow. Alessa tiptoed back to her room. She was careful to stay close to the wall, knowing exactly which sections of the floor had the tendency to squeak.

Climbing back into bed, she wrapped herself tightly in her blankets.

CHAPTER 3

She faced the wall that separated her room from her sister's. The silence from the other side was comforting. She pressed her forehead against the wall. Alessa could feel sleep coming. She welcomed it readily, her eyelids fluttering shut.

The creak of her bedroom door opening made her eyes fly open. Alessa went rigid, doing her best to feign sleep. She opened one eye just enough to see her mother's shadow on her wall. Lily did not move and she did not speak. She simply stood with one hand resting on the doorknob... watching. Alessa's heart hammered.

Lily finally stepped away, closing the door behind her. Alessa let out a pained breath and rolled onto her back; her heartbeat finally returning to a normal rhythm. Once again, she tried to rest but every time she closed her eyes, she saw her mother's tall, faceless shadow; an ever present, silent ghoul watching over her.

Chapter 4

Time had lost all meaning to Alessa. How long had she been sitting in the back of Roswell's squad car? She couldn't remember getting in the car to begin with. The world was a white haze, a tapestry of snow and sleet. Alessa watched the color drain from the world.

Even their exit from the woods remained a blur. Alessa couldn't lock on to one decipherable thought. Her brain was liquefied, swimming in red. The vague image of Shirley practically carrying her useless body through the woods, rushed to the front of her mind.

Alessa stared, unblinking out the window of the patrol car. Her body sagged with exhaustion, her heavy limbs weighing her down. When she finally blinked, she saw the jawbone again, only this time she imagined it attached to Aria's lifeless face, broken and gushing blood. She hunched forward on her legs, her hands rubbing at her temples. Alessa wanted to dig her fingertips in, through her flesh and straight into her brain to swirl around the white matter and pull the memories out of existence.

The car stopped. When did it stop? Both the driver and front passenger seats were empty. Alessa pressed her forehead to the cold glass of the window. Roswell and Shirley were outside her house talking with her father. Everyone knew Joshua Hale for his warmth and neighborly attitude. Today, he stared into the squad car at the pale moon of his daughter's face, gnawing on his thumbnail with exasperation. Alessa couldn't hold his eyes, instead, her head fell in shame. As mad as she had been with her father, the reality of disappointing him still broke her heart.

Alessa kept her gaze on the ground in front of her as she let Shirley escort her back inside. Her parents remained silent as she shuffled past, but the intensity of their stares burned into her back as she headed inside.

Alessa collapsed onto the couch and squeezed a pillow close to her chest. She needed to hang on to something tangible, something that could keep her anchored in reality. Through the open door, she heard her father sending the officers on their way. "I'm sorry again for all the trouble. I'll speak with her," her father said, "thank you both for giving her a ride back."

Roswell's response was indistinct and muffled. She flinched a bit when the door finally shut. The suffocating silence that followed made Alessa's teeth hurt. He cleared his throat, preparing his latest speech. Before he had the chance to speak, Alessa's mouth was open, and the words were flying out.

"Did they tell you what they found out there?"

The sharpness of her voice sliced through the tension. She hesitantly looked up and finally met her dad's gaze.

"What on Earth were you doing out there?" He was simmering, red beginning to creep up his neck. He gestured to her hiking gear sitting on the floor.

"Where did you even get all of this? How long has this been going on?"

She looked away again, unable to face him, unable to face any of it. Lily sat on the edge of the coffee table in front of her.

"Alessa, please, just let us in," Lily pleaded, "you know you can't go running off into the woods alone. How many times do we have to have this conversation?"

Alessa's face flushed, her lips curling into a snarl.

"Until you listen!" she snapped, startling all of them. "I've been looking for Ari!"

Alessa jumped to her feet, nearly knocking her mother over as she stood. She wrenched her hiking bag open and yanked out the crumpled map.

"I've been looking relentlessly for weeks," she growled. Alessa's hands shook as she unfolded the map, slamming it on the table for her parents to see. Lily paled when she saw the red markings across the page.

"Alessa!" Joshua shouted.

"What?" Her eyes were wild. "It's not like anyone else is looking for her!"

That did it. The red had made its way to his face now, and the vein in his left temple was pulsing.

"Alessa..." Lily spoke her daughter's name, a soft warning that she was nearing a line she ought not to cross.

"No!" Alessa yelled. She would not be guilted back into silence. The floodgates were open. Every bit of anger, fear, sadness, and resentment she had pushed down over the past two months came rushing to the surface.

"It's like everyone woke up one day and forgot she was gone! It's been two months and they've got nothing to show for it. What the hell have they been doing all this time?"

"Enough!" Joshua exploded, silencing her. "That's enough. Chief Roswell is a good man, and he has done everything in his power to help us. He has been nothing but transparent with us every step of the way, but their resources are limited."

Alessa opened her mouth to argue, but he lifted his hand to stop her.

"This is just something we have to accept. No amount of arguing and disparaging them will change anything."

Alessa clenched her teeth, sinking into the nearest chair. Joshua towered over her. Alessa had never felt smaller.

"We have been over this, Alessa. We leave the investigating to the professionals. You can't go into the woods alone, you know this. Do you have any idea what can happen to you out there? One wrong step, one wrong turn, and you're gone."

Joshua snapped his fingers for emphasis, but his voice wavered, anger faltering as the pain bled through.

Gone. The word felt like a fist to the stomach, knocking the wind out of her. An invisible weight was crushing her chest. She didn't know what to say. There was nothing she *could* say.

"This stops now. No more skipping school. From now on we drop you off and we pick you up. This is the last time we are going to have this conversation." He paused for emphasis. "Do we have an understanding?"

Her father crossed his arms and planted his feet in a wider stance, attempting to look stern as he waited for his daughter's answer. Alessa felt so deflated–it would be easy to say yes and give it all up.

Gone. The word slithered back to the forefront of her mind, only this time as a hiss, a cruel and needless reminder of the gaping wound in her heart. A storm of emotions rippled through her. She heard the word gone as she remembered her sister's empty bedroom. She heard it when she saw the pictures overturned on the mantel, and when she stared up at her father, she heard it louder than ever before. Alessa shook her head, her expression hardening.

"No." Her voice was a low and vicious rumble. "No, we do not have an understanding."

Lily's head jerked up. "Alessa, watch your tone."

Alessa pushed herself back to her feet.

"You and I haven't been on the same page since Ari went missing!

You've barely spoken to me in weeks and what, now you're suddenly interested in if I'm going to school—now you suddenly care?" she spat out, venom dripping from every word.

Joshua's jaw went slack. "That's not fair."

A burst of laughter escaped her. "Not fair? Really?"

Alessa wanted to shriek. She wanted to grab him and shake him and scream in his face. Every ounce of her self-control had been depleted by holding it in.

"Fine, we can talk about fair." Her voice broke a little, but she soldiered on. "Do you realize that this is the first time you've even so much as looked at me in weeks?"

The creases around his eyes deepened with confusion. She held firm and watched as his expression crumbled. Seeing her father's shattered face stung. The child in her wanted desperately to comfort him.

"It's been two months, and where have you been? You're like a ghost, you're gone before I wake up, you hide away after dinner. And don't think I haven't noticed the pictures!"

Alessa pointed to the fireplace mantle. Joshua winced and looked away.

"Dad," she said. He did not reply, nor did he bother to lift his head. The ache of his refusal to acknowledge her was all-encompassing like a hungry, metastasizing cancer.

"Dad, look at me," her bottom lip trembled. The wrath that burned inside of her was warring with the little girl who just wanted her dad to hold her and tell her that everything was going to be all right.

"Dad!"

His head shot up. She gasped when she saw tears sparkling in the corners of his eyes. Alessa expected disappointment from him, perhaps even anger, but not this. He suddenly didn't look like the indignant, and often combative patriarch she knew him to be.

Joshua finally opened his mouth. "I'm sorry."

Silence followed, and Alessa waited, thinking there had to be more, but he only pressed his lips together.

"That's it? You're sorry?"

Joshua tensed. "What else do you want me to say?"

The dam cracked within her; her anger suddenly too great to be expressed by any combination of words. Alessa charged at him. Her small hands curled into tight fists, and she nearly knocked her dad over as she crashed into him, pounding on his chest and whatever parts of him she could reach. Stumbling back, he raised his arms to block the blows, but hesitated in pushing her off.

"Alessa, stop!" Lily shouted, mortified.

"I want you to see me. I *need* you to see me!" Alessa wailed, her red cheeks damp with tears, "I need you to tell me that she'll come back and that she's okay. I need you to be my dad!"

Her arms ached, and her movements slowed as she grew tired, giving Joshua an opportunity to lower his arms and wrap them around her. She thrashed at first, his touch reigniting her anger, but he only held tighter, bringing her closer to his chest.

"Okay, okay, it's okay," Joshua whispered. The soothing timbre of his voice turned her muscles to jelly. Alessa went limp in his arms. She had nothing left, no energy–no fight. Her hands clawed at her father's shirt, clinging to him even tighter. She let out a stream of sobs.

"I want her back! I just want her back..."

Joshua shushed her, continuing to stroke her hair and swayed them back and forth. He placed a kiss on Alessa's temple.

"Breathe, Lessa, breathe."

So, she did. Pressing to her father's chest, she followed the rhythmic flow of his breathing until it matched her own.

"You're right."

She leaned back, and he cupped her cheeks, carefully brushing the tears away with his thumbs.

"You're absolutely right."

Alessa blinked up at him. A deer caught in the headlights.

"I did disappear on you, I just—I couldn't bring myself to look at you... after what happened to her," Joshua said, tears slipped from the corners of his eyes, "because—because how could I look at you after I failed her so horribly?"

Her breathing slowed as his words sunk in. The lingering haze of her exhaustion made the world take on a dream-like hue. It made her believe, only briefly, that this was all in her head.

"I wasn't fair to you, and I failed you both. Every time I close my eyes, I can't help but imagine what was going through her head that night, if she knew what was happening. If—if she tried to call for help."

He stared at her, toying with the ends of her hair and brushing his palm against her cheek, as if afraid to touch her. They rested on her shoulders, and his lips flickered into a fleeting smile. It died when he glanced at the mantle of overturned pictures.

"Alessa, I love you and your sister more than you'll ever know. I know you want her back. I do too, with all of my heart."

Joshua choked back a sob. "I'm sorry I've been such a shitty father."

The stoicism he normally portrayed was nothing more now than a thin pane of cracked glass in danger of shattering at any second. Alessa circled her small arms around his neck. "You're not a shitty father," she whispered.

His body tensed under her embrace, releasing a quiet chuckle as he hugged her back.

"Agree to disagree," he replied.

"Did they tell you what they found out there?" Alessa asked again. Joshua exhaled sharply.

"Yes, they did."

"Do you think it's her?"

CHAPTER 4

When she pressed her chin to his chest to look up at him, he was watching her mother. She glanced between her parents, a silent understanding passing between them. They'd always been able to communicate without words. Alessa always admired that connection, but right now it just made her feel excluded.

"I'm praying it isn't," he said.

Lily turned to the window, looking out towards the street. Joshua gave his daughter a hollow smile. She wanted to ask him what conclusion they had come to, but the cold and unreadable expression of her mother's profile gave her pause. She knew in her gut that even if she asked, she would not like the answer. Instead, she burrowed deeper into her father's arms, enjoying the embrace for as long as she could.

Frost shimmered in the brisk night air. Snowflakes froze instantly against the windows of the house, making starburst patterns on the glass. The alluring glitter of the untouched snow captivated Alessa. She longingly gazed out the window, her hands moving from muscle memory, mindlessly finishing her evening chores. After the argument with her father, Alessa felt drained and detached. As if reality and her imaginings had become hard to tell apart. She looked at her hands from time to time, rubbing her fingers together to feel the skin, grounding herself with the sensation, reminding herself that what was happening in the present was real. The barrier between her and her father was not entirely broken, but it was fractured, and for now it soothed the gnawing ache in her stomach.

Joshua was in the process of unfolding the pullout couch when she entered the living room. She lingered at the bottom of the stairs.

"Dad."

Dropping a pillow in place on the couch, her father turned to look at her.

"I love you," she said.

As the words sank in, his face lit up with a warm grin. It was as if he had needed to hear the words from her just as much as she had needed it from him.

"I love you too, Alessa. Get some sleep."

Alessa smiled, and for the first time in a while, she did as she was told without argument.

Chapter 5

9 Months Ago

Green had always been Aria's favorite color. Sage, Chartreuse, Olive, Emerald, any shade of green, really. Aria adored them all. So Alessa was not only surprised but delighted to find Aria traipsing down the stairs in a lovely new pine-colored dress. Aria's joyful mood was tangible. She greeted her sibling with a contagious smile that naturally brought Alessa own sheepish grin to the surface.

"Morning, Squirt!" Aria gently teased as she ruffled the top of Alessa's blonde head. The two of them spun around in a mass of giggles and tangled limbs.

"Happy Birthday, Ari."

Aria grinned.

"Thanks. Can you believe Mom left this hanging on my door this morning?" Aria spun around; the skirt of the dress fluttered around her knees.

"It's so pretty," Alessa marveled. The fabric glistened in the light, reflecting various shades of green embedded in the threads. At first glance, Alessa could tell it was expensive, far pricier than the gifts their mother was typically known for. Alessa felt the gentle gnawing of jealousy pinching in her gut but covered it with a smile, not wanting to steal from Aria's moment.

Let her enjoy this, Alessa thought, *she deserves it.*

Aria finally ceased her spinning, laughing when she wobbled to catch her balance. "She left a note claiming that seventeen was an important birthday, or something like that."

Aria looked Alessa up and down, and in that moment it left her feeling exposed. Could Ari see how much Alessa envied her? She placed a hand on Alessa's shoulder and leaned in closer.

"You know, I bet you Mom is planning something super special for *your* seventeenth birthday," she said in a whisper, "I'll just have to make sure she knows exactly what you like."

Alessa's insides melted to butter. No matter how hard she tried to wrestle against her envy and guilt, Aria always knew just how to calm her and put her mind at ease.

"Thanks, Ari."

Aria patted her shoulder in response before swiping a fresh orange off the table and tossing it back and forth in her hands.

"No worries." Aria's eyes narrowed strangely at her. "Your favorite color is bright neon orange, right? I'll have to make sure Mom has these specifics, you know, for your dress."

Alessa scoffed in disgust and shoved her playfully. "Ew, no!"

Aria raised her hands in surrender and began peeling back the skin of her fruit.

"Forgive me, I must have misremembered," Aria smirked. Alessa rolled her eyes but softened the gesture with an amused smile.

"So, will you be seeing Noah at church, or is he not coming until the party?"

The sound of Noah's name caused Aria to nearly choke on her fruit. She cleared her throat carefully, rubbing at her neck as a flush of embarrassment colored her neck and cheeks red. Alessa muffled her giggle beneath her hand.

Aria shot a sharp glance over her shoulder and down the hall, checking to make sure neither of their parents were listening.

"Church," she mumbled, forcing down the smile that played at the corners of her mouth.

"Girls!" their father shouted from the other room; Aria flinched, "are you ready for service?"

As his footsteps drew nearer, Aria held a single finger over her pursed lips. Alessa gave discreet nod, not needing any further clarification. Under the watchful eyes of their devout parents, Aria and Noah were close friends and nothing more. Joshua and Lily were adamant that they not only practice abstinence, but they also forbade them from dating until they were eighteen. As archaic as it seemed Alessa never questioned the rule. Nearly everyone in Pine Hollow raised their children the same, at least those who went to their church.

Both girls flashed their warmest smiles at their father as he entered the room. He smiled back at them, oblivious to their mischief. Their mother entered just a moment later. Alessa frowned as she watched her sister's shine dull the moment her mother walked into the room. Lily's eyes eventually settling on Aria, a slow smile stretching across her face. Alessa couldn't help but feel struck by the genuine affection she saw in her mother's eyes. Lily's smiles were usually as rigid as her personality. Aria preened under the sudden and unusual display of devotion, grinning as their mother cupped her cheeks, gazing at her with a reverence she reserved only for the heavenly cross.

"You look absolutely beautiful, sweetheart."

The smile on Aria's face was blinding. Lily pressed a gentle kiss to Aria's forehead, lightly dabbing at the lipstick mark she left behind.

"Thanks, Mom."

Aria leaned into her touch but shook out of her momentary stupor when Lily pulled away. Alessa saw longing swim in Aria's eyes as she watched her mother walk away.

"Let's go, girls. We don't want to be late!"

The moment was over, Aria was the first to turn away, scurrying after their parents. Alessa was quick on her heels.

The sanctuary was teeming with people when the family arrived. Alessa immediately got a strange feeling just watching the crowd move toward the building. Friends and neighbors smiled and waved to them as they parked and joined the throng. While their church was always well attended, there were definitely more people than normal for a typical Sunday sermon.

"Wow, it's packed in here," Aria grumbled, shifting in her seat.

Alessa knew Aria loathed going to St. Lawrence. The religious principles that were instilled in them from a young age just never seemed to stick to her. Every prayer, every sermon slid off of her like oil on water. Alessa didn't know why her sister hated secular religion it so much. Maybe conformity wasn't in her sister's nature.

"Happy Birthday to me," Aria sighed to herself.

Alessa slid her hand across the seat to tap her sister's leg. Aria glanced over; lips pursed together in annoyance.

"Just think—you've still got my gift to look forward to," Alessa whispered.

Aria's frown melted into a small grin. "You know just what to say."

Alessa's heart fluttered with excitement, but she played it off with a shrug not wanting to appear over-eager. The truth was that Alessa saved up her allowance for months to buy the perfect gift for her sister's birthday. She hid the package in her closet, where it sat for weeks, taunting her. She was so excited to present it to Ari that she was hardly able to keep the secret to herself. Seeing the look on her face would make suffering through the service worth it.

The gift was a new lens to go with the camera Aria purchased two years prior. The collage of photographs on her bedroom wall was a mere fraction of Aria's portfolio. She stuffed half of her shelves with albums containing all the candid and artistic shots she'd taken since she first learned how to point and shoot. Travel books and National Geographic magazines were bursting from the remaining spaces, all of them marked and dog-eared to Hell.

It took the Hale family almost twenty minutes of slithering through the crowd and before they even entered the building. Their eyes scanned the crowd. Alessa for Maya, Aria for Noah. Aria nudged her.

"There's your girl," Aria nodded off toward the left. Maya, head to toe in her Sunday best, was making her usual rounds, handing out programs and spreading morning joy. Her inky black hair spiraled down her back in buoyant curls.

Alessa cleared her throat, Aria was smirking at her, a knowing look in her eyes that filled Alessa with dread. Aria seemed to recognize the tension and softened. She glanced at their parents, who mingled animatedly with their guests, and pushed Alessa toward her friend with a reassuring poke in the ribs.

"I think Mom and Dad are sufficiently occupied for the moment," she said, "go on, I'll holler when they're ready."

Relief flooded Alessa's veins. She looked around, hunting for a clear path toward Maya, and she noticed Noah as he in turn made his way toward Aria. She saw his smile widen the moment he and Aria locked eyes on each other. "Someone looks excited to see you, Ari."

Aria's gaze flickered up, an enormous grin threatening to split her face. Only Alessa saw Aria's feet tapping against the floor to restraining herself from rushing to meet him in the middle.

Noah looked sleek and handsome in his navy slacks and white button-up. He was the spitting image of his father, but his magnetic smile undoubtedly came from his mother. Noah's family was well loved by their town. His parents owned numerous businesses in the area, and they often used their wealth to give back to their community.

"Wow, he looks..." Aria trailed off, her excitement vibrated in the air around her. She lifted her hand in an enthusiastic wave, and was practically bouncing on her toes, forgetting the world around her. Realizing that Alessa was still eying her, Aria's face bloomed as red as her hair.

Alessa cackled. "Go on!"

Aria flipped her off with a wink before they parted ways.

Maya welcomed Alessa with a jovial smile, passing her half of the programs to help disperse them. The fleeting minutes before service were the only alone time they had, because as soon as the bells chimed, Maya's grandfather would whisk her away.

Church never appealed to Alessa before Maya came along. She enjoyed attending services well enough growing up, but it wasn't until the girl with the million-watt smile handed her a program one Sunday that she finally understood the true potential of this place. Their parents found peace in the cross, Alessa found peace in Maya.

The pair made their way down the pews, passing out programs and catching each other up on the events of the weekend.

"What time's the party again tonight?" Maya asked.

"Around five."

Maya blew a few strands of wayward hair out of her face. "I might be a little late. Is that okay? Sundays are always the super busy for Grandfather, you know."

"Yeah, no worries, just show up when you can. Mom invited practically the whole town, so I'm sure there will be people trickling in for a few hours."

An eruption of laughter in the distance made Alessa turn her head. Aria and Noah were standing near the opposite wall, concealed partially by the crowd, hovering dangerously close together. Her sister threw her head back with a cackle while Noah hid snorts behind a clenched fist. Aria reached for him with her left hand which remained somewhat concealed by their bodies, and looped her fingers around his pinky. A private, intimate gesture.

A heavy unease immediately settled in Alessa's stomach; she knew what was coming next. Lily, who had been conferring with Father Samuel and Joshua, turned her stone-cold gaze toward Aria from across the room.

Alessa's heart pounded, a yell rising in her throat. She desperately wanted to warn Aria, but there was no way without drawing the attention of everyone in the room. Again, Aria burst into laughter, the noise rippling across the crowd and drawing a few curious and judgmental eyes. Lily sauntered through the crowd toward the discordant sound of joy. She watched Aria distance herself from Noah just before their mother emerged before them. Noah greeted Lily with a smile, and even through the chaos, Alessa could see Aria's trademark smirk. It was one Alessa recognized well. It meant she thought she was getting away with something.

Noah peeled away, shooting Aria one final lingering look, before rejoining his parents. Lily stepped in front of Aria, and from that point on, the rest of the conversation was beyond what she could see.

"Hey, I missed a seat. Can you throw one over there?"

Maya's question caught her attention. "Got it!"

She continued placing programs down in empty seats. When she was finished, she looked up to see Lily towering over Aria in the shadows of the ceiling arches.

"That can't be good." Maya reappeared next to her, watching the scene unfold.

"It never is."

Maya gripped Alessa's wrist delicately, thumb grazing the skin over her racing pulse and adding just the slightest pressure to remind her of her presence. A lump formed in Alessa's throat, lodged like a stone. Across the room Lily's arm jerked roughly before she smoothed out the front of her blouse and walked away. Aria lingered behind watching as her mother seamlessly blended back into the crowd. Her shoulders hunched with defeat as she rubbed at a spot on her left arm. Alessa swore she saw her sister wince, and she cradled the arm she was holding against her chest. A sliver of crimson light slashed across Aria's face from the stained-glass windows above, the furious color making her look feral.

Father Samuel took his place at the front of the church. The parishioners began to settle in. Maya parted from Alessa with a quick hug, and she too rejoined her family. The buzz of a dozen of conversations dulled into faint whispers as everyone took their seats. Finding their pew, Alessa planted herself next to her sister. Squishing in close, Aria jerked away as if burned, yanking her favored arm away when Alessa pressed against her side.

"You okay?" Alessa asked.

Her sister glanced nervously at her parents and then back to Alessa. Lily smiled peacefully with her hands folded neatly in her lap as she awaited the beginning of the service. Aria smiled, but it didn't meet her eyes.

"Yeah, of course," she let out a weak laugh, "just another one of Mom's lectures. You know how it is."

"Are you sure?"

Aria shrugged, slipping right back into her nonchalant skin, a bright smile at the ready as if the last few minutes hadn't happened at all.

"No need to worry, Squirt."

Aria reached over to pat Alessa's leg reassuringly, but while the gesture was kind, Alessa saw Aria's hand shaking.

The service was no more exciting than usual, but Aria was quieter than ever. Normally, she would be in Alessa's ear, whispering jokes and sarcastic quips about the sermon. Alessa figured Aria didn't want to anger their mother more than she already had, but her sister's silence made the service drag on for what felt like years. Before they concluded the service, Father Samuel encouraged the entire room to wish Aria a happy birthday. She smiled, all teeth and tension, while everyone clapped for her. Alessa couldn't stomach applauding along with them.

The rest of the afternoon passed in a blur of well-wishes, followed by hours of cleaning and preparation for the party that evening. Their father always seemed to be hovering nearby ready to jump in with a soothing smile and quick kiss to soften Lily's edges when the stress was piling on.

Aria had been mostly silent since the confrontation with their mother, sequestering herself for most of the afternoon and taking on tasks that kept her out of Lily's path. In between chores, Alessa attempted to make her laugh, joking about their father's inability to frost the cake, but she only managed a half-smile. Whatever their mother said to her, it successfully drained every ounce of joy out of her sister.

Neighbors and family friends began trickling in at precisely five o'clock. Aria and Alessa stood by the entrance as their parents greeted guests at the door. They posed like beautiful little statues, politely welcoming every guest who crossed the threshold. Alessa's jaw began to ache within the first fifteen minutes, and Aria didn't look much better, her exceedingly wide smile fading a little more after each handshake. Joshua took each perfectly wrapped gift that was presented to display proudly on a pyramid that was forming on the living room table.

Once about a dozen people had arrived, Alessa realized none of them were Aria's age. The guests consisted mostly of their parents' friends by the time Noah arrived. Aria hugged him eagerly, face falling when he parted from her. Maya was thankfully not far behind, but the only other teenagers to arrive were a trio of girls who Alessa couldn't recall Aria ever spending time with.

The clinking of glasses, and bursts of haughty laughter fluttered through the halls of the Hale house. Alessa and Maya remained huddled near the snack table. Snickering under their breath, they gorged themselves on skewered cubes of cheese and fruit; the luscious array of finger foods was arranged to draw attention to the extravagant birthday cake in the center. Alessa lost sight of her sister not long after Noah arrived and hoped she was enjoying herself.

"Alessa."

She was midway to shoving another piece of cheese into her mouth when her mother's voice jolted her to attention. Lily appeared calm, but Alessa knew by the way her jaw muscles were clenched, she was anything but.

"Have you seen your sister?" she bit out, "people have been asking for her for the last twenty minutes. Father Samuel wants to have a word with her."

"I haven't seen her." Alessa didn't dare speak Noah's name after the events of that morning. She scrambled for something else to say. "I can go look for her. I'll bring her right back."

That seemed to do the trick. Lily smiled and let out a sigh, her shoulders relaxing. She cupped Alessa's cheek and patted it lovingly. Alessa melted into her touch almost immediately.

"I'm thankful I can always count on you, dear."

Her words were a plush cocoon that Alessa wanted to wrap herself in forever, but it was short-lived, and Lily pulled away. "Please, be quick. This is no way for her to be treating her guests."

The ice in her tone made Alessa nauseous, her appetite instantly gone. She tossed her plate and mouthed a quick 'sorry' to Maya before darting into the next room. She checked the kitchen, then the living room, and even knocked on the bathroom door a few times, but Aria was nowhere to be found. The sounds of the party faded into the background as she delved deeper into the house. She noticed the door of her father's office was slightly open, the light from inside coloring the hallway. Alessa realized she hadn't seen her father in a while, and carefully treaded down the hall, inching silently closer to the door.

"This is getting ridiculous, Aria." Her ears perked at the sound of her father's voice. "You two can't keep bickering like this. She's your mother, treat her with respect."

"So, the whole give respect to get respect thing you taught us was just a bunch of bullshit?"

Alessa pressed herself as close to the opening of the door as possible without being seen. She heard Joshua scoff; through the crack, she saw him shaking his head fiercely.

"Sarcasm is not the way to get yourself out of his hole."

An explosion of laughter from down the hall muffled Aria's response.

"She went to a lot of trouble to plan this party for you. The very least you could do is smile and act like you're having a nice time."

Her responding chuckle was thick with annoyance.

"All that effort and she couldn't invite any of the girls I actually like?"

Joshua was at a loss for words, but his silence spoke volumes. Aria scoffed, bitterly. He mumbled something, but Alessa couldn't make it out. She figured this was her best chance. She knocked softly on the door, pushing it open to stick her head in.

"Aria?"

The two stood were clearly in a standoff, Joshua's arms crossed tightly over his chest, Aria's shoulders heaving with barely contained rage. Alessa smiled to defuse the tension. Her father noticed her, brows flying to his hairline in surprise.

"Oh, Alessa, I didn't hear you."

"It's okay. Mom was just asking for Aria. Father Samuel wants to talk to her."

Aria slowly uncoiled with relief at Alessa's presence. Gliding past their father, she paused just once, her lips morphing into a smile that looked more like a snarl.

"Wouldn't want to keep her waiting," she said, a sickly sweetness tainting every syllable. He tensed but remained quiet until she walked away. She brushed by Alessa, gathering herself with a long inhale before trudging back to the party. A woman walking the plank.

Alessa looked at Joshua. He was facing away from her now, shaking his head and rubbing his temples. He flinched when he saw her still standing in the doorway and smiled, tired lines creasing around his eyes.

"I'll be right there, Lessa, just give me a minute."

Nodding slowly, she closed the door, shutting him away with his thoughts.

When Alessa returned to the festivities, Aria was gone again. She weaved through the walls of people, bristling each time one of them accidentally bumped her. The three girls from Aria's grade huddled in the far corner of the living room, speaking, and giggling quietly to themselves.

A flash of red hair bobbing toward the back porch alerted her to Aria's whereabouts. Lily and Father Samuel were right beside her; Lily opened the door to allow the both of them outside and closed it behind them. Once it latched shut, she leaned back against the door, her eyes drifting closed while she took a deep breath. In a snap, she was the perfect host again, traipsing around the party with a winning smile and not a single hair out of place. Alessa wrinkled her nose in distaste, but a smiling Maya distracted her with a plate of food.

"Might I interest you in some absolutely exquisite quiche?"

Alessa gladly took a piece from the plate. "Don't mind if I do."

Aria didn't emerge again until nearly an hour later.

Minutes before it was time to cut the cake, the back door creaked open and banged against the frame, the frosty night air whistling throughout the house. The party barely noticed, but Alessa did, the icy breeze trailing up the inside of her dress.

Mouth still full of quiche, Alessa's head jerked in the direction of the back door. Aria stood, arms hanging limp at her sides, her eyes glazed over with a blank stare that looked both perplexing and grim. Shadows danced across her sister's face. She seemed... haunted–it was the only word that came to Alessa's mind.

"There she is!"

In a flurry, their mother was at Aria's side, drawing the attention of the entire room.

"Time for cake," Lily beamed.

Without a word, Aria allowed herself to be steered toward the impossibly extravagant cake on display in the other room. Alessa scrambled to keep up with the crowd, quietly praising the fact that she was on the smaller side, allowing her to maneuver through the bodies with relative ease. When she broke through, she noticed her father was out and socializing once more, and Lily, still gripping her daughter's slim shoulders, was standing in the center. The smile fell from Aria's face, and she instead stared at the flickering candles, two big numbers to commemorate her big day.

The off-key chorus of Happy Birthday made the inside of Alessa's ears itch, but she kept her eyes on her sister the whole time. Their gazes locked across the room, and the world seemed far away. Alessa mouthed something.

"*You good?*"

It wasn't until that moment that Aria finally smiled. When she blew out her candles, Alessa wondered what she wished for.

At exactly nine o'clock, their mother was ushering guests out the door, thanking them for their presence and gifts. Alessa lost Aria immediately after the cutting of the cake. After blowing out her candles, she swept up her plate and vanished into the chaos. Lily stuck Alessa with cleanup duty in the dining room before she had the chance to go searching for her, so with a huff she craned her neck every time she heard someone walk by the door, aching for a flash of ginger hair. Within minutes, the next best thing arrived.

"Noah!" Alessa hissed when she saw him. He came to an abrupt stop and peered in, smiling when he noticed her.

"Hey, I thought I missed ya. We were just about to head out."

Noah stepped into the room; hands buried in the pockets of his pants. There was always an effortlessness in the way he carried himself. He never seemed uncomfortable, like no matter where he ended up, even if unintentionally, he could make you believe it was his idea all along.

"Have you seen Ari? I lost her in the cake stampede."

Noah chuckled. She held out a plate with some leftover quiche; he snatched one and took a bite that removed half of it before answering.

"My guess is she's hiding out in her room. I caught her after the vultures swarmed and she seemed really out of it. I don't exactly blame her."

"Yeah," Alessa muttered, "today's been a mess."

They both knew today had not gone the way Aria imagined it.

"Anyway, she said she had a headache and wanted to lie down. I offered to keep her company, but she was pretty confident your parents would not be okay with that."

"That's a fair guess," Alessa sighed.

Noah's smile faltered; his disappointment was as potent as his cologne. She wanted to reassure him otherwise and tell him it wasn't true. But she'd just be lying to him.

"It's not because they don't like you," Alessa added. She felt the need to soften the blow, even if all she had were feeble words.

"I know. Can you check on her for me? I told her to call me if she needs anything, but you know her."

They both snickered. Alessa nodded.

CHAPTER 5

"Of course."

Two hours of tidying later and Alessa finally had enough spare consecutive minutes to give Aria her present. The gift bag, elegant and silver, with an expertly tied ribbon around the handle, was burning a hole in her closet. Every time she looked at it, the overwhelming urge to spill the beans to Aria seized her. Her stomach buzzed with anticipation as she rushed upstairs.

Before barging into her room, she splashed cold water on her face to wake herself up. The weight of the long, busy day was starting to take its toll. Distantly, she heard the rumblings of her father doing his nightly activities. Two doors down, Lily was chatting with Aria in her room.

As she rummaged through the back of her closet, Alessa didn't notice the voices down the hall become louder and more terse than before. It wasn't until she was standing outside Aria's doorway that she realized her sister and mother were arguing. Alessa held the gift bag tight between her fingers. She tried to quiet the sound of her heart beating in her ears so that she could hear what was being said behind the partially open door.

"It's enough you were disrespectful to your guests, but this." Lily snarled. "This is unacceptable!"

Nothing from Aria, but Alessa could hear Lily's foot tapping, like it always did when she was wound up.

"I raised you better than this, Aria. Everyone was here to celebrate you. We spent weeks planning all of this for you!"

Aria snorted. "Please, you can stop pretending any of this was for me."

The lack of an immediate response from Lily filled the air with a tangible chill. Alessa struggled to swallow while she awaited the inevitable explosion.

"Tell me when all of this started." Lily demanded.

"I've never done it before."

"Don't lie to me." The quiver in Lily's voice hinted at the rage Alessa knew was boiling under the surface.

Aria held firm. "I'm not lying."

Alessa peered around the corner, holding the gift bag away from herself in order to prevent crinkling. Lily was standing just a few feet from Aria, who crossed her arms defiantly over her chest. Lily clutched something small between her fingers and her hands were shaking as she lifted the strange object into the light. It was thin and cylindrical, composed of a nearly transparent tan paper that was twisted at the very tip.

"I'll ask one more time. How *fucking* long have you been smoking for?"

Shadows cut across the delicate slants of Aria's face as she grinned. Her eyes were vicious, she was ready to go for the jugular.

"Profanity, wow, Mom, that's not very Godly of you."

Alessa heard the slap before she saw it, a resounding and sharp crack that ripped the air from her lungs. Papers rustled as the gift bag in her hand fell to the floor.

Aria's head snapped to the side and remained there for a long moment; her eyes were wide with disbelief. Her hand rose to her cheek, the skin growing redder by the second, tears glimmered in her eyes. Lily said nothing when Aria finally looked at her again. Instead, she smoothed out the sides of her hair and cleared her throat.

"Alessa."

Alessa started turning to see her father down the hall. He threw a quick glance at Aria's bedroom door, his face never betraying his thoughts.

"Go to bed. It's late."

Alessa didn't know what to say. A million questions screamed from within. He had to have heard it too. He had to know what was going on. Why didn't he stop it? Joshua started toward her and picked up the bag, handing it back to her.

"You can give this to her in the morning. Come on."

The protests died on her tongue, and he redirected her to her room. Once inside, he wished her goodnight, hardly giving her a chance to reply before closing the door behind him as he left.

Helpless–aimless, that's how it felt, standing in the middle of her darkened room trying to process what was going on while her mother slammed Aria's door. She didn't dare go back out, not with Lily tearing up and down the hall and spewing flames from her lips. With a wrenching sigh, Alessa resigned herself to the fact that Aria would not receive her birthday gift until the next day.

Later that night, when the sky was black, and the world slumbered, Alessa woke to Aria climbing into bed with her. Alessa kept her back turned, waiting until her sister settled. Bleary-eyed and exhausted, Alessa closed her eyes when she heard the soothing rhythm of her sister's peaceful breathing.

When they awoke the next morning, neither of them brought up the night's events, and they didn't discuss it the next day, or the day after that.

In fact, they never spoke about the night of Aria's birthday again.

She wished, now more than ever, that they had.

Chapter 6

Monday morning arrived like it always had. Unfortunately, for once, her parents did exactly as they threatened. One of them was in the car waiting to drive her to school every morning and the other would wait on the curb at the end of the day to take her home. Her forest excursions had swiftly and effectively come to an end. The extra super vision did nothing, however, to stop Alessa from searching for her sister everywhere she went; in every car that passed, in every window of every building they drove by. She kept right on searching for any hint at all of Aria's existence. Having Maya by her side was the only thing truly keeping her sane. She walked Alessa to all her classes and texted her during their separate periods to check in on her. Her parents didn't want her to spend time with Maya outside of school after what happened, so she was relieved to have the opportunity to interact with her at church. It was the only thing giving her motivation to get out of bed.

The doll-like reflection that stared back at Alessa in the mirror made her cringe. Her finger prodded at the high neckline of her top. The pristine white fabric was rough and starchy. Golden hair tumbled down her back in a braid, and the hem of her ruffled skirt drifted softly above the floor, dusting her ankles. It used to belong to Aria. The fabric was worn and faded in places, but it was soft, and when she looked at the little white daisies that decorated her skirt, she thought of Aria sitting in their garden, skirt hiked up around her thighs as she sat in the grass and read. Alessa glanced out the window, out of habit, eyes searching the garden. It was barren and cold.

"Alessa, time to go!"

Alessa gave over the mirror one last look and wondered as she looked at the deep circles under her eyes, and the pale lifelessness of her complexion, if she would ever look like herself again. Usually, she could find reminders of Aria in the curve of her jaw and the slope of her brows, but now she struggled to find even that.

The ride to the Sunday mass was deathly quiet, a growing line of parishioners filed outside the church's doors. Alessa knew attendance had gone up since Aria's disappearance, but she didn't quite understand the magnitude. Being inside of the car was like being trapped in a fishbowl, all eyes on them, mouths twisted with sadness and pity. Alessa felt sick regret for coming.

Alessa remained sandwiched between Joshua and Lily as they approached the wide-open church doors. Her small fingers gripped the sleeve of her father's jacket as the crowd ushered them along. He glanced down at her and smiled with reassurance.

"Lily, Joshua!"

Alessa stiffened at the loud boom of Father Samuel's voice. When she looked up, he was already coming toward them, smile bright and arms outstretched in welcome. Her parents grinned back at him with equal fervor.

"Father Samuel! Good morning," Lily said.

Father Samuel took her hand carefully into his, squeezing it gently. His expression was the perfect mix of genuine concern and openness. He then moved to Joshua. Giving him a firm handshake, Alessa instinctually scanned the room for Maya.

"I am so pleased to see you both," he turned to Alessa, his brown eyes lighting up. "And isn't this a wonderful surprise? We weren't sure you were going to make it, Alessa."

She flinched when he suddenly grabbed both of her hands, holding them in a bundle close to his chest. The stale smell of his cologne wafted into her nostrils. She choked back a gag. His hands were slick and clammy, but she resisted the rising urge to pull away, not wanting to seem impolite.

"Welcome back, dear. It is truly so wonderful to have you here again." He relaxed his grip on her hands. "We missed you."

She smiled and shifted uncomfortably. "Thank you, Father."

Samuel finally let go. She discretely rubbed her wet palms over her skirt. Ever since the night of Aria's seventeenth birthday, her sister never acted the same toward the priest. Her relationship with him even before was tenuous at best, but after that night, it all fell apart. She'd always despised how religion stifled every aspect of their lives in Pine Hollow: the conservative clothing, the abstinence teachings, and the crosses on every door.

Alessa never put much stock in it, and while their lifestyle never truly bothered her, she could see Aria's perspective and respected her ability to voice her opinions the way she did. But after that day, something changed. She never told Alessa what transpired between her and the priest that night, but whatever it was, Aria's reaction was enough to give Alessa pause.

"Please, it's just such a pleasure to have you all here. I know Maya has missed having you around as well."

He gestured toward the podium where Maya stood. Maya's hand fluttered in a nervous wave and the sight of her relaxed Alessa instantly. When she turned back to Father Samuel, all eyes were on her, and she realized they were awaiting a response. She cleared her throat.

"I heard you were adding a prayer for Aria in the service today."

"Yes, absolutely. We all miss your sister terribly. It's the least I can do to wish her a safe return."

"And we very much appreciate it," Joshua chimed in.

"Aria is always in my thoughts," Samuel said.

"I'm sorry I haven't attended the last few services, Father."

Samuel placed a hand on Alessa's shoulder.

"Fret not, Alessa, you're here now and that's what matters." He removed his hand and folded his arms behind him. Once again, he was the picture of divine authority, exuding strength that seemed impossible for a man his age.

"The service is starting shortly. Please take your time and get comfortable."

"Thank you, Father," Lily said. They leaned in, planting a quick parting kiss on each other's cheeks before Samuel departed.

Alessa's eyes followed the priest as he greeted Noah's parents, who just happened to be standing nearby. Their son stood right behind them, hunched and barely visible amongst the chaos of the crowd. His hair knotted and unkempt, and his normally perfect collar was wrinkled. He looked like he hadn't slept in weeks.

Seeing that Lily and Joshua were otherwise occupied, she took her chance to slip away. Squeezing through the bodies, she poked his shoulder, and he slowly turned to her. Noah's eyes widened a bit, blinking rapidly, as if he didn't believe she was there.

"Alessa," he choked out, "hey."

He shot a glance over his shoulder, but neither his parents nor Samuel seemed to realize he wasn't part of their conversation.

"It's been a while, huh?" Noah's strained chuckle tore a fresh wound in Alessa's heart. "It's nice to see you back here."

He sounded genuine. Alessa shrugged, attempting a smile of her own that was equally pathetic.

"Yeah, Maya said they were doing a prayer for Aria, so..."

Pain flashed across his face. "Yeah, yeah, I heard about that. That's nice of them."

"How are you doing?" Alessa muttered, acid swimming in her stomach. This was not the boy she knew; this was not the Noah whose smile could light up a room.

He looked surprised and then embarrassed by the question.

"Oh God, Alessa, I should be the one asking you that," Noah said, his voice on the verge of breaking. Tears shimmered in his eyes. Alessa's entire body itched to hug him, to do anything to lessen his pain. His teeth grazed over his trembling bottom lip. Noah sniffed and aggressively wiped his eyes with the sleeve of his shirt.

"Shit, here," he said under his breath. Noah tugged her away from the others, leading them to a slightly less crowded area.

"Sorry, I just really didn't want to talk about this around them."

Alessa's eyes bounced from Noah back to his parents.

"Look." She turned back to him. "I'm really fucking sorry; I meant to reach out after what happened—I swear—I just..."

Noah morphed into a child before her eyes. This time, he couldn't prevent the tears that rushed forth, spilling down his cheeks.

"Noah, please, you really don't have to apologize."

He raised his hand, and she paused.

"No, I-I owe you that much—hell, I owe you more than that," Noah trailed off, folding his arms so tightly over his chest she was afraid he would crush it. "I owe her more than that."

For a second, she thought she lost him, but with a firm shake of his head, he returned to Earth once more, his expression clear and focused.

"I am sorry, truly, I should have come by to check on you after—or at the very least called." Noah shrugged, but his remorse was leaking from every pore. "I freaked out and didn't know what to say to you. I had no idea how to comfort you. I still don't—I don't even know how to comfort myself."

CHAPTER 6

The agonized laugh that followed cut into her core.

"It's no excuse, I know—I got into this loop in my head. I just kept thinking, Aria would know what to say, she would know just what to do."

Noah ran a hand down his face, and then slid his fingers through his messy curls, yanking harshly at the roots.

"But she... she's not here."

The final words came out in a whisper, the bitter truth of them making a shiver dance down her spine. He spaced out again for a few seconds; she wondered where he went when it happened. Wherever it was, it had to be better than here.

"It felt wrong to reach out... because there was nothing I could do for you—nothing I could ever say that would make this any better, but that was selfish of me. If Ari could see me now, she'd be pissed."

Alessa stepped forward, allowing her gut instinct to lead her as she wrapped her slender arms around him. He stood, stunned at first. She closed her eyes and squeezed him with all the strength she could muster. His heart was pounding against her ear.

"Please, stop saying sorry." Alessa's insides ached and the urge to cry rose in the back of her throat. "That's all people ever say to me is sorry—sorry this, sorry that—from them I can take it. But not from you."

One tear slid down the bridge of her nose and soaked into the fabric of his shirt.

"You were there. You helped look for her, I remember," she continued, "I always knew you were there, even if you didn't say it."

Noah was one of the first people Alessa called when Aria went missing, and that call would stick with her forever. She could still hear the terrible, unending silence on the other end, that torturous moment where he hovered in limbo before the weight of their new reality pulled him under. She'd felt the same thing when her parents sat her down. For several seconds after they broke the news, her brain disconnected, refusing all the information. Alessa hovered in that silent space just like Noah did, wanting to live forever in a world where Aria wasn't lost.

Slowly, his arms encircled her, first awkwardly, but the longer she held on the more comfortable he became. Eventually, Alessa felt him relax against her. Noah patted her back in the warm, brotherly way he always did, and before they knew it, they were falling back into their old patterns.

Noah completed the embrace with his trademark last squeeze, the kind that lifted her slightly off her toes. Alessa giggled, and for a moment the world seemed to right itself. She was happy to take whatever fleeting moments of normalcy she could get. As they parted, Noah was smiling, looking more peaceful than she'd seen him in weeks.

"Seriously, Noah, you don't need to be sorry. You were there in all the ways that counted, and I know Aria would be more than grateful to see what you've done."

The gossip mill, as in any small town, worked overtime in Pine Hollow. Nothing ever remained secret for very long. Early on, she found out Noah was canvassing neighborhoods in the evenings to check for sightings and was using his limited internet access to investigate viable leads outside of town–much to the dismay of his parents. So, even if Noah avoided their family, Alessa knew he had never abandoned them.

He smiled. The pink hue of his cheeks was slowly returning, the color bringing life to his face.

"You're being way nicer than I deserve, kid." He sniffled, but there was a teasing glint in his eye. "Are you sure you're a Hale?"

Alessa bubbled with a surprising second burst of laughter.

"Uh, thank you, though." He cleared his throat. "But I should have tried harder. I pussied out and I gotta own that."

"If you're looking for me to get pissed and yell at you, you're barking up the wrong tree."

He chuckled, and pride swelled in the center of her chest.

"Besides, you were like Ari's favorite person."

She recalled a memory of Aria, of the way she looked at Noah from across the room. The world could have been crumbling around her and she never would have noticed.

Tears threatened the strength of her voice. "If she wouldn't judge you, why should I?"

His expression softened, the ragged lines of grief around his reddened eyes lightened a bit. Noah scrutinized her, curious and unbelieving. The intensity of his stare made her skin tickle. Alessa didn't like people to see her discomfort, to see her fiddling and fidgeting like a terrified little child.

"What?" she asked.

Noah snapped out of it, giving a swift shake of his head.

"Nothing, I just..." He paused, and his smile returned. "Alessa, you were always Aria's favorite person. Not me. Not by a long shot."

Alessa's chest tightened, and based on Noah's amused expression her shock must have been evident on her face.

"You have no idea, do you?" Noah continued, no trace of judgment, only genuine confusion. "To Aria, everyone was always in second place compared to you."

Alessa swayed back and forth, weightless, shoulder to shoulder with her parents while the grating cluster of voices in the church half-yelled and half-sang "How Great is Our God?" Her jaw worked up and down like a ventriloquist dummy, devoid of emotion. Noah's voice was all she could hear, a broken record that spun endlessly. *You were her favorite. Her favorite. Her favorite.*

The rapid thoughts made her head spin, so she squeezed her eyes shut, blocking out the sea of moving people and vibrations of the music around her.

When she opened her eyes, she saw Maya watching her with rapt attention from her place in the choir. The room was sweltering and growing worse by the second. Sweat beaded and trickled down her back. Maya's lips curved into a faint smile. Alessa's temples pulsed with the beginnings of a headache. She nodded but didn't smile back.

Alessa nearly thanked God himself when the singing finally ceased, and they all sank back onto the bench. Father Samuel rose to the podium and held out his arms to each side as if to embrace them all and then tucked his hands into his chest. The church was silent. Everyone seemed to sit at the edge of their chairs, inching forward as they waited for their beloved clergy to make the first move.

"I want to take a moment to welcome all of you on this beautiful Sunday morning," he finally spoke, and a collective sigh washed over the crowd.

"Our town has seen much despair in the last few weeks," Father Samuel continued, eyes growing dark, "both fear and grief have seized our hearts, so today I would like to use this service to bring everyone together, to foster hope and optimism."

He turned his gaze on Alessa, and her fists clenched tightly on her lap.

"Because when the members of this town stand with their neighbors, there is nothing we cannot achieve."

Alessa glanced down when she felt something brush her fingers. Her father's warm hand was resting over hers. She gripped it tightly.

"Please, join me in a prayer for Aria Hale and her family. May she return home quickly and safely."

Alessa reached tentatively across her mother's lap to grab her hand. She expected her to shake it off, but became surprised when Lily's delicate fingers clutched hers back. Father Samuel's strong, controlled voice was a warm honey that spread through Alessa's veins. She squeezed her parent's hands.

"We will begin with a reading of Romans 5:3-13."

The sound of a dozen hands rustling through fragile paper filled the room, led by the priest himself. His beautifully bound Bible, wrapped in genuine leather, and hand-stitched with gold thread, was something to be marveled at. Alessa watched the hungry and envious eyes of her neighbors as Father Samuel lifted it above their heads. He swept his cloaked arm theatrically; Samuel opened his Bible to the exact page he needed. Alessa couldn't tear her eyes from him. He was magnetic.

Father Samuel cleared his throat softly, and the room held its breath while they waited for him to continue. It was in that brief second Alessa realized she could see herself believing in anything he told her.

"Not only so, but we also glory in our sufferings, because we know that suffering produces perseverance." He paused, scanning the intent expressions of his audience. "Perseverance, character; and character, hope."

"And hope does not put us to shame, because God's love has been poured out into our hearts through the Holy Spirit, who has been given to us."

Alessa's eyelids drifted closed. A cold tremor ripped through her bones, and she suddenly remembered the chill in the air that morning when her life fell apart. The snow was coming down in steady droves, covering the world's imperfections in a blanket of white. The sun was peering into her room, casting rainbows as it reflected off the ice on her window. How beautiful she remembered that morning being. Terrible days weren't supposed to be beautiful.

"You see, at just the right time, when we were still powerless, Christ died for the Ungodly," Samuel continued.

Alessa's palms were slick with sweat. Why had she not gotten up earlier that day? She spent nearly an hour gazing at those silly rainbows. So many minutes wasted.

"Very rarely will anyone die for a righteous person." His eyes landed on the Hale family. "Though for a good person, someone might possibly dare to die."

Father Samuel smiled, bolstered in strength by his faith. The attention of the room only fueled him.

"But God demonstrates his own love for us in this: While we were still sinners, Christ died for us." Samuel's hand balled into a fist, and he banged it on the podium. "Since we have now been justified by his blood, how much more shall we be saved from God's wrath through him?"

As he articulated each verse, his gesticulation grew wilder and bolder.

"For if, while we were God's enemies, we were reconciled to him through the death of his Son, how much more, having been reconciled, shall we be saved through this life?"

How much did an hour matter? Alessa wondered. Could sixty minutes have made a difference in the search for her sister? She saw herself in the mirror that morning, fiddling with her hair, as if she had all the time in the world. If only she knew then how precious time really was.

"Not only is this so, but we also boast in God through our Lord Jesus Christ, through whom we have now received reconciliation."

Reconciliation. Alessa wasn't sure such a word was applicable to her anymore. She could barely reconcile her choices with herself, let alone expect anyone else to. Alessa forced her eyes open, focusing on Father Samuel's words.

"Therefore, just as sin entered the world through one man, and death through sin, and in this way, death came to all people, because

CHAPTER 6

all sinned." A serenity washed over him, smoothing out the tense lines of his face, it made him look ten years younger.

"To be sure, sin was in the world before the law was given, but sin is not charged against anyone's account where there is no law."

The icy winter air felt heavenly as the church doors opened at the end of the service. It cooled the sweat that was pooling under Alessa's thick clothing. She breathed in deeply until it pained her lungs. From inside her thoughts, Alessa was jolted by the sound of her friend sounding completely out of breath as she rushed to catch up with her. "Everyone's talking about her now," Maya said.

Alessa glanced over at the crowd. Everyone sectioned off in their chosen groups to chat and catch up. She smirked.

"You know, the funny thing s is that Aria probably would have hated that he held a service for her," Alessa replied.

Maya shrugged, taking no offense. "Yeah, she never struck me as the God-fearing type."

"Not even a little."

They looked at each other and devolved into a fit of giggles. Maya's gloved hand brush against hers, and her stomach flipped. Alessa steeled herself, ignoring the jackhammering in her chest.

"I want to thank you," Alessa said; Maya looked puzzled, "for always talking about Ari, for remembering her as she was, and not the girl they painted her out to be."

Her smile fell at Alessa's words, but Alessa wasn't looking at her anymore. She was staring blankly into the crowd of people, a hollow ache in her chest.

"Hey," Maya murmured, her pinky swiping over Alessa's knuckles, "it's you and me, remember? Till we're old and bitchy, and sitting in rocking chairs."

When Alessa didn't immediately respond, Maya wrapped her arm around Alessa's shoulders. Her hot breath dusted across Alessa's cold cheek as she spoke.

"I mean it. You know, I really do."

Alessa opened her mouth to question what she meant but she was interrupted by the sound of someone loudly clearing their throat. Alessa tensed when she saw Gavin Roswell approaching. Freshly shaved and wearing a newly pressed uniform, the chief removed his hat respectfully as he stopped in front of them.

"Sorry for the interruption, ladies" he began, fiddling with the brim of his hat. Maya shot Alessa a quick glance, her eyebrows raised with questions. Alessa pursed her lips and shrugged in response. Gavin Roswell was the last person she wanted to see today. Despite her distaste for his policework, Alessa let any verbal thrashings she wanted to give him shrivel up and die in her chest.

"I'm sure your mom and dad already gave you a good talking-to, so I'll spare you the lecture."

Neither of them replied. Roswell's gaze softened, as he clipped his sunglasses to the collar of his shirt.

"I wanted to apologize for what you witnessed out there. It was scary... for all of us. I wanted to make sure you were all right."

Alessa didn't know why she felt the need to look at Maya for reassurance, but Maya gave it to her anyway, nodding in response. She chalked it up to shock at Roswell's concern, because while he was a good man, he was also infamous for his firm hand.

"I'm okay, thanks."

"I know things have been hard, but I want to reassure you we have not given up on your sister. Understandably, none of this is going as quickly or as easily as you or I want it to, but I promise we'll keep going for as long as it takes."

Roswell held her eyes without blinking. And in spite of all the anger she had harbored toward the Chief, she sincerely believed he meant it.

"Thank you, Chief Roswell."

Lily approached her shortly after, placing a hand on her shoulder, Joshua waiting close behind. She smiled down at Alessa.

"Ready to go?"

Alessa nodded. "Yeah."

A shattering scream rippled over the crowd, stopping everyone dead in their tracks. A sea of heads shifted, seeking the source of the distress. Alessa turned to her parents. Lily's skin was stark white in terror, her eyes wide. Joshua didn't look any better, and it was challenging to see anything through the cluster of people. Gasps erupted around her, whispers and questions fluttered in the air.

"Roswell! ROSWELL!"

It was Officer Shirley's voice.

Bodies moved abruptly around her, the crowd parting like the red sea around Roswell as he clawed his way down the aisle. Alessa didn't hesitate. She felt like she was being pulled forward, compelled by an invisible force. She charged after him, ignoring the distant pleas of her mother.

Roswell continued on, unaware of the girl biting at his heels, until finally the crowd dispersed at the entrance of the building. When he reached the front, he came to a grinding halt, the wood squealing beneath the soles of his boots. The color drained from his skin; his usual pink flush replaced with a ghostly white that reached from his hairline to his toes.

"Jesus Christ," he whispered.

Alessa brushed past him easily. She stumbled to a stop once Roswell was behind her, almost dropping to the ground when her legs locked up. Many seconds passed where Alessa convinced herself that what she was seeing had to be a lie. It couldn't be real. She rubbed at her eyes, trying to awaken from the nightmare she was sure she was in. When she opened them again, she unleashed a sob that was ripped from her very core.

Aria Hale stood in the doorway of the church. Her pale body was naked from head-to-toe, and the sunlight streaming through the stained glass illuminated the blood, dark and thick, that was caked to her skin, mixing with dirt and mud. It smeared across her stomach, thighs, and forearms. The darkest stain blackened her lips and her long hair dangled around her face in greasy strands.

"Aria," Alessa said, breathless.

"Oh my God," another, vaguely familiar voice rang out, followed by a chaotic explosion of questions and accusations. The meaningless banter faded into a blur behind Alessa.

The crowd fell silent again, everyone sucking in a frantic breath when Aria seized a step, and then another. Distantly, Alessa heard Roswell's voice again.

"For God's sake, someone get me a damn coat!"

Aria continued, undeterred by the swelling madness around her. Slick, sticky footprints followed her with each step until she came to a stop in front of the crowd. Her shoulders rose and fell, and slow, steady breaths rasped from between her slightly parted lips. Blue eyes, bright against her filthy skin, remained locked on Alessa. She never blinked.

Coat in hand, Roswell rushed to Aria's aid. He hesitated when he approached her, his arms arching carefully around her as he draped it over her shoulders. She remained still as his trembling hands buttoned the top of the coat to cover her. Roswell stood right in front of her, but she appeared to be staring right through him.

"Aria," Roswell said carefully, keeping his hands close to but never touching her, "Aria, do you remember who I am? Do you know where you are?"

She said nothing.

Aria took another step, and then another, brushing by Roswell entirely. Despite the waver in her step, she took each one with purpose, each one of them leading to her sister. Alessa blinked out of her trance then, her brain shrieking back to life, and she bolted to Aria, arms outstretched. Aria's legs buckled from under her, and she collapsed to the floor just as Alessa reached her. She threw herself under her sister's weight, catching the worst of the fall, and they landed in a tangled heap of limbs. Gasps and shouts of horror ricocheted against the walls, and everyone crowded around them.

Alessa rose to her knees, cradling Aria's head delicately in her arms before resting it on her lap. Matted clumps of red hair cascaded over her thighs and tumbled onto the shiny wood floor. Aria blinked up at her wearily.

"I'm here, Ari," Alessa wept, "I'm here."

Tears raked angry streaks down Alessa's cheeks, but Aria's stare remained unfocused, scanning over her features repeatedly. It was as if she didn't recognize her at all.

Father Samuel remained behind the podium; feet rooted to the floor. He folded his hands over the hard wooden edge of the podium, squeezing until his knuckles turned into white marbles against his flesh.

Alessa froze when Aria reached up a blood soaked, shaky hand. It fell just short of her face, instead clamping tightly around the fabric of her blouse. Aria dragged Alessa closer until their noses nearly brushed. Alessa caught a whiff of the bitter and vile stench clinging to her sister's body. All of her energy went into not reeling back at the scent. She couldn't, even if she wanted to. Aria's hold kept her firmly in place.

Aria's mouth parted with a sickening snap, the dried blood breaking as her lips moved, her slick tongue coming out to wet them desperately. She held Alessa's stare, tiny sounds emitting from the back of her throat, but no words. Aria continued to move her lips, trying to form something Alessa couldn't decipher. Her eyes fluttered, irises rolling all the way back to reveal the red veins in her sclera. Alessa held her close as her body fell limp. Frantically, she jostled her, only stopping when she saw the rise and fall of Aria's chest. She was alive.

Alessa's head lifted. The swarm of people tightened around them, but she was looking at Roswell. The two stared at each other with a shared look of horror.

Aria Hale had come home.

Chapter 7

Aria jerked back into consciousness. She caught flashes of a door opening and a small waiting room. A seamless blob of figures moved around her, but she couldn't make out any of their features. Voices clamored, each one louder than the next. But it all felt so far away. Her face was pressed into something warm and soft, arms cradling her from underneath. Fingers pried open her eye, shining in a bright light and sending a scattershot of pain bursting in her temples. She tucked her face into the body carrying her.

Aria winced with each movement. Her ears were beginning to ring, a screeching sound that lacerated her ear drums from the inside. The voices, while indistinguishable, grew louder, each word like a tiny explosion of untenable pain inside her skull. Aria's eyes widened, fluttering frantically, as the voices swelled to an unbearable crescendo. A dark, hollow gnawing tore at her insides. It took the air right out of her. Her breaths came shallow and ragged. Each one sounded like pebbles scraping across gravel. A soft hand caressed her cheek.

"Sweetheart, can you hear me?"

A blonde woman hovered beside her, moving with them. Hands grazed and patted her, but she roughly turned her head away every time they had a tenuous grip.

She scanned the woman's face, searching her mind for any recognition, but came up blank. Their expressions were sharpening, each voice becoming more distinct from the next. Blood was pounding in her ears.

"Do we have an exam room open?" the doctor called above the rest of them.

"Yes, sir, just down the hall!" A nurse replied.

Not only were the voices steadily becoming clearer, but she could now hear beyond them. Layered under the chatter, she heard the frost crunching under their boots. She heard a phone ringing from down the hall and the grinding of her teeth in the bowels of her brain.

Beads of sweat formed on her upper lip and temples. Aria started wriggling uncomfortably as the world spun around her. Her senses were becoming painfully overwhelmed. Too many sounds. Too many things touching her. Her skin crawled like spiders were dancing under her flesh. The person holding her, whom she recognized as the man who'd given her the jacket, tried to grip her tighter.

"Aria, just breathe, honey," the blonde cooed, "it's all right."

Suddenly, the woman's voice exploded into a deafening decibel. Aria thrashed, releasing a cry of pain that drew the entire group to a screeching halt.

"I can't keep hold of her!" the man shouted, straining to contain her writhing.

"Bring her in here!" Another voice from a man in a white coat sounded as they rounded the next corner. They practically threw her down on an examination table. Aria kicked and flailed, her howls echoing down each hall and spilling into every room.

"Roswell, help me hold her down," the man in the white coat commanded. They each grabbed one of her arms. "Nurse!"

A young lady in pink scrubs rushed forth to grab her legs. The brunette man pulled the other woman away, their expressions equally distraught.

CHAPTER 7

Aria scratched her blood-soaked fingers down her arms, itching to tear it directly from the muscle, to strip herself down to the bone. The gnawing in her gut bloomed, pulsing as it expanded. Her insides screamed. Hungry. She was so hungry.

The one they called Roswell attempting to pin her arm to the table. Aria used the man's grip to yank him down to her level. Tense fingers latched around his bicep and Roswell lifted his head, brown irises meeting blue depths as dark and fathomless as the sea. Aria snarled; bloody teeth bared.

He barely had time to blink before she launched him like a paper airplane across the room and into the wall. The blonde screamed; Joshua pulled her deeper into his embrace. The man in white turned to the nurse.

"I need five milligrams of Haldol and two milligrams of Ativan."

"Yes, Doctor Sutton." She rushed out.

"Joshua, Lily, I need you!" The couple hovered by the door hesitantly. "Now!"

They jumped to attention, grabbing her limbs to keep her still. Aria jerked and struggled; the nurse returned seconds later.

They passed the syringe from hand to hand, and they barely keeping Aria from propelling off the table. Their necks were red and wrung with tension. Doctor Sutton grabbed her and pressed the tip of the needle into the pale, spongy flesh of her upper arm. He pressed down on the plunger, the medicine shooting into her body down to the very last drop. Aria hardly felt it, the pinch swallowed by the gaping hole tearing open in her guts. Making room for something she couldn't possibly fathom. She couldn't think. She could barely breathe. It was so hot.

They held her and waited as the sedative took effect, rushing cool and smooth in her bloodstream. Thirty seconds passed, and then sixty. Even when the seconds stretched beyond a minute, Aria continued to move, her strength barely impeded. Her screams finally died down into groans and growls, and she rocked her head furiously back and forth.

"How the hell is she still awake?" Someone whispered.

Eventually, after five minutes ticked by and Aria still didn't succumb to the sedative entirely, the doctor sighed to himself. The fight was seeping out of her. She felt heavy.

"Okay, let's get started," he said, once more gaining control of the room. The nurses ushered the couple out as Doctor Sutton tended to Roswell. He'd only suffered a few bumps and bruises, but they provided him with an icepack as they helped him to his feet and led him out.

There were three of them, two nurses and the doctor. They darted around Aria in the small exam room. The walls were a pale purple, although there were cracks in the paint that were chipped with age. Aria grimaced at the scent of the stale air.

Whatever they injected her with depleted most of her energy. She felt fuzzy now, every movement dragging as if in slow motion. Aria blinked dazedly as the nurses propped her in a sitting position. She swayed slightly, her balance off. It was constant action, gloved hands grasping silver instruments, pushing her hair away, and swabbing soft cotton across her sticky cheeks.

She didn't move this time when Doctor Sutton pointed a flashlight into her eyes and her pupils dilated in response. He was pulling away when a flash of color gave him pause. His bottom lip snagged between his teeth, and he brought the light back up.

"Everything all right, Doctor Sutton?" one nurse asked.

He checked again, his words catching in his throat. The doctor reeled back, ashen, and shoved the light into his pocket. Aria watched him, face blank.

"Yes," he finally replied, "yes, fine. Please, make sure you get as many samples of the blood as possible."

They were gentle as they wiped the blood from her face and neck, layers and layers caked under dirt and grime. She remained still as the medicine soothed her muscles and cast a thick fog over her brain. Her mouth opened easily when the doctor checked her throat, shining the same light inside.

Later, after switching her into a gown that slit open in the back, Harris pressed the cold drum of his stethoscope to her back, but she didn't react. Not even a shiver. The ridges of her spine practically protruded from her skin, like it wasn't enough to contain her skeleton. Every blue vein that threaded a web inside of her blossomed brightly under her nearly translucent flesh.

"A deep breath for me," he requested.

Aria did as she was told, drawing in slow, deep breaths so he could listen to her lungs. He adjusted the drum after each breath.

"And one more time."

She turned to watch him as he pressed the drum to her back one last time. Her lips gently parted, eyes trailing down to his neck where his Adam's apple bobbed up and down. A shimmer of sweat glistened under his chin.

His skin looked soft, Aria thought, soft enough to give with the slightest amount of pressure. It would tear with little effort. Hot saliva pooled in her mouth. Doctor Sutton cleared his throat and backed away.

For nearly an hour, Aria remained on the bed, twisted, and turned—positioned in whatever manner necessary to conduct their tests. Their hands, poking and prodding, were like sandpaper dragging over her skin, but the drugs had softened and exhausted her. When it finally ceased, she curled tightly into herself at the corner of the bed, wedged against the wall with her knees hugged to her chest. Her attention, however, remained steady on the people who cycled in and out of her room.

Sutton opened the door to allow Lily back inside, and the two remained sequestered on the opposite side of the room. They turned their backs to her, mumbling quietly, but she heard them clear and sharp.

"It's very strange. I can't really make sense of it," he said to her.

"What do you mean?"

Doctor Sutton fiddled with his glasses, the artificial light reflecting off the lenses. He flipped through her chart.

"Aside from being malnourished, it appears Aria is in remarkably adequate health."

Lily's face twisted in confusion. She glanced at Aria, who glowered at them from the corner of the room.

"I don't understand."

"Frankly, neither do I, Mrs. Hale. We've done a full physical, and taken a slew of blood samples for testing, and from what I can tell, she isn't ill, and she's not injured."

Baffled, he continued to read through the chart over and over again.

"Aria appears..." He searched for the right words. "For lack of a better term: normal. Although, her resistance to the sedatives is... alarming."

"That doesn't make sense," Lily fumed, "she's been gone for two months – God knows where – and what about all the blood... I mean, she's covered..."

Two months? Aria wondered. What the hell were these people talking about? The only glimpses of her memories she conjured were fleeting. The woods. A church. The girl in the floral skirt.

The girl. She'd been heading right toward her. Aria's heart sped up. She didn't know why, but she wanted to see that girl again. It felt important.

"I wish I knew. I'm sorry. We should know more when the blood tests come back. We're running a complete metabolic panel, and we've taken various samples of the fluids found on her body. But there was a lot, as you know, so it could take one to two days."

Lily exhaled sharply and nibbled on her thumbnail.

"God, I think I'm going to be sick."

"I promise I will make you aware of the results as soon as we have them but take solace that she is here now. She's safe. There is a distinct possibility that the blood could come from an animal."

Lily cringed. "Is that supposed to make me feel better?"

"It means Aria probably foraged for food while she was in the woods. The blood doesn't have to mean anything sinister. It could simply mean survival. The best thing you can do right now is focus on moving forward."

Doctor Sutton turned to exit the exam room but paused as his hand touched the knob. "Might I make a suggestion?"

Lily nodded, eager for any advice that might help.

"Find out where she's been. I think that will benefit everyone."

Without giving her a second to reply, he was out the door. Silence thickened the air as soon as the door clicked shut. They were alone. Aria continued to watch her intensely, hands resting on her knees., dark lashes fanning shadows across her cheeks. Lily squared her shoulders and stepped toward Aria.

"Aria, sweetie, how are you feeling?"

Aria. Why did they keep calling her that? Was it supposed to be her name? She had no memory of being called by any name. Truly, she had no memory of anything before this place.

She didn't answer, didn't even twitch in recognition of the question. However, there was something familiar about Lily. This woman knew her. That much was easy to tell, but Aria couldn't understand how. Despite her confusion, she was drawn to the blonde woman in a way that defied explanation. Whoever this woman was, Aria felt linked to her. But a feeling did not equate trust. She continued to stare, unblinking, until Lily was standing directly next to her at the edge of the bed.

"Sweetheart?" Lily pleaded, gnawing on her bottom lip. Aria's head rose with interest. A pebble of blood formed at the corner of her mother's mouth, thick and dark.

Aria jumped to her feet; knees bent in an awkward squat on the feeble mattress to stay at eye level with the woman. Lily gasped but stayed put, hands clenching into fists.

"Aria, please talk to me."

Still, she gave no response. Her eyes instead took in every detail of this strange woman. The golden hair, verging on white in places, with barely a strand in disarray. Lily tilted her head in confusion; Aria mirrored her movements. She tilted her head as well, keeping her unnerving eye contact the entire time. Aria caught a powerful gust of the woman's perfume, floral and sickening. Her heart was thrumming.

Lily bit back a squeal when Aria's hand darted out, gripping her jaw forcefully. Aria's fingertips pressed into her skin as she adjusted Lily's head to examine it. Lily attempted to pull away, but she couldn't move. Aria's hand kept her immobile. Aria drew her closer until she felt puffs of hot breath caressing her cheeks.

"A-Ari," she barely squeaked out, but it was lost before reaching Aria's ears. She cared for nothing aside from the shimmering pebble of blood that now streamed from the corner of Lily's mouth down her chin. Aria caught it with her thumb, smearing beautiful red across the woman's previously flawless complexion.

Lily stumbled back when Aria finally released her, stroking her cheek. Without a second thought, Aria plunged her blood covered finger into her wet and waiting mouth, swirling her tongue decadently around the appendage.

CHAPTER 7

The blood was dense, the taste of iron exploding on her tastebuds, but there was something more—a taste underneath the iron—a taste she couldn't pinpoint that was unmistakably tied to this woman. It made the hunger inside of her rise like a blossoming flower. The fluid slid across her teeth, and she sucked her finger dry. A string of saliva connected her lips to her hand when she finally removed it from her mouth. It broke when Aria let out a low, contented sigh.

Her eyes flickered to Lily once more and the woman tensed. Aria saw she was quivering, and her hands twitched with anticipation. She could have more. She could have as much as she wanted. Lily opened her mouth to speak, but only mustered one breathless word.

"Aria?"

A small patch of red lingered on Aria's bottom lip, and she slowly and deliberately dragged her tongue across it, trying to catch every last drop. The sound rushed out of the room, like someone had taken a vacuum to the atmosphere and pulled the switch.

The door opened and the hustling and bustling of the hallway leaked into the room, breaking the tension. The two women turned and saw Joshua enter. He stood hesitantly by the door, a paper bag dangling in his hand. Joshua glanced between the two of them.

"I, uh... I brought you some fresh clothes."

Lily darted to his side. "Thank you, dear."

When Lily didn't motion to take the bag, he approached Aria himself, smiling softly, before dropping the object on the bed next to her. His presence startled Aria. This man was unlike the one she'd seen earlier. Again, he was familiar, the curves and indents of his expression lighting a bare spark of recognition in her. She continued to watch him cautiously and backed herself into the corner again when he got close enough. Their eyes met briefly, and she immediately turned away, her shoulders hunched. Joshua looked her up and down, poised to speak, but no words emerged. Shock and devastation warred over his face.

Joshua reached out, his hand coming within a hair's breadth of her; she recoiled and knocked the back of her skull against the wall. He hissed in pain, reeling back, and retracting his arm. Aria was shaking, her tremors vibrating through the mattress.

"I'm sorry, I'm sorry," he whispered and backed away, "it's okay, it's just me, honey."

She peered at him suspiciously.

"It's your dad, sweetie," he choked out. Aria sensed the hurt in his words, but it brought her no closer to understanding who these people were. Joshua turned back to Lily, crestfallen.

"What did Doctor Sutton say?"

Lily regaled the details to him, everything from the doctor's confusion down to awaiting the results of the blood tests.

"How can this be possible?" Joshua asked absently. Lily frowned, gaze hardening.

"I have no idea, but Doctor Sutton suggested we do our best to figure out where exactly she's been this whole time."

"This is fucking insanity, Lily."

Her hands clenched around her knees, nails digging into her skirt. "Joshua, please."

A knock at the door stole their attention. Doctor Sutton poked his head in, his face relaxing when he saw they were both present.

"Oh good, you're both here. I'm so sorry to interrupt, but Roswell and Shirley would like a word."

They shared a simultaneous look of concern and followed him out without glancing back at Aria once. When they were out of sight, Aria slid off the bed. She stood in the center of the exam room and faced the mirror that was flush against the wall. The thin gown the nurses forced upon her dropped to her feet, leaving her skin naked. Chilled air spilled out of the vents on the ceiling. It was heavenly to Aria, drying the patches of sweat that pebbled on her neck and back. She examined her reflection, the sharp curves of her ribs, the pale-bordering-on-blue hue of her complexion. Bony fingers pressed into protruding hip bones and brushed the bumps of her spine that lead up the back of her neck.

She looked both like and unlike herself. *Was that right?* Aria thought. What did she look like before? Aria's lashes fluttered. Before. *Before what?*

She leaned in close to her reflection, prodding at her cheekbones and eyes. Within her blue irises were glimmers of gold clinging to the edges of her pupils. Faint ringing burned deep in her ear canal, and a splitting pain burst in the front of her brain. Her thoughts erupted into confetti, memories fading to dust.

When did she move back to the bed?

Aria blinked and saw the folded pile of clothes on the bed directly in front of her. Over her shoulder, across the room, stood the mirror. Taking a deep breath, she picked up the top item of clothing by the very tips of her fingers. Warm, heavy fabric with long sleeves. It appeared similar to the piece of clothing the man who had just left was wearing. She stroked it between her fingers. It was far better than the gown she was previously wearing.

The woman instructed her to put them on before they left. In her mind, it felt right, but her stomach thrashed at the idea of putting anything against her skin. This time, her mind won out, and she slipped on the sweater.

"This is ridiculous!"

An exclamation from the hallway caught Aria's attention. She slowly and quietly crept to the door until she was right in front of it.

"S-Surely you don't think Aria had anything to do with that, do you?" the same voice said, crystal clear, as if they were standing in the same room.

"We can't make any definitive statements yet, but we'll be comparing the blood samples of the body we found to what on Aria." someone explained.

"You can't seriously be considering Aria for this; I mean, you both know her—you've known her for her entire life!" This one she recognized as the blonde.

"We can't ignore the facts. Now we promise to keep you informed. We don't want any problems, but we have a responsibility to this town."

"Can this at least wait until tomorrow?" Lily asked.

Aria backed away from the door when she heard movement from the other side and retreated to the bed. It opened to reveal Lily and Joshua, both of them wearing uneasy smiles. Joshua was the first to take a tentative step closer.

"Ready to go home?"

Aria didn't know of any home. These strange people were relentless, but they seemed to know her, or at least they believed they did.

"Your sister is waiting outside; I know she's going to be so happy to see you."

Sister? This made her perk up. She remembered the young girl from the church. Had she been looking for her? Aria couldn't recall. All she knew was when their eyes locked from across the room, she was certain she was exactly where she needed to be.

Aria slid off the bed, her curiosity overwhelming, and followed the two without a word. Lily and Joshua flanked her as they led her from the examination room and down the short hall to the main lobby. Now that she had a better look at it, Aria noticed how small the building was. The lobby was barely bigger than the room she was just in and had a line of five chairs leaning against the front window that faced the street.

"I-I don't... I don't understand," a small voice stammered, "why did she look like that?"

CHAPTER 7

"I don't know. But she's here now, she's home. That's what matters."

"Alessa," Lily said.

Two girls were sitting side by side, practically entangled in their chairs. The girl in question perked up and bolted from her chair. She wore a brown coat over her Sunday best now and clutched it to her chest like a safety blanket. Alessa, as they called her, took a step closer.

"Ari?" Her question came out as a whisper.

Aria flinched. It was strange hearing the name come out of her mouth. Her instinct was to back away, tucking herself behind Lily and James. There were far too many eyes on her.

"We should get home," Lily interrupted.

"Oh, sure," Alessa said, stunned.

Joshua directed Aria to the exit. Aria followed closely behind not wanting to be out in the open anymore. She felt exposed. Alessa gave her friend one last nod before scurrying after them.

A small but rambunctious crowd gathered outside the doctor's office, flinging constant questions at them, but Aria kept her head down. Joshua threw open the door to his car and ushered her in. Alessa slid in next to her. Aria leaned her forehead against the window, eyes on the crowd, and noticed someone standing still in the center of it all. Through the madness, she noticed a man in black robes with a white collar watching her, his face a blank slate of emotion.

Their eyes locked, Joshua revved the engine, and as the car pulled away, Aria lifted her hand to the odd man, and waved.

Chapter 8

Alessa had never seen so many people gathered in one place. She thought the church was bad, but the entire town appeared to be gathering across the street from their home as their car pulled into the driveway. Aria didn't seem to pay them any mind. Alessa wished she was as calm, but she truly had no idea how Aria was feeling.

"Vultures," Joshua spit venomously. Alessa agreed wholeheartedly.

The car rolled to a slow stop; Joshua gripped the steering wheel tightly.

"All right, everyone just head inside. Don't engage." He glanced in the rearview mirror to catch Alessa's eye. She nodded.

All at once, the family opened their doors, Joshua taking care of Aria's. Alessa glanced across the street at the crowd. Oddly, they were all adults. Alessa didn't see anyone her age, or any of the kids from her school. She figured they would be just as desperate for some town drama. Joshua was helping Aria out of the car as Alessa took a headcount. Anger bubbled beneath her ribs. There were far more people present now than there ever were in the searches for Aria. Vulture was too kind a word for these people.

A constant hum of murmured chatter came from across the street, questions blended with gossip and judgmental glares.

A wave of silence befell them when Aria emerged from the car. Joshua allowed her space but hovered close, trying to lead her to the house. Aria stayed stiff but turned to face the crowd. It surprised Alessa to see a couple of people suddenly gather their belongings and shuffle away, heads downcast and shielding their faces.

"Aria!" Lily called softly from the front steps.

Alessa followed their gazes to her sister.

Oh god, Ari. She thought.

Aria was smiling; though it was not Aria's smile, not the one Alessa knew. This was something awful—something sinister. Alessa's veins filled with ice.

"A-Ari."

Smile gone; Aria whipped around to face her. Alessa steadied her breathing.

"Come on, let's go inside."

Aria stared blankly at Alessa for a moment before turning and following their parents inside. Lily was quick to close the curtains, not wanting the onlookers to have any more access to their family than they already had. She muttered angrily under her breath while Alessa watched Aria wander the living room.

Aria scanned the mantel above the fireplace, where most of the photos remained overturned. Her eyes passed over them with a carelessness that surprised Alessa. Aria ascended the stairs and while Alessa ached to follow, she figured it best to allow her sister some space. She was here now; she had to remind herself. Aria was home, and she was safe.

But maybe just a quick peak? That couldn't hurt, right?

As soon as her parents' backs were turned, Alessa crept quietly up the stairs. Aria was standing in front of her now open bedroom door, staring inside with an unreadable gaze. Alessa gripped the railing until her palm was sweating. Eventually, Aria stepped inside. Alessa snuck up the rest of the way, pressing her back to the wall and inching closer.

Aria looked out of place in her room. As if the idea of being confined to these four walls disgusted her. While her body should have been weakened by malnourishment, Aria exuded a powerful energy that Alessa struggled to put her finger on. It pulsed from every pore and ran in rivulets to the floor. The energy reminded Alessa of the cold and unwelcoming aura of the surrounding woods.

Alessa kept to the shadows in case Aria saw her. Taking a shallow breath, she glanced down for just an instant to wipe her palms on her jeans when suddenly the light shifted in the corner of her eye. Alessa jumped when she realized Aria had already been watching her.

"Jesus!" Alessa gasped, her heart racing.

Aria simply stared at her, analyzing.

"S-Sorry, Ari," she started, "I just wanted to check and make sure you were settling in, okay."

There was no response to her apology, no nod, not even a twitch of the lips, to show Aria understood what she was saying. The intensity of her sister's gaze made a surge of guilt overcome her senses; despair crept into the corners of Alessa's mind.

"Everything is where you left it. I didn't mess with anything, I promise."

Still no response. Alessa's face fell, and she wrung her hands together, skin red and raw. Her eyes glistened with fresh tears, and she mustered a trembling smile. A grating voice hissed in the back of her mind: *This is not her. This is not your sister.*

Of course, it occurred to Alessa that if Aria were to return, she would be different. Long absences had the tendency to do that, especially given their suspicious and traumatic circumstances. She wasn't naïve enough to believe that Aria would come home normal, vibrant, and full of joy, but she never expected this. She couldn't have predicted that her own sister wouldn't recognize her.

"I'll leave you alone, I just..." Alessa sniffled and wiped a tear away that escaped. "I-I'm really happy you're back. We missed you."

Alessa paused and held Aria's eyes when she spoke again.

"*I* missed you," she emphasized.

Aria's blank stare softened ever-so-slightly, almost imperceptibly, but it made Alessa perk up with hope. She waited just a moment hoping that her sister would respond, but she continued to hold her silence. Alessa knew it was time to retreat, she could feel the tears damming up behind her eyes and they were getting hard to fight. She gave a little nod, turning on her heels, heading back toward the safety of her own space.

"Wait."

She whipped back around, nearly falling over.

Aria's voice was hoarse and gravelly from a lack of use, but the sound of it rolled over Alessa like a warm wave of honey.

"Stay?"

Alessa was confused but refused to question the sudden change. Alessa flashed her sister a watery smile and nodded. She followed Aria into the bedroom and closed the door behind them.

Aria returned to standing awkwardly in the center of the room. It was as if she was unsure how to occupy this space. Alessa, muscles weak with exhaustion, crawled into the bed. Her sister watched her; eyes curious but uncomprehending. Alessa gently patted the mattress next to her, encouraging Aria to join. After brief consideration, she did.

The two young women rested on their sides, facing one another. Alessa's eyes fluttered. She fought to keep her consciousness but was failing. Sleep chased her for the first time in months. She smiled blearily at Aria, struggling to speak through her drowsiness.

"I'm afraid if I close my eyes, you'll disappear again," she whispered.

CHAPTER 8

Aria reached out and grabbed Alessa's hand, surprising her. Aria clasped it tightly.

"I'm here." Aria said, renewed intensity flashing on her face before returning to a flat, and vaguely lost expression.

Alessa bit back tears. "Promise?"

Tentatively, Alessa reached out and wrapped pinky finger around Aria's. She noted how cold her sister's skin was. Aria furrowed her brows at their tangled fingers, a storm brewing in her irises.

"I... promise."

A flicker of recognition sparkled in Aria's eyes. And just like that, it was gone, replaced with detached uncertainty, but at least Aria wasn't running. She was still here. The mantra repeated in a cyclical but soothing rhythm in Alessa's mind until sleep enveloped her.

She woke with a start, her brain shrieking back to life as the foggy remnants of a nightmare dissipated like smoke. It took a while for her mind to catch up to the events of the day.

Aria.

She instantly turned over to find the spot next to her was empty. Alessa touched the mattress. It was cold. Panic shot through her like an electric wire. The bedroom door was open. Alessa imagined Aria outside, heading for the woods, and jumped to her feet.

The house was quiet, and she pulled on a sweater as she tiptoed into the hallway, whispering her sister's name but getting no response. Amber light poured into the hall, and she noticed the door to her parent's room was slightly ajar. It was unlike either of them to be up at this hour.

Alessa heard mumbling as she approached their room. She peered through the crack in the door and saw her mother hunched on her knees on the mattress, hands clasped in prayer in front of her forehead. Lily faced the wooden cross dangling above her headboard. Her shoulders trembled, small gasps and whimpers escaping her.

"Dearest Lord," Lily whispered, "I humbly request your forgiveness. I am lost and I need your guidance. I'm afraid I don't know where to turn."

Alessa stayed out of sight. The flame of a lone candle on the nightstand twitched.

"Show me the way, show me the right path, so I may do right by her."

Tightly wound hands shook, and tears spilled down Lily's red cheeks.

"None of this," she continued, "none of this should have ever happened... I'm sorry – I'm sorry!"

The fragile floorboards creaked under Alessa's weight, and she abruptly pressed herself into the shadows to avoid being seen. She waited, back to the wall and holding her breath, until she could hear the desperation in her mother's prayers again before making her way downstairs.

Joshua sprawled haphazardly on the couch in the living room, bundled and snoring, with his cheek smashed against the pillow. Alessa breathed out in relief when she saw Aria staring out the window.

"Aria," Alessa whispered, moving to stand beside her., "what are you doing down here?"

When her sister didn't reply, Alessa followed her gaze out the window. Across the street, lit by the dim glow of a streetlamp, was a young couple walking their dog. She watched as they teased, playfully shoving at each other before the man dropped a loving kiss to the woman's forehead. The dog's pink tongue lolled out the side of its mouth.

Suddenly, the boyfriend noticed them and with a soft tug on his girlfriend's jacket; they slowed to a stop. Their eyes were wide and wary, shifting repeatedly from the girls back to each other. The impenetrable darkness of the woods behind them only made the couple

CHAPTER 8

appear smaller.

Aria pressed her fingertips to the chilled glass of the window, and then her whole palm. The woman flinched when she moved, tucking herself into the man's side as if shielding herself. Alessa watched in silence. Eventually, the couple took off, hurrying down the road and away from their house. The girlfriend continually threw concerned glances over her shoulder until eventually they turned the corner and were out of sight.

Chapter 9

Fresh beams of sunlight warmed Alessa's cheeks the following morning, gently rousing her from her slumber. Alessa turned over to make sure Aria was still there, that everything that happened before wasn't just a product of her own feverish imagination. But Aria was no longer in bed.

Instead, she was standing in front of the window facing their backyard, still as a statue. Alessa couldn't even see the rise and fall of her shoulders to indicate she was breathing. Her mouth, however, was moving. Lips forming odd patterns, voice barely floating above a whisper. Alessa threw the covers off.

"Ari?"

Alessa rushed to Aria's side, but she did not acknowledge her. Wanting to see what she was seeing, Alessa looked out the window as well, but saw only an endless stretch of forest. Darkness permeated through the gaps in the trees, but nothing appeared unusual or concerning.

Aria's gaze was distant and locked on something seemingly intangible. Her body did not move, but her lips kept going, quietly repeating the same words. She did not seem to register that her sister had joined her, in fact her eyes glazed over, as if the rhythmic chanting of these strange phrases had lured her into a trance. "We did not come to be served, but to serve, and to give our lives as a ransom to many," Aria spoke, "whomever is the first to open..."

"Ari," Alessa said again.

Nothing.

"... to give our lives as ransom to many..."

Perturbed, Alessa grabbed her arm and shook her. This seemed to snap Aria out of it, and she blinked rapidly. Her brows narrowed in confusion.

"Are you okay?"

Aria finally looked at Alessa, the fog in her eyes a little clearer now. She shot a glance out the window to where the trees danced.

"What's wrong?" Alessa asked.

Aria flinched. "Nothing." She spoke so abruptly it startled Alessa. "I just thought I heard... something?"

When Aria didn't elaborate, Alessa pressed her. "What did you hear?"

Her nose wrinkled the way it used to when something stumped her. Alessa almost smiled at the sight, pleased to find a piece of the old Aria still lingering.

"My name," she finally said, "like someone calling my name."

The silhouette of Lily Hale was framed in slate grey. She stood before the front window; the sky was churning. A storm was coming. Maybe a day or two away, but if the darkening of the sky was any indication, it would be a bad one. Outside, the accumulation of curious neighbors had grown even larger.

"You'd think they'd give us just a second of peace," she grumbled.

Joshua fluffed the pillow on the couch and folded his blanket in tight, practiced squares until it was small enough to wedge in their storage ottoman.

"Roswell will take care of them."

"Fucking parasites," Lily hissed.

"Lily, please," Joshua tried to reach her, his fingers barely brushing her shoulders when she coldly shrugged him off. She turned on him with a look of icy fury.

"I don't want your excuses, Joshua. I want you to handle it."

He sank to the couch as he watched her stalk away from him; his shoulders sagged. As Aria and Alessa rounded the corner, he threw on a smile.

"Good morning, girls. Did you both sleep well?"

"Fine," Alessa said quietly.

"Oh good, you're both up!"

Lily swept in gracefully, all smiles and teeth. She looked manic, Alessa thought. Lily immediately crowded their space, mania replaced with motherly affection.

"I hope you got some good rest."

Aria's lip pulled back in a sneer, but she didn't respond. Alessa noticed her sister visibly tense and tense and shift away from their mother. Thankfully, this time Lily took the hint and took a step back.

"Anyway, I made your favorite breakfast, Aria. Bacon and blueberry waffles with orange juice!"

Even Alessa was stunned. She couldn't remember the last time their mother made Aria's favorite meal - breakfast, lunch, or dinner. But she supposed these circumstances warranted a change of heart. Aria, however, looked anything but pleased.

"I'm not hungry," she said.

Lily simply stared at her, and Alessa briefly thought she didn't hear Aria.

"How can you not be hungry?"

Lily asked, bewildered, but Alessa felt the undercurrent of anger simmering under her words. When Aria didn't answer, she tried a different approach.

CHAPTER 9

"The doctor said you were malnourished, really it would be best if you ate something. You need to get your strength back up."

"Your mother's right, you really should have at least a few bites, get some protein in you," Joshua argued readily. .

Aria looked to Alessa, scanning her face as if asking for help. While it was surprising in her current state, Aria apparently trusted her enough to seek her wisdom. Alessa gave her a nod.

"Later, maybe? I just don't feel very well."

Aria laid her hand on her abdomen. It was difficult to argue against, Aria did not look good.

"Of course, sweetheart, I'll just package it up and you can have some in an hour or so, okay?" Lily offered. Aria shrugged one shoulder, placating their parents for now.

Roswell and Shirley arrived an hour later. They were the picture of professionalism as they stood waiting on the front steps; the door swinging wide as Joshua greeted them. After Lily insisted on getting beverages for everyone, the family and the officers gathered in the living room.

"We're very sorry to be putting you through this. As I mentioned yesterday, we're going to be questioning Aria regarding her whereabouts over the previous two months— specifically where she was the last few days before she returned," Roswell started.

Shirley looked at Aria. "This won't take long, and you're welcome to stop us at any point if you need to take a break," she said.

Aria gave a curt nod. Alessa sat next to her, alert and eager. Roswell pulled out his notepad and clicked the top of his pen several times.

"All right, let's get started."

"Let's start with the night you went missing. What can you tell us about that evening?"

Everyone in the room held their breath. Alessa's leg bounced. Her nerves were on fire. Shuddering, Aria's eyes shot open.

"I-I don't know."

"You don't know?"

She gazed up at them helplessly, shaking her head. "I'm sorry, I don't remember."

How could someone be gone for two months and recall none of the experience? Alessa wondered in horror. What could cause a person to lose so much time?

"Is there anything you do remember?" Shirley interjected.

Alessa noticed Aria's long nails leaving indentations on the skin of her knees. Again, she closed her eyes as if to will the memories to the surface.

"Snow," she finally said, "a lot of snow."

Aria stayed that way for a while, her jaw clenched and her eyelids rapidly fluttering. She jerked back to the present, her eyes flying open. She inhaled shakily.

"I guess I got lost."

The gentle scratching of pen on paper filled the room as Roswell jotted down the scant details.

"Do you know why you were in the woods in the first place?"

"No."

"Okay, do you recall seeing anyone? Did someone help you?" Shirley questioned next.

Alessa knew the continued questioning was a lost cause. If Aria couldn't remember, their pestering certainly wouldn't force an epiphany.

"Take your time," she added when Aria raised a hand to rub her temple.

Alessa wanted to tell them to screw off, but kept quiet, giving her sister a reassuring smile. She reached over and grasped her sister's hand gently. Aria surprised them all by gripping her fingers softly in return.

"Maybe," Aria finally answered. Roswell and Shirley shared a worried look.

"What do you mean by maybe, Aria?" the chief asked.

"It's hazy... but I-I remember seeing... something out there."

They waited, hanging on her words with bated breath. Aria groaned.

"That's all I can give you. I'm sorry."

Roswell had become just as frustrated as Aria. He ran a hand down his face, sighing. The tension in the room was becoming palpable.

"So, you're telling us you have absolutely no memory of the last two months?"

"How is that possible?" Lily barked.

Shirley reached her hand out in a calming gesture to draw their attention.

"It's quite common for traumatic events to result in temporary memory loss, Mrs. Hale. It's likely these memories will return to her over time; we just have to be patient."

Lily, however, pushed aside the officer's advice. She turned to Aria with a smile that was smoldering with fury and wrought with a strange desperation.

"Please, honey," she started, leaning into them, "just take a moment and really think about it."

"I did," Aria spat. Unfortunately, this answer did not deter Lily's need for immediate answers.

"You must remember something, Aria. You can't just forget two whole months!"

"Mrs. Hale," Shirley tried to interrupt.

"I mean, this is ridiculous!"

"Lillian." The simmering authority of Roswell's baritone voice effectively quieted her. When she looked at him, there was a warning in his eyes. His expression was stern.

"That's enough. Now if Aria is having problems with her memory, there's nothing we can do about it. We'll work with what we have."

When his attention was back on Aria, he was smiling, his previous irritation completely gone.

"And when you do remember, we hope you'll inform us of anything that comes to you."

Aria said nothing, but she did nod. Joshua pulled Lily back to his side. Her head lowered, successfully cowed for the time being. Satisfied, the officers continued.

"We just have one more question for you, Aria. Can you tell us anything about the blood that was found on you when you returned to the church?"

Aria gave the smallest shake of her head. Shirley looked at Roswell with a shrug.

"Well, in honor of being completely transparent with you, we are having the blood that was found on you tested against a body we found in the woods the other day."

"Body?" Aria asked.

A cold sweat drenched Alessa's back when she thought back to the horrors she'd seen in those woods. The blood, the bones, and the carnage. She felt sick, thinking Aria could ever do anything so awful.

"Are you saying she did something?" Alessa asked.

"Of course not. We aren't making any assumptions."

"They're just doing their job, Alessa," Joshua chimed in.

"But Dad, this is insane! Aria would never hurt anybody! Tell them Ari."

Alessa gazed pleadingly at her sister and tugged on her hand, but Aria did not even acknowledge her.

"We've known your family for many years, Alessa. We know Aria is a good person, we would never assume the worst of her. But we can't leave any stone left un-turned."

CHAPTER 9

Alessa lowered her head and watched her lap while the others turned to Aria expectantly.

"It's just... blank," she replied.

Roswell tapped his pen on the pad a few more times before shutting it.

"All right. Well, please call us if any new memories return. Every single detail matters, no matter how small. So even if you think it isn't important, it may point us in the right direction. We want to find out what happened just as much as you do," Shirley added.

"We won't take up much more of your time. You've been through something very traumatic. It makes sense that your body and your mind need time to recuperate."

Chief Roswell stood and Shirley was quick behind him, but first she turned to Lily and Joshua.

"May we speak with both of you in private?"

They followed the officers outside. Aria watched, her eyes tracking their every move until the front door closed behind them. Aria slid from Alessa's grip and approached the window facing the lawn.

"Ari?" Alessa squeaked, Aria lifted her hand to silence her. Alessa moved to stand next to her, seeing the group of four huddled outside in a tight circle. Aria watched the adults as intensely as Alessa watched her. The force of her stare gave Alessa the impression she was reading their lips, but she'd never been capable of such a thing before. She remembered Aria staring out the window this morning, how she claimed someone was calling for her.

"Can you tell what they're saying?"

Aria arched a brow at her, Alessa sighed.

Aria returned to her seat as Alessa watched. Roswell and Shirley disappeared down the street and their parents swiftly returned inside.

"What time did you girls go to bed last night?" Joshua asked. It sounded casual enough, but Alessa noted a slight hitch in his voice.

"Um, I think 9:45, maybe ten—but it wasn't long after you and Mom," Alessa said.

Their parents stared at each other, their expressions constantly shifting.

"Why? What's going on?"

"It looks like Thomas and Gretchen Singer's daughter reported them missing this morning. They went to walk the dog sometime after ten last night and never came home," he explained.

Alessa's jaw dropped. That must have been the couple from the night before. They were gone? Her mind reeled with possibilities — none of them pleasant. She did her best to keep a straight face.

"Did either of you see anything last night?" Lily asked.

Alessa considered her words carefully. She had to tell the truth, but she wasn't sure she wanted their father to know Aria was awake in the middle of the night, alone for who knows how long. Everyone already made it clear how suspicious they were of Aria, and she wasn't going to make it worse by giving them unnecessary details.

"I woke up late to go to the bathroom, but I'm not sure what time it was. I saw them walk by with their dog out the window when I came down for a glass of water, but nothing looked strange to me. They turned the corner a minute later, and I finished my drink and went back to bed."

Joshua turned his sights on Aria. "Aria, did you see anything?"

Aria looked him dead in his eyes. Was she smirking? Alessa blinked, but when she opened her eyes, Aria's face had returned to its usual blank stare. Oh God, she was losing it.

"No." Aria said.

Joshua exhaled, and it was as if someone finally popped the balloon of tension between them, the pressure slowly leaking out.

"Good, then."

Water rushed out of the kitchen sink; Lily's glove clad hands were

CHAPTER 9

elbow deep in a mountain of suds as she scrubbed up the breakfast dishes.

"You need to eat something, Aria. Doctor Sutton was very concerned about your nutrition," she insisted.

Aria lingered in the doorway like a ghoul. Only now she was absently scratching at the skin of her left arm. The redhead glanced at Alessa, who was munching on a bag of carrots; she extended one to her sister with a smile. Aria's face flashed with intense disgust.

"I'm fine."

Alessa's face fell, and she retracted the carrot. The rubber gloves came off Lily's arms with a wet snap. She chucked them to the side and dried her hands.

"Well, I would really love it if you tried, even if it's just something small, while your father and I go meet with Doctor Sutton. He has a few things he wants to discuss with us regarding your recovery plan."

Aria's nails were still raking over her flesh, angry red marks rising in response. She kept going, even as she broke skin, blood beading at the surface and smearing with every swipe of her fingers.

"What on Earth..."

Lily tossed the drying cloth to the side and snatched Aria's wrist with a surprising roughness that made Alessa flinch. Aria looked eerily calm in response. The two stared at each other. Lily's expression remained stony even as her irises flared with warning.

"That's enough. You're going to hurt yourself," she stated.

Darkness fell over Aria's face. Taken aback, Lily's grip around Aria's arm loosened.

"Please, Aria," Lily said, softer this time.

Alessa held her breath. Suddenly, Aria ripped her arm from her mother's grasp with enough force to make Lily stumble backwards. Aria's eyes held her until she slowly turned around and walked out of the kitchen, her hand continuing its work on the bloody patch it created.

Alessa was rooted to her chair, and her mother was shaken. Lily rolled it off with a deep breath and straightened her shoulders. She wasn't sure if she should be amazed or terrified by how easily her mother regained her composure.

"Alessa." She jumped at Lily's voice. "Please look after your sister while we're gone, and for God's sake, try to get her to eat something."

"Of course, Mom."

When Aria didn't reappear within the hour, Joshua and Lily decided to leave without disrupting her. Alessa waved them off. Aria stepped back into the main foyer as soon as their parent's car cleared their street. Even as anxiety ravaged her insides, Alessa smiled.

"Want to watch some TV?"

The two sisters sat side by side like the old days, another mind-numbing reality show on their small television, a show they would normally be relentlessly making fun of. Only now there was no laughter, and no pile of salty snacks on the table. They sat on opposite ends of the couch, with what felt like the entire world nestled between them. Moments passed where Alessa found something funny about the show, and she would giggle, only to turn to her sister and see her staring absently ahead. It was as though the television, and even Alessa herself, did not exist.

For an hour she sat there, trying to conjure up a conversation. But she didn't know what she would even talk about. Alessa never felt so disconnected from her sister. She hated herself for thinking about it, but this was almost worse than Aria being gone. She hated herself even more over the relief she felt when the phone rang.

"Shit, Alessa!" Her entire body relaxed at the sound of Maya's voice on the other end of the line. "Where have you been? I told you to call me! I've been worried sick."

Despite the harshness of her tone, Alessa grinned. Maya was exactly who she needed right now.

"Maya!" Alessa choked out, blinking back an onslaught of tears, "hey, I'm so sorry. Things were just so crazy last night when we got home. I was exhausted and fell asleep early."

"I'm such an ass, you shouldn't be apologizing to me," Maya replied, "God, it's just since Ari showed up in church yesterday. It's been all I can think about."

"I can relate," Alessa teased.

"Glad to see you still have your sense of humor. Are you okay?"

"As okay as I can be, I guess." Alessa peered around the corner into the living room. Aria was still sitting on the couch.

"She's completely different, she told Maya in hushed tones. It's like she doesn't recognize any of us, and she can't remember anything that happened after she left."

"What? How?"

Alessa recounted the entire afternoon in as much detail as she could recall. Maya sat in stunned silence for at least thirty seconds after the tale was done. Alessa returned to the kitchen, phone snug between her ear and shoulder. On the counter was a plate she slowly filled with a small lunch for Aria.

"Mom and Dad are meeting with Doctor Sutton right now, so I'm keeping an eye on her."

"This is all going to get resolved. Everyone knows Aria wouldn't hurt a fly. The test results are going to prove it. It's just a matter of time."

Alessa crossed the room in search of milk, but something in the corner of her eye made her pause. Aria was no longer on the couch. Stepping a little further into the hall, she arched her neck to check the rest of the living room and a sigh of relief escaped her. Aria was standing at the window, gazing out. Still, she held that same dead stare. It made Alessa's stomach turn. When she was confident her sister wasn't going anywhere, she went back to her conversation and meal prep.

"I'll keep you posted," Alessa said, her nerves beginning to settle.

"Please do! And if there's anything you need–seriously anything, I've got you. Ari's strong. Alessa, she's going to be okay."

"Thanks, Maya, you always know what to say."

"It's a gift," she said with a weak laugh.

The two said their goodbyes. The click of the phone connecting to the receiver filled Alessa with an odd sense of dread. She didn't want to look in the other room and see this new Aria. What she would give to go back out there and find Aria smiling at her, arms outstretched and waiting while she said, *"I've missed you."*

But that was not going to happen. All she could do now was be patient and support her sister in whatever she needed to heal from this experience. No matter how challenging it might be in the moment. Alessa rolled her shoulders and steeled herself. Aria would do the same for her. It was time to put up or shut up.

Alessa walked back into the living room armed with a plate of food and a bright smile, but Aria was no longer there. She swallowed down her worry. Her sister was likely somewhere else in the house. Instinct told her to go upstairs, knowing that if Aria was going to go anywhere, it was her room.

The door was closed. Alessa carefully turned the knob and pushed it open a sliver to see inside. A mass of red hair rested at the top of a bundle covered in blankets on her bed.

"Ari?" she whispered, but received no reply.

Alessa was glad Aria was getting some rest. She could only imagine how long she went without. Gently, Alessa tiptoed inside her sister's room and plate of food on her desk in case she woke up hungry. Content with her effort, she snuck out of her sister's room as quietly as she had come in.

Chapter 10

Five Months Ago

The Hale house was never quiet. More often than not it was filled with the sounds of girls giggling, the television blaring or the occasional disagreement around the family dinner table. Tonight, however, the aftermath of a heated argument left the house in a suffocating silence. Alessa groaned when Lily's bedroom door slammed and then, as expected Aria's door slammed shut shortly after.

The announcement that Aria was planning on leaving home immediately after graduation sparked their most recent argument. Originally, she planned to stay in Pine Hollow, at least for the summer. The sudden change in Aria's plans was as jarring to Alessa as it was to her parents.

Just as she was about to enter her bedroom, she heard rustling and movement from within Aria's room. A sudden spark of indignation burned to life inside of Alessa. She barged in without knocking. Aria did not appear surprised to see her. Alessa's irritation ebbed into confusion when she saw the open bag on her bed, half-stuffed with food, the lone arm of a sweater hanging out.

"What are you doing?"

Aria shushed her. "Close the door."

She did as she was told. Aria continued to throw miscellaneous items into her bag. She mumbled a string of curse words under her breath, seemingly in search of something.

"Are you going somewhere?"

"Out."

"Where?"

"To see Noah," she replied with ease.

"Why are you going to meet Noah right now?"

The cherry red flush that shaded Aria's cheeks made Alessa feel incredibly stupid, but also incredibly annoyed.

"That's not a good idea, Ari."

Both were taken aback by the force of her tone. Alessa strained to keep her expression cool and confident, even though her heart was racing. Aria smirked, a bit of pride gleaming in her eyes.

"It's gonna be fine, Alessa. Not like this is my first rodeo."

This time Alessa couldn't control her surprise. "How long have you been sneaking out for?"

First, the revelation of Aria's new plans, and now this. They normally told each other everything.

"Why are you freaking out? It's no big deal. We just like to spend time together when our parents aren't around."

"It's bad enough that you two are dating behind their backs. If Mom or Dad finds out about this, you two are toast, you know that right?"

Aria's eyes darkened, her smirk sliding away. "It's none of their business, Alessa, and besides, we haven't... done any of that yet."

Aria's voice wavered, her confidence faltering. Alessa took a deep breath, doing her best to reel in her anger. She knew how much Aria loved Noah. Alessa didn't want to interfere with her sister's happiness, she only she wished Aria understood the consequences of her often-impulsive decisions.

"Look, things are already super tense with Mom and Dad right now.

CHAPTER 10

I really wouldn't push it if I were you."

"It's not my fault Mom's pissed off. She's always looking for reasons to be upset with me!"

Alessa bristled. "But you know how she is. You knew how she'd react to something like this!"

"So, I'm just supposed to let her emotions run my life?"

Even though Alessa's rational mind was telling her that Aria was right, her pain and her wrath won out.

"Do you really want to get away from us so badly?" Alessa asked, trying to mask the hurt in her voice.

A black fog rolled over Aria's gaze, and Alessa's first instinct was to run. She held her ground.

"I thought you of all people would understand, Alessa." Her voice was colder than her sister had ever heard it. "There's an entire world outside this place. Aren't you curious about what it's like?"

The question hovered in the air between them. Alessa dared not answer.

"Don't you want to spend your weekends with your friends? Don't you want to go to a late-night movie now and then? Wear what you want, curse if you want?"

A smile stretched across Aria's lips that made Alessa grimace. Of course, she wanted all of that, but they were minor problems in the grand scheme of things. If she had to suffer a few years of strict parental rules until she forged out on her own, that was a small price to pay.

"Our parents being strict isn't the worst thing in the world, Ari. Quit being dramatic."

"I'm sick of wasting my life in a town that can't see past its front doorstep. And I am sick to fucking death of being surrounded by people whose entire personalities are based around an invisible man in the sky!" Aria seethed, ripples of fury rolling off her skin. If Alessa opened her mouth, she knew she'd be able to taste it.

Alessa wasn't sure how much more fighting she could take. Pressure built behind her eyes; the tears were coming.

"I guess I didn't know how much you hated your life here," Alessa sniffled. The darkness suddenly faded out of Aria's expression. She looked as if Alessa had struck her.

"That's not fair."

"It's not?" Alessa sneered, "why else would you keep it a secret from me?"

"Alessa, this isn't about you."

Aria looked genuinely distraught, but Alessa couldn't see past her rage.

"You're being selfish, Ari. You should have told me," Alessa snarled.

"I'm not like you, Alessa. I'm not content with being trapped in my little bubble." Every word was slow, deliberate. "Unlike you, I don't want to spend one more second pretending to be someone I'm not—constantly lying to the world about who I am and what I want."

The tears came unimpeded and silent. Alessa choked down a sob. Aria paled. Her fury turning to horror. They stared at each other in shock. This wasn't like them. Sure, they argued, but nothing that was ever said could not be forgiven, because no matter what, they never went for the jugular. Aria had not only ripped Alessa's jugular out, but she proceeded to devour it and spit blood on the floor.

Maybe Alessa was a liar, but it was only because she had to be. She didn't have the luxury of even considering being her true self. This town would never allow it. It didn't matter if Alessa had known them all her life, or that she was kind and generous—these people would never accept who she really was. Their unspoken judgements haunted her every time her heart stuttered at the lovely chime of Maya's laugh, and kept her awake in a cold sweat when her dreams drifted to her friend's perfect, sly smile.

CHAPTER 10

"Alessa," Aria started, but hesitated, "I'm sorry, I shouldn't have said that."

The shame and guilt were evident on Aria's face. Her frown deepened and tears filled her eyes. Aria lifted her arms with open hands, signifying a peaceful approach.

"I'm so sorry."

Alessa allowed Aria to wrap her in an embrace but she did not return it.

"I didn't mean it," Aria mumbled, "Mom and Dad, they've just been more... difficult recently. You're not the one I'm upset with, I just..."

Alessa waited.

"You're right, I'm the one who's the liar, not you." Aria pulled away. "Just because I'm pissed about my life doesn't mean I have any right to pass judgement on you or anyone else."

Aria sagged into a chair she placed by the window; a hazardous stack of National Geographic magazines rested next to it. "The truth is, Alessa, I've always admired you."

"What are you talking about?" Alessa asked with a sniffle.

"I don't think it's any secret that I've never really felt... at home here." Alessa agreed. Even as a child, Aria felt bigger than this town, like a star just waiting to go supernova. "I've always known that I belonged somewhere else, and every day that I'm still here, I can feel myself crawling more and more out of my skin."

The way the light hit Aria's face, crisscrossing with shadows, made her look haunted – like a different person.

"It's the people here – the way they look at me," Aria shook her head slightly. "I don't know how to explain it, like they know something about me that I don't. I've always felt it – like my existence is a burden and no matter what I do, it's never right."

Alessa saw with her own eyes how Aria minimized herself in the presence of others, shaving off pieces of herself to make it just the tiniest bit easier to get through the day.

"Ari," Alessa started, but Aria stopped her.

"No, I'm not saying all this, so you'll forgive me. I just... you've always been such a bright light, Alessa. No matter how rude or stuffy the people in this town are, you're never let any of it get to you. The wind changes, you adapt." Aria smiled. "You don't know how many times I've wished I was more like you."

It was everything Alessa wanted to hear and more, but it also made her insides splinter into a million painful shards. She never wanted Aria to see her value at the cost of her own.

"I stuff things down too, you know," Alessa said. Aria perked up.

She looked away, suddenly bashful. "I don't always want to be adaptable or have to be adaptable, if that makes any sense. This town isn't my favorite, but it's my home... and if they found out what I've been stuffing down, I don't think it would feel much like home anymore. I'm just not ready to give that up yet."

"Oh, Squirt." It sounded like the wind had been knocked out of her. "If I'm being honest, I was scared shitless to tell you. The school I'm going to has a photography program that takes place over the summer. Honestly, it was so spur of the moment, I didn't even think twice but the second I decided to do it I felt so guilty because I knew I'd broken my promise."

Alessa held her sister's gaze even when it was hard. She needed to hear this, and it was clear Aria needed to say it.

"So, you were right when you said I was being selfish for keeping it to myself. I was." She turned back to the window, the same look of longing coming over her face. "I didn't even think twice about what you were going through, and I'm sorry for that."

Alessa didn't even need to question if Aria was being truthful. She already knew.

"It's okay. I'm sorry too."

CHAPTER 10

The look of shock Aria bore would have been comical if it weren't for the situation.

"What in the hell do you have to be sorry for? I'm the asshole here."

"I shouldn't have come at you so hard." Alessa wiped at her damp cheeks as she spoke. "I was just so pissed at you—so pissed - for dropping it on me like that. I just wanted to know why. And coming in here and seeing you so... so calm, well, it seemed like you didn't care at all."

"It's not that I don't care," Aria said.

"Maybe not, but you were probably right to be freaked. No matter how you decided to tell me, I think I would have had the same reaction."

She imagined dozens of ways in which Aria could have sat her down to break the news, and in every scenario, she felt just as broken and angry.

Now, she had to admit that her desire for Aria to stay was just as selfish as Aria's desire to keep information to herself. Aria was not leaving to spite Alessa, she was leaving because she'd been waiting for this kind of chance her entire life. Tonight, she was meeting with Noah, not because she didn't care how Alessa felt, but because she was a teenage girl who was in love with a boy. A boy she was rarely allowed to see.

She knew exactly what that felt like, Alessa realized with a sharp intake of breath.

"Noah..." Aria started, her voice cracking as she fiddled with her fingers in her lap, "he's sweet. We don't... we don't do anything bad when we sneak out, we just like to spend time just the two of us. Without our parents breathing down our necks."

A small smile curled on Aria's lips, but it was glowing with love. Her adoration for that boy was written all over her face. Alessa found it impossible not to grin in return.

"I get that."

"We usually just drive out somewhere quiet, lay on the roof of his car and look at the stars. I can never remember what's what but Noah..." She hesitated, timid as her smile grew. "He knows the name of every star, and every constellation. And he gets this crazy-big smile on his face when he talks about them. He's... special, you know?"

Alessa bobbed her head in silent agreement, and her voice became teasing.

"So, what are you wearing tonight?"

A cherry red blush bloomed over the apples of Aria's cheeks as her face crumbled.

"I don't know, actually," Aria replied. A girlish nervousness coming over her. Alessa couldn't remember the last time she saw her sister like this. It was sweet.

"What time are you meeting him?"

Aria checked the clock and cursed, leaping to her feet.

"In like ten minutes, shit!"

She raced to her closet, Alessa quick on her heels.

"Chill, how about you pick out three options and I'll help you choose?"

A slow but grateful grin spread over Aria's face.

"You're a lifesaver."

Alessa brightened, renewed with positive energy and purpose, and sat on the bed, waiting. Aria emerged with her options and one by one tried them on. The first dress choice did not fit over the curve of her hips, the second one would not zip, and by the third Alessa saw frustrated tears building in Aria's eyes.

"Shit, this is why I was having trouble before," she muttered and angrily wiped the corner of her eye, "none of my stuff fits me like it used to. I knew I gained some weight but..."

Aria wilted before her, but Alessa was quick to intercept. She helped

CHAPTER 10

to pull the last dress up and over her shoulders, clipping the neckline into place before zipping the back. This time, the zipper slid home with minor struggle. Aria deflated with relief. The navy-blue fabric draped over her like a second skin. Alessa peered at Aria in the mirror.

"You're beautiful," she said.

Aria grabbed for Alessa's hand again, giving it a gentle squeeze.

"Thanks."

A light flashed dimly in the window. Alessa just barely caught it out of the corner of her eye. She looked out to see a distant vehicle, cloaked in shadow, parking down the street. The headlights of the car blinked twice and then went out.

"Your ride's here."

Alessa flashed Aria a wink, and her sister laughed, but it was tense with fresh anxiety. Aria approached the window, and all her muscles unwound at once when she saw Noah's car.

"Keep look out for me?" Aria asked.

Immediately, Alessa nodded. And just like that, they were a team again.

Within sixty seconds, Aria was securing her backpack over her shoulders and hovering on the sill of her now open window. One foot dangled inside her room, the other placed firmly on the slats of roofing outside.

"Be safe," Alessa said.

"Always," Aria smirked.

Aria slipped out and into the darkness. A few seconds passed before her head popped back into view.

"Oh, almost forgot, I have this really pretty sky-blue dress in the back of my closet. You should take it, wear it soon. It's Maya's favorite color."

Now it was Alessa's turn to blush, only it felt like her entire face was burning, not just her cheeks. Before she could reply, Aria gave a wink that much resembled her own.

"Night, Squirt."

And she was gone again. Alessa rushed to the window to make sure Aria reached the ground safely. Her sister maneuvered the uneven roof with expert precision until she reached the left side of the house where a trellis was secured to the framing. When she reached the bottom, she sprinted across their large yard and down the street. Alessa saw the smile that lit up her sister's face under the blue glow of the streetlamps.

She waited until Aria was in the car before she sat down in the chair her sister once occupied. Propping an elbow on the sill, she rested her chin in her hand and watched the taillights of the car dim as it receded into the distance.

When the tiny orbs of red light vanished into the darkness, Alessa imagined what it would be like to watch Aria's car drive away as she bid farewell to Pine Hollow one final time.

Chapter 11

Aria's insides burned, a raging flame charring the inside of her chest as she ran. Every desperate gasp of frigid air sent sharp, stabbing pains through her lungs. Aria could no longer feel her feet. Her toes were blue and blackening at the tips. She'd been out here for too long. Right now, that was the only thing she was certain of.

Despite the freezing temperature, Aria couldn't feel the cold anymore. In fact, she was sweating from head to toe, the shreds of her tattered clothing clinging to damp skin. Damp with sweat or ice or tears, she didn't know.

Aria stumbled into a nearby tree, the bark tearing through her already abused flesh. She leaned against it, her weak arms wrapping around the trunk to keep steady. The sky was swiftly darkening, another pitch-black night rapidly approaching. Aria stared at the tops of the dark trees. The world spun. Stars shimmered through the thick forest canopy, tiny pinpricks in the darkness. The sight of them brought her a drop of comfort.

A sharp cracking noise in the brush nearby brought her deepest fears to the forefront of her imagination.

She whipped around; a wave of adrenaline pushing her forward. Something shifted in the shadows, bushes rustled, and even the trees held their breath. The baby hairs on the back of her neck tingled. In the dark, something growled.

She took off running again, moving as fast as her weary legs could carry her. As the last of the sun's color left the sky, it became harder to navigate. She could no longer recognize landmarks or tell what direction she was moving— but she knew she couldn't stop. The silence of the dense woods was shattered by a shriek as her foot caught in a tree root sending her tumbling down hill. Bones bruised and snapped on rocks and massive, fallen branches, until she rolled to a halt in the dirt and grime. Every inch of her body radiated with pain; warmth bloomed at the front of her head. Sticky liquid tangled in her hair and eyelashes, obstructing her view. She looked up again trying to find the stars, but she was in the denser part of the forest now, where no light shone through.

Her vision swam. She'd never been so exhausted, she felt it in her soul. The hairs on her arms stood at attention. The air changed, only the leaves rustled gently in the breeze. The sounds of the forest had suddenly disappeared, there were no birds fluttering, no insects chirping. Nothing but the slow, measured intake and expulsion of a breath that didn't belong to her.

And then the woods themselves seemed to speak.

"Aria..."

Aria was thrust, heart pounding, and temples throbbing back into the world. Her skin was flush was heat, and the cotton fabric of the sheets felt like a sizzling iron being pressed against her. She kicked and clawed them off as though they were melting her down to the bone. Amid her distress, her ankles tangled further in the blankets, and she rolled over the edge, landing with a thud on the floor.

She was soaked in her own sweat, and soon her clothing followed the growing pile of damp linens the floor. Down to her undergarments, she managed to steady herself on her hands and knees, the room tilting and whirling.

An ache spread, like the gaping maw of some horrific eldritch creature, from the center of her stomach to the rest of her body. Hungry. She was so hungry. Aria turned desperately to the plate of food that was still sitting by the door. The hunger clawed at her insides, a rake scraping over tender organs. Her stomach pulsed as she crawled to the plate. Her hands trembled over the food. She pawed at it like an animal.

She brought a small bite to her lips, but the pungent scent of egg and grease made her stomach lurch with such force that she immediately dropped what she was holding onto the floor. Acid scorched the back of her throat and tongue, and she swallowed down every last drop, the struggle of it bringing tears to her eyes.

"Aria..."

Her brain jostled inside her skull as she turned to face the source of the whisper. She barely heard it over her own breathing. The window was open now. Had it been opened before? Trees danced at the border of their property; mesmerized, Aria rose to her feet to watch them.

"Aria..."

This time, it was more distinct. Aria's eyes widened. It was coming from the woods. She dragged her fingertips across the windowsill and opened the window further. A cold gust of air instantly swept into the room and sent a few loose papers fluttering about. She smelled the damp earth, the pine, and the evergreen. They were calling for her.

"Aria..."

A singsong voice this time, light and lovely, trickled over her like a healing balm. They wanted her; they needed her. She had to find them; she had to go back.

Her hand shot out, ripping right through the flimsy screen as she tore it directly out of the frame. Bits and pieces of splintered wood fell to the floor, the wire screen now a tangled mess. Aria paid it no mind as she climbed over the mess with ease and shot out the window.

Aria hit the ground running, bare feet pounding on frozen earth as she darted toward the woods. The crowd across the street caught sight of her and erupted in panic. They pointed at her and screamed but Aria didn't miss a step. The door of the back porch flew open, banging against the outside wall of the house. Aria glanced over her shoulder and saw Alessa launch over the back steps, forgoing shoes entirely as she raced after her sister. Aria was fast approaching the trees.

"Ari! Wait!" Aria's pounding heart swallowed Alessa's cries.

"She's running!" one of the onlookers yelled.

"Ari, please!"

This time, Alessa broke through. Aria's run stuttered to a speedy walk and then stopped altogether. She turned on unsteady legs back to Alessa, a haunted and almost hypnotic look in her eyes. Alessa slowed down to approach her at a calm pace.

"Aria," Alessa said, softer this time, "please, come back inside with me. Where are you going?"

Again, she turned to the woods, looking at them as if they would answer for her. But the whispering had ceased, her name fading on the wind like a memory.

"Ari," Alessa pleaded.

Aria blinked at her. "They were calling my name," she replied, her confidence waning along with the strength of her voice.

"They... they were calling my name..." she repeated, now attempting to convince herself more than Alessa. The trees had ceased in their in melodic lullaby, the cord tugging her toward the forest fractured. Gone in an instant. She expected to feel some sense of relief but was astonished to find that the pull inside of her had only been replaced by a longing so consuming it nearly crippled her.

"Who, Ari? Who was calling your name?" Alessa tried to regain her attention.

When the woods did not reply, Aria shook her head, the soft buzzing of their murmuring slithering from her mind to make room for the gasps of shock, and exclamations of horror and disgust that pinged back and forth in her brain, searing everything they touched. Aria released a cry that was an awful combination of agony and outrage. Alessa flinched and took a few cautious steps closer.

"Ari, please just come back home, okay? It's gonna be all right, I promise!"

"Where did you go?" Aria pleaded to the trees, pain and anger dueling ferociously inside of her, sending her to the edge of delirium. Her body ached, bones shrieking in protest at the slightest movement. Fists balled tightly at her sides, she faced the forest and squeezed her eyes shut, unleashing her fury.

"Where did you go?!" she shouted into the wind but again there was no answer. Everyone was silent. Spent, Aria's body sagged, and she opened her eyes.

Standing just beyond the brush, partially cloaked in shadow, stood a petite figure clad in white. Aria blinked, but the girl remained. Her eyes trailed from the bottom of her tattered, lacy dress that completely obscured her feet, to the perfectly tailored neckline that tucked under her chin. When their eyes met, her heart stuttered in her chest, terror gripping it so viciously she forgot to breathe.

Aria was looking at herself. Sort of. She was looking at some *other* version of herself. Someone wrapped this other's hair in an elaborate updo, which seamlessly fused a mixture of flowers and braids. And she was smiling, only it was anything but comforting. This was brittle and full of hate. Her eyes were wide but devoid of life, and when they locked with Aria's, she couldn't look away. The doppelgänger's frighteningly familiar eyes quivered and rolled into the back of her head, leaving white orbs dotted by red veins. Her body twitched and spasmed, and her teeth stayed locked together even when the blood leaked between their crevices. Trails of red dripped from her chin and stained her dress.

Eventually, her jaw creaked open as if under great strain, her psychotic grin still in place. Aria's vision went black when out of the dark open hole of the doppelgänger's mouth came a fresh wave of crimson, bathing her entirely in blood.

Her body hit the ground, the sounds of Alessa's terrified screaming turned to white noise as she faded in and out of consciousness.

The rest came to her in flashes. She saw the tops of the black trees swaying against the background of a stormy sky. She felt the icy dirt under her nails and her throbbing fingers. Her body was on fire, her blood boiling; Aria wanted to tear her skin off.

Distantly, she realized she was being moved, but couldn't push beyond her own exhaustion. The doppelgänger appeared in her mind's eyes, grinning her bloody grin, white eyes becoming back pits, and another flurry of images flooded her brain.

Aria sitting in the garden, taking pictures of insects and birds.

A boy with curly hair smiling at her over a textbook.

Alessa, watching her with a smile as she taught her how to apply makeup.

The creature's bloody lips began to move, so quickly they morphed into a formless, red blur. Eventually, the words it spoke materialized in Aria's brain, but they were delayed, mismatched with her mouth.

Do you hear them, Aria? It asked. *They waited so long for you.*

Aria saw a snapshot of the forest, black silhouettes with gleaming red eyes watching her from between the trees. They were mesmerizing and horrifying all at once.

She came to briefly, glimpsing Alessa and someone else dragging her back into the house. Cool relief washed over her when they placed her on the ground, the tile floor soothing her scorching flesh.

"Ari, can you hear me?" a distant voice called.

CHAPTER 11

The images pulled her under again. She saw Alessa greeting her after a long day of school. Alessa giggling madly in front of a television set. Alessa pointing at all the photographs on her wall, picking out which ones she liked best.

Alessa.

Alessa.

Alessa.

Her eyes popped open. She was back in the house, resting on the kitchen floor, skin cloaked in a layer of sweat. Her blurred vision took several blinks to clear, and when they did, she saw Alessa kneeling over her, face damp, and another girl with raven colored hair at her side.

Aria gazed up at her sister. She lifted a trembling hand and cupped Alessa's soft cheek, startling her. Alessa's eyes widened, and she opened her mouth to speak, but nothing came out. The corner of Aria's mouth quirked up into a small smile.

"Oh, Squirt... you know... I hate to see you cry..."

The noise that escaped Alessa was caught between a laugh and a sob.

"Where did you go, Ari?" Alessa asked in a whisper, raising her hand to grip Aria's.

Aria's mind instantly went blank.

"Ari?"

She blinked up at her, struggling to remain conscious. Aria pushed through; her mind clear for the first time in... how long? She couldn't recall. The fog was rolling in again, threatening to suffocate her—to fill every crevice of her brain until there was nothing left of the original Aria.

NO! She screamed internally; she wasn't ready to give up her clarity yet. She didn't want to go back to that distant, black space in the furthest reaches of her subconscious. A place where she hovered in darkness, privy to the actions of her body but unable to control it. No, not again. Aria wanted to stay with her sister, if only for a little while longer.

"The woods..." Aria finally spoke. Alessa sucked in a sharp breath. The girls listened silently.

Fear painted Aria's face white. "Stay...stay away from the woods..."

Just as the words left her mouth, her entire body seized up, muscles locking in place and forcing her jaw to clamp tightly shut. Aria's nostrils flared with each shallow, frantic breath, and her eyes rolled back. All at once, her body fell limp to the floor, but her eyes still fluttered, head teetering back and forth.

"Ari? Ari!" Alessa cried out.

Time moved in a blur of light and color. Aria could feel herself being moved again but had no control over her limbs. Soon, warm cloth replaced the cold tile floor. A fresh wave of chaotic noise crashed over her, but she couldn't see or make out any of it. Heat enveloped her body, her mind struggled to sift through the sludge that was holding her inside herself. A few distinct words rose to the surface.

"She woke up... just for a second, but... she recognized me."

"Aria needs to draw upon our strength right now," a voice she didn't recognize piped up, "please, let us join hands."

An image flickered in Aria's brain, a tight circle of bodies forming around her.

"Lord Jesus Christ, by your patience in suffering you hallowed earthly pain and gave us the example of obedience to your Father's will."

Her temperature began rising, her skin radiating heat.

"Cleansing."

The black trees called for her to come closer.

"Purifying."

She felt hands on her, everywhere and all at once.

"Restoring her to wholeness and strength for service in your kingdom. Amen."

A hand touched her.

Aria came thrashing out of the darkness with a harsh gasp of breath. The circle shattered as everyone stumbled back. Maya yanked Alessa to her side when Aria swiped at the air. Her sharp nails tore into the couch as she got her bearings, head shaking as an image slipped from her mental grasp. The image of a white dress, tattered and stained with blood, lying in the snow.

"My God, Aria, are you all right?" Lily asked.

Aria didn't answer. Once she was sure she was no longer in the woods, she felt an ache in her hand. Glancing down, she unclenched her aching fingers to unveil a crucifix. It sliced her palms open, blood smearing on skin.

"Aria," a man in black said, leaning closer. He was the same man she had seen the day before outside the doctor's office as they were leaving. "Can you tell us what happened? Your sister said you were attempting to return to the woods."

Aria heard him but did not reply or look up. Her eyes remained rooted to the crucifix, now stained with her blood. She slowly rose to her feet.

"Please, Aria, you had us all terribly worried," he continued, completely undeterred by her attitude.

She finally raised her head. The cloaked man leaned forward as he smiled at her. Their eyes met, and the room went still. Aria saw concern briefly flicker in the man's eyes. He recovered himself before anyone else could notice. "Do you recognize me, Aria?" He patted his chest. "Father Samuel, I've known you since you were just a little bundle in your mother's arms. I baptized you and your sister."

As he spoke, something black and cold came over Aria. His voice crept into her brain, dredging up flashes of nightmarish horrors. Or were they memories? She saw a night sky, glittering with stars, as the snow tipped trees drifted by.

"Can you tell us what you remember? Why were you heading for the woods?"

She heard his voice but not his words; the sound only amplifying the image in her mind. Aria lifted her hand, reaching it toward the sky. She was tired—so, so tired. Her mouth felt dry and fuzzy, like someone had stuffed it with cotton.

"You have to give us something. We cannot help you and God cannot help you unless you take the first steps," he continued, his tone harsher. Aria merely continued to hold her hand out and stare at her own palm.

"Aria, please!" Father Samuel's hand glided to Aria's wrist.

Aria floated, gazing upon the night sky, shooting stars burning streaks of fire across the horizon. A rough hand shot out, snatching her wrist in an iron grip that made her bones ache. A flash of light caught her eye, and she saw a large, elaborate ring with black engraved designs on the person's ring finger.

Aria gasped, wrenched from the memory and into the present moment. She was back in the living room, with Samuel's hand gripping her own. There was no gold ring, but the feel of his skin brushing hers made a blazing rage envelop every cell inside her body.

Aria threw herself at Father Samuel like a rabid animal. Unleashing a cry that was measured somewhere between a growl and a shriek, Aria slammed the elderly priest against the wall. The foundation trembled beneath the impact, knocking a few pictures off the mantle.

"Aria!" Lillian screamed in terror.

Joshua was quick on his feet, launching himself over the couch to pry Aria off of him.

"Grandfather!" the dark-haired girl called.

"Ari! Let go!"

Another growl bellowed from Aria's throat, a growl that was distinctly not human. She turned on her father and shoved him aside as though he were weightless. Joshua went rolling over the back of the couch and into the coffee table. As he crashed to the ground Lily released another fearful cry.

"Aria, stop please!" Alessa pleaded.

"Oh God, oh Lord, protect me," Father Samuel whispered, his trembling hand frantically patting at his side in search of his rosary.

Aria braced him against the wall and leaned in close, their noses barely brushing. He flinched, trying to turn away when she opened her mouth and released an ear-splitting roar. The sound filled the room and vibrated inside their skulls, expanding beyond the barriers of the house.

The scream was endless. Maya and Alessa covered their ears. Gusts of furious wind picked up outside, branches smacking the exterior of the house. Alessa squeezed one eye open and glanced out the window. The trees moved as one, as if taunting them.

"Aria, stop!" Alessa begged.

Something heavy slammed into the side of Aria's head, cutting off her scream. She hit the floor — hard. The room faded into darkness as Aria looked up to see Lily standing and heaving over her, the end table lamp in her shaking fingers. Father Samuel leaned against the wall, hand to his heart, and eyes remaining locked on Aria in case she moved again.

"Lillian?" Aria barely registered Joshua's voice, so faint and stunned.

Aria tried to speak, but words failed her. The sight of them all standing around her faded out of existence as a black tide swept her under.

Chapter 12

Aria couldn't remember a time when she wasn't in these woods. Distantly, she recalled the image of a home. She had a home once, right? A house with a fireplace, where she could curl up with a blanket and her camera, to sift through the day's shots. It sounded familiar like a distant childhood bedtime story. She'd been so cold, and so hungry, for so long. Home was but a memory now.

She stumbled on numb feet. She had cast away any last vestiges of fabric on her body, leaving her pallid skin exposed to the elements. Arctic wind sliced through her bones, her shivering becoming full-blown teeth-chattering tremors. Something clawed at her insides, making her hunch over in pain. Aria grit her teeth, but the monster in her stomach roared, desperate and demanding.

When was the last time she ate?

It took her ages to form a single thought. The words jumbled, flitting into her mind one minute and then dissolving the next. She struggled to hold them in place, but they slipped through her fingers like water—just like her memories.

Aria stood still for a moment, wheezing shallow breaths, her heart barely fluttering in her chest. Only this time, the pain didn't pass. The vicious hunger ripped through her gut, and branched further out, gripping Aria with a splitting agony that made every muscle in her body tense at once. For a single, brutal second, she froze in pain. She refused to even blink, afraid the movement would send her into violent spasms, or worse, make her lose consciousness completely.

Please. Aria's thoughts bounced around like ping-pong balls. *Please, I don't wanna die.*

Wind howled through the trees, casting her in a spray of frost. This time, the wind carried something with it—a voice. Not close enough for her to catch what they were saying, but it was a person! She had no idea when she last saw a person. This one sounded like a man. Maybe he could help her out of the woods.

Finally, finally she could leave these mountains behind. She would grab Alessa, and they would leave Pine Hollow behind for good. A smile, bright in its lunacy, crossed Aria's face. Yes, they would run, and she'd finally be free.

The man spoke again, only this time he sounded closer. Apprehension and excitement battled within her. This could be her only chance to escape this hell. She needed to make sure he found her. Aria opened her mouth to speak, but the noise that came out was more of a hoarse, choked garble. Her throat was scorching from thirst and the burn of icy air, but she forced herself to swallow, licking her lips to stimulate some saliva.

"H-Help!" Louder this time, but still not enough. She coughed, a wet hack that had her spitting phlegm on the pristine snow. Through blurred eyes, she saw pebbles of red dotting the ground. Aria gently touched her fingers to her lips; they were damp and warm.

Blood. There was blood on her fingers.

"Help! Help me!"

He had to have heard it this time. Her smile grew when she heard him call out again, and then the crunch of feet charging through the snow. He was coming.

Aria took a step forward, eager to meet her savior, but as her foot touched the ground, she stilled. The corners of her vision flooded with shadow, the voracious beast inside of her drew attention to itself once more and the blinding pain rushed back tenfold. It sent her to the ground, a pile of brittle skin and bones. She was already so chilled she didn't even feel herself sinking into the tall snow. Aria felt like an exposed nerve, raw and bloody.

Her bones were singing, and as they struggled to hold her up, she swore she felt them shifting and moving, clicking, and snapping. Aria watched her hands in horror, palms flat on the ground, as her slender fingers stretched and lengthened before her eyes.

This isn't happening! It couldn't be. Aria shriveled into a tiny, trembling ball. She tried to open her mouth one last time, to call just once more for help. Colors smeared around her, the sharp edges of the world becoming blurred. She thought she saw the bushes parting, maybe a shadow breaking through the undergrowth. But before Aria could speak, it dragged her into depths of darkness so black and so endless; she was sure she would never come up for air again.

"Aria?"

Aria drifted softly out of unconsciousness, a razor-sharp pain stabbing through her temple and the left side of her jaw. She tried to find the source of the voice through her bleary vision. Darkness threatened to grab hold of her once more. Dozens of slithering shadows beckoned her back inside, whispering so sweetly to her to let go and that it was okay. *Just let go, Aria.*

Aria whimpered. No, she wasn't ready to let go just yet. She was finally somewhat lucid again, and she pushed furiously against her mounting fatigue even as it smothered every cell in her body. Aria had to hang on for as long as she could. She had no idea how much time she had before she got sucked back inside herself; before she became a mere passenger in her own body. Whatever this was—this darkness that came over her—the darkness that was still calling to her now—it

CHAPTER 12

had sentience. A mind all its own.

"Dad?" she whispered.

Joshua hurried to her side, hands gripping hers. She squeezed them obsessively, needing to feel them firm around her fingers. One second, she felt him, the next her fingers were cold and numb to the touch. She was lying down in her bedroom with her father resting in a chair at her bedside. Aria had no idea how she ended up here. Her only guess was that he carried her.

Aria saw the world through a prism. She saw herself now, lying in the dark and clawing at her father in desperation. But as the light shifted, she also saw herself as a child, with the warmth of her father's large hand resting upon her forehead to check her fever. In the present, her father looked haunted. In the past, he smiled.

Tears filled her eyes, and spilled over, her bottom lip quivering as Joshua wiped them away.

"Oh, sweetie. I'm sorry. Does it hurt? Tell me what I can do."

Her grip around his hand tightened. He grimaced. "Do you remember what happened, Ari?"

She only half heard him. Her skull ached, and the darkness beckoned with a chilling lullaby, waiting eagerly to sweep her away. It tugged her into a frigid oblivion that rivaled the black expanse between the stars.

"D-Daddy..."

"Yes, honey, I'm here." He patted her hand.

"Am I... am I dying?"

The color dimmed from his cheeks. "N-No, no of course not, Aria! You're going to be just fine, you hear me?"

He continued to wipe her endless stream of tears away. Aria sucked back a sob. She was too tired to cry. The shadows at the corners of her eyes inched closer, and Aria felt herself slipping away again. Her body felt weak, and something intuitively told her that she didn't have much time left.

She tried to focus on the details of her father's face, the dark blue of his irises, and the laugh lines etched into the corners of his mouth and eyes. Her vision wavered in and out. Aria tried embedding the sensation of skin on skin inside her mind. His hand against her cheek. That sensation meant she was still here.

"Listen to me, okay?" Joshua took a breath to steady his voice. "You're home, honey. You're home and we are all here for you. You're safe now."

She blinked slowly, trying to keep her vision clear of the shadows just a little longer.

"Safe?" Aria asked.

"Yes, yes, you're safe! Everything is okay now. I'm won't let anything else happen to you, I promise."

Joshua tried to hold her gaze,

"Do you understand, Aria? It's all going to be okay."

His voice was getting further away, but she held onto his words. Aria fought through the exhaustion to offer him one faint smile.

"Aria?" Joshua spoke in soft tones, trying to keep her awake.

The dark tunnel between Aria and her father stretched on. She knew she only had a few seconds left.

"I... love you..." Aria whispered. She needed him to know in case he could not keep his promise.

As the darkness took her over, she suddenly realized how much she missed that little girl, and the way her dad would check for a fever, even when she only had a sniffle. She nearly forgot who that little girl was.

Chapter 13

Alessa counted her breaths: in for four counts, out for six. It was the only thing keeping the room from spinning entirely out of control. Losing Maya's hand left her own feeling cold and afraid. She sat on the couch, grasping the cushions, and picking at the already worn fabric. Despite their house being warm, her body shivered uncontrollably with anxiety.

Only minutes had passed since her mother cracked a lamp across her sister's skull. Alessa kept rerunning those seconds in her mind, hoping somehow that she had just imagined it. Time suddenly seemed to slow to an intolerable crawl. Had it really only been minutes? Alessa questioned herself, teeth gently gnawing at her bottom lip.

Aria. A girl who would never hurt a fly, a girl who cried herself into a stupor after accidentally running over an opossum with their father's car. Her sister always had more bark than bite, although that wasn't to say her bark wasn't ferocious. Aria knew how to hold her own, but she didn't hurt people. Even after seeing it with her own two eyes, Alessa couldn't believe it.

Her father checked Aria for any immediate injuries before carrying her up to her room, avoiding Lily's gaze the entire time. Thankfully, it appeared the lamp didn't even break the skin, and she was breathing evenly. Alessa knew they should call the doctor—someone who knew what they were doing, but she couldn't bring herself to say anything. How would he react if he knew what Aria had done? Rumors were already circulating that Aria had done something terrible in the woods. This would only fuel the fire.

What would Chief Roswell say? A chill came over her. He was already suspicious of Aria, despite saying otherwise. It didn't matter that he'd known them their whole lives. If there was one thing Alessa knew about Roswell, it was that he was a cop first, and a friend second. Roswell's duty to the badge overwhelmed any sentiment he held toward them the second he got a whiff of any wrongdoing.

Lily and Maya hovered over Father Samuel, carefully ushering him back to his feet. Lily placed the lamp to the side in a daze before attending to her guest as any proper hostess would. She cooed and fussed over him more than she did her own children, leaving Joshua in utterly stunned silence as she abandoned him to check on Aria alone.

"I'm terribly sorry, Father!" Lily said. Samuel steadied himself and smoothed out his robe. A thin sheen of sweat formed just below his collar and the color had not yet returned to his cheeks. "I'm absolutely mortified. I can't believe Aria would do such a thing," she rambled on, "she's just feeling very unlike herself these days. Please don't hold this against us."

Alessa winced. Lily's eldest daughter assaulted someone after returning, traumatized, from an experience none of them could understand—and Lily was worried about their beloved priest holding a grudge?

She suddenly saw her mother in a glaring and gritty light that horrified her. Alessa always gave her mother the benefit of the doubt. She wasn't anywhere near perfect, but she wasn't a monster either. Now, she wondered, if this was the mother Aria saw every day, the one she kept Alessa blissfully ignorant of.

"Is there anything I can get you? Please, please sit—I'll grab you some water!"

Again, Lily's desire to help came off more desperate than helpful. Father Samuel stepped away from her, despite the obvious pain it caused him. Maya remained at his side, sniffling through the last of her frightened tears.

"Are you okay, Grandfather?"

His wrinkled lips curled back in a snarl. He turned to Lily, wincing with every movement, and grumbling ferociously under his breath. Alessa saw his rage stemmed from something deeper than just physical pain. It wasn't just his body that was bruised; it was his ego.

"Grandfather?" Maya pried, but he remained fixated on Lily.

She withered under the heat of his glare The priest's eyes were tar black, devoid of any previous sympathy or tenderness. A vein throbbed in his temple.

"Never in all my years of service to the Lord have I ever experienced such–such..." Father Samuel gritted his teeth. "Vile behavior."

He practically spit the last word, as if it were poison scorching the tip of his tongue. Disgust colored every syllable, sharpening them to a brutal point. Even Maya flinched. Alessa's head shot up again, too surprised to mutter a word. She'd never seen him raise his voice, let alone yell at another person, and he never described them with such vitriol.

"And to think it would come from someone as dear to my heart as Aria," he continued.

"Please Father, you know what she's been through–she's not herself! She needs you," Lily said, holding her ground despite the waver in her voice.

Alessa didn't understand why she was trying so hard to keep him there, when all he did was cause more problems.

"I can't give that girl what she needs," he sneered, "perhaps she truly is not herself, but whatever has taken her place is beyond my reach."

This only heightened her mother's visible terror. Alessa marveled at the sight. She'd never seen her mother this scared. Not even, much to her own horror, when Aria went missing.

Guilt clawed at her heart. It was because Aria had been their mother's primary target, upon which she projected all her expectations, disappointments, and rage. Alessa kept herself blind to the worst of it because she was too afraid to end up in Lily's crosshairs.

"What would you suggest we do?" Lily asked.

Alessa looked at Maya, both sharing a look of pure bewilderment.

Father Samuel finished adjusting his clothes and patted down the frail bits of hair he had left. He cast one more passing glance over at Lily. In just a few seconds, she went from the primary target of his ire to not being worthy of eye contact.

"I suggest you turn her over to the appropriate authorities, Mrs. Hale. It is quite obvious your family is out of its depth."

Alessa shot him a baffled look. He met it with a cutting glare. She flinched, much to her dismay. She hated how this man had the power to make her feel so small. Using just a look, he reduced her to a little girl, desperate and insecure, wanting the approval of the most influential man in their town. Maya looked mortified.

"D-Do you intend to press charges, Father?"

"I *intend* on doing what I must in order to protect myself and the people of this good town. It would seem fit you do the same."

Father Samuel turned on his heel and grabbed Maya's arm, dragging her to the front door.

"Wait—Grandfather!"

His stride didn't break, even though Alessa noticed an obvious new limp to his gait. Maya shot a panicked look at her over her shoulder. Alessa jumped to her feet.

"Father, please, don't go!" Lillian raced after him. "What exactly do you mean?"

She faltered when he turned on her, tugging Maya behind him so close that he wedged her between his body and the door. His words seethed with venom.

"I mean, if you and Mister Hale are incapable of doing what is right, I will be forced to involve Chief Roswell."

Alessa and Maya locked eyes across the room; a shared moment of dread.

"Aria is already being investigated for another act of violence, Lillian. Now she turns her viciousness toward me, toward the word of the Lord! You know exactly what needs to be done."

"Grandfather, please, they need help..." Maya whispered. Samuel lifted his hand. Her mouth clicked shut.

"We will be taking our leave now." He looked them over, analyzing.

To Alessa, it looked like he was trying to memorize every detail of their terror, of how easily they cowered under his authority. Apparently, the only one of them courageous enough to stand up to the priest was the very person who needed his help the most.

"I suggest you give some serious thought to what we've discussed, Lillian."

He slipped out the door, pulling Maya with him. Maya caught Alessa's eye one last time, her lips mouthing something.

Alessa couldn't be one-hundred percent sure, but she was pretty certain the word she mouthed was 'sorry.'

She was alone with her mother, standing in the living room like an idiot, and staring at the closed door. That was it, then? Alessa felt tears prickling the backs of her eyes. One attempt at salvation was all Aria was worthy of? Even after all she had been through, they still saw her as a burden, just as Aria said all those months ago.

Alessa stared at the back of her mother's head, at her perfect hair and her perfect clothes. She hated her at that moment.

"Where the *hell* is your father?" Lillian spat, shattering the silence into jagged little pieces.

Alessa flinched when the house phone rang, in what she didn't know at the time was just the first of many unwanted calls.

Lily slammed the receiver down, following the third phone call in a row. Alessa remained slumped in the armchair, staring at the lamp on the table. She scanned the base, searching for any bits of blood and hair, and let out a breath of the relief when she found none.

This time Alessa was ready when the shrill ring from the phone sliced through the room again. From eavesdropping on the first few, an easy feat since Lily was clearly in no mood to keep her usual decorum and inside voice, Alessa gathered they were friends from church. The rumor mill of Pine Hollow never ceased to amaze her. Father Samuel was barely gone for ten minutes before news had traveled of the town's beloved priest seen leaving the Hale home in a rage.

No wonder Aria hated this town so much. Alessa would have done anything to go back in time, to not only encourage her sister to leave this town behind but join her as well.

"Enough of this!"

Lily ripped the phone off the receiver and crashed it back down without a word. She fisted the red wire that fed into the wall and tore it out. The silence stretched on forever, and all Alessa could hear was the ticking of the clock on the wall.

"What the hell happened today?"

Lily stood in the doorway that led to the kitchen. Her voice was the tip of an ice pick dragging up Alessa's spine. "What do you mean?"

Lily smiled, full of poison, and rolled her eyes with a haughty laugh.

"Oh, don't you dare play dumb with me, Alessa. It's incredibly unbecoming. I would expect such behavior from your sister, but not from you."

Alessa recoiled, the stab at Aria feeling like a stab at her own self-worth. Lily stepped further into the room. Alessa wanted to shrink away from her, to dissolve into the furniture and never be seen again.

"Now, tell me what happened. Why was Aria out there in the first place? She was supposed to be resting, and you were supposed to be watching her."

The sheer disdain of her tone ignited a spark of defiance in Alessa's chest.

"And you were supposed to bring the doctor, not the priest."

Lillian's face flushed red hot, stunned at her daughter's boldness. Alessa sucked down her fear, feeling it grate through her throat as if she'd dry swallowed a large pill. She dragged herself out of the chair, feeling vulnerable without the cushions to protect her, but she didn't let it deter her.

"Ari needed help; she needed a doctor! Why did you bring him when you know how Ari feels about Father Samuel?"

Lily closed the gap between them. Alessa felt the urge to back away but held her ground.

"How dare you? Of all the times to bring this up, Alessa."

The anger waned, much to Alessa's shock, instead melting into bitter disappointment. It made her insides shrivel.

"Your father and I went to see Father Samuel to get his advice, to clear our minds, so we can properly care for our daughter. When you called, well, your father was in such a panic, we barely had any time to think."

Somehow, the disappointment was worse. Lily looked down upon her, as if she should know all of this already. As if she were nothing more than a stupid child for ever questioning her parents.

"We were desperate. Alessa, you were crying, and Father Samuel offered his services. He saw we were in distress, and he lent a helping hand."

Her lips curled into an ugly frown. "So, forgive me for trying to do everything in my power to help my child, and for accepting help in our family's time of need!"

Alessa felt as though she'd been slapped and physically recoiled. Lily was one step ahead, however, keeping on her even as she backed away. A lion cornering a gazelle, only this gazelle was her own daughter.

"Forgive me, Alessa, for forgetting, ever so briefly, about your sister's little gripes with church because I hoped that maybe—*finally*, someone might be able to help her!"

The echo of her anger resonated in the air. Alessa held her breath, terrified to speak the first word and break the safety of the silence. Her eyes stung, and she blinked back tears. How easy it was for her mother to reduce her into nothing more than a bumbling, weepy child.

Every harsh comment Aria made about their mother behind her back, the ones that Alessa always used to find overly cruel, all came rushing back to her with a new kind of clarity. The smallness, and the inferiority she felt now, was only a drop in the bucket of what Aria must have felt for so many years.

Her mother withdrew, the space between them widening again. Alessa watched Lily compose herself; the heat receding from her neck and a normal, pink hue shading her cheeks. A few pats here and an adjustment or two there, and she was back to the picture of perfection. Her expression remained soft, the hard edges of her resentment smoothing out.

"Well, now that someone is saying she can't be helped," Alessa blurted out before she could stop herself.

Alessa wasn't sure if Lily's gob smacked expression was because of the substance of her words or the audacity of them, but she used her mother's momentary shock to power through.

"Aria was in bed; she was sleeping, and I left her some food. Maya called, and we were talking and then I heard a noise from upstairs. I don't know what happened! But I saw Ari running to the woods, so I went after her."

A few of the tears spilled over. She swiped at them furiously with the sleeve of her shirt. Lily opened her mouth to reply, but Alessa charged on.

"I was screaming at her—begging her to stop! And she did, but she seemed confused, like she didn't know where or why she was running. She said she heard them calling her name—something from the woods calling her name, Mom! And I tried to ask her who, but she just freaked out—it was like she saw something in the woods and then she was on the ground, and she wouldn't wake up."

Alessa pulled at the ends of her hair. Her head spun, the events from the day finally closing in around her. She choked through the last details of Maya's miraculous rescue.

"So, forgive me, Mom, for being scared and for not knowing exactly what to do. Forgive me for doing your job!"

She pushed past her mother, their shoulders brushing. Lily stumbled.

"Alessa, wait!"

She whipped around and reached out to her retreating daughter but was too late. Alessa rounded the corner and sprinted up the stairs.

"I'm sorry!" Lily called up to her.

Alessa slammed her bedroom door hard enough to shake the frame.

She didn't know how long she remained in the same spot, curled into a little ball, in the center of her bed. Minutes? Hours? Not that it mattered, she would have stayed there forever if she could.

Her tears had long since dried, and snot crusted around her nose and mouth. Crippling exhaustion replaced sharp, metallic agony. She distantly recalled the tensing of her entire body when she heard her mother's heels as she ascended the staircase. She remained alert even when Lily paused at her door and only relaxed when she knew the woman had moved on.

She remained there, locked tightly away even when through layers of wood and plaster she heard the echoes of her parent's muffled shouting. Alessa couldn't make out their words, but she didn't need to, and she didn't want to. This was their life now, one screaming match after another.

Alessa's aching joints forced her to unravel, her limbs coming undone from their makeshift cocoon. She took a moment to listen. The yelling dimmed into frustrated grumbles and passive aggressive jabs. For now, they kept their battle relegated to their bedroom.

Alessa stretched her arms, forcing the blood to flow back through them, her skin sizzling with a buzzing, static sensation from having fallen asleep while tucked into her small form. Aside from the indistinct noises of her parents arguing, she heard nothing else. Alessa prayed this meant Aria was finally getting some proper rest.

Would she wake up again, kicking and screaming, to return to the woods? Who's to say that whatever Aria heard that morning wouldn't come back, sweeping in like a dense fog to lure her away?

A thought came to her then: Noah. She hadn't heard from him since Aria first showed up at St. Lawrence. She was shocked he hadn't tried to contact them by now to see how she was doing. Alessa bottled the instant burst of frustration she felt. There had to be a reasonable explanation. Her brain burned, and she rubbed her tired eyes. It was difficult to hold on to the threads of logic when she could barely see straight.

Certainly, he would have called by now, right?

She remembered her mother jerking the cable out of the wall and cursed under her breath. If he had called, they never would have known. Alessa was in the hallway before she could second guess herself, creeping at a glacial pace so her parents wouldn't hear. Although, based on what she heard, they were still otherwise occupied. Alessa slipped slowly down the hall and descended the stairs, careful to avoid the ones she knew would creak.

As seamlessly as a shadow fading into the night, she reached the kitchen without incident. The silver glow of the moon provided her with enough light to work with, and she followed the wire from the telephone to where it hooked into a port on the wall. It took two tries before she managed to get it plugged back in. Alessa held her breath for a horrified second and raced back to the phone. It occurred to her the phone could still end up ringing due to nosy neighbors.

Alessa let out the breath when she took the phone off the receiver, preserving the silence. She waited for her heartbeat to steady before dialing Noah's number. Like most kids in their town, his parents didn't allow him to have a cell, but during one rogue day of internet exploration at the library, he ordered himself a burner. It was the most basic model available, a lone flip phone in a world of touch screens, and it was banged to hell, but it worked. According to Aria, Noah hid it in the false drawer in his desk at home.

Noah answered in under three rings. "Alessa?"

"It's me."

"Thank God, I've been trying to call your house all day, but I just kept getting a busy tone."

While she expected this, it was still a relief to hear him say it.

"Mom unplugged the phone. It's been ringing off the hook, sorry."

"No, don't apologize, please. I'm just so relieved you called. How are you? How's Aria?"

Alessa was perplexed. Had no one told him what was going on? It seemed like everyone, and their mothers, knew the dirty little details of their family drama.

"You haven't heard anything?"

Noah mumbled something vaguely explicit. "Not anything I can actually trust! Look, I don't know why, but my parents have completely shut down since Aria came back. They won't let me go see her. Hell, they didn't even want me talking to you or asking about her."

Sharp prickles of dread delicately traced the back of her neck.

"What do you mean, they won't let you see her? Why not?"

Alessa knew, in her bones, and in her very soul, that Aria would want to see Noah. Someone she loved - someone she actually trusted.

"I have no idea. They said they spoke with your parents, and they all agreed it was in my *best interest* to stay away." He gave a dry chuckle. "What the fuck does that even mean?"

Alessa didn't know what to say. For his parents to wish him away was one thing, but her mother and father were actively encouraging this. They wanted to keep him away from her, Aria's choices be damned.

"Just please, tell me she's okay." Noah's voice faded to a whimper, and it tugged at Alessa's heart.

"She's okay," she said resolutely. A sad smile pulled at her lips when he exhaled in relief.

"Y-Yeah?"

His voice was thick, and she was pretty sure he was crying. Alessa clenched her hand into a fist and choked down the acidic ball of pain that slid up her throat.

"B-But look, she's... she's not the same." She groaned at her choice of words. "I don't know how to explain it but, she doesn't remember anything from the last two months. And she's acting... strange."

There was a long pause on the other end of the line. For a second, she thought she lost him until he spoke up again.

"What do you mean, strange?"

Throwing one last look over her shoulder to make sure her parents weren't coming; she took a deep breath and told him everything. Right down to the moment she slammed her bedroom door behind her after escaping the wrath of her mother.

"Holy shit, Alessa," came his stunned response.

"I don't know what's going on," Alessa sniffled. The tears she thought dried up came back with a vengeance. "I'm scared."

"Hey, listen to me. We're going to figure this out."

It was as if hearing her own distress flipped a switch in him. He had gone from the one needing reassurance to protective brother mode. Now he sounded controlled.

"I don't know what the hell is happening, but... well, it seems like her memories are coming in bits and pieces. You said she remembered you for a second. Even the doctor said her memory loss could be temporary."

Alessa nodded until she realized he couldn't see her.

"I guess, but I'm not sure that's what I'm really scared of."

"What is it then?"

She turned and looked out the window, beyond their yard, beyond the trees, and into the darkness within.

"I'm more scared of what we'll find out when she does remember."

Alessa ended the call with a promise to give him a ring again the next day. He did his best to comfort her, but she knew he wanted to fall apart just as much as she did. She appreciated his effort, but she was becoming less confident.

However, one thing she knew for sure, is that Noah had a right to see Aria, and she didn't give a damn what their parent's reasons were for keeping him away. Even if it got her into more trouble, she was going to do whatever she could to help Noah.

Alessa lingered in front of her bed for a bit. Even though the mattress looked inviting, she was unable to sit. Every time she thought about lying down, her stomach swirled with anxiety. Minutes passed as she battled this internal war until, eventually, she ripped the blankets and a pillow from her bed and stormed back out of the room. She was careful when she opened Aria's door and slipped in.

She kept her eyes on her sister's motionless form on the bed as she laid out her blankets on the floor below the window. They stayed on

Aria even when sleep threatened to pull her under. She didn't know how long she was awake, but she knew if Aria tried to run again, she would be there, and she would be ready.

Chapter 14

Aria didn't remember waking up the next morning. One moment she was hovering in a sea of black, and the next she was standing over Alessa, who slept soundly below her window. She blinked in confusion, trying to recall when she'd gotten out of bed in the first place. She vaguely remembered pain spreading across her face and jaw, but she felt none of that now. Aria ran her finger along her hairline, searching for any sign of a wound, but the skin was unblemished.

"Ari?"

Her eyes met Alessa's, and the girl flinched.

The scent of bacon and sausage filled the air. Groggily, Alessa peeled herself from her makeshift bed and stood beside Aria, both of them looking out at the forest.

"Do you hear them?" Alessa asked.

It stirred something in her. Aria's brow twitched, and she turned her icy stare on Alessa without a word.

"You said they were calling your name. Do you hear them now?"

Aria's brows furrowed and a point of tension flexed in the middle of her forehead. She faced the window. The corners of her delicate mouth fell, and a palpable longing emitting from her like an aura.

"No."

"What else do they say, Ari? Anything else besides your name?" she asked in desperation, but Aria struggled to form words.

"Ari, please." Alessa wrapped her index and middle fingers around Aria's. "I just want to understand."

Aria's lips moved, mouthing something.

"What?" Alessa whispered.

"Home. They want me to come home."

Aria gazed at her, eyes unfocused, with a dreamy, hopeful smile on her face.

"I'd like to go home."

Alessa tugged her hand, wiping the eerie grin from her sister's lips.

"You are home, Ari! This is your home!" she retorted.

Alessa roughly grabbed her other hand and squeezed them both against her chest. Aria looked to her in surprise and felt the rocketing force of Alessa's heart beating furiously beneath her ribs.

"Please, tell me you understand that Ari," Alessa continued, her words catching painfully in her throat, "*this* is your home. We're your family, and I'm your sister…"

Aria stared at her.

"Sister," she repeated. The word tasted strange on her tongue. Strange but familiar. Alessa nodded.

Aria nodded back, even though she couldn't conceive of why. Her instincts, her very core, screamed for the woods—for the snow—and the damp, dark cold. A voice emerged from the furthest reaches of her mind, quiet and relentless. She tried to listen, but only made out a couple of words.

Trust her.

This voice differed from the one she heard in the woods. It's lure less seductive but still powerful. It looped around her heart like a noose, yanking her toward Alessa. Aria was torn between the two, but she nodded because this voice, unlike the dissonant call of the wilderness, felt familiar.

"Exactly," Alessa said. She carefully unraveled her hands from Aria's, but their pinkies remained latched. The gesture sparked a memory in Aria, the image of her and Alessa linking their fingers and making promises known only to each other suddenly blinded her. The picture slipped away before she could hold on to it, but her pinky squeezed around Alessa's a little tighter.

"I'm going to help you figure this out, I promise."

A knock on the door caused both of their heads to pop up. The door popped open a few inches to reveal Joshua.

"Oh, you're both up!" He said with surprise. A smile blew wide across his face. "Ari, you look like you're feeling better. How's your head?"

His booming voice was grating to Aria's ears. Aria wrenched her hand from Alessa's, dragging her sharp nails across the flesh of her neck as she started scratching again.

Joshua's smile collapsed, the hope drained from his eyes, taking the light with it.

"Your mother made breakfast."

Aria turned her back to them and returned to the window. Her nails scraped continuously beneath her ear and along her neck.

"Not hungry."

Joshua didn't look surprised, more disappointed, like he'd been expecting it. He looked both wired and exhausted, his clothes ruffled and hair sprouting in every direction.

"Aria," Joshua began carefully, she continued to scratch, "your mother is really sorry about what she did yesterday. She's just torn up about it. I completely understand if you're upset, but if you would just come down... we can talk it out."

Aria's nails only dug in further, raising angry, red slashes. She felt both pairs of eyes on her, her skin flaring with heat. A slick layer of sweat coated her. The air was sweltering. Her eyes flickered outside; the snow looked inviting. Aria wanted to cocoon herself in it, to feel the cold deep in her marrow.

Joshua's voice was like nails dragging across her ear drum. Too loud even though he stood several feet away. She didn't understand how Alessa didn't find him absolutely deafening.

"Aria, at least look at me."

She flinched away but did as requested. Her body ached, every bone from the top of her head to the arches of her feet blazed with pain. The constant throb that her want to rip off her flesh and bare her skeleton to the ice and wind.

A light pulse beat in her temple from the night before, but it was nothing compared to the fresh stabbing in her gums. She clenched her teeth. The right side of her jaw popped, back molars screeching in protest. Aria fought the urge to plunge her fingers into her mouth to rip them out. Bloody root and all.

Her body felt wrong. All wrong.

"Honey, are you feeling all right?"

She drew back. If only they would leave her alone. She needed to breathe, but all she could smell was the thick grease and butter from the floor below. It threatened to choke her, and despite her insurmountable hunger, the idea of eating whatever they were cooking was enough to make her sick. It smelled toxic. She could taste it in the back of her throat when she swallowed. Sour and rotten.

One of her arms cradled her stomach when she nausea swept through her. She gritted out a response.

"Not. Hungry."

"Okay, it's okay," he floundered. His eyes shot to Alessa, pleading.

She held his stare for a while before giving in. "You know, Ari, if you're not feeling well, it might feel good to take a shower."

Aria brightened with interest. She shot Alessa a curious look.

CHAPTER 14

"A nice, hot shower," Alessa said, "you can take a breather. Have some time alone."

Aria's head rose even further. Yes, she thought, what she wanted more than anything was just to be alone. A moment away from all the noise and the pestering. And even though she was warm, hot water rushing over her aching joints sounded very appealing.

"That's a good idea, Alessa," Joshua said with a new smile, "take a nice, long shower, and you can try to eat after if you're feeling up to it."

Aria considered it. If it got this man to leave her alone, she supposed it was a small price to pay.

Aria finally nodded. A brilliant grin broke out on Alessa's face. Joshua let out a quiet breath of relief.

"Don't worry, I'll let your mother know. Alessa, help get your sister set up in the bathroom."

And just like that, he was out the door.

Aria heard Lily's reaction from upstairs. The telltale stomp of annoyance and the affronted griping traveled up the stairs and down the hall, halting only when Alessa closed them into the bathroom.

She immediately went about preparing the shower, whipping the water on, and arranging the hair and body wash products. Aria was grateful for the white noise of the rushing water. While Alessa busied herself with finding towels, Aria faced herself in the mirror.

The mirror was huge and covered almost the entirety of one wall opposite the shower itself, with bright bulbs lining the top. The intense light they emitted enhanced every detail of Aria's appearance.

Aria stared at the person looking back at her. Even though she knew she was looking at herself, the face staring back was both familiar and unfamiliar. She moved her head back and forth, as if to test whether the reflection would abide. She prodded at the flesh around her jaw, pinching and pulling, only to let go and watch it snap promptly back into place.

Clearly it was her skin. So why did it feel like it didn't belong to her? The spaces below her sharp cheekbones sunken in, giving her already wide eyes a bulging appearance. She looked extremely thin. The rounded ends of her bones pressed up against her nearly translucent skin.

Her fingers continued to travel over the expanse of her face, feeling every dip and curve. Her tongue poked at the insides of her cheeks before running along her bottom row of teeth. Aria committed every detail to memory, certain that when she turned away, something would automatically wipe it from her brain. She hissed when her tongue caught a particularly sensitive back molar on the right side of her mouth. The more she adjusted her mouth to accommodate her curious tongue, the louder her jaw snapped. Although Alessa didn't seem to notice. Her tongue pressed into the side of the burning tooth. It wiggled loose. She tasted iron.

"There." Aria turned, Alessa was looking at her with a satisfied smile. "You should be all set; we've got fresh towels. I set the heat pretty high to start out, but feel free to adjust it. Just toggle the knob a little hard. It gets stuck a lot."

Aria simply stared at her. Alessa proceeded to leave but stopped before pulling open the door.

"Ari, have you heard from Noah at all?"

Aria's brows furrowed, eyes creasing in thought.

Noah?

"Noah," she said, more to herself than Alessa, feeling the sound of it on her tongue.

Noah. Just the sound of it filled her chest and stomach with warmth. It was the sun peeking through the clouds. She couldn't put a face to the name, but she saw his outline, a blur of brown hair and shadows. Her heart fluttered. Aria sucked in an alarmed gasp at the unfamiliar sensation. She shook her head.

"Okay, no problem," she said, and opened the door, "I'll see you in a bit. Just call if you need anything."

Alessa waited until Aria gave her the barest nod of acknowledgment before leaving her to her own devices.

Aria faced the mirror again before the door clicked all the way shut. Alessa's steps faded down the hall and descended the stairs. Finally, she was alone.

For a few minutes, she closed her eyes and listened to the calming rush of the streaming water. Her tongue brushed the sensitive tooth again, and her eyes popped back open. Aria's ghoulish face stared back at her.

Aria leaned over the sink, getting closer to her haunting reflection. Her gut churned, part of her wanting desperately to turn away. Instead, she opened her mouth as wide as she could, arching her neck to angle herself in the light. The bulbs shined into the dark spaces, but only to a certain extent. She hooked her finger on the inside of her cheek, pulling it to the side to get a better visual, but still, the angle wasn't quite right.

The taste of iron trickled down the back of her throat. She burrowed the tip of her tongue into the crevice under the molar, feeling the warm, slick hole. A lightning flash of pain shot through her mouth, but she barely acknowledged it. All she felt was the damn tooth. It overrode everything else. She just wanted it out.

A whimper died in the back of her throat as she slipped her nail under the tooth. Ignoring the wet heat of the wound, and agony shooting through her gums, she shoved the finger in as deep as she could. Eventually, mouth pooling with blood, she got a good grip on the tooth.

Black, blown pupils connected in the mirror. She stared at herself. Bracing herself with a breath and the balling of her free fist, she ripped the tooth right from the root. Crimson, bloody nerves still dangled from the bottom, dripping red into the basin of the sink and all over the white counter. The rest spilled in a thick line down her chin.

Her hand trembled, wide eyes locked on the gnarled tooth. It fell from her grasp, bouncing into the sink until it settled near the drain. Aria spit out a thick glob of blood, wiping her mouth sloppily with the side of her arm.

She stared at herself in the mirror again, lips smeared in red. Her brain flashed with the vague memory of herself, hunched in the snow with something hot and moist on her tongue. Eyes facing the ground, not daring to look around in fear of what she would find watching her from between the trees.

Aria grabbed one of the towels Alessa left for her, trying, and somehow failing in using it to cover up her mess. No matter what she tried, it only made things worse. She tried to stifle the slow but steady stream of blood pumping from the hole in her gums with the tip of her tongue.

She paused. The soft muscle brushed over something sharp. Her stomach clenched in anticipation as she dragged her tongue across the wound again. Beneath the blood and a layer of muscle, there was a point, something firm and sharp protruding from the gum. A new tooth? Aria leaned into the mirror; her breath was close enough to fog the glass. Steam billowed from the shower.

Her jaw ached as she opened her mouth wide, stretching it to its limit, but no angle she chose was enough for her to get a good look. Aria shoved her fingers deeper. They hooked around her jaw to tug it down further. Her mandible quivered with stabbing pains, the corners of her lips smarting, but even as tears spilled down her cheeks, she did not cease.

None of that mattered. She had to see.

She pulled one last time and with a resonating crack, the pain was gone. Aria's hands fell to her sides, and she blinked dumbly at her reflection. Even as she stared at herself, she couldn't fully comprehend what she was seeing.

Aria had unhinged her own jaw. The skin was torn at the edges of her mouth in what looked like a psychotic joker's smile. When before she saw nothing, now she was witness to every horrifying detail. Not just rows of white teeth smeared in blood, but the ridges on the roof of her mouth, as well as the uvula dangling at the entrance of her dark throat.

Aria's heart slammed against her ribcage, breath coming in quicker and quicker pants. Her hands trembled, and tears raced down the apples of her cheeks and into her gaping mouth. She tasted their salt, and instinctively attempted to clench her jaw shut, but it wouldn't budge. Dread knotted in her stomach when her eyes met her own in the mirror again. This time she was met with coal-black pits where her eyes should have been.

The reflective copy of her grinned. Aria didn't know how it was possible with her jaw in this condition, but she could tell from the amused arch of the doppelganger's brow that it was so. She tried to scream but a wretched gargling noise emerged instead.

Do you see? The words echoed in Aria's mind even though her reflection's mouth never moved. *Do you see what you are? What you could be?*

Aria frantically grabbed the bottom of her jaw, trying and failing to force it closed. Layers of spit and blood drenched her fingers. It didn't budge. She couldn't stop looking at the brilliant red of the inside of her mouth, and even her tongue which appeared longer to her than usual, because now she could see every inch of it as it disappeared into the back of her throat. It resembled a large, undulating snake.

Her dark reflection continued to watch her, still as stone while she thrashed wildly. Its' gaze burned her skin. The steam from the shower made it difficult to catch her breath, and through choked, quiet sobs, she continued to push her palms up against her jaw. Even using all of her strength, it fought against her. The reflection tilted its' head with interest.

Aria slammed her hand against the mirror in frustration, and the glass gave way. It shattered against her palm, shards slicing into her skin. She yanked her arm back and looked at the wound, fresh blood mixing with old. Pieces of mirror littered the floor and in each one the doppelganger lingered, still watching.

Doesn't it feel... miraculous? The copy's voice multiplied with every shard of glass it occupied.

Her mind buzzed with static. Aria stumbled to the shower and threw the curtain back, staining it with streaks of red. She made a strange, garbled noise in the back of her gaping throat when she felt the hot water singe her skin. Fumbling for the knob, one of her slick hands twisted it all the way to the coldest setting.

Simpering, she pressed her still clothed back to the wall of the shower. She gripped her jaw with both hands, grunting in fierce determination, and pushed with all her might. Another crack burst like a gunshot in the small room, and her jaw locked back into its proper place. However, she refused to move her hands, terrified that if she let go, it would fall back open.

Aria's quivering body slid to the floor of the tub, palms sealed firmly over her mouth, with the frigid water beating on her scalp. Despite the shivers it brought, it soothed the heat radiating off her skin, and numbed her aching joints.

A heavy knot of dread crushed her intestines like a lead weight. Every time she closed her eyes, the image of her deformed and bloody face appeared, making them fly back open again. Aria only had enough strength to lower her head between her bent knees.

Aria remained on the floor of the shower, trembling and swaying,

CHAPTER 14

as the water washed over her. She wilted like a dying flower, beaten in a frozen storm.

Aria didn't know how long she'd been lying in the same spot. She lifted her head when she heard a light drumming on the bathroom door.

"Ari? Everything good in there?" Alessa called, her words muffled.

Aria's cheek pressed against the floor of the tub. She opened her mouth to reply, but she was too exhausted. Time meant nothing to her anymore. Alessa might as well be millions of miles away.

"Ari, come on, answer me!"

Her laugh carried a ragged edge of fear.

"I'm coming in!"

Aria was fading fast, eyes closing as her mind filled with a labyrinth of dark trees.

"Aria?"

Deep within the labyrinth, Aria heard Alessa's cries. They seemed so far away.

"Oh my God, Ari!"

Something jostled Aria, catapulting her from the dark and into the light.

Aria's eyes opened slowly, and she stared at Alessa through damp strands of hair. She hovered over Aria, the shower curtain tossed back. Alessa stared back at her in horror. Aria merely smiled.

"Lessa."

As the word left her lips, Joshua and Lily piled into the room.

"Ale–oh dear God." Lily cupped her demure hands over her gaping mouth.

"What the hell?"

"Joshua!" Lily spat.

Aria gripped Lily's arms, her lashes flittering like the legs of a spider, and mouth twisting in discomfort. Her gaze darted in every direction, confused one second and clear the next. Her brain dipped in and out of a nightmarish dreamscape. When she opened her eyes, she saw the ransacked bathroom and the worried eyes of her sister, but when she blinked, she saw an entirely new world.

A world bathed in fire and blood. Trees broken and blackened, blades catching the reflection of moonlight. Snow—no *ash* falling from the sky and layering the charred earth.

Aria's breathing came in shallow pants. She slammed her eyes shut and popped them open again. She was back in the bathroom.

"Are you okay?" Alessa's soft tone drew Aria's attention, but she strained to keep her eyes open – terrified to blink.

"Where am I?" she whispered.

"You're home, Ari—it's okay."

Alessa whipped around to see her mother and father still staring at the mess. Their faces were ashen.

"Mom!" Alessa yelped, and the woman startled.

Lily stared at them for a second, a look of puzzlement on her face before all the pieces finally clicked into place. Lily ushered Joshua out of the room. Once he was gone, she rushed to their sides with an armful of towels.

"Aria, honey," Lily kneeled by the tub and handed Alessa one. She immediately draped it over Aria. Lily cupped Aria's wet cheek, picking away strands of hair that clung to her face.

"What happened? Did you hurt yourself?"

Aria's bulging and stinging eyes slowly slid to meet Lily's. It was difficult to hold them open, and she wasn't sure how much longer she could do it. That other world lurked at the darkest edges of her vision, voices from another universe echoing like a monstrous war cry from somewhere deep in her soul. An ancient and heavy pain settled in her bones.

When her gaze landed on her mother, she nearly crumbled.

CHAPTER 14

"Mom..." Aria whimpered.

Both Alessa and Lily straightened when she spoke, their expressions caught somewhere between astonishment and despair.

"Mommy?" she said next, and Lily went rigid. She was motionless for a while, but finally came out of it with the shake of her head.

"I'm here, sweetie, right here."

As Lily cradled her face, Aria lost the battle. She blinked, and she was back in the dark, standing alone and surrounded by the tallest trees she had ever seen. White snow buried her feet and a black sky loomed over her. She spun in endless circles, terrified to turn her back to the woods but ultimately having no choice. Something large, a thick branch perhaps, sent a loud crack splitting through the gaps in the trees. Aria looked over her shoulder, back slick with sweat, but all she saw was darkness.

That is... until the trees moved.

She closed her eyes again, blacking them out further with her hands.

"Ari, look at me, please—did you hit your head?"

Aria lowered her palms and saw her mother once more staring back at her. Both she and Alessa watched her with bewilderment, as if she was crazy.

And wasn't she? Aria could barely hold on to her own consciousness long enough to have a conversation and having mental flashes of a place she didn't recognize. An explosive cackle erupted from deep in her chest. Aria's sopping form convulsed as a horrifying blend of sobs and laughter poured out of her. One blink and she was there with her mother and sister, their gentle hands cradling her. Another blink and those same hands were soaked in blood, blackened nails cutting into her flesh before being dragged into an abyss beyond what her subconscious could fathom.

A chasm ripped through the middle of Aria's skull. Her brain was at war with itself, overloaded with memories that were both hers and not hers. The pain was a splitting, cold steel.

"Ari," Lily tried, but Aria responded with a whine so long and low it resembled a wounded animal, "Aria, please, you have to breathe, honey! You're going to pass out."

"We did not come to be served, but to serve!" Aria wailed. The words repeated in a loop in her mind. It was spoken, not by one voice, but by many. Each tone layered over the other, slicing through her brain matter like butter.

"A-And to give our lives as... as ransom to many!"

Her mouth lifted into a sardonic grin even as the tears continued to spill down her cheeks. Aria squeezed her eyes shut, so afraid of what images she would see next that she blocked them out altogether.

"Keep talking to her, Alessa!"

Alessa gripped Aria's hand, her thumb landing on Aria's hammering pulse point. She put a bit of pressure there, moving it in steady circles.

"We're here, Ari. Just keep listening to us, okay?"

Lily continued to stroke Aria's cheek, keeping her voice as level as possible. She murmured soothing words of encouragement.

"Whomever is..." Aria's tongue was heavy, and she tripped over her words. "Whomever is the first to open..."

The screams gradually faded. Aria tried to focus on the warmth of Lily's palm and Alessa's sturdy grasp. Their voices were so distant, but it reminded her of where she truly was. She mentally chased those voices, muscling past shearing pain that had taken over ever synapse of her brain. Louder and louder, the voices became.

"We got you, Ari. We're not going anywhere," Alessa said, and her serene timbre melted away the remaining screams.

When her mind fell silent once again, she finally mustered the courage to open her eyes. Lily and Alessa gazed upon her with hope. Lily patted Aria's cheek.

"There she is," she whispered.

Aria stared at her, mouth hanging open like a dead fish. She willed herself to speak, to form any words at all, but her brain was overwhelmed, both flooded with a million questions, and dumbstruck by the reality of her mother's face up close.

"I'm sorry," Aria replied. She didn't know why, only that she was. So very, very sorry.

Lily frowned, a knot of confusion forming between her brows.

Aria.

She heard it, clear as day. Far away, but distinct. Only her mother's lips hadn't moved. Aria shot a frantic look at Alessa.

"Did you hear that?"

Her question snuffed out the light in Alessa's face. "N-No, Aria. We didn't say anything."

Aria...

Her head jerked to the other side, ripping her face from Lily's hands. The voice danced in the air, the source coming from all around her.

"Aria, what are you..."

Aria lifted her hand, sharply cutting Lily off mid-sentence. Aria continued to look away from them, eyes wide and searching.

Sweet Aria...

They were both inside and around her. She pictured her name drifting on the winter wind, weaving through the trees. The voices from the forest called to her again.

Her eyes still flooding with tears, Aria's quivering lips stretched into a marionette smile. It was like someone was pulling at the corners of her mouth with hooks, exposing all of her teeth. Her heart tugged in two different directions, part yearning to remain with Alessa, and the other screeching and clawing to get back to the woods.

"Can't you hear them?" Aria whimpered, her grin a horrid yet permanent fixture.

"Hear who, honey?" Lily asked. Aria's pupils swallowed the blue of her irises like tiny, ferocious black holes.

She cried out when Aria grabbed her by the arms, bringing their faces close. Aria pressed her skeletal fingers into Lily's skin until the woman whimpered, and she felt bone grinding on bone. Aria yanked her even closer, lips brushing her mother's earlobe as she spoke.

"They're all around us."

Chapter 15

All around us.

Alessa hadn't been able to get the words out of her head. A creeping unease curled its way around her spine, higher and higher until it latched onto the base of where her neck met her skull. It took her mother several, infinitely long seconds to recover and ask Aria what she meant. But Aria had become unreachable again.

When they realized she wasn't going to elaborate further, they hauled her out of the tub as Lily obsessively tucked and re-tucked a warm, dry towel around her. Alessa followed behind her parents like a lost puppy, to Aria's bedroom and watched them place her gently on the bed.

Alessa leaned against the doorway as Lily checked for the fifth time to make sure the towel was covering her sufficiently. Aria looked past them at the wall, but her focus was somewhere beyond it—beyond all of them.

They're all around us.

A vicious chill threaded through Alessa's nervous system, down to her atoms. It made her head spin.

"Joshua, there isn't a scratch on her, it's just like in the church—all of that blood."

Lily's complexion soured into a sickly green. Joshua shook his head as they entered the hallway.

"I found a tooth in the sink," he replied. Alessa's vision briefly tilted as the image of a bloody tooth flashed in her mind.

Lily and Joshua seemed to think better of continuing the conversation when they noticed Alessa was close enough to hear them. Joshua cleared his throat and gestured toward the stairs. Lily followed him down wordlessly.

"Noah... Noah..."

At first Alessa thought she was hearing things, but when she heard it a second time, she whirled around to find Aria still sitting in the same spot, clutching the blanket like a small child. Her lips moved rapidly as her head tilted to face the floor. Alessa darted into the bedroom and shut the door behind her.

"What did you say, Ari?" She rushed to Aria's side, kneeling before the bed. "Did you say Noah?"

Aria shook her head at Alessa's question, but from the way she denied eye contact, Alessa wasn't buying it.

"It's okay if you did, Ari. You remember Noah, right?"

Aria still seemed reluctant to answer or even acknowledge the question. Alessa's eyes landed on the dozens of photographs intermingled in a giant collage above her desk. A small smile danced across her lips, and she jumped up, zeroing in on and plucking one particular photo from the wall.

Alessa approached her with more caution this time, the photograph pressed against her chest. She had half a mind not to give it over, knowing it was possible that in her current state of mind, Aria might damage or destroy it. But she reminded herself that Aria would rather have the memory at the expense of the photograph, rather than the other way around.

"I want you to look at this—I mean *really* look—take your time. And tell me if you recognize him. Okay?"

CHAPTER 15

It took a while before Aria lifted her head, curiosity getting the better of her. She stared at the piece of paper. Alessa held it out for her to take at her own pace. Golden beams of sunlight sliced across Aria's bony wrist as she took it between her long fingers.

The picture was of her, from before, with full freckled cheeks, vibrant eyes and burying a brilliant smile in the base of a boy's neck. Her arms were around him, his chocolate curls tumbling over his forehead in a wild but completely endearing way. They were laughing. Both of them looked so utterly happy.

She traced her index finger along the line of his jawbone and followed the tangled mass of her hair, billowing in the air behind her.

"Noah..." she said again, "I... I think I do..." Aria replied with hesitance.

"Yeah?"

Aria nodded, continuing to stare at the picture.

"Noah," she said it with more confidence this time.

"Yes! Exactly, that's Noah," Alessa encouraged, "your boyfriend."

Aria's nose wrinkled. She glanced back up at Alessa.

"Can I... can I see him?"

Alessa pushed away any and all concerns she had about their parent's rules.

"Yeah! Yeah, of course."

The corner of Aria's mouth twitched into the barest of smiles, but it was all the encouragement Alessa needed.

"He really, really wants to see you too. He really missed you," Alessa added.

The look Aria gave her then was that of pure, childlike hope.

"Yeah?" Aria whispered. Alessa swallowed her tears, willing herself to nod.

"Yeah," she breathed out in one heaving exhale, "God, you have no idea how much."

Aria still held the photograph when Alessa left the room, following one last promise to bring Noah to her no matter what it cost. Renewed energy pulsed in her veins, and Alessa returned downstairs. Having a new mission helped her focus, enabling her to rest her tunnel vision on something other than what was currently warping her sister's mind. This, she could handle.

Lily and Joshua stood huddled in the kitchen. Their exchange was mumbled, too quiet and fast for her to make any of it out. She cleared her throat and both of them straightened. Her mother plastered on a smile that didn't reach her eyes.

"How is she?"

Alessa shrugged. She refused to mention anything about Noah. The only way she'd be able to sneak him over was if her parents believed nothing was amiss.

"What were you guys talking about?"

She swore she saw panic flicker in Joshua's eyes, but he tossed on a convincing smile.

"Your mother and I were just discussing our plan for the day, after I take care of the mess upstairs, we need to make another stop by the doctor's office."

"Again?" Alessa sneered. After what happened the day before? If something like that happened again, Alessa wasn't confident she'd catch Aria.

Sensing her mounting stress, Joshua placed a reassuring hand on her shoulder.

"We won't be gone long, two hours at most, we promise. But we got a call from Doctor Sutton, and he really needs us to swing by and discuss a few more test results."

Her brows furrowed, upper lip curling in disbelief and irritation.

"I didn't hear the phone ring."

CHAPTER 15

Alessa always heard it when it rang. The thing was so old; the ringtone was shrill enough to crack the sound barrier; it was impossible to find a room in the house the noise didn't reach. Joshua seemed taken aback.

"That's because he called on my cell," he replied, his nervous stammer fading.

Alessa didn't know if she bought it. He very likely could have been telling the truth, he often kept his phone on vibrate so she wouldn't have heard it. But after finding out about their agreement with Noah's parents, she couldn't be sure.

"But what if something happens again?"

"It's going to be fine; we won't be gone as long this time, but it's really important we get down there."

Alessa deflated, but she perked up when she remembered Noah. Even though she didn't want her parents to go, it presented the perfect opportunity to sneak him in. She had an exact timeline, two hours, she could make that work. Her heart pounded as the idea took root.

"Fine," she muttered. Joshua smiled with relief.

"And of course, you can call my cell if you need anything, okay?"

"Sure, Dad."

Perhaps this time, they'd be able to get some help from someone who was qualified. So long as they didn't come rushing back with the priest in tow, she could live two hours without their presence.

Alessa dutifully waved them off when they departed, waiting to close the door until the exact moment they shut themselves into their car. As soon as she was alone, she rushed to the phone. Every second counted. It didn't take much to convince Noah, and their exchange took barely 60 seconds.

Alessa wasn't sure whether God was real or not, but she prayed to whoever listened that this helped.

Alessa waited on the couch, leg bouncing furiously, as her hands wrung the circulation out of her wrists. The skin was red and raw when she heard the faint knock coming from the back of the house. She jumped to her feet, wanting to let him in before the nosey neighbors got too curious. Their stalkers across the road had dwindled since the day before but they still had lingerers. Alessa didn't care to give them another spectacle to obsess over.

However, when she threw open the door to greet him, she wished she'd given herself a moment longer to prepare. Maybe then she would have been able to mask her shock.

Noah looked bad. Worse than that fateful morning in church. From just a brief glance she gathered he hadn't slept, at least since Aria came home. Her heart ached for him.

Noah's dark hair, damp from the misty air, flattened against his forehead. It accentuated the deep circles under his eyes. His winter jacket looked like it was going to swallow him whole.

"Hey," he said as he scurried inside, kicking off his boots. His wide eyes kept darting from her to the stairwell.

"Thanks for sneaking me over."

Finally, his gaze landed on Alessa and stayed there, but he was still fidgety.

"You've got a little less than two hours, hope that's okay."

"Please, it's more than enough." Noah closed the distance between them, tugging her into a warm, brotherly hug. He patted her back. "I can't thank you enough."

Alessa pulled away after one more squeeze. "You don't have to. Come on, I'll take you to her."

Noah followed in silence behind her. At one point she had to peek over her shoulder to make sure he was still there and hadn't bolted in terror. But there he remained, stiff as a board, his eyes wide like saucers. She waited until he nodded at her, a signal that he was ready, before opening Aria's door.

CHAPTER 15

Noah stepped slowly into the room, arms locked at his sides, his hands buried in his pockets. Aria still sat on the bed, cradling the photograph Alessa gave her.

Once Aria lifted her head, and Alessa saw the clearness in her eyes, she shut the door, leaving them to their privacy.

Alessa kept herself otherwise occupied by watching the television on the lowest volume setting, simultaneously listening to the show and for any outside sounds in case their parents decided to come home early. She jumped from her spot on the couch every single time she heard something that sounded even remotely out of place. Her heart pounded, the constant awareness and caution threatening to split her apart until she was nothing but a bundle of raging nerves.

Alessa was just sitting down again when the ear-splitting ring of their landline pierced the air.

"Fuck!" She exclaimed, sucking in a terrified gasp, and sprung to action.

"Hale residence, Alessa speaking." The words were automatic, a polite and required greeting drilled into them by their mother.

"Lessa! It's me!"

"Maya, holy shit," Alessa breathed out, "I didn't think I'd hear from you so soon after yesterday. How are you? Are you okay? I'm so sorry you had to see that."

"I'm fine, oh my God, I should be asking *you* that!"

Their words toppled over each other until they both suddenly went quiet at the same moment. The dam broke, cracking through the tension, and they both fell into a string of quiet giggles. Hearing Maya's laugh lifted Alessa's spirit instantly.

"How are things over there? How is Ari?"

Alessa was stunned her friend was even considering Aria's wellbeing given her previous actions. She wouldn't have blamed Maya if she never wanted to interact with anyone in the Hale family again.

"I don't know. I mean... one minute she seems clear, she remembers us, and she can talk to us – and then one minute later she's stuck in some weird fog, impossible to reach."

Alessa glanced at the stairs, imagining what might be going on between Noah and Aria. She figured as long as she didn't hear any strange noises; they were in the clear.

"Noah is visiting with her right now." She looked back to the front door, checking for movement. "Did you hear his parents banned him from coming over, or even asking about her?"

"What the hell?" Maya spat, disgust coloring her tone, "what is with these people?"

"He said they talked with our parents, that they all agreed it was best for him to stay away." She unconsciously shook her head, still in disbelief. However, with everything that had been going on, and her parent's sudden shadiness, she wasn't sure what she could trust them with anymore.

"I mean I know your parents are weird about dating but God... they've been friends since we were kids, how do they think this is okay?"

The rush of affection she felt for Maya intensified. Maya didn't have to care, she didn't have to stick around or give her insane family the time of day, yet there she was. A beam of light in never ending darkness.

"Well, he's with her now."

"You're a wonderful sister for doing that for her."

Alessa's lips quivered into a small smile. "She would do the same for me."

"Still," Maya continued, "you're a damn good sister, Lessa. You should know that."

Alessa tongued the inside of her mouth, eyelids fluttering as tears welled to the surface. She blinked them back and cleared her throat.

CHAPTER 15

"Thanks," Alessa sniffled, "I am really sorry... about yesterday. I didn't think she would ever do anything like that."

"Please. The whole thing was destined to crash and burn the minute your parents brought Grandfather into the room. I don't understand why he agreed to go at all, he should have known she would need a doctor."

Alessa sighed quietly but with intense relief to know she felt the same.

"He's... he's never been like that before... never claimed someone was beyond help even when they were at their worst," Maya said.

Father Samuel was arguably the most important figurehead in their town. He had his hands in everything, knew a little about everyone, and was widely respected. As was his father, the former priest of St. Lawrence, and his father before him. Their church and their family lineage were as old as the town and known as generous folks with a desire to help even the darkest of souls. It was their calling, Father Samuel always claimed.

"I've never seen him so angry..."

Alessa swore she heard a muffled sniffle on the other end of the line but said nothing about it. Maya wouldn't have wanted her to. She waited until her friend was ready.

"Don't worry about me, okay? You got enough on your plate. I don't wanna be another headache."

"You could never be a headache," Alessa whispered, just loud enough for Maya to hear, "never."

Maya let out a slight, choked breath of air. She giggled and Alessa's heart hurtled into the stratosphere.

"Listen," Maya said, her tone serious, "there is another reason I called."

Creeping, aching dread crawled back into the very center of Alessa's being. She forced herself to swallow before she replied, needing the extra seconds to push past the fear clamping around her throat.

"You mean you didn't just call to hear my pretty voice?"

"No, although that is a huge bonus," she said, humoring her friend, "I saw something earlier and couldn't get it out of my head, so I had to ask. Did your parents talk to my grandfather after last night?"

Alessa frowned in confusion. After the way Father Samuel left things, she highly doubted they were on speaking terms again already. He'd made his distaste for them abundantly clear.

"Uh, no. Not that I know of, at least."

A memory struck her.

We need to make another stop at the doctor's office.

She recalled her father's stammer when she pointed out the phone didn't ring, how for a brief instant, he seemed to be internally scrambling for an excuse. Their dad had always been the weakest liar in the family.

"They said Doctor Sutton called and needed to see them again today. That's how I was able to sneak Noah over."

"Well, I don't know if they were at the doctor's or what, but I was helping Grandfather clean the pews this morning and as I was leaving," she hesitated, "I saw your parents pull in."

The searing knot residing in Alessa's gut burst. A sudden but intense bout of dizziness slammed into her, and she placed a clammy hand on the wall to right herself.

"Why.... why would they be there?"

"I don't know. I thought maybe you would have an idea."

Alessa shook her head, even though Maya couldn't see it. She took a few deep breaths, each one harder than the last. It was like someone was sitting on her chest.

"That doesn't make any sense. Father Samuel wanted nothing to do with us—I thought he made that pretty clear."

"Believe me, so do I. I thought I was crazy at first, did a double take

CHAPTER 15

and everything—ducked behind some bushes like a lunatic, just to be sure."

Alessa's brows narrowed as she racked her brain, trying to fathom why they were visiting the priest. Every scenario stalled at a dead end.

"Maybe they went over to apologize again in person?" Alessa guessed, but it sounded ridiculous even to her own ears.

"Could be. I don't blame them for trying."

"Either way, it's odd. I don't know why Dad would lie about where they were going."

Maya had nothing to offer in that regard.

"Could mean nothing but, I thought you should know."

"Thank you, really." Alessa gripped the phone tighter. "I'm glad you called."

"Me too."

They both idled, neither one of them wanting to hang up just yet. Alessa opened her mouth to grunt out a reluctant goodbye, but Maya beat her to the punch.

"I can keep an eye out for them if you want. I don't really know what I'm looking for, but—if I find anything out, I'll keep you in the loop."

"Yeah," Alessa grinned, "that would be helpful. Thanks."

"Anything you need. *Anything*. We'll figure this out, Alessa. I know it."

One lone tear escaped down Alessa's cheek. She swiftly wiped it away.

"I know. I know we will."

She didn't know what that would mean, but it was the closest thing to hope she had right now.

Chapter 16

The silence was all-encompassing. Aria couldn't believe what she was seeing.

Aria's fractured mind had calmed significantly since receiving the picture. Something about the comforting weight in her hand, and the sight of their smiles, joyous and burning, put her at ease. This person, this version of her, had been happy. Aria followed the feeling right back to the forefront of her consciousness so she could once again take the reins.

There he stood, flesh and blood before her. The boy from the picture. Aria walked toward him, slowly and carefully. It took all her physical and mental strength to keep control over her own body. Her mind begged her to succumb to the darkness again. Every second she kept her sentience exhausted her, and every time she reemerged, it was harder and harder to hold on to.

But right now, she was in control, and she had to make it count.

"Noah?" she muttered; her voice hoarse. His eyes shimmered with a fresh wave of tears. Noah leaned forward, unconsciously seeking her touch, but he continued to hold himself back.

Aria smiled.

"Noah."

That was all it took. It happened in the span of one breath, his long arms encircling her as she collapsed against him. He kept her up even

CHAPTER 16

as her knees buckled. Aria shook, like a fragile branch whipping in the wind of a hurricane, as quiet sobs wracked her body.

Aria clawed at his coat blindly, her face buried in his chest, clutching him as if to mold their bodies into one being. Noah was here. She felt secure and comforted in his arms.

"God, oh God, I missed you," Noah whispered into her hair, breathing her in, "I'm so sorry I didn't get here sooner—so fucking sorry—but my parents, they wouldn't allow it. I don't know what the hell has gotten into them. It's like they just wanted me to forget about you."

He shook his head miserably.

"I just didn't want you to think that I abandoned you."

Noah leaned back and gently nudged her chin, lifting her gaze to meet his.

"I would never just leave you like that," he continued with an emphatic shake of his head. Aria cupped his cheek, and he shivered.

"I know, Noah," she replied, "I know."

He gave a wobbly smile. They fell silent again, only this time, it was peaceful. Their foreheads touched, noses brushing as he cradled her close. Aria's finger danced along his cheekbone; his skin was hot to the touch despite the cold weather.

Neither one of them knew who moved first, nor did they care to second guess it. But suddenly his lips were on hers, delicate but steady, and lightning flashes of color burst behind her eyelids. Aria gripped him tighter, her body buzzing. She wanted to bask in this moment forever. Her head spun from lack of air when they parted, and the smile that crossed his face only made her dizzier.

"I can't believe you're here," she said after, breathless.

"Are you okay? Alessa told me what's been going on, but are you all right? Are you hurt or anything?"

Noah began frantically searching every inch he could see for any visible cuts or wounds. Aria shook her head, gripping his arms to get his attention.

"I'm not hurt."

Every word she spoke was a conscious effort, each one threatening to be the last until she was eventually kicked out of the driver's seat once more. Aria tried focusing on the fabric of his jacket between her fingers, grounding herself physically in the present to combat the shadows that wriggled in her peripheral vision.

"Alessa said you were having trouble remembering."

Aria furrowed her brows in concentration and nodded.

"So, you really don't remember anything from the last two months?"

Aria thought of the man with the gold ring, the endless night sky, and running from something in a tattered white dress.

"I remember... bits and pieces."

She led him to the bed to sit, but they never let go of each other. Noah waited, staring at her in reverence until she continued.

"They come in flashes, out of order and jumbled together," she said, a deep shiver running through her, "some of them I don't recognize."

"What do you mean?"

She recalled ash falling from a dark sky, and hands bathed in red.

"Some of the memories... they feel wrong, like they were plucked from someone else's head and put into mine."

Aria tapped her temple, her eyes glazing as she tried to explain it.

"They don't feel like they belong to me."

She knew it sounded ludicrous, but she didn't know how else to explain it.

"I don't recognize where I am. They're places I've never been before–things I've never seen." Aria shook her head at the insanity of it all. "But it's like I'm there all the same."

She lifted her eyes to check Noah's reaction, but his expression was unreadable.

CHAPTER 16

"You must think I went crazy out there. I know how it sounds."

"Hey, no," Noah firmly cut in, "I don't care how it sounds. If you say that's how it is, that's how it is."

She looked to him in surprise, his lack of hesitation catching her completely off guard.

"I'm on your side, Ari. Always. Crazy sounding or not."

Aria didn't know how to express just how grateful she felt for him. Anyone else would have run for the hills much sooner. But Noah was special, always had been. She leaned into him.

"Tell me what you can. I want to hear all of it."

Aria looked down at her hands, still gripping his jacket, the whites of her knuckles shining. She stared at the skin sealed tightly over her bones, like cling wrap. Skin that itched and burned with every movement. Skin she had the undying urge to tear right from the muscle.

How do you explain to someone that your body no longer feels like your own? That she felt like a passenger, battling for control against something she couldn't see but knew was hiding in the fathomless corners of her mind. How did she explain the unexplainable?

"I feel like I'm losing myself... like maybe I lost a bit already."

It wasn't everything she wanted to say, but it was the best her scattered brain could come up with. Aria searched his expression for any traces of fear. Noah curled a wayward strand of her hair behind her ear. It was a familiar gesture that filled her with warmth and comforted her even at her most anxious.

"How about we start with what you remember? And maybe I can help find the pieces of you that you're looking for."

Tears threatened to spill from her eyes once more, his unending empathy and kindness consistently surprising her. The shadows continued to taunt her, whispering promises of rest and peace. Aria charged forward. It would be hard to articulate what she remembered.

A lot of it was hazy and out of order, but she had to try.

And so, she began.

She told him everything, from the flashes of a war-torn world, and ash raining from the sky to the dreams of her in a white dress, stumbling through the snow. Even with all of it laid bare before them, none of it made sense. Aria knew they needed more, but recounting these memories stole what little energy she had left. The shadows never abated. They merely lingered in her periphery, singing their sacred songs, and draining her bit by bit. The invisible force churned to life inside of her again, twisting her intestines and putting pressure on her brain.

Her vision faded in and out, the darkness becoming ever more enticing. Even though Noah cradled her hand, she felt detached from it, no longer able to feel the soft warmth of his skin on hers.

She was running out of time.

Aria wasn't sure how long she had left before the darkness took over, replacing her with a stone - cold husk of the girl she'd once been. Every time it fought its way back to the forefront, shards of Aria broke away, disintegrating into a black sea. If this continued for much longer, there would be nothing left to chisel away.

A piercing pain cut through Aria's stomach, leaving behind a now-familiar hollow ache. The hunger was returning. She couldn't let Noah see her like this. Aria remembered the satisfying crunch of Father Samuel's frail bones when she slammed him against the wall and was immediately sick at the rush of gratification it instilled in her.

No, he had to go. Now. There was no telling what she was capable of when she lost control. Aria didn't want him to see her fade away.

Aria tore her hand from his grasp, Noah blinked at her in surprise.

"You should go," she said.

Panic flashed across his face. "Go? Is everything okay? Did I do something?"

The raw fear saturating his words made her eyes sting with tears. Aria bit her bottom lip until blood pebbled under her teeth. She shook her head and sprung to her feet when he reached out again, the tips of his fingers brushing her arm. Her vision whirled, the darkness at the edges of her eyes growing. The world shrank, her perception tunneling, and Noah seemed to drift further away. Aria turned away from him, unable to stomach the torment on his beautiful face.

"No, no. It's not you," she whimpered, facing the wall of photographs above her desk, "there's something wrong with me, Noah. You have to go."

She didn't hear him but felt him draw closer to her. The heat radiated from his body as he hovered behind her, hands suspended in midair.

"Please, Ari. I don't want to leave you."

His soft, pleading whisper almost made her cave. She wanted to curl into his embrace, to mold her body into his, and forget the world. But the twinge in her gut sent her hurtling back down into reality.

"Please, Noah," she would beg him if she had to, "I *need* you to go."

Aria wrapped her arms around her middle, hoping to physically stifle the agonizing hunger from spreading to the rest of her. She saw how badly he wanted to protest; to soothe and hold her, to take her pain away. His desperation was palpable. "Okay, if that's what you need, I'll go."

Somehow, it hurt even worse to hear not a single drop of resentment in his voice. He was too good, she thought, far too good for someone like her.

His warmth dissipated from the surrounding air when he backed away and gathered his belongings. She didn't turn to face him until he opened the door, afraid that if she did so even a second sooner she would second guess her decision and run to him. Noah paused when he was halfway out the door.

"Oh," he glanced up, eyes widening as he patted his left coat pocket.

Noah pulled something out and stared at it for a long moment before glancing back at her.

"I almost forgot. I brought you something."

Noah shifted from one foot to the other, nervous. Eventually, he outstretched his free hand toward her.

"Can I?"

She hesitated. Aria wasn't sure she could handle touching him again, but the shimmer in his red-rimmed eyes tugged at her heart. He kept his hand out until she laid her own in it. Noah opened his fist to reveal a bracelet with a delicate gold chain, and a small diamond 'A' dangling in the center. Noah wrapped the piece of jewelry around her wrist.

"The chain broke, and it fell off in my car," Noah said as he latched it, "you thought you lost it, and you were so upset you didn't even want to tell me. And when you did, you cried so hard."

Aria saw flashes of herself turning her bedroom inside out to find it, and then blubbering in the hallway at school when she finally confessed her misdeed. Noah had simply squeezed her close and told her he'd be happy to get her another.

"I remember," she said.

He smiled, and she marveled at how effortlessly he made her heart flip.

"I found it after you went missing." His smile faded, "I got the chain fixed and promised myself I would give it back to you when you came home."

Noah continued to hold her hand even when the bracelet was secure. They stared at it for a long while, and when Aria lifted her head to look at him again, his face was damp with tears. He was so beautiful, she thought, effortlessly so, right down to his very soul. How lucky she had been to bask in the rays of his light for as long as she did. She forced herself to pull away. Every second he was here prolonged the inevitable.

CHAPTER 16

Her stomach convulsed, the pressure in her brain releasing in bursts of splitting pain. It pulled Aria in deeper, hot saliva filled her mouth, and her vision darkened. She smelled the salt on his skin and was overcome with the urge to bury her teeth in his doughy flesh and tear.

"Ari."

His voice brought her back to reality, but she felt beads of sweat forming on her temples. Her heart crashed in her ears. Aria gritted her teeth, determined to muscle through it. She just needed a little longer.

Noah gave her one last look over and sucked in a long, shuddering breath.

"I just want you to know, no matter what happened to you out there, I will always love you."

Aria's lip trembled, and she nearly broke right then. But then she saw Noah, limbs splayed before her, and dark blood streaming from a gash ripped open in his neck. She backed away from him as the vision disappeared, shaking her head.

"I love you," she whimpered and grabbed the door, "I'm sorry."

Aria did not look at him again and turned her back to the door as it slammed shut. Placing her palms and forehead against the wood, she allowed the torrent of sobs to escape her. The force of them made her crumble to the floor, and curl into a tiny ball. There Aria remained, quaking with tears, a noose cinched around her heart and throat, for how long she didn't know. Then, all at once, the tears dried and her eyes glazed over, agony contorting into an impassive stare that remained as the sunlight from the window faded into night.

Chapter 17

Aria didn't leave her room for the rest of the night, even for dinner. They all took turns knocking on her door, and when that predictably did nothing, Lily and Joshua forced their way in. Aria, however, stonewalled them. Whether she was truly sleeping, Alessa couldn't tell. After their failed attempts, Lily stormed out of the room, her face twisted into a grimace of barely contained rage with Joshua close on her heels.

They retired to their bedroom after dinner. Alessa noticed her dad was no longer camping on the couch and wondered which of them had finally caved. He stopped sleeping in their room days after Aria went missing. They never talked about why. Honestly, Alessa was so preoccupied, she didn't give it much thought.

Now her eyes were wide open, and she was curious. Did Lily force him out? Or did he leave voluntarily, seeking a modicum of peace in the chaos? Alessa groaned; exhausted, her eyelids threatened to seal shut every time she blinked. Her brain hummed, more awake than ever.

She watched TV for a few hours to distract herself until she couldn't keep her eyes open any longer. Every time she blinked, she lost a chunk of time, and winced at the bright blue glare of the screen. Sleep, she needed sleep.

Alessa was to return to school tomorrow. Lily made it clear over

CHAPTER 17

dinner. She'd missed far too many days in the year already. Her mother never glanced up from her plate as she spoke, but her tone made her intention perfectly clear. Unfortunately, no matter how much Alessa loathed it, there wasn't much she could do about it. She knew she pushed her luck by having Maya cover for her so many times, now it was biting her in the ass.

Alessa rubbed her eyes and squinted at the clock. She had less than four hours before she had to get up. The cruel assurance of how difficult it would be to wake up the next day was enough motivation to get her off the couch. She bumped her shin against the coffee table as she stumbled out. Her bladder twinged.

Alessa hit the second-floor landing and walked past Aria's door, heading to the bathroom at the other end of the hall. She yawned, stretching her arms over her head when she heard a creaking sound. At the end of the hall stood a figure partially immersed in shadow. Alessa blinked a few times; she swore it was just her eyes playing tricks on her, but the figure remained.

A pale sliver of moonlight illuminated a pair of bony feet attached to skeletal legs. The darkness concealed most of their torso, but when Alessa peered closely, she realized they weren't wearing any clothes. Based on thinness alone, she guessed it had to be Aria. Maybe she needed to use the restroom too?

"Ari? You okay? I didn't wake you, did I?" Alessa asked, stepping closer. Aria did not respond, nor did she move. Alessa made it halfway to her when Aria stepped back.

Alessa stopped. Aria's torso and chest hit the light, only they weren't as naked as Alessa thought. Something dark and thick created a glistening wet trail from her mouth, down her neck and beyond.

"Ari?"

A resounding snap caused Alessa to whip around, fear bleeding into her system and waking her right back up. The hall was empty.

Something flickered in the corner of her vision. A tree branch smacked the window, bobbing wildly as the winter wind whipped it against the side of the house.

"Jesus," she exhaled, turning back around.

Aria was gone.

Alessa darted down the hall and turned the corner, but Aria was nowhere to be found. She opened the bathroom door and checked inside. No luck. It was as though she had dissipated into thin air.

She was at a loss. Alessa was sure she'd been there. Had the stress of everything finally gotten into her head? Was she too losing her sanity to the point of hallucinations? Alessa couldn't handle where that line of thought was taking her. Instead of letting it fester further, she shrugged it off as she washed her hands, splashing some water on her face for good measure. Whatever the case, there was nothing she could do about it right this second.

Still, Alessa remained cautious as she left the bathroom, keeping her eyes peeled for any sudden movements as she headed back toward Aria's room. Satisfied the ghoul twin of her sister wouldn't reappear, she went inside.

Aria was still trapped within a bundle of pillows and blankets. It didn't appear that she'd moved at all, even to switch positions. She leaned over for a closer look. Aria had the blanket pulled up to her nose, shielding her mouth from view. Alessa thought of the dark stains she'd seen, how they made Aria's mouth look like a black hole.

She had to know, had to be sure.

Alessa bent over Aria's sleeping form and carefully pinched the top of the blanket between her fingers. Her skin flushed hot, and she held her breath. Alessa lifted it millimeter by millimeter.

Aria grunted and shifted, pulling the blanket almost completely over her head. Alessa ripped her hand away and nearly tripped over her own feet as she backed away. Disappointment burned in her, but she resisted the urge to try again. There was no way she could check now without waking her.

Alessa would merely have to accept for now that she imagined what she saw in the hallway. Her tired mind was playing tricks on her. That's all it was.

Alessa returned to her spot on the floor below the window. She was already forgetting about it as her head hit the pillow, and in seconds, the claws of sleep ensnared her.

Had her eyes been closed for ten hours or ten minutes? Crawling from the dredges of slumber was treacherous for Alessa that morning. A headache beat at her temples, karmic retribution for not going to bed at a reasonable hour. Her eyes were in her shoes. Despite it all, she forced herself from the floor, knowing it wouldn't be long before Lily came barging in.

Aria remained in bed as Alessa got ready for school. She dragged her feet, doing every task as slowly as possible, hoping to extend her time at home. Alessa dreaded school. She wasn't a fan of it before, but now that Aria was home, there was bound to be gossip. The vultures would swarm with their insensitive and incessant questions before she even hit the front door. Also, she wasn't exactly keen on leaving Aria to the mercy of their parents. Lily was one bad day away from an eruption, and Joshua was hanging on by a thread. Now, there would be no one to buffer Aria from their codependent insanity.

"Alessa! Are you almost ready? You can't be late!"

Her mother's morning reminders used to irritate her only mildly, but now they were unbearable, like nails dragging across a chalkboard.

"Coming!" she replied and took one last look at the mound of her sleeping sister before tearing herself away.

"Grab yourself a snack before you go," Lily insisted, and knowing Aria's propensity of denying food as of late, Alessa grabbed an apple. She didn't need to give her mom anymore reasons to be upset.

"I'm going out the back today."

She slipped past her mother as she entered the kitchen, wanting to avoid the onlookers across the street. There would be enough eyes following her today.

"Alessa, wait!"

She paused, hand on the screen door.

"We got a call from your school this morning. The night janitor, Mr. Archer, never returned home from his shift this morning."

Another person missing. Alessa forced herself to breathe, her brain racing to catch up. That was three people missing now. Three people snatched out of existence in the short time since Aria's return.

"Just be extra cautious on your way home this afternoon, eyes and ears peeled, please."

Her mom's words whipped right over her head. After the news regarding Mr. Archer sank in, everything else she said turned to dust. She nodded to satisfy Lily until her mom shooed her out the door.

Crisp mountain air slapped her awake when she stepped outside. The door slammed behind her and suddenly she felt miles away. Just one wall separating her from an alien world. The cold forced her forward, and she walked straight to the tree line, checking over her shoulder repeatedly until she knew the spectators could no longer see her. She blazed a trail behind the row of houses that lined her street. On her right, the path laid before her was dotted with perfectly manicured lawns. On her left, the trees stood guard before an unimaginably vast wilderness.

Alessa paused, thinking of Mr. Archer, and of the Singer couple and their dog. She pictured them standing just beyond the tree line–far enough so she couldn't see them–but close enough for her to still feel their gaze. She pictured them naked, skin clinging to boney frames, and wearing blood-black grins. Alessa tore her eyes from the woods. But they found something else.

CHAPTER 17

A small, dark mound rested about ten feet away from her. Frayed, wiry fur fluttered in the wind. It looked too small to be a dog, but maybe a cat or an oversized rat. Alessa stepped closer, her brain lagging a few seconds behind, only registering that she'd begun moving toward it when she was halfway there.

Nestled in the crunchy, frozen grass were the remains of a rather large raccoon. Wrinkling her nose at the rotten stench, she realized she was wrong about the fur. It wasn't brown but discolored by dirt and drying blood.

Something tore the animal's chest cavity open. A pile of pink intestines rested beside the carcass. The mouth remained open in a silent scream. Flies buzzed around oozing, open wounds that revealed the tips of white bone. Most of the creature's body was gone, devoured by the predator that happened upon it.

Alessa quivered, bundling deeper into her winter coat. She wasn't ready to face the possibility last night hadn't been a dream, or the possibility that Aria really had been there, waiting in the dark with blood on her lips.

A tingle tickled the back of her neck. Alessa turned back to the house, a line of sweat dribbling down her spine. She had to blink past the tears and squint in order to truly see, but she swore she saw movement in Aria's window.

Alessa swiveled, immediately ducking her head, and resumed her walk. As the distance between Alessa and her house grew, she tried to forget the raccoon. The smell, thick as honey though not remotely as sweet, glued to the walls of her nasal cavity. Even when she turned the corner and could no longer see her house, she still felt that tingle smoldering at the base of her neck. Like someone was watching her. The feeling followed her all the way to school.

It didn't stop there. Soon, the imagined eyes from the woods became real eyes, dozens of them belonging to her peers. The whispers started before she even hit the sidewalk in front of the school. Everywhere she turned, gazes flickered away. She could tell by the way they avoided her stare and muffled their comments behind their hands that they were talking about her.

Alessa kept her head down and kept moving. She wasn't going to give them anything. All of them were so quick to drop Aria the second things started to look grim. The town that claimed to love and cherish its own was ready to discard her sister at the drop of a hat. She viewed her fellow students a lot differently now. Actually, she viewed everyone in her life a lot differently now.

"Alessa, hey, wait!"

Maya emerged through the thickening crowd of kids traversing up the school steps like a tidal wave. Alessa didn't hesitate to throw her arms around her friend, crushing their bodies in a bruising hug. Maya's scent washed over her, fresh like wildflowers.

"It's so good to see you," Alessa said as they parted.

"Same," Maya replied, "I'm not even technically supposed to be talking to you right now."

Alessa arched her brow. "What do you mean?"

Students surrounded the two in every direction, their collective movement forcing the two girls toward the entrance as well. The pair linked their arms to keep from being separated.

"Grandfather still isn't happy about what happened the other night. He thinks it's dangerous to associate with your family now." Maya shook her head with a scoff at Alessa's stunned expression. "Believe me, I know how crazy it sounds. I even tried to talk to him, try to describe the situation from Aria's point of view–but he wasn't hearing any of it."

"So, she makes one mistake, and that's it?" Alessa chuckled in utter disbelief. Maya shrugged; a deep frown on her lips.

"I'd like to say no, but... I guess I didn't know him like I thought I did."

Alessa saw how this pained her friend. Despite being heavily involved in the church, Maya didn't care much about religion on its own. She told Alessa she mostly enjoyed it for the company. She loved seeing her friends attending the church events, and loved to be helpful, but above all, she was just happy to be spending time with her family. Father Samuel was someone she admired and sought to emulate. Alessa knew that had to be driving Maya crazy.

"I'm sorry my family drug your family into all of this."

Maya nudged Alessa's hip. "Nonsense. You know as well as I do, Grandfather went there willingly."

Alessa shrugged. The surrounding crowd dissipated as students parted ways to visit their lockers or dip into classrooms. This, however, did not dispel the magnetic pull that had everyone looking in Alessa's direction. She caught a few snippets of conversations here and there.

"*She came back to the church covered in blood; I was sick that day, but my little sister saw the whole thing!*"

"*My aunt saw her bolting from the house the other day. She was running BACK to the woods; guess she didn't want to be back as bad as we thought.*"

"*The girl was always weird, barely had any friends. Never got why Noah wasted so much time with her. Always acting like she was better than all of us. I'm not surprised she snapped.*"

Maya laid a hand on her arm and squeezed. Alessa saw red. She wanted to scream at them, to tear them down as they were doing Aria, and show them even just a drop of the pain she'd experienced over the last few months. But they would never listen. They would nod their heads and go back to their sniggering the moment she turned her back.

"Did you hear about Mr. Archer?"

Maya's question broke her from her rage haze. "My mom told me this morning; how did you find out?"

They turned down the next hall, walking slowly, wanting to prolong parting ways for as long as they could.

"He lives a few doors down from us," Maya said, "likes to bike to work. He waves to Dad on the porch when he's on his way to the school. It really freaked both my parents out that it was someone so close to us."

"Did they ever find his bike?" Alessa inquired.

Maya's lips pursed. "Actually, I don't know."

Alessa groaned, unsettled by the continuing lack of information. Three people were missing, and no one had heard anything. In a town where everyone talked about everything, it rung as strange to Alessa. She was sure she'd have heard something from another student by now, but the only name on their lips was Aria's.

"First the Singers now, Mr. Archer," Alessa lamented.

"I know. I don't like it either."

They stopped outside of Alessa's first period class. Biology. Her stomach churned. After what she saw this morning, biology was the last thing she wanted to think about. Maya separated herself and busied her hands with the straps of her backpack.

"How many people know about Mr. Archer, do you think?" Alessa asked.

"Not many, I imagine. Most people don't notice him too much, he keeps to himself. From how my parents told it, seems like they don't want a lot of details spread before the police learn more."

"I just feel like it's something everyone should be worried about, don't you? Three people going missing after what happened to Ari. Does no one else find it strange?"

Glancing around at the dwindling sea of students, Alessa was suddenly very aware of just how alone they were. No one else had seen the things they'd seen—what Alessa alone had experienced. To the rest of the town, this was nothing more than passing gossip to

CHAPTER 17

entertain their friends and families, until it faded into nothing more than a tired old story.

"Maybe the local paper wrote about it. I didn't have time to check this morning, but it's hard to believe this wouldn't make the news," Maya said.

Alessa lit up when a metaphorical light bulb burst in her head.

"If we meet in the library at lunch, we can check online to see if anything's been written about it."

Easy enough. It was normal for students to ditch their lunch period in favor of using the library to study or get some homework done. Maya didn't take any convincing. Alessa could see it on her face. She was just as curious and eager to put this mess to bed.

Both of them lifted their heads when the first bell sounded, sending the remaining kids in the hall into a flurry. If they waited until the next bell, they would officially be late.

"Meet me there later?" Alessa asked, trying to keep the desperate hopefulness from her tone. Maya rolled her eyes, but the slight smile on her lips told Alessa it was playful.

"Like I'd ever leave you to deal with this shit on your own."

Alessa giggled, and the two parted with one last brief hug. She wished she could make it last longer, but she didn't want to be responsible for Maya being late either, so she let her go and darted into her classroom.

She knew she should have been paying attention, that she'd missed enough school already and was woefully behind on her assignments. Alessa couldn't bring herself to care. Even the teachers looked at her oddly, either out of pity or fear. She didn't know which was worse. The morning classes passed in a blur. Every lecture sounded the same, one word bleeding into the next. She checked the clock every few minutes, and it made the morning drag on for eons.

Alessa leapt to her feet when the bell chimed to signal that lunch period had begun and breezed past whoever stood in her way to be the first out the door before the rush started.

Maya was already on the computer when Alessa arrived. No words needed to be spoken. They began scouring the internet, avoiding any blocked sites, and seeking any hint that someone knew what was going on in this town. Fifteen minutes into their search, they were still coming up empty. Alessa's eyes continually darted to the bottom of the screen, watching their window of time get smaller. Five more minutes of clicking, scrolling, and scanning articles and blogs, and Alessa was ready to put her fist through the screen.

"You guys lookin' up stuff about Mr. Archer?"

Maya gasped and Alessa nearly came out of her skin. Behind them stood the editor of their school paper, Cleo Thompson. She often spent her free periods in the library and was fiendishly dedicated to her position. Outside of her passion for the paper, she was also a notorious gossip, only she had the journalistic skills to back her gossip up with facts. Alessa always thought she was a nice girl, and she tended to only use her powers for good.

"Hey, Cleo." Alessa let out a breath and relaxed. "Yeah, actually. You haven't heard anything about it, have you? We can't find anything online."

"We figured we'd be able to find at least something after what happened to the Singers," Maya added.

Cleo wrinkled her nose and shrugged, although she didn't seem all too concerned.

"Well, you gotta remember, the Pine Hollow Post isn't exactly the New York Times. Mr. Buchanan and his wife run that operation all by themselves, and they're pushing seventy."

Alessa frowned. Cleo had a point.

Sensing Alessa's disappointment, Cleo continued.

"That's not to say they won't, knowing Mr. Buchanan he's likely

CHAPTER 17

trying to get all his facts lined up before he publishes. He may be old, but the guy is a stickler for the journalistic process."

She had a point there, too. But Alessa couldn't ignore the nagging whisper in the back of her brain that something wasn't right.

"What have you heard, Cleo?" Maya plunged ahead, "I know you have to have heard something."

Cleo adjusted the stack of books she had in the crook of her arm, and smirked.

"I'm flattered," she said, but then her smirk fell, "honestly, though. I probably don't know much more than you guys do."

"But you do know something?" Maya pressed.

Cleo was quiet for a second, as if considering her options.

"About Mr. Archer, I don't really know much other than the police found his bike this morning. I'm not sure where they found it, only that they did."

"Do they think this could be connected to what happened to the Singers?"

"It's possible, nothing confirmed but, they're definitely not ruling it out."

Cleo fidgeted and looked around, growing more self-conscious. "But when it comes to Mr. Archer, that's really all I know. His wife must be devastated."

The way Cleo was avoiding her eyes made Alessa wonder if there was more she wanted to tell them.

"Is there something else, Cleo? Something not about Mr. Archer, that you want to tell us?"

Alessa watched Cleo's tongue nervously prod at the insides of her cheeks. Her leg bounced up and down, and she did one last check to see if anyone was within hearing range before inching closer to them. Her voice was low when she spoke.

"I have to admit I was... curious when your sister went missing,

Alessa. I guess I never really expected something that terrible could happen in a place like this, but the whole thing really got to me, I guess."

Alessa appreciated her candidness and was actually quite pleased to hear someone else was shaken by the ordeal.

"I started doing my own research after seeing you constantly putting up fliers and never giving up. I figured if I could find just a hint that something like this happened before, maybe it could lead the cops in the right direction."

Alessa teetered on the edge of her seat.

"Did you find anything?"

Cleo sighed; dejected. "No, nothing but rumors. Eventually, my workload got a little too crazy, with the paper and everything and because I wasn't turning anything up, I kind of just... let it go."

The guilt clouded her face, but Alessa felt no anger or disdain toward her. This was not her life, and these were not her problems. She had done more than most by at least trying to look into it.

"And then your sister came home, and I let myself believe that was the end of it." She looked down, dark bangs shading her eyes. "I always felt bad for not looking into it more. I should have."

"It's okay, Cleo," Alessa reassured her, "it wasn't your job, and I appreciate you trying. Really, I do."

Cleo smiled gratefully. However, there was something else bothering Alessa.

"These rumors, though. What did you hear?"

Rumors in Pine Hollow were almost as valuable as the facts themselves. They always came from somewhere, and even if what you heard wasn't the truth, it was usually never that far from it. Cleo shifted her weight from one foot to the other. She looked like she wanted to bolt, and for a second Alessa thought she might.

"Well, there was one that *really* stood out to me, but you both have

CHAPTER 17

to swear not to say a word, and if someone else finds out you didn't hear this from me."

The girls nodded without hesitation.

"Supposedly, and again, this is just a rumor. But word is that Officer Shirley used to have an older brother."

Alessa cocked her head, confused about what this had to do with Aria and also surprised by the information itself. A close-knit community like this. How did they not know Shirley had a brother? No one ever mentioned him or saw him, and as far as Alessa knew, Shirley was the only child in her family to attend her parent's funeral. Surely, by now, they would have seen or met her brother if she had one.

"What does that have to do with Ari?"

"Well, as the rumor goes, supposedly he went missing too, and he was around the same age as Aria when it happened, right after his eighteenth birthday."

Chapter 18

When Aria awoke, she had regained some control, but she felt muffled as if she were behind a thick, invisible curtain. She watched the world through a pinhole. Her body moved according to her brain's commands, but they were slow, like she was a glitchy character from one of the video games Noah had taught her to play. She scratched her sharp nails, long and slow along her right arm, but felt nothing.

The hunger remained constant now.

Alessa left early. She'd listened to the girl depart but had no desire to move. Maneuvering her body felt like operating a slow, heavy puppet. She could dictate the movements and arrange her limbs, but her consciousness was just watching from the back seat along for the ride. She eventually dragged herself from the bed and watched Alessa pause at the edge of their property and look back.

Aria knew Alessa saw her and watched until she was gone. Something about Alessa walking too close to the forest's edge made Aria nervous. She imagined pale, gnarled hands darting from between the trees and dragging Alessa into the earth, her mouth filling with dirt.

Aria turned to the mirror, standing so close to the glass that her nose almost brushed the glass. Puffs of steam from her breath fogged her reflection.

Crack!

CHAPTER 18

Her open palm connected harshly with her cheek; she gritted her teeth on impact but the tiny burst of pain that lit up her jaw finally made her feel connected to her body. However, briefly, it kept Aria present. She did it again.

Slap!

And again.

SLAP!

Aria glared at herself, at the shadow of the girl she used to be. Bloodless skin, thin as a rail and, despite the strength behind her blows, the pain barely registered. It felt no worse than being pinched. All that mattered, however; was that she felt something. That she could still feel at all. It gave her a small sliver of hope.

She thought of Noah, and the pain in his eyes when she turned away from him. It was the only way to ensure his safety. Aria didn't trust herself around anyone anymore.

But something he said stuck out to her.

Maybe I can help find the pieces of you that you're looking for.

Her memories were the key. She didn't know what they would tell her, but if she didn't fit the pieces together soon, there was a chance she might stay lost forever. Talking about them with Noah helped set them free and helped loosen the tangles of time and memory in her brain, but they were slippery and hard to hold on to. Aria looked at her desk, and the piles of notebooks and papers sitting on it.

She knew it was a longshot when she grabbed pen and paper, but it didn't stop her from sitting cross-legged on the floor and getting to work. If the memories were tangible, if she could hold them, then she might be able to make sense of the timeline. And maybe—just maybe—it would open up her mind to new memories.

Soon, torn shreds of paper with furious scribbles on them surrounded her. Aria tried not to skip any details, not knowing what could end up being important. None of it was in order, but the sight of them brought her comfort. Now, even if she couldn't figure this out, there was something physical, some sort of proof that her experience was real.

She ripped off another piece of paper. Her hand was cramping around the pen. The tip of the ballpoint grazed the crisp white sheet when a fresh memory exploded in her mind's eye. First came the sounds, the delicate scratching of a pen on paper, the crinkle of a page turning, and then the colors bled in, gradually sharping into a fully fleshed picture.

Aria saw herself sitting on her bed. The old her. The girl before the woods. She sat with her knees drawn to her chest, as she scribbled on something resting on her legs. It was small and made of a shimmering brown material. A journal, possibly. The girl's cheeks sparkled with tears. Whatever was going through her turbulent mind was gushing out on the page. Her focus was unwavering. Until a knock at the door.

Both of their heads, the Aria's of past and present, turned to the door.

The spell broke, and the remaining echoes of the memory dispelled, like dew drops evaporating in the morning sun. When Aria landed firmly back in the present, she heard another distant thud. It was the sound of a car door slamming. Outside their house? Perhaps. It was hard to be sure.

Aria scrambled to her feet, but her eyesight was wobbly. Being spit back out into the present smacked her with vertigo. The wind whipped the trees, raking their branches along the sides of the house. Each scrape split through her skull like tissue paper. Another sound echoed beneath the scratches, a mishmash of lingering whispers continually overlapping and growing in volume. Soon, the dragging of the branches and the voices were one and the same.

She returned to the window, and every step was a tilt-a-whirl. She braced her hands on either side of the window frame. Her swaying vision made settled when she saw the woods. The movement of the trees and pine needles dancing in the wind was soothing, hypnotic, even. Aria pressed close to the glass, weak against their magnetic pull.

The dozens of voices soon coalesced into one last word, all of them speaking in one distorted but emotionless cadence.

ARIA.

Her grip around the frame tightened. Wood splintered beneath her palms, splinters piercing her skin. The black slices of darkness between the trees seemed to stain the deep green of the leaves, expanding like a parasite over the property line. A million shadow hands lurked in the grass, inching closer.

"What is.... happening?" she droned, eyes blurring in and out of focus.

Something stepped out of the woods. Her ghoulish doppelgänger emerged into the cold morning light; black eye sockets stared up at her. Its white lips stretched into an uncanny smile that Aria couldn't decipher as being welcoming or sinister.

When the doppelgänger spoke, the trees spoke with her, their voices sent tremors through the air. "Patience. It's almost time."

Three thuds, like a fist striking wood, sounded from downstairs. They thundered like drums in her ears. Someone was here. Aria tilted her head away from the window and listened. Through the floor she heard footsteps, the jingling of keys, and then the creaking of the door being opened.

"Chief Roswell! What a surprise!" Joshua greeted.

All at once, Aria was overcome with a torrent of clashing emotions. Vivid blistering rage and electrifying terror sent paralyzing shockwaves through her body. Her soul splintered and twisted in and around itself until it was impossible to tell which emotions belonged to her and which came from this other force inside of her. In the end, she decided it didn't matter. All she knew was she couldn't see Roswell.

She wasn't sure how she would react if she did. There was no way to know if the rage or the fear would take over when they walked through her door, but she had seen what the rage could do, and it was enough for her.

Aria lunged at the window. In lieu of just boarding it up, Joshua drilled nails into top and bottom rails of the windowpane to keep it closed. It barely slowed her down. Aria punched her fist through the glass and shards spewed in every direction. She didn't hesitate when a few of their sharpened points sliced her arms open.

Following her muscle memory, Aria darted to the trellis and practically threw herself down. Her feet slipped in and out of place a few times on her way, but within minutes, she was safely on the ground.

Aria ran, only this time she followed Alessa's footsteps. She slipped quickly and quietly away and directly into town.

Bare feet pounded on cold, damp pavement. The back of Aria's thin shirt clutched her sweat-drenched back. Houses and trees blurred in at the corners of her vision. Each time she glanced over her shoulder, or paused for a breath, she felt blackened eyes blazing a hole in her back. Her dark doppelganger lurked around every corner, in the alleys between the buildings, in the reflection of a car window, and in the slivers of shadow between the imposing evergreens.

Aria knew if she stopped for too long, it would catch up to her, and she didn't want to know what would happen if it did.

Chapter 19

The sound of glass crashing echoed all the way downstairs. Roswell's hand shot to the weapon on his hip, his thumb lingered over the button of his holster. Lily rushed to the bottom of the stairs.

"Aria! Sweetie, are you okay?"

The only response was a resounding thud, and the three of them barreled up the stairs to her room.

"Wait! Both of you!"

Roswell thrust his arm out ahead of them, urging them to remain near the wall. He knocked once but loudly, hand still gripping his holster, palm slick against leather.

"Aria, it's Chief Roswell! Are you all right in there?"

No response. He looked at Joshua and Lily, brows arching in a silent request. Lily shooed him forth without hesitation.

"I'm coming in!"

Roswell shoved the door open with his shoulder. They rushed in, one after the other, Lily shoving her way to the front. Glass shards littered the floor. Cold air poured in from the broken window, sending the discarded bits of paper fluttering under Aria's bed.

Roswell checked the corners of the room and threw her closet open. Aria was gone.

"Shit!" he spat, and rushed to the window.

A flash of red caught his eye. The end of her long, flowing hair lashed the air behind her as she turned the corner that led into the town square. Roswell's heart leapt into his throat.

"She's heading into town."

The officer immediately turned and bounded down the stairs, leaving Lily gaping and Joshua struggling to keep up.

"Please, Chief, she's just frightened! She needs help."

"That's the plan, Mr. Hale. Believe me, I'm the last person who wants any trouble, but we have to locate her as soon as we can. We still don't know how much of a danger she is to herself or others."

"I'm sure she just panicked; you can't imagine just how difficult things have been. But I know she's trying."

Roswell clapped a reassuring hand on Joshua's shoulder and smiled in soft understanding.

"I'll be back before you know it, Mr. Hale. And I'm sure you and Lillian will do everything you can to ensure Aria gets the help she needs."

His grip tightened; Joshua's lips rose into a trembling smile.

"Of course, that's all we want."

Roswell grinned, satisfied, and let go.

"I'll have her back here as soon as I can, but you and Lily stay put in case she circles back. If she does, call me immediately."

"Yes, of course."

Roswell raced to his car, threw it into drive, and peeled off into the same direction as Aria.

Roswell's patrol car drifted slowly along the streets of Pine Hollow, windows down, and the siren silently flashing. He kept his eyes peeled and flagging people down until he was lucky enough to find a neighbor who'd been having coffee on their back porch when they saw a smear of red hair darting by. The elderly man almost missed her. She was running so fast, and his weary eyes struggled to keep up, but there was no mistaking it. After he pointed Roswell in the general direction he'd seen her take off, the chief continued his tracking on foot.

As he approached the outskirts of the town square, the more people he saw. A few claimed they heard she was seen in town, but others were sure they'd witnessed her divert to the woods. Roswell was split, unsure where to focus his attention and, as a compromise, kept close to the tree line as he approached town.

Winter sludge squelched beneath his boots, the ice and mud getting slicker the closer he got to the brush. His head remained on a swivel, and he was careful to remain as quiet as possible to listen for any unusual activity.

Roswell halted when a sharp snap to his right fractured the stillness in the air. He turned to face the woods, hand flying to his holster. His jaw clenched, but he waited and listened. Birds screeched from above and peppered the silver sky like splashes of black ink. He cautiously approached the woods.

Another crack burst through the trees, only this time it sounded further away, like the splitting of a thick branch. He stopped again, goosebumps raising across his flesh and setting his hair on edge all over his body. After a moment, he continued, pushing against the needling feeling that something or someone was watching him. For the first time in his life, he wasn't sure what the danger was or from which direction it was coming. In all these years as a cop his gut instincts rarely let him down, but now his intestines were so warped with unease, he couldn't derive any message from them at all.

"Aria!" he bellowed. His voice echoed, morphing into a ghostly whimper the further it traveled. "Aria Hale! It's Chief Roswell. If you're out here, your parents sent me to bring you home! They are very worried about you!"

A debilitating surge of déjà vu crashed over him. Suddenly, it was two months ago. He was back in the same woods, screaming hopelessly into the air as he searched for the same girl. Roswell's heart hammered ferociously against his ribs. He drew in a few deep, almost painful breaths and when the world stopped spinning, he charged on.

"Aria, we only want to help you! There's nothing to be afraid of." Roswell didn't know if she could hear him, or if it was even Aria that was listening. But he sensed a presence and watchful eyes on him. He cleared his throat to keep his voice from shaking.

"Just follow my voice if you can hear me! You're not in any trouble!"

A rustling sounded from behind him; Roswell spun in a complete circle chasing the sound like a dog chases its tail. Still, he saw nothing. His inner voice flickered back to life, intuition kicking in once again to raise the alarm bells. Roswell was struck with the realization that whatever was out here definitely wasn't Aria.

Roswell followed the rustling through the increasingly dense undergrowth. Pushing past gnarled branches that scraped at his skin, he stumbled upon a patch of shallow snow with deep grooves carved into it. Heaping chunks of Earth were tossed in every direction, like something had been dragged.

Whoever, or whatever, was being dragged had obviously lost the fight. He walked alongside the trenches carved into the dirt to where they stopped in front of a tall, sturdy pine tree. However, the markings did not cease. Up they went, higher and higher, until the gashes embedded in the bark vanished into its grand abundance of needles. He lifted his hand and traced his palm along the gouges in the wood and estimated them to be about an inch deep. Some markings were shallow, bark shavings torn off in random places as if something were trying to grab onto it, but their grip kept slipping.

Roswell flashed back to the carnage he and Shirley had happened upon in the woods only days prior. Had it truly only been days? It felt like a lifetime ago. The scene was very similar, only without bloody carnage. Everything from the drag marks to the indents in the trees.

CHAPTER 19

He still didn't know how to make heads or tails of it. The markings held no resemblance to any animal Roswell had ever come in contact with. A bear was the closest he could guess, but there were no tracks nearby, which made it unlikely.

"What in God's name?" he whispered, and when nothing answered back Roswell realized just how isolated he was out here. He looked over his shoulder, his spine prickling.

He was not alone.

Sweat ran down his back, and he could barely feel the cold anymore. The evidence of this mad struggle seemed like it would never end.

Finally, he came to where he guessed the battle was decided. It wasn't nearly as horrific as what he'd seen the other day. This time the gore was in one area, a puddle of blood and pale meat. A few specks of red were splashed across the trees. Roswell stood above the remains, hand pinching his nose. Juicy black flies danced in the air. There was so little left, he couldn't tell if it belonged to a human or an animal. His immediate thoughts were of the trio of folks who'd just gone missing, and his stomach roiled. Praying to God it wasn't one of them.

Burrowing his face into the crevice of his elbow, he took shots of the scene with his phone. It would be hours before they could get authorities out to do a proper investigation, and he wanted to capture as many details as possible. When he was done, he slid his phone into his back pocket. Roswell let out a little cough and was startled by how loud the sound was against the heavy silence of the woods. In that moment, it dawned on him how quiet the forest had become in just the last few moments. He stood stock still, not daring to even breath as he listened. There were no chittering squirrels, or chirping birds, not even the slightest breeze to shake the branches. Everything had gone completely and utterly silent. He adjusted his stance, the crunching of his boots in the snow suddenly too loud.

The same sensation of fingers creeping up his neck returned, the sensation of eyes boring into him from the distance. The sensation of being stalked like prey. Roswell inhaled sharply. It came from behind him. Roswell clenched his fists, nails digging crescent moon shapes into his palms, and turned just his head to glance over his shoulder.

A large, pale form standing taller than Roswell's brain could comprehend shifted out from behind a nearby tree trunk. Ice crushed under its movements. Roswell couldn't even hear it breathe, but he could feel it in the air—the enormity of it. His eyes trailed up, higher and higher, until he glimpsed a pair of gold irises buried in black sockets.

Roswell ran. He didn't chance another look and didn't stop until his lungs burned, and he burst safely through the tree line, reentering Pine Hollow.

Chapter 20

After Cleo dropped her bomb, nothing else mattered. Alessa thought about nothing else for the rest of the day. Before they parted ways for their afternoon classes, Maya and Alessa agreed to meet after school to continue their research. There, they would have more freedom and access to sites their administration had blocked, as well as town records dating back to its inception. If a document existed to prove Shirley's brother existed and disappeared, it would be there.

Cleo had been kind enough to give them everything she gathered when she was researching Aria's disappearance. She also dictated the details of the rumors that she could remember before she bid them good luck. Cleo didn't have much, but it gave them somewhere to start.

"Good afternoon, Mrs. Anderson!" Maya cheerfully greeted the elderly librarian seated at the reception desk. The woman startled and let out a small but bright laugh when she recognized them. She set down the returned books she'd been organizing.

"Goodness, Maya, you scared me!"

"Sorry!" Maya replied, genuinely apologetic.

Gloria Anderson, however, was a good sport and waved it off. The thick, golden bangles hanging around her thin wrists clinked together with every movement.

"Oh, don't worry about little old me. I'm easily startled. What brings you girls in this afternoon? It's been a long time since I've seen either of you down here."

Alessa didn't hesitate to reply with their pre-planned spiel.

"With Aria going missing, I got behind on a lot of assignments. I really need to buckle down if I don't want to be held back a year. Maya's helping me and I thought it would be a good idea to just hole up in here, get rid of any distractions, and get as much done as I can."

Alessa shocked herself at how easily the lie came out. Aria always used to be the better liar of the two of them. My, how things had changed.

"Good on you for being so studious, Alessa, and quite blessed to have a friend as generous as Maya here."

The girls beamed.

"Yes, I'm very lucky to have her." That she didn't need to lie about.

"Anything I can help with?" Gloria asked, eager to be of service.

"We're actually working on a project and were wondering if you had any old newspapers or yearbooks," Alessa fabricated, but it grabbed Gloria hook, line, and sinker.

"Sounds interesting! I think we may have some stuff in the back."

Alessa felt guilty for lying to get what she wanted, but she forced that out of her mind for now. She discreetly removed a folded piece of paper from her pocket. It contained the notes Cleo gave them in haphazard script. Cleo narrowed down the possible timeline during which Shirley's alleged brother was born and then went missing. Unfortunately, because she only knew Officer Shirley's birthday and nothing else, she had to do a lot of guesses work and only whittled down the window of time so much. She thumbed the numbers immortalized in black ink: 1965–1985.

Gloria flounced around the desk, happy to be of service. Alessa didn't imagine the woman got asked for help regularly. They followed her to the back of the building. The scent of books, both old and new, wafted in the surrounding air, rows towering above them on either side, arranged neatly on wooden shelves.

Aria used to come here from time to time, returning with an armful of photography and travel books stacked high against her chest. Alessa often found her sister lying on her stomach in the center of her room, books open, and fanned around her as she flipped meticulously through each picture.

Gloria stopped in front of a room labeled 'Employees Only' and they waited patiently as she took her time picking the right key out of the mass jingling on her keyring. When she finally opened it, she entered the dark office and turned on a light that flickered ominously. Slate grey filing cabinets lined the walls. Gloria mumbled to herself as she hunted for the right one.

"Ah! Here it is."

The girls stayed in the doorway, marveling at the sheer volume of the files. Each of them labeled differently, everything from old maps of Pine Hollow, and documents of the town's construction, to footage of the now abandoned railroad up the mountain.

"Here they are. Grab that footstool, will you? I'm not as limber as I used to be, so one of you will have to do the heavy lifting," Gloria requested.

Maya stepped forward and unfolded the stool she found in the corner. She carefully grabbed the handles cut into the sides of the box and lifted them off the cabinet, passing them into Alessa's safe hands. A cloud of dust filled her nostrils and her eyes watered when she held back a burning sneeze. She was grateful to be rid of the stale stench that clung to the air in the back room when they followed Gloria to one of the open tables. They placed their spoils in the center.

"Is there anything else I can do for you girls?"

As much as Alessa wanted to rush her off, she didn't want to appear suspicious.

"I think that's everything, Mrs. Anderson. Thank you so much for all of your help."

"If we think of anything else, you'll be the first person we ask," Maya replied.

Butter her up. It was the quickest way to make her leave. Alessa didn't feel good about it, but she figured anything was better than being cruel. Gloria smiled, eyes shimmering behind her thick-rimmed glasses. She folded a trembling, blue veined hand over her heart.

"Nothing would make me happier. You know where to find me."

She bid them one last good luck before returning to her post. Maya and Alessa looked at each other, both of them releasing great breaths of relief as they sank into their chairs. Alessa stared at the stacks of documents to her left.

"Shall we?" she asked. Maya nodded.

They covered their table with newspapers and splayed open yearbooks dating from the 60s to mid-80's. Alessa put Maya in charge of scanning the papers with a fine-toothed comb, while she dove headfirst into the yearbooks, beginning in 1980 and working her way backwards. She figured it would be the easiest way to determine the year he disappeared, rather than trace the entirety of his school career. Maya searched for anything even remotely referencing Shirley's surname: Powell, and missing persons' reports.

Dozens upon dozens of static smiles stared back at Alessa from the pages of the yearbooks as she worked her way through the years. After three books, her eyes stung, and she rubbed them periodically to keep them clear. She flipped her way through 1987 to 1984 and found nothing. Alessa glanced over the table at Maya, who looked up at her only to frown in disappointment, before she continued reading. Alessa grabbed the book with the dull, gold lettering that read 1983. Blowing off the layer of dust that gathered on the cover, she turned immediately to the photographs of the graduating class.

Five pages in, and she froze. There it was in the senior class of 1983, a faded but clear picture of a young, handsome boy with dark skin and a warm smile. Dominic Powell. But Alessa wanted to be sure, and grabbed an earlier yearbook from the 70s, this time from the middle school stack. Maya noticed her frantic movements and lifted her head with interest.

"Everything okay?"

"Yeah! Yeah." She didn't even look up, tunnel vision singularly focused on the fragile thread of thought weaving a path through her mind. Her hands moved of their own accord, rapidly flipping pages, sharp corners and thin edges slicing shallow cuts into her fingers. All she needed was one photo, and she knew exactly the one to look for.

Pine Hollow Middle School had a tradition of dedicating a section in the back of their yearbooks to pictures of students who were moving on to Pine Hollow High to be with their older siblings. The photography club posed the pairs, and sometimes trios of siblings together on the middle school lawn and take portraits of them. Alessa and Aria participated in Alessa's final year of middle school.

Finally, she found it. Buried in the last pages of Pine Hollow Middle in 1982 was Dominic Powell, towering over a much shorter and stockier female student. He was a lean boy, and his clothes looked about two sizes too big, but his grin was one of joy and confidence. The girl at his side was unmistakably related to him. They shared everything down to the same cheekbones and slope of the nose. The photo captured her mid-laugh, head thrown back and releasing her unbridled amusement into the sky. Just below the picture was the caption: Dominic and Shirley Powell.

She really did have a brother. It was true. Alessa's jaw dropped. Maya lowered the paper she was reading.

"Alessa?"

"Here." Alessa slammed the book down, and Maya jumped. "It's right here!"

Her finger landed on the picture, and she watched the realization dawn over Maya's face. They stared at it in silence, as though neither of them believed it was actually true. In the back of her mind, Alessa was genuinely worried Cleo's research would be a dead end. But here it was, forever preserved in black and white.

"Holy shit," Maya said; awestruck.

"Are there any papers from 1983?"

Maya surveyed her messy stack and pulled out a handful. They split the pile in half.

"Look for anything mentioning a Dominic Powell. If Cleo was right and he vanished right after he turned eighteen, that means it probably happened not long after he graduated."

Just like Aria. A disquieting shiver trembled in the ridges of Alessa's spine.

"Oh my God."

Alessa's head snapped up. Maya's blood seemed to drain from her cheeks. Slowly, their eyes met, and Alessa knew what Maya was going to say before she even opened her mouth.

"I found it."

Carefully, she placed the newspaper in Alessa's hands and listened as she read the small headline aloud.

"Pine Hollow alumni Dominic Powell, 18, missing now for three weeks," Alessa read, the words washing over her like a cold mist, "Powell was last seen by his younger sister Shirley Powell, 15, who said goodnight to him around 11 P.M. on the night of December 15th. His mother entered his room the next morning to wake him for school, but Powell was gone, and his bed had been freshly made."

Maya unconsciously leaned closer as Alessa read, completely riveted.

"Officers initially suspected he was a runaway, as some items of clothing and his wallet were missing from his bedroom and have yet to be recovered. However, searches of the surrounding area continue."

Alessa swallowed and the sensitive tissue in her throat stung, like she was being force-fed a handful of needles. It was all too familiar. After Aria went missing, the paper ran a few minor stories, just like this one. Alessa became accustomed to checking them every day for new information, but the more days that past the more the stories dwindled. After all, it was just like Cleo said. It was a small-town paper run by an elderly couple on the cusp of retirement. There was only so much they could write about before the well ran dry. Their resources were finite, just like everything else in this dead-end town.

The details were strikingly similar. There was some suspicion that Aria ran away when the police began their investigation. Despite Alessa's protests, she supposed it was a fair assumption for an outsider to make. Aria let everyone know exactly what she thought of this place, and how much she wanted to spread her wings to explore the world. This theory only lasted so long, as it was only days before they traced her final whereabouts to the woods. The same place Dominic's trail went cold.

"This is..." Alessa trailed off.

"Afternoon, girls."

Alessa's head pivoted so fast it strained her neck, and she instinctively slapped the newspaper closed. Officer Shirley stood at the far end of the table, emerging from between the shelves that cloaked her approach. She wore a pleasant smile that softened the steely intensity in her eyes.

"What have we got going on here?"

Alessa forced a smile. The Deputy Chief looked as professional and polished as always, not a wrinkle in sight or hair out of place.

"Deputy Shirley! You spooked us," she greeted as cheerfully as she could manage.

Shirley grinned and, as far as Alessa could tell, it was genuine.

"My apologies. I didn't mean to scare you girls. I was on my way back to the station and saw you two through the window." Shirley gestured to the window in question, which faced the front of the building. "Thought I'd stop in and see how things were going."

Alessa immediately sensed the double meaning behind Shirley's statement. She wasn't just checking in on them. She was hoping Alessa had more information about how Aria was doing.

During their initial questioning, Alessa could see just how frustrated Shirley and Roswell had been in response to her sister's memory loss. She knew it only made their job twice as challenging, but Alessa wasn't sure how comfortable she was with their current tactic of acquiring information. It felt like a betrayal of Aria's confidence somehow.

Shirley rounded the corner of the table, leisurely approaching Alessa's side. She held the officer's gaze; her smile straining. Alessa carefully folded the newspaper she was holding and placed it casually over the picture of the young Shirley and Dominic.

By the time Shirley reached her side, both the picture and the article were out of sight. Alessa finally chanced a look at Maya and saw the girl mindlessly tearing at the skin on her thumb. Guilt tugged at Alessa's stomach. Maya looked utterly exhausted already; she hated herself for putting her through this. Maya, of all people, deserved more.

"Oh, things are fine," Alessa replied, "I'm sure you already guessed, but I missed a lot of school when Aria went missing, so Maya's helping me play catchup."

"Mrs. Anderson mentioned you were working on a project. That's a nice way to take your mind off of things, I'm sure."

Alessa bypassed the comment with a flippant shrug, hoping if she kept the conversation light, it would steer Shirley away from asking too many questions. There was, after all, nothing more to tell than they already knew. Her sister's memory was still spotty. She couldn't

CHAPTER 20

tell the difference between what she had directly experienced and what her imagination conjured up. There was no sense in muddying up the police investigation with unconfirmed information and wild stories. She resolved to keep what she knew to herself, at least for now.

"It's all right, I guess."

Alessa made a show of tidying the discarded papers into one enormous pile, further burying the evidence under an ever-growing stack. Keeping Aria's secrets was one thing, but Alessa didn't want to know how Shirley would react if she discovered they were looking into her brother as well. Even if it existed in the public sphere, it felt like a flagrant disregard of her privacy.

"Mrs. Anderson was super helpful and fished out some old papers and yearbooks for us," Maya finally chimed in, "you could probably give us some good stories from back then!"

Shirley let out a hearty chuckle, and Alessa echoed it, hoping Shirley would take the bait.

"I'm not so sure about that. I was a bit of a homebody back in those days. Didn't get out much."

Maya pursed her lips in disappointment. "Oh, come on! Nothing of note? No wild tales? There had to be something worth passing on to the next generation."

Shirley's laughter dissipated and she tilted her head with a thoughtful hum, eyes scanning the ceiling as if she were sifting through memories like books on a shelf. She shook her head.

"Sorry to disappoint girls. I have to admit, I was a bit of a nerd when I was your age. I unsurprisingly have led a very standard, boring life," she said with a smirk.

However, Alessa knew for a fact that Shirley was lying. She had not lived a standard, boring life. That's not how Alessa would define the experience of losing a sibling. Maybe Shirley didn't like to address it; everyone had their secrets. But it sent off alarm bells in Alessa's head.

She caught Maya's perplexed expression; she noticed it, too.

Shirley turned back to Alessa. "How are things, Alessa? How is Aria's recovery coming?"

"She's okay," she said, perhaps a bit too fast. Aria was anything but okay, but Alessa knew how the police would react if they found out half of the things she'd done since she came home. They couldn't know about her outbursts or how she attacked the priest. They'd assume she was beyond help and lock her up. Alessa wouldn't allow it, not when there was more to the story, and not when Alessa just got her sister back.

"That's good to hear." She straightened, the soft edges of her expression subtly sharpening into something more inquisitive. "Of course, you know if anything were to happen, Roswell and I are just a phone call away. We want to help in any way we can."

"Thank you, we appreciate all you and the Chief have done to help."

"And if she remembers anything, please let us know. Any detail could be the key to figuring out what happened to her out there."

Alessa turned away from her. Noticing her friend's growing discomfort, Maya swooped in.

"Actually, Deputy Shirley, there is something you can help us with."

Mercifully, the officer tore her eyes away from Alessa, allowing the girl a moment to breathe.

"Speaking of Aria," Maya started, "we were wondering. I mean, you were born and raised here. Have there ever been any other disappearances like this? It's pretty remote out here. I'm sure it isn't out of the ordinary for people to get lost in the woods, especially hikers and tourists."

Alessa watched as Shirley's reaction to Maya's inquiry flicker over her face. She looked taken aback, but that didn't necessarily mean anything. Maybe she was just surprised by the abrupt change in the subject. She considered the question. Both girls studied her expression, but it was a blank canvas, utterly unreadable. Alessa flinched when she finally responded.

"No," she said in a low voice, "at least, not as far back as I can remember. People get lost in the woods from time to time, sure." She came off so casual and matter of fact, Alessa wanted to believe her, but Dominic's face blazed bright in her memory.

"Really?" Maya pressed.

"Really," Shirley stated firmly, leaving no room for argument, and looked at Alessa, "what occurred with Aria is a unique case. Which is why getting to the bottom of her memory loss is so imperative."

Alessa's grip tightened around the stack of papers. A cold sweat was working its way down her back. Shirley was lying to them. Why?

Shirley scanned their table again. "Is that what you girls are doing?" She narrowed her eyes. "Looking for patterns?"

Shit. Alessa groaned internally. Her mind scrambled for a way to salvage this.

"No! Honestly, we really were just working on the assignment, but... seeing everything from the past really got our heads spinning."

She couldn't tell if Shirley bought it, so she resolved to give the woman just a crumb of what she wanted in order to placate her. Hell, the best lies were the ones colored with a bit of truth.

"It's been really hard since Ari came home. It's all I can think about, so it's tough not to want to see patterns everywhere. I guess I just hoped what happened to us wasn't a one-off. Like that would somehow make it easier."

Alessa shrugged lamely, selling it with a somber pout.

"Of course. It must feel extremely isolating for you and your family, wading through this insanity." Shirley placed a comforting hand on her shoulder. Alessa resisted the urge to shrug it off. "But you have to trust the process, Alessa. You need to have faith that Roswell and I are investigating every lead."

She gestured to the newspapers with a sigh. "Dwelling on the past will only keep you trapped there."

A surge of anger bubbled up inside of Alessa. She didn't understand how Shirley could say these things, how she could look Alessa in the face and lie about not feeling the same pain. If anyone could understand what Alessa had gone through, it was Shirley, but here she was, acting as if it had never happened.

"I just want to help my sister," Alessa grumbled. Shirley reeled back, surprised.

"Well, of course, Alessa. I don't mean to argue otherwise. I only want you to trust us to do our job. Digging into all of this will only make it more challenging for you to move on."

To hear Shirley so nonchalantly dismiss her concerns only made Alessa's anger more powerful.

"I only want justice for my sister, Deputy Shirley," she said, measuring her words carefully, "wouldn't you want the same if you were in my position?"

Shirley's lips pressed into a tense line. Alessa held their eye contact, not wanting to miss a second of her reaction. Shirley blinked a few times before recovering, her expression shifting into something stern and curious.

"I may not understand your exact circumstances, Alessa, but I assure you, we are only looking out for you and your family."

Alessa was about to reply when a buzzing in Shirley's pocket interrupted them. She held up a finger as she rummaged through her pocket and took out her work cell.

"One moment, girls," she replied before stepping into the nearest aisle. As soon as she was out of sight, Maya and Alessa began cleaning and stuffing their materials back into their assigned boxes. They were securing the lids in place when Shirley reemerged, her expression grave.

CHAPTER 20

"You girls need to come with me right away."

"Is everything okay?" Maya asked. Shirley rested her eyes solely on Alessa.

"I just spoke with Roswell. Your sister broke out of the house and was last seen scaring people on her way into town. Roswell was waylaid and having three sets of eyes is better than one. Do you have any idea where Aria might go?"

Alessa's heart sputtered. She shook her head, words failing her.

"She might be heading toward something familiar; can you direct me to the spots she used to frequent?"

Finding it impossible to form words, Alessa grabbed her belongings in a daze. Shirley led them both out the front door and into her squad car, all of her instructions going in one ear and out the other.

Alessa thought of her sister, frantic and alone, and wondered if history was about to repeat itself.

Chapter 21

3 Months Ago

Alessa loved Christmas. The twinkling lights, the smell of freshly baked cookies, and even the caroling. In a small, religious town it wasn't a surprise that everyone went all out this time of year. Colorful bulbs decorated every building, casting a festive glow over the entire town, and the community always erected a large tree in the town square.

This year, however, things felt different. Ever since Aria's birthday, things in the Hale house had been more tense than usual. Her sister was more reserved, and any former antagonistic feelings she held toward their mother had depleted. Aria merely seemed tired now.

Aria never brought up her birthday, and Alessa never asked, believing it was what her sister wanted. But the guilt ate away at her. That night something had irrevocably changed in Aria. She was jumpy and nervous, emerging from her room less and less. Then the nightmares came, and Alessa often awoke to find Aria curled up against her back, having snuck in during the night. On the nights when she struggled to sleep at all, Lily gave her some Xanax to calm her nerves.

It felt strange to think this was all caused by one slap, and she wondered if there was more at play, but it had become impossible to weasel anything out of Aria these days.

CHAPTER 21

Alessa sat in the kitchen, slogging her way through a bowl of cereal even though she barely had an appetite. She stared out the window and allowed herself to be swept away by the rhythmic flashing of the Christmas lights outside. Lily shuffled into the room, keys jingling.

"There are leftovers in the fridge, and if you girls need anything, your father will have his cell on him."

She managed a small smile. Their parents were heading with the church into the town square to help decorate the large tree that was installed the night before. They normally participated as a family, but Aria wasn't feeling well, and when Alessa elected to stay behind to watch her, their parents didn't argue.

"Thanks, Mom. We'll be fine."

Lily rushed over to plant a quick kiss on the crown of Alessa's head and gave her one last affectionate pat on the cheek before rushing out. After a shouted farewell, they were gone. The house was quiet.

For the next hour, she killed time watching trash TV shows. Her stomach gurgled. Alessa stood at the bottom of the stairs and called up to the second floor.

"Ari! I'm gonna reheat the leftovers. Do you want any?"

Aside from a few soft thuds, she received no response. Shrugging, she decided she would make enough for both of them anyway and went to the kitchen to preheat the oven. She hummed a Christmas carol as she pulled the tray filled with casserole out of the fridge and peeled the tinfoil from the top. After the oven beeped to signal it was ready, she carefully placed it inside and slammed it shut.

Aria was standing in the entrance to the kitchen when Alessa turned around. She let out a startled yelp and fell back against the counter.

"Jesus, Ari! You scared me," she said, chuckling.

Aria only stared at her with a perturbed expression, her fingers fidgeting wildly and leg bouncing as if she was going to come bursting out of her skin. Her anxiety was palpable, and it made Alessa straighten.

"Is everything okay? Are you hungry? I just put the food in the oven. It should finish in about twenty."

Aria's eyes flickered to the oven and then back to her. Her brows furrowed a bit, lips pursing like she wanted to speak, but she never opened her mouth. Alessa waited. Whenever she tried to push Aria for more in the past, she only clammed up. She realized over time the best way to get to her sister was to give her space until she was ready, no matter how much the curiosity nagged at her.

"If you want, you can pick a movie and I'll make a plate for you when it's ready."

"Are they gone?" Aria interrupted.

"Uh, yeah, they left like an hour ago." She thought it strange that Aria didn't hear them leave but considered that she might have been napping. Aria had been doing that a lot recently.

"Do you know when they're coming back?"

"Not for a few hours, probably. You know how long those things go; everyone wants the tree to look perfect." Again, she giggled, attempting to lighten the mood. Aria shot a disgusted look at the oven.

"Is it the casserole again?"

Alessa nodded and watched as Aria raised a hand to pinch the fleshy softness of her belly between her fingers.

"It's a little weird, isn't it? All the fatty foods Mom's been making. She's usually such a pillar of health."

Alessa frowned in thought. It was odd. Lily had always been a healthy food type of parent, putting in the effort to balance every meal. She didn't allow them to have more than one pack of junk food in the house at one time. Joshua was definitely more relaxed with these rules.

However, since Aria's birthday, she'd been much more generous with the variety of dinners she prepared. They went from having barely seasoned chicken with vegetables to macaroni and cheese skillet, pasta with creamy sauce, and many, many casseroles. Alessa didn't give it a second thought because she was so happy to have the variety.

"I guess so."

Maybe Lily felt bad for how she acted at the party, and cooking was the only way to assuage her guilt for putting a hand on her child. Aria glared down at her stomach; she'd gained a bit of weight in the last few months since Lily implemented all these diet changes. It was only a few pounds, and Alessa couldn't even tell when she looked at her, but it was obvious Aria was insecure about it. Clothes she wore all the time suddenly fit a bit too snug. Alessa imagined that would take a toll on anyone. She only wished her sister saw how beautiful she still was.

"You don't have to have any if you don't want. I'm sure we could whip up something else."

"No, it's fine," Aria mumbled, "doesn't matter."

"What?"

"Nothing," Aria said and threw a quick glance over her shoulder, "can you do something for me?"

"Uh, sure. With what?"

Aria waved for her to follow and wordlessly exited the room. Confused but curious, Alessa trailed behind. They stopped in front of their father's office.

"I need you to keep an ear out for me while I look for something."

Alessa arched her brow, perplexed. "What do you mean, an ear out? What are you looking for?"

Aria's expression turned stony. "In case Mom and Dad come home early or whatever." She appeared frustrated Alessa was even asking, but Alessa wasn't giving in that easily. Their dad gave them strict instructions not to enter his office when he wasn't home, and he usually kept it locked tight. If Alessa was going to risk her neck to help, she wanted to know why she was helping.

"You didn't answer my second question, Ari. You know we're not supposed to go in there."

Aria ran a defeated hand down her face.

"Fine," she snapped, "I snuck into Dad's office the other day to use his laptop and dropped one of my rings. I wanted to dip in and find it before he does."

Alessa studied Aria's expression. She wanted to believe her sister was telling her the truth, but she also knew the girl was an adept liar. Seconds ticked on as Alessa considered it, but when Aria never faltered, she finally gave in.

"Okay! But I don't know how you're going to get in there without a key."

Aria pulled a key out of her pocket.

Alessa blanched. "Where did you get that?"

Her sister smirked, eyes twinkling with rebellion. "Made a copy about a year ago. Had one too many times where I needed to finish a last-minute assignment and couldn't get to the library. I made a copy so when he's out or asleep, I can finish them on his computer."

Their parents had always been stingy about internet use, limiting them to a certain amount of screen time per day. In their minds, too much technology would stunt their growth. Their rules had made things challenging for them in the past when they really needed the extra time, so despite Alessa's surprise, she didn't blame her. She also had to admit, Aria's sneakiness impressed her.

Alessa watched with genuine intrigue as Aria slid the key into the lock and opened the door with ease. She remained outside and leaned against the wall, listening to Aria's shuffling while also checking for the sounds of a car pulling into the driveway. Tension grew in her shoulders the more time her sister spent in there, and even if she was confident their parents wouldn't come home for a few more hours, paranoia was setting in. There was still a chance the church could finish early, or that their parents would simply become tired and return soon, only to discover their betrayal.

After fifteen minutes of searching, Alessa checked her watch.

"Are you almost done?"

She only received a grunt and more thuds of movement in response. Alessa rolled her eyes. How long did it take to find a ring? There were only so many places it could be. The jostling in the office only got louder and more frantic. Drawers slammed, and papers rustled, peppered by the increasingly distraught mumbles from Aria.

Another fifteen minutes passed and Alessa bounded into the office.

"Ari, come on, what's taking so long?" Alessa stopped short when she found Aria crumpled on the floor in the center of the room, head in her heads and shoulders shaking. Joshua's desk was cluttered, and Alessa noticed a few books out of place. A trashcan overflowing with papers laid turned over on the ground. Her sister whimpered. She rushed to her side.

"Ari? What's wrong?"

Aria refused to look up, tears dripping from her hands into her lap.

"It's gonna be okay. Can I help look for it?"

"It's not here."

Aria finally looked up. Her eyes were shiny and red-rimmed. When she spoke again, it was softer, more resigned. "It's not here."

Alessa's face fell, but she tried to remain positive. "I'm sure we can get you a new one. Which one was it?"

Aria shook her head. "It's fine."

She peeled herself off the floor and wiped at her face. Alessa felt useless standing there. Aria began cleaning the mess she left, putting the trash back in the receptacle and tidying Joshua's desk so he'd never know anyone was there. She did it so smoothly and without thought, Alessa could tell Aria had done this dozens of times.

"Are you sure you're all right, Ari?" she asked, and Aria paused.

There was something massive and unsaid between them, and Alessa didn't know what it was, but she sensed it didn't have anything to do with a lost ring. "You can always talk to me. You know that."

Aria turned to her and gave her a long look. Alessa flinched when Aria suddenly stepped toward her and gripped her arms, a crazed smile on her lips.

"You're a good kid, Squirt."

Startled, Alessa floundered for something to say, but Aria barreled over her. "What do you think about coming with me this summer?"

"What... what do you mean?"

Hundreds of micro expressions rippled over Aria's face until the smile returned. Her lips were trembling.

"When I go to my summer program! You can just come with. Haul out of this town and never look back, just you and me! That would be fun, right?"

"Ari... you know I can't come with you; I still have to finish school."

Aria's grip on her sister's arms tightened, her grin faltering.

"Oh, come on, since when do you care about school?" She laughed, but it sounded sharp and forced. "It would be so great. We could travel, we could see the ocean. We'd be able to do whatever we wanted!" It felt like she was trying more to convince herself than Alessa.

At first, Alessa was too bewildered to speak. She tried to convince herself that Aria would snap out of it any second. She didn't.

"Aria," Alessa said slowly and firmly, Aria blinked at her with mounting hope, "it would never work. Mom and Dad would freak."

The smile dropped from Aria's face. Alessa scrambled for a way to lessen the blow.

"Don't get me wrong, I'm gonna miss you like crazy. There's nothing I'd rather do than travel with you, Ari. But there are still things I need to do. I can't just up and leave. But you're gonna have so much fun without me, and I only have one year left! I'll be right behind you."

Aria didn't answer immediately, but she seemed to be taking in what Alessa was saying. All at once, Aria cleared her throat and uncurled her fingers from Alessa's arms. As she rolled back her shoulders, the wild light in her eyes diminished.

"You're right," she said, "I was just getting ahead of myself. I guess I'm anxious about leaving home. Sorry if I freaked you out."

"Of course. This town is all you've ever known. It makes sense. But you're gonna kill it out there, you're going to make a ton of new friends and go to a ton of cool places. And you can always call me and give me a detailed report. In fact, I expect you to," Alessa replied with a giggle.

Aria's hands fidgeted, and she slipped around Alessa to exit the office without another word. Alessa's eyes followed her. The creeping suspicion that there was still something left unsaid pestered her.

"Ari."

Aria frozen, took a breath, and turned to Alessa.

"I love you," she said.

This time, when Aria smiled, it was genuine. "Love you too, Squirt."

Aria was gone with a wink and a nod, leaving Alessa standing alone in the center of their father's office.

Chapter 22

Darting and dipping into alleys between houses and stores, Aria finally felt like she'd outrun her shadow-self. She felt like she'd been running forever until the town became nothing but a distant blur around her. As the day crept into late afternoon, more people were out and about, and it was harder not to take notice of her.

Aria never relented, even as a few faces she distantly recognized hissed at her in disdain and disappointment, praying their Hail Mary's. She wanted to duck away from prying eyes to a place where she could be alone.

The crowds of people finally thinned out by the time Aria reached the outskirts of town. Aria slowed to a hurried walk and finally took a moment to observe her surroundings. She stopped dead in her tracks.

Moments later, she found herself on the sidewalk just outside St. Lawrence, unsure of how she got there. The building cast a long, menacing shadow over the snow that seemed to reach right for her. Dark clouds rolled leisurely in the slate grey sky, giving the church an even more foreboding appearance. Large black crows balanced precariously on the roof, keeping an eye on everything from above.

When the doppelgänger stepped out from behind the building, Aria realized her ending up here was no mistake. The darkness had led her here. It didn't matter how fast or how far she ran, it would always find her.

The doppelgänger gradually made its way around the building, one palm flat against the white paneled exterior. Aria was unable to turn away. It looked up at the cross resting atop the church's spire. When it spoke, the air vibrated with a tangible energy.

"It will end where it began," it spoke.

A headache split through Aria's skull, blurring her vision, and making her cry out into the wind. Pressure throbbed in her forehead; warmth trickling down her lips. She licked them and tasted iron. Aria brushed her fingers under her nose, her hand came back smeared with red. The doppelgänger looked back at her.

"It will all be over soon."

Black spots dotted her vision as her copy stepped closer. Her feet cemented to the ground, and as the distanced between them shortened, the darkness inside her raged with renewed energy. Aria blinked rapidly and swayed from side to side. Her surroundings faded until there was nothing but the creature inching ever closer. Its gore crusted lips stretched into a smile and extended its arms to her. Behind it, the front door of the church opened.

"Aria," the creature drawled.

Father Samuel stepped out, and darkness took control of her body once again. Her shadow-self vanished before it had the chance to close the gap between them.

"Aria," Father Samuel scowled from the stoop, "you shouldn't be here. Where are your parents? I thought I made my stance abundantly clear."

He didn't yell, but he didn't need to. Inside the shadows of her mind Aria could hear him, but she couldn't respond. A silent abyss sucked her screams away as her body moved forward of its own accord, propelled by this other thing inside of her. Father Samuel flinched when she stepped closer.

"Are you listening to me, Ms. Hale?"

She kept going, movements slow and jerky.

"You are no longer permitted on these premises, Aria! If you do not leave, I will have you removed," he called even more forcefully, but she heard the tremor in his voice. He was afraid. She liked it. Wanted more of it. She was a mere fifteen feet away from the first step.

"Aria Hale, that is enough! You will cease this absurd behavior this instant!" Veins pulsed in his neck. "Your vicious spirit is no longer welcome in these holy halls. Until you repent for your sinful ways, I ban you from this house of God."

Aria halted then; her expression hauntingly devoid of emotion. She tilted her head curiously at him.

"Whose God?"

Tires screeched across the asphalt, and Shirley's squad car tore down the street. Father Samuel pressed against the door, one hand on the crucifix around his neck and the other fumbling for the doorknob. They all piled out of the car; Shirley raised her arm to keep Maya and Alessa behind her.

"Everything all right here, Father Samuel?"

His bulging eyes shot to her; he shook his head. "I want this girl off my property this instant, Deputy! She is not to set foot in this church."

"Of course, Father. I'm very sorry for the inconvenience."

"I told her mother she was not welcome here. She has exhibited disturbing and abominable conduct. This girl is a danger to me and my family. I'll have you know. She assaulted me."

Shirley made her way up the path. Aria stood between her and the priest, her eyes never leaving him. For now, Aria wasn't moving.

"I-I apologize, Father. I was unaware."

Samuel cut her off with a sharp jerk of his hand. "I don't want apologies. I want her gone!"

"She's not a danger! She's scared!" Alessa yelled.

CHAPTER 22

The priest scowled at her.

"You defend such behavior, Ms. Hale?" he sneered, giving her a measured look of disgust, "I shouldn't be surprised. Girls of your age are so easily influenced."

Alessa's jaw dropped, and even Maya was speechless. Samuel locked eyes with his granddaughter, his expression morphing into a mask of unbridled rage.

"I want her out of my sight."

There was nothing left to be said. Shirley took over, approaching Aria from the side.

"Aria, come with me, it's time to go home." She reached her arm out, but did not force physical contact, Aria did not look at her. "Your parents are extremely worried about you. Just follow me and I'll give you a lift."

Nothing. Father Samuel writhed under her increasingly unsettling stare. Aria didn't even blink. Shirley stole a glance at Alessa, who stood at a respectable distance.

"I have your sister with me. Alessa."

The name sparked something inside of Aria, snapping her from her trance. She finally looked at Shirley, who waited with a placating smile. Encouraged by the response, Shirley continued.

"See, she's right over there." She pointed. Aria's gaze followed. Alessa wiggled her fingers in a hesitant wave.

"Let's go home, Ari."

Aria felt her head move up and down in a nod. Beside her, Shirley released an intense sigh. She kept herself at a distance as she walked Aria back to the car.

"Maya!" Father Samuel barked, pointing at the spot next to him with a firm hand. Alessa nudged her and offered a reassuring smile.

"It's okay, we'll talk later."

Alessa grabbed her hand and gave it a squeeze. Reluctantly, Maya pulled away. She crossed paths with Shirley and Aria as she approached the stairs.

Aria stopped and watched Maya go by, her curly hair bouncing behind her, and continued to do so until she was standing next to her grandfather. Shirley stopped with her.

"Everything okay, Aria?" she mumbled.

Samuel noticed Aria staring at him again. They all went still as Aria smiled; a chilling grin full of teeth and bloody promises. Samuel's face turned ashen.

"Come on, Aria. It's time to go," Shirley said, and Aria's smile vanished just as quickly as it appeared. There was a shared, palpable relief when Shirley finally got Aria to the car. Without so much as a goodbye, Samuel shuffled Maya inside and slammed the door behind him.

Alessa buckled herself in and helped Aria do so as well. The ride back to the Hale house was silent and choked with tension. Shirley rolled to a stop and glanced in her rearview mirror, adjusting it to better match her preferred field of view. Aria caught the deputy's stare in the reflection. Shirley's eyes widened.

Aria's heart raced, tasting Shirley's terror. The car behind them blared its horn impatiently and Shirley almost leapt out of her skin. Aria turned back to the window and watched the town whisk by, her now bright gold eyes gazing back at her in the glass.

Chapter 23

Alessa was so fraught with anticipation it sapped her energy completely by the time they pulled into the driveway. Shirley didn't stay long after making sure the girls got in safely, citing an emergency call from Roswell that summoned her back to the station. When the door clicked shut, Alessa held her breath, waiting for the explosion.

It never came. Lily was furious. That much was obvious from the tension in her clenched jaw and the flush on her neck. Their father was less tense. As soon as Shirley was gone, he crossed the room in barely three strides, glancing them up and down, checking for injuries.

"You girls all right?"

Alessa nodded, looking befuddled. Since when did concern outweigh punishment for her parents? It was usually consequences first, ask questions later.

"Where did you run off to, Aria?"

When she predictably met his question with a blank look, Alessa chimed in.

"We found her at the church, on Father Samuel's doorstep."

Both of her parents straightened, the anger in their mother's eyes abating, only to be replaced with an instant flash of fear.

"What in God's name was she doing at the church?" Lily spat, "what were you thinking, Aria? After all that you've already done."

Alessa flinched at the acidity in her words, but Aria didn't even deign to look in their mother's direction. Joshua whirled on her.

"That's enough, Lily. That isn't helpful."

His confidence and stern delivery surprised both Alessa and Lily. But for the moment, it got their mom to shut up. The muscles in her face tightened into an expression of reluctant acceptance. Satisfied, Joshua turned back to Aria, speaking calmly.

"You really scared us, Aria. We thought... well, we didn't know what to think. We just want to make sure you're okay, sweetheart. Did something scare you? Were you... were you trying to get back into the woods again?"

Her head tilted to look at him, slow and strange, as if she were being adjusted by invisible hands. It didn't look natural. Alessa's skin crawled, watching it.

"I was... startled." Even Aria's voice sounded hollow, as if it were echoing from some dark cavern.

"Startled by what? Was it Roswell? Were you nervous about seeing him again?"

She nodded, her eyes betraying no emotion.

"He was only here to tell us that your school janitor, Mr. Archer, went missing last night. I know it's a bit nerve-wracking to talk to him, especially after all you've been through, but he's only doing his job, he's trying to keep everyone safe."

Aria blinked but gave no indication she understood. Lily fidgeted behind Joshua, itching to burst. He eventually sighed.

"She wasn't doing anything wrong," Alessa added, "she was just standing there, and she seemed confused."

Joshua smiled at her. "It's okay, Alessa. She's not in trouble. You have been through more than we can imagine, and we understand that. We don't want to punish you; we want to help you. Although I'm boarding your window up, so we don't have another incident like this."

As expected, Aria didn't argue.

"I'm sure Alessa will let you rest in her room until I'm done?" Alessa immediately nodded. He patted her shoulder gratefully.

"Great, shouldn't take me long."

Joshua immediately got to work, taking a small stack of wooden planks from the kitchen up the stairs. Ice crept up the back of her neck, and Alessa turned to find her mother inches away.

"Get your homework done and be ready for dinner at seven." Her tone left no room for argument, and Alessa didn't have time to agree before her mother was darting out of the room.

Aria still refused to eat. Immediately after Joshua finished boarding up her window, she secluded herself in her room and locked the door. Both Joshua and Lily attempted to persuade Aria into joining them for a meal but to no avail. Short of breaking down her door and dragging her down the stairs, there wasn't much they could do. Lily reluctantly gave in, yet again, and angrily brushed off her husband's endeavors to comfort her. The three of them sat at the dinner table and ate in pensive silence.

For almost a full hour that night, Lily prayed on her knees at the edge of her bed, her cross necklace between interlocked fingers. Alessa had never seen her pray for so long before. She only stopped when Joshua entered, but kept her eyes averted when Alessa wished them goodnight.

Alessa waited up for as long as she could, but when she could no longer keep her eyes open, she accepted that she'd be sleeping in her own room this time. Even if the thought brought her anxiety, she had no choice. She had to trust that her father's work boarding up the window would do the job. On her way to bed, she paused in front of Aria's door. Alessa tapped on it with her finger, talking just loud enough so her sister would hear.

"I'm going to bed, Ari, just wanted to stop by and say goodnight."

She lingered there, hoping against all hope that Aria would prove her wrong. The door remained closed.

"I love you, Ari," she continued, "and everything is gonna be okay, I promise. We're gonna figure this out. I'm not giving up on you."

Alessa let the words dangle until she knew for sure she wasn't getting a response. For now, she would have to settle by trusting that Aria heard her. She pressed her forehead to the door and sucked in one final, deep breath before retreating to her room.

Alessa woke to a series of bangs and the sounds of arguing. Barely out of her sleepy haze, she shot out of bed when her mother's voice rose to a yell. She rushed toward the sounds of distress. Aria's bedroom door was wide open, and Joshua's shadow shifted in the entrance. She wiggled in behind him.

"What have you done, Aria?" She heard her mother wail. "What have YOU DONE?"

Alessa's veins ran cold when she finally saw what her mother was screaming about. Crosses. Red crosses. On every free space of wall available, there were upside down crosses painted in crimson streaks. Joshua looked just as stunned as Alessa.

Eventually, Alessa's eyes landed on Aria, who remained quiet in the chaos. She sat on the edge of her bed, hands resting on her knees as she stared at the wall across from her, ignoring Lily's comments and accusations. However, it wasn't Aria's demeanor that unnerved Alessa; it was the reverse cross she'd painted on her own face. One streak of red trailed down the center of her face, over her nose and stopping at the tip of her chin. She'd slashed another horizontal line of red across her mouth. Dried blood stained her hands.

Lily flitted about the room, hands moving so fast they were a blur. She didn't seem to know where to start, but Alessa could see her growing more harried by the second.

"I can't... I can't believe," she mumbled, forcing down tears, "Joshua, *do* something!"

His eyes widened. "W-What?"

Her expression distorted with fury; she shot her husband a dark look. "Useless," Lily growled. Both Alessa and Joshua recoiled.

Lily turned to Aria and stepped closer, only to stop herself. She wrinkled her nose, upper lip curling in disgust, as she finally looked at Alessa.

"You deal with your sister," Lily commanded, "I have to focus on this... this disaster."

Alessa rushed to Aria's side, too afraid of being on the receiving end of Lily's rage to speak.

"Come on, let's go to the bathroom."

Aria complied readily. Alessa tugged on her arm, and she allowed herself to be led to down the hall. Alessa held her breath until they were alone, letting it out when she knew they were out of Lily's hearing range. She got to work and wet a washcloth under some cold water, starting on Aria's hands first.

"What happened, Ari?" she whispered, "what did you do?"

Of course, she received no response, but then again, she hadn't really expected one. Alessa continued on with her silent cleaning, and carefully wiped every bit of red from her sister's fingers. Watery blood filled the sink when she rinsed the cloth and wrung it out. When she was done, she scanned Aria's hands, looking for scratches, but they were unblemished.

She tried to ignore the sinking feeling in her stomach and instead focused on removing the blood from Aria's face. Her sister watched her with a vacant expression. When Alessa finished, she took both of Aria's hands into hers.

"I wish you would talk to me, Ari," Alessa lamented.

A harsh knock on the door ripped her out of her thoughts. "Hurry up, Alessa! You're going to be late!"

"Be right there!"

When the girls finished in the bathroom, they retreated back to Alessa's room so she could finish getting ready for school, Joshua was waiting in the hall. He was on his cell when she stepped out, talking in hushed tones.

"Yes, of course. We'll be there. Thank you, we truly appreciate it. See you then." He hung up.

"Who was that?" Alessa asked.

Joshua's head bounced up, a startled look on his face. "Oh! That was Father Samuel." Alessa's eyes widened.

"Why is he calling?"

Joshua's lips curled into a placating smile; his once nervous disposition replaced with a strange, eager energy.

"A peace offering. He invited us over to the church tonight to talk, so we can all make amends and figure out how to move forward as a unit."

For a minute, Alessa was sure she was hallucinating the words coming out of his mouth. Joshua seemed genuinely pleased to be graced by the priest's generosity. Alessa didn't know if she wanted to cry or smack her father in the face.

"Dad, I don't get it. Why do we need to make amends right now? What exactly can he do for Aria? She's sick, Dad. She needs real help!" Finally asking the questions that had been plaguing her felt like a monumental weight was being lifted from her shoulders. "Why is he suddenly so eager to give a peace offering? You should have seen the way he looked at her yesterday."

She watched as his smile slowly fell. "Like she was nothing, Dad. *Nothing.* Why do you even want his help?"

Pain flickered in his eyes, but he held himself together. He cleared his throat, expression turning hopeful.

"I know you're scared for your sister, Alessa. We all are. We thought if... when... she came home, things would be okay again. It would be hard, of course, but we'd be a family again. Things didn't turn out like we all hoped. Your mother and I, we're in over our heads and... despite what you believe of Father Samuel, he has always been a dear and supportive friend to this family. He held you both as babies.

"But Aria attacked him. It frightened him. He had every reason to walk out that door, Alessa. He could have done much worse. We've all made mistakes since your sister came home, but your mom and I can't do this alone. We need help too."

Each word felt like a punch to her gut, but she knew he was right. Aria was the violent one — the attacker. Father Samuel was only responding to what she had done to him. Still, Alessa felt uneasy.

"It's just one chat. He wants to apologize in person, and we'd like to do the same. If we can all come together in the end, it will be even better for Aria. She needs more people in her corner, Alessa."

That she definitely couldn't argue with. Joshua smiled, still looking at her with those desperate eyes.

"Okay," Alessa finally said.

"Okay?" he parroted, his smile brightening, "okay." He planted a quick kiss against her hairline.

"Love you, sweetheart. Now go on, before you're late."

Joshua rushed her off, and with one last look at her sister over her shoulder, she headed to school.

Maya and Noah were already together and waiting for Alessa on the front steps when she rounded the corner. She was more than a little surprised to see them together, but she rushed up to them anyway, meeting Maya in a quick hug. The trio stood in awkward silence, all of them looking worse for wear. Alessa was sure they were quite the sight. Maya was the first to speak.

"I filled Noah in on what happened yesterday."

"I hope you didn't get into too much trouble with your grandfather," Alessa said.

"I've never seen him so pissed," Maya said, trying to act nonchalant, but Alessa knew differently. Her friend was hanging on by a thread. They all were. "I was given express instructions not to associate with the Hale family in any way, shape, or form."

"That's weird. He was just on the phone with my dad this morning and invited my parents over for a peace offering or something."

Maya squinted at her in bewilderment. "But... why would he..." she trailed off with an exasperated groan, "what the fuck is going on?"

Alessa didn't know how to answer her, but she had a hunch. It could still lead nowhere. Anything was better than stumbling around in the dark.

"I think we need to go look at the church."

Now there were two shocked pairs of eyes on her. "Just hear me out."

Alessa recounted what she saw that morning, the crosses on the walls and the blood on Aria's arms. Nothing made sense, but there remained one fact threading through every detail: Aria had a connection to the church.

"I don't know what it means, but it would explain why she reacted to Father Samuel so violently, and why she ended up at the church yesterday. Maybe I'm looking for patterns that aren't there, or maybe I'm crazy but, it seems as good a place to start as any."

Alessa expected them to argue, to laugh in her face, to tell her she was losing her mind. She wouldn't blame them if they did. Noah and Maya took one long look at each other before turning back to Alessa with an answer.

"We're in."

Chapter 24

Alessa, Maya, and Noah decided their best chance to investigate the church was during their lunch break. Alessa couldn't afford to miss anymore classes, and students frequently traveled into town for food during lunch period. If they were seen departing the school, everyone would assume they were going to eat. Maya informed them that Father Samuel usually spent his afternoons volunteering, and the church would likely be empty during this time.

For the first half of the day, it was all Alessa could think about, and she felt a swell of relief when the bell finally rang to signal it was time. She practically flew out of the room to meet Maya and Noah at the foot of the front steps.

"So, what exactly are we looking for?" Maya asked.

"I don't know, I just have a gut feeling the church is important," Alessa replied. She felt guilty she was taking them on what could be a wild goose chase, but she couldn't ignore how she felt. Maya stopped walking, causing Noah and Alessa to pause as well.

"You don't... you don't think my grandfather had anything to do with what happened to Ari, do you?" Maya fiddled nervously with the strap of her bag. Alessa frowned.

"I'm sure that's not it." She didn't know what else to say, or how to convince her. Hell, she was having trouble convincing herself.

"Maybe she's drawn to it because of how often your family spends time there. Maybe that's why she showed up there on the first day, because she knows it's safe," Noah offered.

Alessa could tell he didn't have faith in his own words. They both knew just how much Aria disliked the church, how she rebelled against it any chance she had, but it wasn't a bad theory and if it comforted Maya, that was enough. It did the trick. Maya's shoulders relaxed, and they continued walking.

When they arrived at the church, it was empty, just like Maya said. Using her key, Maya let them in the side door. Being inside the empty church was strange. Normally, it teemed with life, and you could barely hear yourself think. Now she only heard the echoing of their shoes against the hardwood floor. Dust particles danced in the air, illuminated by the sun pouring in through the windows.

"We can start in his office," Maya said, "he usually keeps it locked, but he gave me a copy of his key for emergencies."

Alessa's heart was pounding as she waited for Maya to open the door. His office was about what she expected. He kept it simply decorated and very organized, with a large oak desk in the center of the room. Tall windows doused the small space in a dusky glow.

"Look for anything weird or out of the ordinary especially anything that might have even the slightest bit to do with Ari." Perhaps Alessa was reaching, and this would all be for naught, but her intuition argued otherwise.

The trio went to work, each covering a different area of the office. Maya flipped through Samuel's dusty bookshelf, Alessa focused on the filing cabinets, and Noah sifted through the desk. None of them spoke.

"Guys, I think I found something."

The girls turned away from their respective searches to join him at the desk. Maya arched over him, trying to see what Noah was doing.

CHAPTER 24

"What's up?"

Noah jostled the drawer some more before pulling the whole thing out. "I think this drawer has a false bottom."

Noah dislodged the wooden slat from the bottom of the drawer and slid it out of place, revealing more space underneath. Alessa grit her teeth when she saw what was inside: a single, golden skeleton key. They stared at it in silence, none of them wanting to touch it.

"I've never seen that key before," Maya whispered.

"What do you think it goes to?" Alessa asked just as quietly.

"I have no idea."

The sound of a door opening followed by a series of muffled voices stopped Alessa cold before she responded. Maya's eyes shot to the door. They hadn't closed it all the way behind them.

"Shit!" Maya hissed and ducked behind the desk, yanking Alessa down with her. The trio huddled together. "Put it back!" Maya gestured to the drawer and Noah didn't argue. He slid the false bottom back in place and put back the supplies.

Sweat pearled on Noah's upper lip when the drawer clicked back into its slot. The voices and footsteps were drawing closer. Maya crept across the floor until she reached the cracked door and listened.

"It's grandfather!" she said, anxious, "he's with Roswell and Shirley—shit! We have to go!"

Noah zeroed in on the drawer and held his breath until it slid home. Once complete, he and Alessa crawled on all fours to Maya's side. Maya poked her head out.

"What the hell are they even doing here?" Maya spat, fear bleeding into frustration.

"Why don't I put on some tea and then we can discuss this in my office?" They heard Father Samuel say.

"When they get into the kitchen, turn right, and go straight down the hall. Last door on the left will take you to the basement. We can wait them out down there," Maya instructed.

"But we don't know how long they're planning on staying. What if we're down there all afternoon?" Noah asked. Maya shot him a glare.

"Do you have any better ideas?"

Noah's face fell. Alessa jumped in, "we'll cross that bridge when we come to it. Let's just go!"

Maya held her hand up and peered into the hallway once more. She watched and waited until she saw her grandfather's figure round the corner and head toward the kitchen, Roswell, and Shirley close behind. The second they were out of sight, she leapt into action.

"Okay–go, go!"

Alessa and Noah shuffled their feet as they rushed to the correct door. Maya lingered behind to close and relock the door behind her to avoid any excess suspicion. Alessa cringed every time her foot landed on a loose floorboard, but soon the three of them were inching down the stairwell leading to the basement.

The cold air smelled stale, and the basement spanned almost the entire length of the first floor. Maya flicked on the single, dim bulb to illuminate the space. They kept it remarkably well organized. Filing cabinets lined the wall to their left and several packed boxes stood stacked in the corner near an old wire bookshelf that held heavy, old tomes layered in dust. The room also contained a few old pieces of furniture that were old or broken, as well as an ancient organ that had stopped functioning years ago.

"I hate it down here," Maya muttered. The light above them flickered precariously.

"What is all this stuff?" Alessa asked as she traced her hand along the tops of the cabinets, gathering dust on the tip of her finger.

"Old church records, some stuff on the town's history. He's big on preserving things like that."

Noah crossed the room, drawn to the thick books sitting on the shelf.

CHAPTER 24

He grabbed the first one he saw, wiping the filth from the cover, and opened it to the first page.

"Oh wow, check these out." The girls joined him, one of them hovering over each shoulder. "Photos of the church from twenty years ago."

He held a photo album, stuffed to the brim with dozens of photographs, all of them either taken inside of the church, outside of it, or at some sort of church function. Alessa recognized the most prevalent man in the pictures as Maya's great-grandfather, Samuel Goddard Sr. His portraits were all over the church halls. It was impossible to live in this town and not know who he was. Looking at the pictures was like being transported back in time. Alessa glanced back at the shelf. There were dates listed on the spine of each book.

"These date all the way back to the founding members," she said in awe. Her eyes landed on one in particular with the dates 1980–1990 printed in gold. Alessa snatched it and immediately began flipping through it.

Reality faded around her as she scanned the faces in every photograph. Her hand remained suspended in midair when she came across a group picture taken on the front steps of the church. There he was: Dominic Powell, positioned behind his sister Shirley, their parents on either side.

"It's Dominic."

The Earth beneath her suddenly felt uneven, and Alessa stumbled backwards, knocking the shelf against the wall. An album fell and landed with a harsh thud. Maya gasped at the sound of footsteps clamoring overhead.

"Shit—hide!"

They didn't need to be told twice. Alessa shut the album and slid it back into place as Maya turned off the light. Fumbling in the dark, white spots dotting her vision, Alessa tucked herself behind a discarded armchair, squeezing herself between the furniture and the wall. She prayed it was enough. Alessa only wished she could see where the other two were hiding. The light clicked back on.

"Hello? Is there someone down here?" It was Roswell.

"Sometimes the school kids like to sneak in and fool around, but I appreciate you taking the time to check." Father Samuel was there too. Alessa saw shadows drifting across the floor. She put a hand over her mouth to quiet her breathing.

"Last chance! If there's anyone in here, come out now!"

Alessa dipped to look under the chair and watched their feet move about the room. The hem of Father Samuel's robes fluttered across the floor.

"Strange. It looks like one of my photo albums fell off the shelf."

Alessa shrank down as much as she could, willing herself to become invisible. She cursed herself for not picking up the fallen book.

"See anything else out of the ordinary, Father?"

"No, not that I can tell."

"Maybe a mouse or a rat knocked it over. There's bound to be a few critters hiding out down here," Roswell offered; Father Samuel hummed in thought.

"It's certainly possible. But I'd like to check something just to make sure. Help me with this, will you?"

Alessa heard more movement, and then something large and heavy being dragged across the floor. It scraped over the concrete ground, and it made Alessa's ears ache. She peeked around the chair. Roswell's veins pulsed in his arms and neck as he pulled the ancient organ out from its resting place against the wall.

Alessa's brows furrowed in confusion when she realized what the organ was concealing.

It was a door. Alessa unconsciously leaned forward, her curiosity getting the better of her. Roswell clapped his hands together to free them of dust. Strange, she ruminated, that he didn't seem at all shocked by its existence. Why was there a hidden door in the church basement? And what the hell was behind it?

Father Samuel stepped forward and presented a small object from within his robes. Alessa bit her tongue so hard she saw stars. He was holding the same skeleton key they found in his office. The priest slid it into the lock with ease and opened the door. From Alessa's angle, she couldn't see what laid within, but she witnessed the glow of another lightbulb being flicked on.

"Everything look good?" Roswell asked.

"Yes, I believe so, thank you. My apologies, I knew it was unlikely as this is the only key, but I like to be sure," Father Samuel replied.

"Of course, never hurts to be cautious."

Alessa dipped back behind the chair when they closed the secret door and locked it. Roswell slid the organ back into place.

"Must have just been a mouse, then. I really should have pest control come through here."

The men chuckled, and soon they were leaving the room. Alessa waited until they turned the light off and she heard the door close before emerging from her hiding place.

"Maya? Noah?"

They, too, slithered from the shadows of their respective hiding spots. Alessa's eyes locked with Maya's, and she didn't need to ask to know her friend had seen everything. Maya immediately went to the old instrument, prodding at the back with her fingers to glimpse what the door it was blocking. She turned to look at both of them, the whites of her eyes shining in the dark.

"I've never seen this door before. I didn't even know it was here."

"Another storage room?" Noah offered.

"I don't see why he'd need it. Everything he owns is up here already, and there's still space. And why would he need to hide it behind this?"

Alessa saw Maya's carefully managed composure beginning to crack. Everywhere they turned, they discovered something new and horrible. Noah checked his watch.

"We don't have time to look, and like he said, he has the only key," he stated.

Maya nodded; eyes glazed as she drifted back toward them.

"I can come check it out after school today. My parents weren't thrilled about me hanging around with you yesterday, so they have me helping grandfather clean the church in the afternoons. I'm sure I can find a chance to slip back down here."

"Are you sure? We don't even know if there's anything down there. I don't want you to risk pissing your family off more by doing this," Alessa argued. She'd already done more than enough to help, and even though Alessa was interested in knowing what the door was hiding, Maya's wellbeing meant more to her.

"I got this. I don't know what the fuck is going on or what it has to do with my grandfather, but the more I find out, the less I like it. And something tells me that door is important."

Alessa could have kissed her then, and it took all the willpower she had to restrain herself. How she got lucky enough to have someone like Maya in her life, she had no clue.

"If you're sure."

The corner of Maya's mouth turned up in a small smirk. "Never been more sure in my life."

Chapter 25

Maya parted from Alessa and Noah after school. Roswell and Shirley left the church only ten minutes after the debacle in the basement, giving them the opportunity to sneak out while Samuel was busy in the kitchen. She left Alessa with a hug and one final promise to call them if she found anything of interest.

"To the library?" Noah asked.

"To the library."

Alessa was eager to peruse the internet with the information she'd gained. They had names and dates now, and they had Dominic Powell, proof that what happened to Aria wasn't a one-off. Noah joined in happily.

They spent most of their walk in comfortable silence. There was an ease to being in his presence. They politely greeted Gloria when they entered the library. She looked pleased to see Alessa had returned and regarded Noah with just as much enthusiasm. She offered to assist once again, but Alessa declined with a smile before tugging Noah over to the computers. They had no time to waste.

"Okay, give me the bullet points. What are we looking for?" he asked, already clicking away.

"Anything on Dominic Powell, or disappearances of seventeen- and eighteen-year-olds around their birthdays, especially if there's any mention of the woods."

They used every search engine at their disposal, trying a million and one different phrasings and keywords. Periodically, Alessa glanced over her shoulder at the front door and Gloria, as if expecting Shirley to materialize and interrogate her again. Noah cleared his throat, grabbing her attention. He looked pained.

"I gotta admit something, Alessa."

Her heart sank. "What do you mean?"

Finally, he looked at her, face grave and miserable. "There was a period, after Aria went missing, where I... I thought she might have run away. That she did it all on purpose. Just up and left."

Alessa frowned, but it wasn't disappointment that plucked at her heartstrings. It was sorrow over his guilt. His confession was surprising, but it didn't anger her.

"She was acting kind of weird towards the end, before she disappeared. I feel weird saying she was paranoid but... God, that's how it seemed, at least to me. Aria was never shy about wanting to leave Pine Hollow, but suddenly it was all she would talk about.

"She snuck over once, after her birthday. Did she ever tell you? Showed up outside my window, throwing pebbles at it like we were in the middle of a rom-com or whatever. I was freaked and thought she was going to wake my parents. When I got down there... she was crying."

The blood rushed out of Alessa's face. "No. She never told me that."

"She said she was having trouble sleeping, but she was so damn tired. I could barely get her to complete a full sentence. She was crying so much. When she got a few words out, it barely made any sense, and all I could gather was that it had to do with your parents."

"Did she say anything else?"

Noah shook his head in defeat. "I tried to get more out of her. But really, I just ended up holding her until she stopped crying. Eventually, she let me drive her home, but it took her a really long time to get out of the car. She was just... dreading going back inside."

Memories of Aria sneaking into their father's office, and of the crazed look in her eyes muddled Alessa's thoughts.

"She asked me to leave with her."

Noah's head reeled back in shock. "What?"

"A few months before she went missing. She was antsy, and she said I should come with her when she leaves for her program, didn't care that I hadn't finished school yet. I obviously told her I couldn't. She never brought it up again."

Noah's lips pursed in consideration, a wrinkle of tension knotting between his brows.

"There was a time where I thought she ran away too, because of that." It felt like a betrayal against Aria to say it out loud. Even though Alessa's suspicions didn't last long, it was the truth. Noah nudged her shin with his foot and smiled sympathetically.

"I pretty quickly realized it was a stupid idea, though. You know why?"

"Why?"

"Because she never would have left without telling us goodbye," Noah replied, as if it were the most obvious answer in the world. Alessa responded with a tender smile.

"Damn right," she agreed, and they got back to work.

No matter what search terms they typed into Google, they still came up dry. They found no other mentions of Dominic Powell, his disappearance, or anything of note happening in Pine Hollow since.

"This is getting us nowhere," Alessa groaned, leaning back in her seat.

"How about you go check out the microfilm machine in the back? It's got some more local stuff, things that might not have been newsworthy enough to make the world wide web. I'll cover things over here."

Alessa completely forgot about the microfilm machine. She looked back at her computer; her eyes were stinging. It might be good to examine things from another angle and stretch her legs a bit. Also, he had a good point. There was likely more information in the filmstrips. Because of the size and age range of their library staff, there were hundreds of strips never converted into digital form. The machine was the only way to view them.

"Let me know if you find something," she said as she gathered her things.

"Same to you," Noah replied.

The library had two microfilm readers in the back, and rarely were they ever used, especially by kids Alessa's age. She had the machines all to herself. Using what she knew already that Aria was the only one to disappear since Dominic Powell, she worked backwards. Forty long years separated them. She felt a stab of uncertainty. There were only a few circumstantial details tying their disappearances together. For all Alessa knew, she was fabricating connections where none existed.

"Forty years," Alessa muttered, chewing on the loose skin of her bottom lip, "I wonder."

Instead of sifting through every year in between, Alessa jumped straight to the film strip labeled 1942. The pictures were all black and white then; the ink faded in certain places. During the 1942, their local paper was only run once a month. Newspapers overall took a hit in the early part of the decade due to the inception of radio, and Pine Hollow wasn't exactly frothing with wealth back then. All Alessa cared about, is it meant there was less for her to sift through.

Alessa clicked through the film so rapidly she had to remind herself to blink. She scrutinized every page, blazing through January, February, and March. She stopped briefly to rub her eyes when she reached April. Flipping through had become so automatic by the time

CHAPTER 25

she reached August; she almost missed it.

In big, blocky letters, it read: MISSING: CONSTANCE PETERSON, 18. Just below it there was a clarifying caption next to a faded headshot of a pretty, fresh-faced brunette. Alessa lapped up the information hungrily, forgetting the world around her.

'Constance Peterson, 18, daughter of Theodore and Elaine Peterson, was reported missing. Peterson's parents, owners of the Pine Hollow's longest standing bakery The Cupcake Corner, were the last people to report seeing her. According to her mother, Constance was last seen doing her nightly prayers before bed. The next morning, she was gone.'

The words went hazy, and it felt like the floor was going to drop out from under her at any second. Alessa's mouth went dry as she continued reading.

'Constance graduated from Pine Hollow High School in June and slated to attend North Dakota State University in the Fall. She was last seen wearing blue pajama pants and a pink tank top. If you or anyone you know as any information regarding this disappearance, please contact...'

A tap on Alessa's shoulder sent her hurtling back and away from the screen. Alessa yelped, pulse roaring as she whipped around.

"Oh, my goodness!" It was Gloria, looking just as startled.

"Oh, God! I'm sorry, Mrs. Anderson. I didn't hear you coming."

"It's all right, dear. I'm the one who should apologize for sneaking up on you. My husband always said I was light-footed. I guess I just never realized how much," Mrs. Anderson replied with a chuckle. Alessa forced a small smile. Mrs. Anderson tilted her head toward the machine.

"We haven't used these machines in so long. Are you still working on that project?"

Alessa positioned herself in front of the screen, obscuring the giant letters that were screaming to be noticed. "Yeah! Yeah, same project."

"Well, I'm thrilled these machines are being put to good use. They can get lonely back here."

Alessa mustered up a giggle and trying her best to look as nonchalant as possible. Gloria lingered for a while longer, a few minutes too long to be comfortable. Alessa fidgeted and cleared her throat, not sure what to say that wouldn't sound impolite, but also wanting the woman to leave her alone. It looked like the woman was waiting for something, but Alessa didn't know what. Was that suspicion in her eyes? Or just genuine curiosity? Finally, she broke the awkward silence.

"You'll let me know if you need anything? I'm here until closing tonight."

It felt like forever before she finally turned around and vanished between the bookshelves. Alessa heaved a great sigh of relief. She turned back to the machine, but she couldn't concentrate long enough on the words to absorb any more information. Her nerves were well and truly shot. She wasn't getting anything else done today. She found what she was looking for.

Alessa hurriedly put the cartridge away and turned the machine off before rejoining Noah. She refused to tell him anything until they were outside and away from Gloria's prying ears. This whole thing felt forbidden–taboo, even. Alessa didn't know who could be listening. It wasn't until they were down the street and around the corner that Alessa laid everything out on the table, watching as Noah's eyes expanded in size with every detail.

"So, with Aria, that makes three disappearances, each about 40 years apart. I mean, that's a lot of time. And Aria's case doesn't even match the other two. She was only seventeen, Dominic and Constance were eighteen."

He was right, this wasn't concrete evidence by any means, but Alessa's gut told her they were onto something bigger. She could see from his expression he didn't believe his own words.

"Could be nothing. Could be something. I just... feel in my bones that there's more going on here, Noah."

He stared at her for a few long seconds, eventually ending in a sigh as he rubbed his forehead with exasperation. "If this has to do with Father Samuel, then what happened to Constance can't be connected. It was too long ago. Do you really think the church is involved in this?"

Alessa shrugged. She didn't have any firm answers right now. She only had her instincts to guide her, and they were all pointing in one direction. "We won't know for sure until we hear from Maya."

That would determine everything. What she did or didn't find in that basement would paint their way forward. All they could do in the meantime was trust her.

"So, we wait?" Noah asked.

"So, we wait," Alessa replied in a firm tone.

Chapter 26

Alessa watched the sun sink deeper into the sky, painting it in blue and purple hues. She stayed in the living room, so rooted to the couch she worried her skin was molding to the leather, but she wanted to be close enough to reach the phone if needed. Maya would be calling to tell her what she did or did not find. Any minute now.

She picked at the tender flesh around her thumbnail, tensing every time the phone rang as she braced herself for the call. Alessa checked the clock. Maya should have been home by now. She supposed it was possible Maya was waiting until later to call, to ensure privacy. The thought did little to calm the static in her brain, but it seemed like a reasonable explanation.

The house filled with a mixture of alluring scents originating from the kitchen where Lily had been hard at work for hours. She made steak, roasted potatoes, steamed greens, and that barely scratched the surface. It was an all-out banquet. Alessa wasn't sure why her mother was going to such an effort. But she was not about to question it. Whatever she needed to do to feel normal was her prerogative.

Lily emerged from the kitchen, white apron stained and wiping her hands with a cloth as the last of the purple drained from the horizon. Her stony expression chilled Alessa's core.

CHAPTER 26

"Dinner is ready. I want you to go upstairs and get your sister, help her get ready if she needs it, and have her down here in ten minutes." Lily's tone left no room for protest, but Alessa hesitated. How her mom expected her to do this boggled her mind. Aria was resistant to food from day one and Alessa didn't see that changing soon. Lily sensed her reluctance and ground her molars so ferociously, Alessa heard her jaw clicking.

"Do not make me ask twice, Alessa. I've had enough of this. Your sister needs to eat, and she is going to come down here even if I have to drag her down the stairs myself," she spat, "tell her if she isn't down here and ready to eat in ten minutes, your father is going to remove her bedroom door from its hinges. This is no longer up for negotiation."

Alessa kept her gaze lowered as she scurried past Lily to get to the stairs. She prayed Aria would come willingly and was so desperate for it to be true she almost convinced herself it was by the time she reached her sister's door. She knocked.

"Aria, it's time for dinner. Mom wants you down there in ten minutes. I can help you get ready!" Alessa didn't want to resort to Lily's threats if she didn't have to. She heard shuffling from inside the room, but Aria didn't answer.

"Ari, please come down. You need to eat. Mom and Dad have been super patient. Can you just give them this one meal? There's only so much mom will tolerate until she loses her shit, you know that."

No one knew Lily like Aria did. No one had faced the sharp edges of their mother like she had. Not even their father. Alessa had to remind Aria what Lily was capable of. This was not the hill Aria needed to die on.

"Just one dinner, that's all. You don't even have to eat that much. A few small bites to show you tried, and she'll be satisfied. But she's pissed, Ari. She said if you don't come down, she's gonna have Dad remove your door. I've never seen her like this. She's not messing around."

Alessa hated being forced to do her mother's dirty work. She understood Lily was concerned for Aria's health, but was this really the way to go about it? Alessa traced patterns into the door with her nail, listening to the faint movements inside, and hoping that her words would be enough. Perhaps the risk of losing the only privacy she had left would put a spring in her step.

The door flew open and ripped the breath right out of Alessa. Aria stood half hidden by a shadow in the doorway. Aria's pallid complexion was moist with a sheen of sweat, and her stick thin arms were trembling. She looked sickly; feverish, worse than before. She stood with a slight hunch to her back, fingers absentmindedly scraping at her concave stomach. When her shirt lifted, Alessa glimpsed her ribs rippling against her skin. She was wasting away, hair dangling in greasy strands around the amber glow of her hollow stare.

Aria slinked by Alessa wordlessly. The surrounding air was colder than the rest of the house. Aria remained close to Alessa's side and followed her downstairs. Aria's movements were slow and calculated, her expression vacant.

Seeing Aria's state caused all of Alessa's previous concerns to come flooding back. This was a bad idea, but the train was moving, and she didn't know how to derail it. Aria stumbled on the last step, and Alessa caught her. Her body felt like a sack of bones, and she was abnormally light. Lily looked none too pleased at Aria's appearance. Joshua busied himself with setting the table.

"I told you to get her cleaned up."

Alessa scrambled for an excuse while trying to balance her sister in her arms. Their father's face was a tense mask.

"Leave it alone, Lily."

Her eyes snapped to him. "What?"

"I said leave it alone. She's here. You got what you wanted. Now, let's eat."

Lily's lips rolled against her teeth, like she was trying to eat the words rising inside of her. Her eyes seared a hole into his skull, but he ignored her and finished laying out the utensils.

"Shall we?"

For the first time since Aria's disappearance, the entire Hale family sat at the dinner table together. Alessa scanned everyone's faces. If you didn't peer too closely, they looked like the picture-perfect family. She felt like she was the only one who noticed the cracks in the foundation.

Lily held out both her hands and looked at them all expectantly. Alessa and Joshua caught on immediately and clasped hands for their pre-dinner prayer. Aria's face froze in an empty stare.

"It's time to say grace, Aria," Lily said. Below her voice, Alessa heard a deep rumble, like the rolling of an earthquake under their feet. Much to Alessa's relief, Aria followed along, one hand in Lily's, and one hand in her sister's. Lily, Joshua, and Alessa bowed their heads as Lily began.

"Dear Lord, make us truly grateful for these and all the other many blessings," their mother droned, smooth as silk.

Aria's hand tightened around Alessa's. She looked up. Aria's eyes screwed shut, and her breath was coming in short pants.

"Bless this food for the nourishment in our bodies, and us to thy service. In Christ's name, we pray. Amen."

"Amen," Joshua and Alessa echoed.

The second their fingers loosened their grip; Aria ripped her hands away and stuffed them between her thighs. Lily glowered at her. Alessa knew what she was waiting for. Aria didn't say 'amen', an insult considered sacrilegious in their house. Lily surprised Alessa by turning away, choosing not to comment. No one made a move to lift their utensils until Lily did.

Soon the room filled with the sounds of forks scraping against plates, and the occasional request to pass another dish around. Alessa glanced at Aria periodically as she filled her plate. Her sister's movements were methodical. She noticed Aria was watching them too, analyzing their choices and how they scooped it from the bowls. When she did the same, it looked more like she was mimicking them. Alessa looked at Aria's plate, a curious wrinkle knitting between her brows. Aria chose the same side dishes as Alessa and arranged them in the same pattern.

Alessa fought against her lack of appetite with every bite. Each one felt like tar gripping her throat as it slid down. She wasn't sure how much more of this silence she could take. Alessa gulped down some water. Her hand was shaking.

"S-So, what time are you guys going to church tonight?"

Lily's eyes rose over the table to meet Alessa's. She took a dainty bite of her steak, unhurried. Another beat passed as she dabbed the corners of her mouth with her napkin.

"Father Samuel is generously giving us an opportunity to plead our case."

Alessa balked at the notion they needed to plead for anything from that man. Lily's glare kept her quiet.

"He admitted that his reactions have been a bit rash, but we need to take responsibility for what happened here the other day. There's no excuse for what Aria did, and him extending an olive branch at all is incredibly kind of him."

All the arguments she wanted to make, all the information Alessa gathered, were burning like hot coals in her mouth. She could tell them what she knew of all her suspicions. Ultimately, she chewed them up and swallowed them down, because without confirmation from Maya, she had nothing firm to back up her claims.

CHAPTER 26

"Everything is delicious, Lily. You've really outdone yourself," Joshua said.

"Thank you, dear."

He turned to Aria. "Ari, is everything okay? Looks like you haven't touched your food."

All heads swiveled. Aria didn't look back. She remained focused on her plate, absently scooting the food around, and never once bringing the fork to her lips.

"Are you still not hungry?" he continued. Lily scowled.

"How can she not be hungry? She's barely eaten in days."

Aria looked awful. Anyone who shot a passing glance her way at this point would notice it. She was thinner than ever, and she looked ill. Alessa saw from Joshua's expression it was plainly obvious to him as well.

"You don't look so good, sweetheart. Are you sure you're feeling up to this?" he asked, ignoring the way Lily's eyes darkened.

Aria shrugged; her food becoming one giant, formless pile. The sharp clang of Lily slamming her fork and knife down made all of them to stiffen. Lily cast a glare full of ice and steel at Aria.

"Enough. I've had enough of this, Aria. I've spent hours slaving away in that kitchen to make a beautiful meal for this family. I took time out of my day to ensure everyone sitting at this table had something they wanted, you most especially. And all you do is turn your nose up at it," Lily taunted.

"Now, Lily..."

She whirled on her husband, cheeks blooming bright red. "I don't want to hear another word out of you. All you've done is enable this ridiculous behavior. She doesn't need you to be her friend Joshua. She needs you to be her father!"

Alessa didn't dare move as her mother's rage unfurled like a corpse flower.

"This is no longer a matter for debate, Aria. Doctor Sutton says you need to eat so, you are going to eat, even if I have to stuff it down your throat myself."

"Mom!" Alessa blanched, horrified.

Aria closed her eyes to block Lily out, but it only fueled her. Pressing her palms into the table, Lily rose from her seat.

"Your father and I have been through enough, young lady! You're going to stop being a disrespectful, little brat and eat this lovely dinner I prepared for you. Do you understand me?"

Aria finally looked at her. Alessa's heart stuttered at the familiarity of the scene. She remembered her mother standing in Aria's room, veins pulsing in her neck and temples as she screamed, waving a joint in her hands.

I'll ask one more time. How fucking long have you been smoking for?

"Are you even fucking listening to me, Aria?" Lily shouted.

Automatically, Aria grinned, her lips tugged as if by puppet strings.

"Profanity, wow Mom, that's not very godly of you."

Alessa stopped-dead, the words hitting her with the force of a semi-truck. She recognized those words, and from Lily's expression, and the sudden ghostly pallor of her face, Alessa could tell she remembered it too.

"What... what did you just say to me?" Lily asked.

"I..." Aria paused, brows narrowing. "I don't remember."

All hell broke loose. Lily, incensed by Aria's comment, kicked her chair to the side and stormed to her daughter's side. Before Alessa or her father had a second to react, she grabbed Aria's jaw in a harsh grip, jerking her head to the side. She snatched Aria's fork and scooped a heaping chunk of food. Lily held it to her Aria's lips, nails forming crescent moon shapes in her chin.

"Mom! What are you doing?" Alessa said, lunging out of her seat. Joshua followed suit, stunned into silence.

"Sit down, Alessa!"

"Lily, just leave her alone. She doesn't feel well," Joshua pleaded. Lily simply ignored him, barely a speed bump on the road to her ultimate goal. Alessa sat helpless and watching.

Aria held Lily's eyes and wordlessly rose to the challenge. She opened her mouth and shoved the fork in, forcing her mouth closed. She refused to let go until Aria swallowed it all down.

Alessa's eyes burned with tears. She wanted to look away but felt pulled to watch, to witness every horrible second. Disgust coiled in her like a venomous snake when she noticed her father's eyes downcast in shame and resignation. So much for being helpful.

Lily finally ripped her hand away and tossed the fork down. She returned to her seat, smoothing her clothes and hair as if nothing ever happened, and sat back down with a content sigh.

"There. That wasn't so difficult."

Lily went back to eating, taking small, delicate bites. Alessa no longer had an appetite. She wanted to say something, to scream at the top of her lungs, and eviscerate her mother with the vilest insults she could fathom. They simmered on her tongue, but she struggled to open her mouth. The placid expression on Lily's face when she stared back at Alessa made all of her courage shrivel and crumble like a dying flower.

The scariest part was not her mother's rage, it was a black emptiness residing behind her eyes. In that darkness, demons writhed. Alessa slowly lowered back into her chair.

A gurgle to her right snatched her attention, and even though she worried breaking eye contact with Lily would somehow cause the woman to lash out, she looked away anyway. The choking noises came from Aria, who looked three shades whiter than before, the pink of her lips fading completely. Her mouth pressed into a razor thin line, hand quivering over her face. Alessa saw it: impending doom, but there was nothing she could do to stop it.

Aria lurched forward and vomited. Stomach bile and chunks of undigested food splattered all over the table. Lily screamed, all three of them scrambling to get out of the line of fire. Aria tried to stop the flow, but a few spurts dribbled from between the gaps between her fingers.

"Jesus Christ!" Joshua yelled, back pressed flat against the nearest wall. Alessa had to smother her nose in the crook of her elbow.

"What the fuck? What *the fuck!*" Lily had well and truly lost it. Vomit covered the table, including the food. Lily held her arms aloft, her body shaking. Some of the puke stained her perfectly assembled outfit, discoloring it with brown and red.

Wait, red? Alessa quirked her head to check the table again. Mixed in with the gnarled chunks of undigested food, and stomach acids, was blood—a lot of it.

Aria gulped in a heaping breath and released a delirious cackle.

"Tastes like shit," Aria snickered, bile and blood still glistening on her lips.

Lily's face went crimson, all her anger frothing at the surface. She released an ungodly, wretched scream and lunged, flat palm raising high in the air. Lily brought it down on Aria's face.

"Mom—STOP!" Alessa shrieked.

The impact never came. Just before her palm cracked across Aria's cheek, Aria snatched her wrist mid swipe, so fast Alessa never saw her arm move. Lily's jaw dropped; dumbfounded. Their eyes locked. All traces of Aria's delirium washed away, replaced with a steely glare. Lily tried to pull away, but Aria's grip was hard as stone and just as immovable.

Screams erupted when Aria shoved their mother onto the table, smashing Lily through the wood. The table split in half, glass shattered, food went flying.

"Oh God, Lily! Lily, are you all right?" Joshua rushed to her aid. Her eyes fluttered, lips flapping as unintelligible whimpers and mumbles escaped her.

"Are you hurt?" Joshua hovered over Lily, checking her for injuries. She squealed with pain as she tried to lift her right arm, which had folded under her body during impact.

Blood ran in rivulets down her arm from a gash sliced into her forearm by the broken glass. Joshua immediately grabbed a few washcloths to staunch the blood, applying pressure even as Lily hissed and tried to lean away.

Aria's eyes were rooted to the blood spurting from her veins. Her gold eyes shined brighter than ever. She licked her lips and stepped toward them.

"Alessa!" Joshua yelled. "Get over here and help me."

It was then that Alessa realized she'd been crying. She wiped her moist face and approached Aria cautiously.

"Ari, Ari, it's okay. It's over now, you don't have to eat anything. Let's just go to bed, okay?" she pleaded. When Aria didn't respond, Alessa placed a trembling hand on her arm.

Aria hardened, her eyes practically shooting out of their sockets the moment Alessa touched her. Aria glanced up to see the carnage, her father pressing a reddening cloth to a cut on her mother's arm. Aria looked at Alessa, glittering with unshed tears. "What did I do?"

"You..." Lily grumbled dangerously as Joshua lifted her to her feet, "I want her out of my sight."

She didn't waste another second. Alessa pulled Aria toward her, hoping to any God that might be listening that she would follow. A relieved sigh left her when Aria moved easily. She stumbled over the edge of the carpet, but Alessa was right there to keep her upright. Aria's bones dug into Alessa's side; she weighed nothing. Aria tried to look back at their parents, but her head lolled like it was too heavy for her shoulders.

"I'm so... I'm sorry," Aria whispered, barely loud enough for them to hear. Alessa didn't stop to check if they did. A dull ache permeated in her chest as she helped her frail sister up the stairs and back into her room. The tears flowed freely from Aria now, each step punctuated with a whimper or a sniffle.

By the time Alessa got them inside Aria's room, her sister was ready to collapse. She fell against Alessa, frantic hands gripping at her clothing, and face shining wet in the light. Alessa thought of that night in their father's office. She tasted the desperation in the air.

"I'm sorry—I'm so sorry! I didn't mean it... I don't—I don't want to hurt anyone!"

The switch in Aria's personality gave Alessa whiplash. It was impossible to keep up. One second, she was wading through a fog, uncaring of the world around her, and the next she was a terrified young girl again.

"Please... please Lessa, you have to know I didn't mean it."

The words broke Alessa from the inside out. Instantly, she threw her arms around Aria, marveling at how fragile she was. Her clavicle was jutting out, pressing into Alessa's chest. Aria wept into her hair, body convulsing, but Alessa only held her tighter. She never wanted to let go again.

"I know, Ari. I know. It's okay," Alessa soothed her, choking back sobs of her own. Aria was always the strong one between the two of them. Now it was Alessa's turn to be strong for her sister.

They stood in the same spot until Aria's convulsions faded into a soft tremble. When her whimpering stopped, Alessa pulled away.

"Let's get you into bed."

"Stay with me?" Aria asked, startling her. Alessa nodded without hesitation.

"Of course. I'm not going anywhere."

CHAPTER 26

Alessa and Aria's hands remained intertwined as they climbed into bed. They settled into the warm mattress, facing each other, and pulled the heavy comforter over themselves. Their woven fingers rested between them. Aria was quiet for so long Alessa started to drift off, but the moment her voice broke the silence, she jerked back awake.

"Tell me a story..."

"A story?" Alessa asked, blinking the sleep from her eyes.

"Something from when we were kids."

Alessa searched her memory. She wanted one with levity, one that could take Aria's mind away from all of this. A tiny smile lifted her expression when she thought of just the right one. She giggled to herself, just thinking about it.

"Okay, well. There was that one time when I got that really bad stomach bug, and Mom let us hang out in their bed while I got better. You were looking after me while Dad was at work, and she went to the store to get me some medicine. I think I was taking a nap.

"Anyway, I felt terrible when I woke up and couldn't make it to the bathroom. Mom's bedsheets were totally ruined! Just puke everywhere. I was freaking out and crying, knowing Mom was going to be pissed, but I could barely stand up. So, you know what you did?"

Aria listened with rapt attention and shook her head. Alessa chuckled but tried to muffle it behind her hand.

"You went into the medicine cabinet and got one of Mom's face masks, put the dishwashing gloves on, and got to work. You stripped the bed, gagging the whole time, and raced around the house trying to get everything clean so she wouldn't find out. I couldn't stop crying, but you kept a cool head, even though you were just as frantic as I was.

"Mom found out anyway, but she let us off pretty easy after she saw all the trouble you went to."

The corners of Aria's mouth twitched into the barest hint of a smile and her eyes drooped. Aria fell asleep first, their pinkies still hooked. Alessa was slipping away, too. When Alessa finally gave in, she pictured her sister standing over their bleeding mother, red splintering through the amber in her irises.

Chapter 27

The energy in the house was indelibly altered when Alessa awoke the next morning. She heard no rustling or movement from downstairs. She dreaded getting out of bed, wishing she could bury her face in the pillow and hide as the world spun on without her. Alessa remained bundled until the last possible second, just listening to the calming rhythm of Aria's breathing. Eventually, she had to get ready for school.

Unsettling nausea lingered as she got dressed, and a tight band of anxiety cinched around her chest. Several times, while picking out an outfit, she leaned on a piece of furniture to catch her breath. She struggled to pinpoint where the fear originated from. It was everywhere, embedded in her skin and hovering in the surrounding air. Her brain droned with static as she went downstairs.

If she hadn't immediately seen her father sipping coffee on the couch, she would have thought the house was empty, it was so quiet. Alessa realized they'd fallen asleep before her parent's trip to the church to meet with Father Samuel. She was immensely curious about what happened, but from the way her dad made a concerted effort not to look at her, she thought it best not to bring it up. Not after what happened at dinner. She dipped into the kitchen to grab a banana.

Lily was standing over the sink staring out the window. She held her bandaged arm across her chest while fiddling with her cross pendant.

The colorful bowl spilling over with bananas and other colorful fruit was sitting on the counter right next to her.

"M-Morning, Mom," Alessa said. "Are you—is your arm okay?"

At first, Lily didn't turn, and Alessa wondered if she heard her. She opened her mouth to reiterate until her mother spoke.

"Fine, dear. I'm just fine."

Lily was shockingly calm. This was the last thing Alessa was expecting. Under any other circumstances, she'd be riding them about their behavior for days—and for much lesser offenses. Alessa had a brief but deeply disquieting sense that she'd somehow hopped into an alternate universe. She pinched her palm until it bled, just to make sure she wasn't dreaming.

Her mother finally turned around, resting her hip against the counter, expression placid and cool. There was even the hint of a smile playing at the corners of her mouth. Alessa ripped a piece of skin from her hand. Lily gestured to the bowl.

"Want a snack for the road?"

Not anymore. The idea of putting anything in her stomach was revolting, but Alessa wasn't about to rock the boat now. Lily held one out to her but didn't make a move to come any closer. Alessa took careful, measured steps forward. Each one felt like she was going to the gallows. Lily only smiled.

"Are you sure that you're okay, Mom?"

Lily tilted her head in a way that made her feel ridiculous for even asking. Alessa sucked in a sharp breath through her nose when her mother moved closer. She was seconds from bolting out the door when Lily tucked her into a gentle embrace. Alessa was too stunned to move.

"Did you sleep well last night?" her mother asked.

"Uh, yeah. Yeah, it was good."

Lily leaned back to examine her face. She brushed a few strands from her face and patted her cheeks warmly. "Promise me you'll be careful getting to and from school?"

What the hell was going on?

"Sure. I-I mean, yes, of course," she replied, eager to keep the peace. Lily smiled.

"Good. Come home straight after, okay? I've been thinking more and more about all these sudden disappearances, and I would just feel better if you were here in the afternoons. At least for a little while."

It was honestly the most reasonable request she'd ever made. Normally, it wouldn't even be a request, it would be a demand. Alessa nodded; dumbstruck. Lily appeared genuinely grateful. She leaned and planted a kiss on Alessa's forehead before returning to the sink. Alessa fiddled with her banana and glanced at the landline. She remembered Maya.

"Did I get any phone calls or messages last night?"

"No, I don't think so. Were you expecting one?"

Alessa shrugged. "Nothing really. Maya said she would call, that's all. Maybe I should try her."

Lily checked the time on the stove. "If you don't go now, you'll be late. I'm sure you'll see her at school."

She had a point. As much as Alessa wanted to make that call there wasn't much point when she'd be seeing her in a few minutes. Talking face-to-face would be better, anyway.

"Okay, love you," Alessa replied with one last wave.

"Love you too, sweetheart. And remember—straight home."

Alessa gave a confirming nod and headed out, giving her father a brief kiss on the cheek as a farewell. He was a mess. His hair was in knots, and dark bags had formed under his eyes. Joshua didn't look at her when he mumbled goodbye, and it reminded her of the days following Aria's disappearance—of how he abandoned her when she needed him most. She tried to ignore the piercing sting it caused. Alessa muttered a quick and clipped goodbye before storming out.

Alessa's first and only thought as she approached the school was finding Maya. She stood in their normal spot at the bottom of the steps, hands clenched in the pockets of her winter coat. She scanned every head of black hair she saw, but none of them were Maya. Hordes of students brushed past her as they made their way inside. To most of them, she was invisible, to others she was a specimen to be stared at. Whispers and gossip bounced around her.

"Did you guys hear about Mrs. Anderson?"

"My grandma is friends with her. I heard she never showed up for her shift this morning. And she never does that."

The chilling winter air seeped into her bones. She pictured Gloria's kind smile and her earnestness. Had she gone missing too?

The bell rang, but Alessa wasn't ready to go inside. There was still no sign of Maya or even Noah. It was possible he was running late, but this was out of character for Maya. On the days she wasn't going to show up, she always left a message. The few remaining students on the front lawn were trickling in and she followed them, but each step felt torturous.

Her stomach felt like it was being pulled apart when she sat down in her first period. The teacher stepped up to the blackboard to start the lesson. It went in one ear and out the other. Alessa told herself she would see Noah at lunch, and God willing Maya too.

Maybe, if she repeated it enough times, she would start to believe it.

By the time lunch rolled around, Alessa was completely wired. Her stomach groaned angrily, but she had no desire to eat. Alessa stared at the food, her mind drifting away as students screamed and cajoled around her.

"Holy crap, finally."

A plastic tray slid into the spot next to hers. Noah fell into the seat to her left. His eyes were puffy and red veins splintered through the whites of his eyes, but his energy was electric.

CHAPTER 27

"Where were you this morning? I was waiting for you!" Her tone was more shaken than accusatory. He grimaced.

"I know, I'm so sorry. My parents were up my ass this morning. It was hard to shake them."

"Everything okay?"

"I think this whole 'librarian going missing thing' is the last straw for them. Mom's been wound tight ever since Aria came home, but now she's ultra-paranoid. She's convinced it's going to happen again."

Alessa didn't disagree with her. Five days since Aria's return and four more people were gone, like they were blipping out of existence.

"Everything is going to hell."

Her head dropped, and Noah frowned. Alessa described what transpired over their family dinner the night before: her mother's cruelty, and her sister's violence. Noah fidgeted in his chair but remained quiet and attentive until she was done. The pain in his eyes seared her soul.

"I don't know how their meeting with Father Samuel went. We fell asleep before they left. And after what happened last night, I didn't want to—"

"Pry?" he filled in with a nod. "I get that. And Maya never called?"

"No. I asked Mom if I got any messages overnight but there weren't any, and she didn't show up for school this morning. She always lets me know when she's going to be out, and with everything going on at the church..." Alessa rambled. Noah grabbed her shoulder reassuringly.

"Hey now—one step at a time," he said. She clamped her mouth shut, embarrassed. He smiled reassuringly and began rummaging through his bag. "How about we try calling her at home? Maybe she just hasn't been able to reach out yet."

Noah held out his burner cell, and every fiber in her being wanted to embrace him. Anything was better than sitting here and waiting.

Her reaction must have been enough because he flipped the phone open and had her type in Maya's number before she ever replied. They huddled together, and he held the phone between them as it rang. On the third chime, Maya's mother Clarissa answered.

"Walker residence." Her voice was smooth and honey-sweet. Alessa had always liked Maya's mother. She was reserved and well-spoken and had a maternal warmth she didn't recognize in her own mom. Hearing her brought immediate comfort.

"Yes, hello Mrs. Walker! It's Alessa. I was just wondering if Maya was home. I was a little worried when she didn't show up for school this morning and wanted to make sure she was okay."

There was a stretch of silence that lasted long enough that Alessa wondered if Clarissa had hung up the phone. Eventually, the woman cleared her throat.

"Oh, Alessa. Hello," Clarissa's tone sharpened into steel. Noah's eyes widened in shock.

So much for honey-sweet.

Clarissa sighed, not bothering to hide her annoyance. "Maya isn't feeling well today. She's sick."

Alessa waited for her to elaborate, but she didn't. What the hell was going on? Normally, Maya's mother was kind, if not downright adoring towards her. Had she done something to piss them off? A dense, cold weight coiled in her stomach. Of course, she had. She dragged Maya into all of this drama. Father Samuel was obviously furious with her family, so it made sense the rest of them would be tense toward her as well.

"Oh. I'm sorry to hear that." Alessa rolled her eyes at herself for sounding so ridiculous. "Would it be all right if I spoke to her?"

Clarissa grunted or scoffed. Alessa wasn't sure. "No, Alessa. You may not. Maya is asleep, and frankly, I find it rude of you to pester us in the middle of the day. You've dragged my daughter into enough of your family's nonsense."

Alessa sucked in a pained gasp as her cutting words, each one a new laceration to her already mangled heart. Noah paled beside her. She felt him squeeze her arm in reassurance.

"M-Mrs. Walker, I'm really sorry—I didn't mean to get Maya into any trouble! She was only trying to be a good friend to me."

"I don't want to hear excuses. You and your family will all face consequences soon enough."

It was like she had doused Alessa in a bucket of ice water. Consequences. Was that supposed to be some sort of threat?

"What do you mean?" Alessa stammered.

"I will pray for you and your sister, Alessa. I will. But do not call us again."

"Wait- Clarissa!" Alessa shouted into the phone, pulling the attention of kids from the surrounding tables, but she'd already hung up.

Alessa could only stare at the phone, jaw gaping. Noah slowly took it from her hands and slid it back into his pocket. They sat in silence for a while after, neither one wanting to speak first.

"I can swing by the church after school," Noah said. Alessa looked at him like he was crazy.

"What?"

"You and I both know Maya isn't sick. Our best option is to go back to the church and see if we can find what she was looking for."

He was right, and honestly, it felt good to have someone else say what she was thinking.

"You'd be alone. My mom wants me back home right after school. No detours for me today."

Noah's expression hardened. "That's fine. Better even. Things are still tense between your family and hers, but I haven't been involved in much. Father Samuel is good friends with my parents. He respects them. If I put on the charm, I might be able to weasel my way in."

As much as she hated the idea of sending him in alone, she didn't have much of a choice. And if anyone was going to get in there, it was Noah. The golden, Christian boy, with the megawatt smile. Everyone in Pine Hollow loved Noah and his parents, they were well-respected business owners and beloved parishioners. Out of the two of them, he had the best chance of succeeding. Alessa gripped his hand with force.

"You better call me after. I'm serious. Swear to me that you will call the second you find anything."

He held her hand back just as tightly. "I swear."

Chapter 28

Aria sat on the floor of her bedroom, surrounded by photographs. After she rose peacefully from the first dreamless sleep she'd had in months, she slid from the bed and poked through the overstuffed bookshelf. She'd barely glanced at it since returning, but she was always aware of it. It loomed like a specter in the corner of the room, the colorful spines of the books and albums calling to her.

It didn't feel right before, to look at them, or even touch them, like it was a violation somehow. Today it was different. She didn't know how or why, but it was in the air. Finality. Ending. Profound and gutting. It compelled her to pick up the leather-bound photo album on the second shelf, and then the red one, and then another, until they encircled her.

The divide that cracked open within her, that separated her and this other, fought to sew itself together. Neurons desperately attempted to transmit information across synapses, connecting in certain places but not others. Aria forced herself to look at every face in every photo, some she instantly recognized, but others remained indistinct and puzzling.

It was becoming harder to bridge those gaps, to press against the hollowness that was spreading like an infection, not only in her blood but in her nerves, in the soft grey matter of her brain. The other was growing stronger, cold, dark, and hungry. Oh, so hungry. It submerged Aria up to her neck.

Should she close her eyes, lie back, and slip into it willingly? It would be so easy; she could finally rest. And she was so tired.

Aria flipped to the next page in the album and found a photograph of her and Alessa right in the center. They were much younger, maybe middle school aged. Alessa's face was still a round like a little cherub, her cheeks full and pink. They were both grinning ear to ear, entangled in each other's arms. The picture brought forth a memory, a thin beam of light in the dark, of the pair playing in the garden at the height of spring, drunk on the childlike energy of just being alive. It was a beautiful day.

Aria placed her palm against the picture and took a deep breath, as if she could drink in the memories and make them part of her again. The light pushed back against the other. Not for good, and she was sure not for long, but it gave her a chance to breathe, her brain fog dissipating. The tiniest of smiles graced her features as she continued to stare at the picture. Alessa. Her sister. Little Squirt.

Aria felt the sudden urge to cry, a painful lump climbing up the back of her throat. She hoped in the deepest parts of her twisted and mangled soul that Alessa knew just how much she loved her. Even through all of this insanity. She hoped she had the chance to tell her.

A knock at the door took her attention away from the albums. She glanced over her shoulder and watched the door creak open, and Joshua's head poked through the gap.

"Can I come in?" Joshua asked. When she met his gaze, it lowered to the floor in shame.

"Yes," she stated, more so out of curiosity than anything else. He smiled, relieved, and entered, the door clicking shut behind him. He stood over her, examining her floor display before sitting on the floor next to her.

"Wow, look at all of this." His face lit up as he began sifting through the pictures.

There was a mixture of photos, some of Aria in groups, some of just her, and others didn't feature her at all, but you knew just at a glance that she was the one behind the camera. Shots of nature, squirrels on branches, leaves falling from trees, the crest of the mountain tops blurred white with mist. Each one expressed her unbridled love for the world around her, and all it had to offer. The visions of a girl eager to explore. They were stunning.

"You did all these?"

Aria nodded without thinking, but she supposed it was true. It felt true, even if she didn't remember all of them.

"They're incredible," he said, his expression faltering, "you really have an amazing talent."

Joshua glanced at the pictures plastered upon the walls as well, each one holding a treasured story. "I guess I didn't realize how much you really loved this stuff."

Aria said nothing. His lips trembled as he tried to hold his smile.

"I guess that's on me for not paying enough attention, huh?"

Joshua finally met her eyes and held them, his filling with tears.

"You've always been so incredibly talented, Aria. I know I haven't said it enough, and I'm sorry for that. I let myself get caught up in other things. But I want you to know how wonderful I've always thought you are. Ever since you were a little girl, you've always been one hundred percent unapologetically you. And I admire you for that."

His voice was raw with emotion. It rattled her. Her hand moved before she could stop it. The desire to comfort was overwhelming. Joshua tensed when she grabbed his hand. He stared at her hand for a few long seconds, but she ripped it away just as he was about to reciprocate, stuffing it back into her lap. Aria turned her attention back to the pictures, flipping through the album again while he watched.

"Are these... um... are they helping at all with your memory?"

Aria only distantly heard his question. She noticed a group picture of the entire family. It was taken in their dining room, and they were standing, framed by balloons, in front of a still lit birthday cake with the words "Happy Birthday, Aria!" in blue icing. In it, Aria was wearing a green dress.

"This one..." she mumbled. Joshua perked up.

"Hm?"

Aria saw a series of images: her and her father sniping at each other in his office, her mother dragging her outside to talk with Father Samuel, and at the end of it all, her mother's slap. Her hand flew to her cheek. It burned with the echo of two vicious hits. Joshua was still talking, but she didn't hear him.

Aria saw herself crying as her mother stormed out of the room and slammed the door behind her. She watched from outside of her body as it immediately moved to the bookshelf and pulled out a hefty photography book from the fourth shelf. It shoved its arm into the space the book left behind and slid out a small, brown journal.

Following the memory, Aria looked over her shoulder at the shelf once again, even as her father rambled on and found the photography book in question. There it was, sitting on the fourth shelf as innocently as ever, where no one would believe she had hidden something.

The memory shattered when another knock reverberated against her door.

"Joshua," Lily spoke through the door, somewhat muffled, "Chief Roswell and Deputy Shirley are here."

Joshua and Aria were silent at first, and he looked just as surprised as she felt. When Lily spoke again, she sounded far less patient.

"You both need to come downstairs. Now."

Aria and Joshua met Lily in the living room, where Roswell and Shirley were waiting patiently. They both sat on the couch, hands

CHAPTER 28

folded. Roswell smiled at Aria directly when she came in, but it looked painfully forced. He knew something.

"Can I get either of you anything to drink? I just finished making another batch of coffee," Lily asked.

"No thank you, Lily. We're all right," Roswell declined, "we won't be long."

"What brings you both here this morning?" Joshua questioned, trying to keep the energy light. Shirley met him with a grim frown.

"We've received some... unfortunate news," she said, looking to Roswell for him to finish.

"What is it?" Joshua continued, sitting across from them with Lily. Aria remained standing; she was too restless to sit still. The urge to run struck her again, but she tampered it down with a few deep breaths. The other inside of her thrashed wildly.

"Well, we have two pieces of information for you. The first is that Mrs. Anderson, our lovely librarian, has been added to the list of missing persons."

"Oh my God," Lily gasped.

Aria didn't flinch. She did not remember, nor care for, this faceless name. It was simply one of many to her. She did notice, however, the other seemed to cease in its relentless fury the moment these words left Roswell's mouth.

"But that's not the main reason we're here," Shirley added, "we received the test results from Doctor Sutton regarding the blood found on Aria when she returned. It turns out the blood is a match for the remains we found in the woods before she came home."

Joshua and Lily looked gob smacked. However, this revelation didn't surprise Aria. When the truth settled in, she felt no different from before—no, that wasn't right—she did feel different. Somehow, she cared even less.

"We are going to need to bring Aria into the station for proper questioning," Roswell finished. Joshua shot up from his seat.

"Wait, wait. There has to be a mistake. There's no way this is possible. Aria isn't capable of something like this!"

"Honey, please," Lily started, but Joshua lifted his hand to shut her down. Her eyes widened.

"No. No, I've had enough of this. Our daughter has done nothing wrong. She's traumatized! And all anyone is concerned about is making sure this awful, terrible thing is tied to her. Aria is not a violent person."

Roswell stood as well. His voice was as calm as the open sea.

"We understand how this all must sound to you, Mr. Hale. But we assure you, Doctor Sutton is a professional. He had the blood tested and re-tested. We know for certain that it matches."

Joshua opened his mouth to speak, but his words failed him.

"There are no mistakes here, Mr. Hale. We've seen the results ourselves," Roswell added.

"This is not us trying to accuse your daughter of anything. But I'm sure you can understand, under these circumstances and what we've been faced with, we need to know what Aria knows," Shirley said.

"But..." he started, trailing off with a pathetic whimper, "she's good. You guys know her—you *both know her!*"

Shirley rose from her seat next. "Please, Joshua. It's the only option we have. We promise, this is not a personal attack on you or your family. But we need to do our job."

Her subdued tone soothed the tension in Joshua's muscles, but his reluctance was evident in his expression. Lily merely sat and watched, face unreadable. She never once spoke up in Aria's defense. She didn't even glance in her direction. Aria scanned everyone in the room. This was only going one way, regardless of if they wanted it or not.

Aria considered running. She could be out the door and behind the tree line before they even noticed. The other preened at the idea.

CHAPTER 28

It longed for the wilderness, but her instincts, the ones she knew belonged to her and only her, told her to stay. The image of her sister's tormented face rose to her mind.

No. Aria would not run again. At least, not without her sister.

While she still had some partial control over her mind, Aria determined the path of least resistance was best. Maybe if they saw how rational she was, they would take it easy on her. Then she could at least avoid further pain.

"I'll go," she said, and all eyes were on her. Their shared expression of shock was comical. None of them expected her to give in so easily. Joshua turned white.

"I can come with you. You shouldn't be alone," he bumbled and hurriedly snatched up his belongings. Roswell cleared his throat.

"Aria is a legal adult now, Mr. Hale. We'll be questioning her on her own. She's not under arrest, at least not yet. For now, we just need information."

Joshua refused to look at him. "Do you want me there? All you need to do is ask."

"Mr. Hale, we currently have enough evidence to bring her in with or without your consent," Roswell's voice boomed, chest puffing up with authority. The air thickened with tension, and Aria could taste it; metallic and bitter.

Irises chiseled from pure ice stared impassively at Aria from the couch. Lily never blinked, but Aria noticed the tiny tick in her jaw. Only Aria heard her grinding her teeth into dust. Heat sizzled and boiled under that wintry façade.

The other pushed against her temples, the pressure making her eyes ache. She rubbed them; God, she was tired.

Sweet Aria...

It was as though the other was whispering over her shoulder. So sweet and gentle. They could lure her right to sleep.

Aria with dark fluid warming her neck and chest. A dark hallway. A familiar figure in the moonlight – Alessa – staring at her in sleepy confusion. Hunger soothed for the first time.

Her head felt like a swelling balloon that was about to pop.

Knees buried in snow. A male voice in the distance. She was screaming for help.

Jason...

...Jason...

Clara.

CLARA.

Aria's eyes flew open. She tried to force her memory further, beyond the names, beyond the pain and the hunger. Who were Jason and Clara? Aria wondered, guilt burrowing its talons into her chest. When she closed her eyes, all she saw was blood. In the snow, on her hands, and in her hair.

Oh, God... Aria thought. *I've done something terrible.*

What felt like minutes to her had apparently only lasted a few milliseconds to the rest of the room. Joshua was becoming increasingly agitated with Roswell's attitude. He looked surprisingly ready for a fight, given that Aria had never seen him raise a hand to anyone. She had to end this before it got out of hand.

"It's fine," Aria interrupted. Joshua looked at her pleadingly.

"Are you sure?"

"She's made her decision," Lily stated.

Aria found it vaguely amusing that out of all the times her mother could have had her back, she chose now.

"I'm sure. I want to help," Aria said. Maybe Chief Roswell and Father Samuel had been right all along. Maybe she truly was something to be feared. She glanced at her mother's bandaged hand, the memory already dull as dishwater, and fading fast.

How much time until there was nothing left of her mind? Nothing but this other? Aria shuddered. She didn't want to imagine it.

Joshua moaned in defeat, mouth pulling into a resigned frown as he shook his head.

"Just let me get my coat," Aria added. Roswell was initially reluctant, but she held his eyes with an open and honest expression, and eventually, he responded.

"All right. Be quick."

Aria responded by nodding in kind and went upstairs to her room. She didn't bother closing the door behind her. Instead, Aria went straight to the bookshelf, and pulled out the huge tome she'd seen in her memories. She peered into the dark space behind it and shoved her arm inside. Her fingers poked and prodded until they brushed smooth leather, and once she had a firm grip, she gave it a tug. Aria marveled at the small object.

A worn, brown journal. Well-loved, frayed at the edges, with an 'A' burned into the bottom corner.

Chapter 29

The interview room at the Pine Hollow Police Station wasn't much to look at. They didn't have the fancy two-way mirrors Aria and Alessa always saw in cop shows. There was no budget for such things. It was simple, with four blank, white walls, a camera sitting on a tripod, and a table with three chairs. Aria sat on one side, the officers on the other. The fluorescent light above their head was peppered with bug carcasses and released a continuous buzzing noise that made Aria's ears ring.

Aria stayed quiet the entire car ride, and though Roswell and Shirley refrained from asking her any questions until she was processed. She sensed their impatience. It was vibrating in the surrounding air. She became distracted by something darting by the window. Her doppelgänger appeared wherever she looked, seamlessly keeping up with their speed despite not moving. It watched her, smiling, from the darkness of the alleys, the reflections of store windows, and from within clusters of people milling about on the sidewalk. An eerie constant in an ever-shifting sea. Aria looked at the seat in front of her just to get away from it.

She wondered if it was still out there now, watching the station. Aria could almost feel its black, hollow eyes on her now.

"Ms. Hale, just so you're aware, we'll be recording this conversation." Aria didn't answer as Shirley pressed the record button on

CHAPTER 29

the camera and the red light blinked to life. She knew it wasn't a question. After they finished setting up the camera, both officers got comfortable at the table across from her.

"The date is September 10th, 2022, and it is currently 4:14 P.M. Questioning is being conducted by myself, Chief Gavin Roswell, and Deputy Chief Shirley Powell." He paused and locked eyes with Aria. "Please state your name for the record."

"Aria Hale."

"Thank you. Aria, we are going to be questioning you regarding the human remains found on September 5th, 2022. Do you understand?"

She nodded.

"Good." Roswell slid out a folder and placed it on the table between them before flipping it open. The first item he pulled out was a glossy photograph of a couple. They wore hiking gear and posed on a cliff overlooking a beautiful golden sunset. A camera dangled around the woman's neck. They looked unbelievably and inexplicably happy.

"Do you recognize this couple?"

He slid it across the table, facing her. Aria leaned forward; arms crossed as she analyzed it. Their faces unveiled nothing within her. There was no spark of recognition, no sudden moment of clarity.

"No."

"You sure you don't want to take a closer look?" he encouraged.

Jaw tightening, she gave the photo one last cursory glance before once more shaking her head. Roswell tensed, his shoulders rising toward his ears.

"Aria, it's extremely important that you're honest with us."

Her lips curled back in a snarl that revealed her teeth, her harsh, amber gaze slicing through him like a knife through butter.

"I told you. I don't remember," she spat. The light continued to buzz incessantly overhead. A migraine prickled at the base of her skull.

Shirley remained quiet but observant, clocking every minute change in Aria's expression. Aria suddenly devolved from calm and collected to frustrated and impatient. Every few seconds, she glanced up at the flickering light hanging above them, her mouth twisted with disdain.

"This is Clara Johansen and Jason Kershaw. They're Pine Hollow natives, both avid hikers, and Clara was a freelance photographer," Roswell explained. Aria merely shrugged. The names meant nothing to her. He sighed.

"All right." He took the photo back and whipped out another, placing it in front of her. "What about this one? Recognize anything?"

This picture was very different from the first. Aria's immediate thought was red, so much red. It depicted a woodland clearing with a thin layer of snow on the ground. All of it was drenched in red. Blood splattered on the ground, and across tree trunks. Puddles formed within trenches on the earth. Chunks of torn flesh and muscle sparkled in the afternoon sun. No immediate reaction came to her, but this photo was far more intriguing to her than the last. Aria slid the photo a little closer to get a better look.

Her head tilted, finger tracing the details on the paper, and her head lowering so much her nose almost brushed it. Blood rushed into Aria's ears the more she stared. The blood was so vivid she felt like she could reach through and touch it. Maybe even taste it. The other residing in her chest, in her mind, in her very soul, writhed like a ravenous beast. Her tongue darted out and wet her bottom lip slowly.

Shirley ripped the picture away from her. The beast in her raged-silent, but relentless. Aria pushed back against it, trying to regain a semblance of control, but she sensed herself fading. She only had so much time before the beast was all that remained. A growl threatened to burst from her throat, but she swallowed it down.

"Well," Roswell pressed; brow raised in challenge, "anything ring a bell?"

Irritation and exhaustion battled within her. She wanted to snap; she

CHAPTER 29

wanted to break something, but she also wanted to find the deepest, darkest hole and hide. Aria gave the picture another glance, but her mind was blank.

"No. Nothing."

"Their blood is an exact match to the blood that was found on your body when you returned from the woods," Roswell stated.

An echo of a long-forgotten shriek sounded from the distance. Aria's head shot up, eyes darting in all directions. Both officers were startled at her abrupt movement. They watched her, curious.

"Is everything all right?" Shirley asked.

Aria shot them a bewildered look. "You didn't hear that?"

They glanced at each other, exchanging some silent communication, before turning back to her.

"No. We didn't. What did you hear, Aria?"

Aria gave the room one more scan before sinking back into her chair. She shook her head, tightening her arms across her chest.

"Nothing."

Aria knew she didn't sound convincing, but she didn't care to. The scream reverberated in her ears. It wasn't even the scream itself that needled at her. It sounded so familiar. She'd heard that scream before.

Out in the woods, stark and freezing. She was on the ground and crying for help. A man broke through the bushes.

Aria snapped back to herself, vision going in and out of focus. Shirley tilted her head in concern as Aria rubbed her eyes. They smoldered in her skull, but the artificial light was inescapable.

"Aria, please. You can help us. We aren't trying to get you into a bind. We want to get to the bottom of this," Roswell said.

Anger flared in her chest. "You think I killed them?"

Roswell flinched, much to her pleasure. To his credit, he recovered quickly.

"That's not what we're saying. We have no idea what you've been through, but we have to work with what we know, and all we have right now are the remains of two people and a girl covered in their blood. Now, I've known you a long time, Aria. I watched you grow up into the lovely young lady you are now, and I can't imagine the sweet, compassionate little girl I once knew is capable of something so terrible. But how can I know without your side of the story?"

His words, his patience. It was enough to make her pride wither and her fury come hurtling back. The other pressed against her organs, expanding like a balloon. Aria pressed her clenched fists into her stomach, wishing she could rip it open and tear into the viscera herself. The nerves in her brain were being plucked like guitar strings, each strum sending a fresh wave of pain rippling across her skull.

Dirt under her fingers, skin split and bleeding. Her reflection in the creek. Gold—no—red eyes staring at her from the dark. They had been watching her... waiting for her.

She bit back a hiss, the memory shooting through her like a bullet. It was growing hot in here. She was sweating again, her clothes fitting too snug. Or was it her skin that was too tight?

"You just have to give us something. Any bit of information helps, even the things you might not think are important. Did you see anything strange? Did you encounter any other people aside from the hikers?"

This made her head shoot back up. She didn't encounter anyone else that she was aware of, but she had seen something out there in the woods. It saw her, too.

Hungry. Oh, she was so goddamn HUNGRY. Limbs made of jelly, her skin smarting with lacerations and purple bruises. A tree branch snapping. A hot growl wafting across the back of her neck.

There was definitely something out there with her. She let this sink in as she stared wide-eyed at the officers, both of them hanging on the edge of their seats and waiting for her to respond. She opened her

CHAPTER 29

mouth, ready to spew it all, but she stopped herself. Aria could tell them about the eyes, about the breath on her neck, and the constant feeling of being pursued, but it suddenly seemed like a terrible idea. Something was out there, but she didn't know if it could be labeled as human. And why would they believe anything she had to say? The truth slithered right back inside of her and curled protectively around her heart.

"What is it, Aria? Is there something you want to tell us?"

Aria leaned back in her chair, forcing her muscles to relax, and shook her head.

"No, nothing."

"Listen, Aria, we've done about all we can do to help you at this point. We're doing our best to be patient, but you need to know that based on the evidence we already have, that we can arrest you. And we will, unless you tell us something that will lead us in the right direction. Every piece of evidence we have points to you and only you. Their blood was on your body. You were missing at the time of the murder, and a few concerned citizens have made us aware of your... violent behavior. Aria, I don't think I have to tell you just how much trouble you're going to be in if you don't give us another story—and quick."

As each word uttered from Shirley's lips, Aria's irritation and headache blossomed into an unignorable state. She was sick of hearing them talk, sick of their words, and sick to death of having them poke and prod where they didn't belong. Could they not see that she had nothing left to give? Aria shook her head with more ferocity and slammed her palms on the table hard enough to make it shake.

"I told you I don't fucking remember!" she hissed, fingers flying to her arms to scratch at her now itching skin. It felt like a million tiny spider legs dancing under her flesh, and she needed to carve them out. Carve down to the bone.

Ashes dancing in the wind, embers flickering against a black sky. Slick blood on hands that are not her own. Blades reflecting in the dark, all of them pointing at her. A dozen faces, none she recognized.

Her brain was an egg, and the unfamiliar memories were trickling out of its cracked shell. The other's rage somewhat quelled when these memories came, its thrashing replaced with a light, humming vibration. This only increased Aria's panic. The room was getting smaller, walls encroaching from every side. The details of the world blurred into smears of color. She didn't realize it was because she was crying.

"I have nothing left, there is nothing LEFT!" she shouted, images flashing in her mind. One of her hands tugged harshly at her hair. "It doesn't matter—none of it matters—nothing fucking matters!"

Roswell paled. He glanced at Shirley and found her equally shocked.

"Aria, it's okay, take a breath," he said.

Aria bared her teeth in a snarl, his attempt at consolation sounding much more like condescension to her.

"It's not okay—nothing is okay! You don't know how bad it is, you have no idea!" Aria raged. The arm she was scratching turned an alarming shade of red. Screams, distant and unheard by anyone else, assaulted her from every direction. A knot of pressure formed in the center of her forehead.

"You're all in danger..." she whispered.

"What do you mean? Who's in danger? From what?"

Aria's eyes rolled back, exposing the red veins creeping across her sclera. Blood, hot and slippery, trickled from her nostrils and down her lips and chin. A few drops splattered on the surface of the table.

"Aria, your nose!" Shirley gasped and moved to grab a tissue from the box on the cabinet next to her. Her fingers brushed the corner of the soft tissue when Aria released a wail so loud it startled them both. It was high-pitched, powerful, and agonizing.

"I don't know! I don't know! I don't know what it is!" she bellowed, spittle and blood flying from her lips, giving her the appearance of a rabid dog. The wailing faded into a deep whine, all of her energy oozing out of her. Aria collapsed onto the table, smearing bits of blood, resting her head on her arm as she whimpered.

"But it's so.... so angry..."

Chapter 30

"What do you mean, she's at the police station?" Alessa exclaimed.

She'd walked into the house just moments ago to find both of her parents waiting for her in the living room. They sat on opposite ends of the couch, with Joshua leaning heavily onto the armrest as if he couldn't get far enough away from his wife.

"You didn't even try to stop them?" she pressed, voice rising.

"There was nothing we could do. The blood on her matched the body in the woods. It was either she go willingly, or they would take her, anyway," Joshua said, looking more defeated than Alessa had ever seen him. Any strength he'd clung to during this entire process was long gone.

She turned to her mother, who seemed completely unbothered. If anything, she looked relaxed with her held high.

"So, you just... let her go. Did they tell you when she can come home?"

Lily rolled her eyes and rose from her seat, casually smoothing down her skirt. "As your father informed you, there was nothing to be done. Roswell and Shirley are doing their jobs and we should respect that. Getting involved will only complicate matters."

It was like Lily considered this a minor offense, no worse than after-school detention. Alessa imagined Aria locked in a small cell,

CHAPTER 30

surrounded by concrete and metal, trapped, isolated, and alone. It brought tears to her eyes. She had failed Aria yet again. She couldn't stop her from disappearing the first time, and she couldn't help her now. All of her rage from months past bubbled to the surface. Her eyes narrowed viciously.

"Fuck you both," she snarled and darted to the stairs.

"Alessa!" Joshua sprang up from the couch but she didn't stop or turn. Alessa didn't care about their excuses. As far as she was concerned, she was the only one who had Aria's best interests in mind.

Alessa slammed her bedroom door for extra effect. She leaned back against it, hot tears rushing down her cheeks. When minutes went by and neither parent came to check on her, she finally felt safe enough to move. She moved sluggishly as she crossed the room and flopped onto her mattress. When her head hit the pillow, it felt hard and lumpy.

She sat back up; curious. Alessa grabbed her pillow and held it up, noticing a small, rectangular imprint on the inside of the pillowcase. She stuffed her hand inside and rummaged around until her fingers clasped something smooth and hard. Aria's leather-bound journal emerged.

Alessa stared at it stupidly for several long seconds, her eyes drawn to the 'A' in the bottom corner. She knew instantly it belonged to her sister, but it didn't quell the shock. She'd never known her sister to keep any type of journal, and definitely never saw her use one. Lily tried gifting her one in the past for one of her birthdays, but Aria left it on her bookshelf to collect dust. And yet, there was a journal here, and it could only belong to one person.

Why would she leave it in here? Alessa wondered, turning it over it in her hands. It looked well-loved and heavily used. But she'd never seen it before today. Maybe, just maybe, Aria left it here on purpose for Alessa to find. A parting gift, or perhaps a last message. If she did indeed leave it here, that meant there was something inside she wanted Alessa to see.

Alessa carefully opened the journal. Aria's trademark sloppy scribble filled the pages. A smile spread across her lips as soon as she saw it.

June 16, 2020

This is really weird. Do I say Dear Diary? Is that still a thing? Seems cliché, but it has a nice ring to it, and it feels weird just starting off by rambling. And yet... here I am. I never thought I'd get one of these, but it felt right somehow, with senior year coming up. I'm gonna be leaving this town as soon as I graduate, or as close to it as I can. So, I had a thought, I've got one year left here—why not record it? Could be fun to look back on!

As much as I want to get the hell out of here, part of me will always miss this shitty town. I'd hate to forget a single moment of the happy times I've had here.

Alessa sank back into the mattress, the pillow puffing up around her head as she delved into Aria's private thoughts. Soon, it was like Aria was resting beside her, whispering her stories. Alessa heard every inflection, every dramatic pause, and fit of laughter. Alessa allowed her smile to grow and drank it all in.

Two hours flew by as Alessa read through Aria's journal. She took her time, tracing the lines with her finger, reading, and then re-reading every page, mesmerized by the smooth strokes of Aria's penmanship. It took at least an hour for the shock to wear off that Aria even had a journal at all, but beneath that shock was a tiny trickle of joy. Joy at being able to see inside Aria's mind before she went missing, and to be trusted with such intimate details.

Most of the entries were mundane, just day-to-day ramblings about events in Aria's life she deemed memorable. Alessa's heart warmed to see how frequently her sister mentioned her. Aria constantly mentioned both her and Noah, remarking on silly jokes Alessa made over dinner, and how they binged trash on TV when their parents weren't around. Peppered throughout the journal were little doodles along the margins: a heart next to Noah's name, and a smiley face with its tongue sticking out next to a retelling of when Aria broke two pairs of headphones in a row.

One memory, in particular, made Alessa giggle to herself as she read.

August 20th, 2020

Dear Diary (lol) – I got grounded today.

Saying it like that sounds so dramatic. I feel like I get grounded every other week. It's Mom's favorite go-to. This time I... might have deserved it? Ha! Either way, it was totally worth it to see the horrified look on her face. Unclench a little, Mom. It won't kill you.

Soooo, this is how it went down. It's Sunday, so of course we went down to church like we do EVERY weekend (ugh). I woke up nauseous and had a headache, so I asked Mom if I could stay behind. Just this ONCE. I go every single weekend. But I felt like shit. She took my temperature, but because I didn't have a fever; she said I have to go, anyway. I was pissed, and of course, Dad did nothing, so I had no choice. She stuffed my sister and I into these AWFUL, scratchy dresses that button all the way to the collar. I was sweating my ass off after ten minutes of wearing it. Asked if I could change into one of my more comfortable dresses, but Mom looked ready to rip my head off, so I let it go when she said no.

Anyway, church was boring, as always. But at least I got to see Noah for a little while beforehand. He knew I wasn't feeling good and brought some hot tea in a thermos for me. Sometimes, I really can't believe I landed him – feels like a dream. If it is – I hope I don't wake up.

The whole service was a blur. But I've mastered the ability to feign interest while also completely disconnecting my brain from what's going on. Father Samuel's ramblings all sound the same. "Praise Him for His mercy!" God this, God that, blah, blah, fucking blah. The idea of having to thank something or praise something I'm not even sure is there always feels really weird to me. Why not thank myself for what I've accomplished? Why does all the credit automatically go to God?

Whatever. Now I'm the one that's rambling. Anyway, Alessa never fails to make me laugh during the service, no matter how mind-numbing it is. She always has just the right jokes loaded up; I swear we spend more time trying not to burst out laughing than anything else. She was in rare form today–everything that came out of her mouth was gold.

I felt like complete crap by the end of the service. I was congested, and pretty much anyone who gave me a passing glance could tell I was sick as hell. Mom, however, was more interested in scolding me for my attitude. It was pouring rain when we left. I accidentally got a little mud on the bottom of my dress when we walked to the car. Mom was raging at that point. How dare I mess up my pristine wardrobe? What would people think? It's always the same shit with her.

Anyway! By the time we got home, I felt terrible, and Mommy Dearest didn't let up the whole way home. I was over it. Done. I tuned her out after a certain point. She waited at the front door. Her face was so red, and I knew I was in for it. Something just clicked. It didn't matter what I said or did, I'd be yelled at and grounded either way. But I didn't want to give Mom even a little satisfaction. If I was gonna go down–why not do it with a bang?

I ran into the rain. It was a downpour. You could barely see across the street and thunder rumbled in the distance. I didn't care. The rain soaked my clothes, and I jumped into the big, murky puddle that had formed at the end of the driveway. I kicked all the mud up and ruined the beautiful, perfect dress Mom loved so much. In the distance, she was screaming. I *laughed and spun in circles and called for Alessa. I wanted her to feel as free and reckless as I did.*

And she did! She actually did it. Alessa came running up to me. At first, she looked skeptical, but soon she was right there with me. Twirling and dancing in a storm.

Mom grounded me for a month. Totally. Fucking. Worth it.

Totally fucking worth it was right. Alessa remembered it like it was yesterday, the warm rain seeping through her clothes, and the soft mud squelching under her shoes. At first, she'd been terrified of her sister's recklessness, of how much trouble she would get in. But after seeing how happy she was, and the ease with which she spun, kicking up water as she went, Alessa knew she wanted to experience it too. Alessa surprised herself by darting into the rain, knowing it would enrage her mom, but it was some of the most fun she'd ever had.

She kept going, wishing she had time to commit all of it to memory. The crashing of a pan, followed by a sharp sigh from downstairs, made her flinch. Alessa stuffed the journal under the covers just in case one of her parents stopped by. After several long seconds of staring at her door, she slid it back out.

Lying within the pages were all the little details that made Aria who she was. It was everything Alessa never knew, and all she did. She felt like she was cradling Aria's fragile heart in her hands, so she treated it with great care.

Alessa saw all of Aria's fights with their mother, and all the times she felt let down and forgotten by their father. But most importantly, she saw all the beautiful, treasured moments she shared with her beloved sister. The bad, the good, and the ridiculous. It wasn't until she hit a certain date that she paused. The date at the top of the page read April 22nd, 2021. Aria's 17th birthday, and her last one before going missing. Heart thudding like a hammer in her chest, she took a few breaths before reading on.

Today was supposed to be amazing. I hated every second of it.

Alessa almost stopped then, eyes immediately shifting away from the paper to protect herself. She wasn't sure she was ready to hear Aria's most intimate thoughts about such a terrible day, a day that should have been special. Immediately, she shoved her anxieties to the side. Aria had been the one to experience it, and she left this book here for a reason. She wanted her sister to see this, all of it.

Mom didn't invite any of my friends aside from Noah. I mean, I know I don't have a lot, but she didn't invite ANY of them! The only girls at my birthday that were my age were the daughters of some of her and Dad's close friends. Girls I don't even like!!! Of course, Dad was useless. What else is new? He could have a gun to his head, and he'd still never stand up to Mom.

Alessa recalled Aria and her father arguing in his office, and how disinterested and exasperated he sounded. Disgust roiled in Alessa's stomach, once again she was faced with the depth of her parent's callousness.

All I wanted for my birthday was to hang out. Maybe sit in the garden or take some new pictures for my portfolio. I just wanted to BE. But I can never just be here...

Everyone we know from church was at the party, all the older people anyway. Mom had me walk around at her side to greet everyone, to play the polite, pretty daughter, and sit quietly and smile as she fawned over me. And not like loveable fawning. It was like being on display, a little puppet soldier to be marched around and marveled at. Everyone's faces just blurred together after a while, all of them complimenting her for how well she'd done raising such a good, well-behaved daughter.

The idea of Aria being tugged along, blank-faced, and dead-eyed by their mother opened up a black hole inside of Alessa. She hadn't noticed their mom parading her around. She must have been with Maya then. Guilt trickled into the black hole, expanding it. If only she'd been paying more attention. Alessa skimmed the rest of the passage. She didn't think she could handle reliving the slap through Aria's eyes.

After her 17th birthday, Aria's journal entries took a noticeable turn. Most, if not all, of the previous entries were positive or contained joyful memories, but everything after took on a much darker tone. It started with Aria's usual impatience to get out of town and have her own life, but it soon morphed into desperation.

Ever since my birthday, I swear people are staring at me all the time. I mean, people in this town are nosey. It's a small place – it happens. But I swear every time I turn around, I see someone looking at me, and it's always someone from church. Smiling. They're always smiling and waving.

I don't know. Maybe I'm nuts. I did just say it's a small place... it's no wonder I run into parishioners so often. Right? I'm sure it's nothing.

I haven't been sleeping as much as usual. Maybe it's stress over graduation coming up, but I can't get my brain to quiet down. I was up most of last night combing through my portfolio until my eyes burned. Sometimes I worry, even though I got into the summer program, that it won't be enough when I actually get there. What if my photos are nothing special? What if everyone is better than me?

The feeling of being watched hasn't gone away. I tried to ignore it, but it's still happening. It's like eyes are on me all the time. Sometimes I think I can feel someone staring at me from outside, in the night.

Mom said she has some sleeping pills that might help. I think I'll ask her for some tomorrow.

Aria's bouts of insomnia were surprising, but it didn't give them cause for concern. They were all convinced it was pre-college jitters, but it continued for months, culminating one day when the school called to pick her up early because she'd collapsed on her desk from exhaustion.

Now Alessa wondered how much of it was school related, and how much of it was paranoia worming its way inside her brain.

I feel like I'm going fucking crazy. I've been waiting on these confirmation papers from the school about the summer program and I still haven't gotten anything. They were supposed to be here a week ago, and when I called the school, they said they sent them out, but where are they?!

I can't get the idea out of my head that Mom and Dad did something with them. They knew the papers were coming and to be on the lookout, and I've asked them every day, but they keep saying no! It's the way Mom looks at me when she says it, smug, with that shitty smirk on her face. And she keeps making these remarks about our plans for the summer, as if I'm part of them, and I have to keep reminding her I won't be here. She should know by now.

CHAPTER 30

I wish someone would tell me I'm not crazy. But I know the second I open my mouth; they'll see me for the lunatic I am.

Was Aria searching for these papers that night when she snuck into their father's office? Alessa remembered the look of disappointment on her sister's face. W She wished Aria had expressed some of these concerns to her. If she had any insight into what Aria was really thinking, Alessa would have dropped everything to help her.

Or would you have thought she was insane? Just like she did.

She immediately shook her head to dispel such thoughts, but they continued to nag intrusively in the back of her mind. Maybe if Alessa had known these things before, she could have put a stop to it. The last entry was dated only days before her disappearance, and it told her nothing that she didn't already know. Alessa shut the book and stared at the wall, limp hands bound to leather.

Telling her parents was a non-starter. Noah was her best option. He might add even more context to some of the events she'd read about. But she didn't want to jeopardize his meeting with Father Samuel. Even though it killed her, she had to wait until he called.

As she settled on this resolution for her best course of action, there was a knock at her door. She shoved the journal back into her pillowcase.

"Come in!"

Lily's pristine, golden hair was the first thing Alessa saw. Her mother stood in the doorway with a grim expression etched in stone. "It's time for dinner, Alessa. Come on down."

Despite having absolutely no appetite, Alessa knew better than to argue. "Be right down."

Her mother wordlessly returned downstairs. Alessa checked the pillow containing the journal, and after making sure it was safe, went to wash her hands before joining her parents.

Admittedly, it smelled phenomenal. The entire house was awash in delicious scents. Her stomach stirred. Maybe she would find it in her to have a full meal after all.

Both of her parents were already at the dining table when she arrived. It was quite an elaborate setup. Beautiful China plates piled with salads, sides of fruit, mashed potatoes, and more, with a juicy roast as the centerpiece. Red, tapered candles flickered among the feast, creating wisps of shadows and light. It was, in a word, heavenly. It was also far more than Alessa expected the three of them to need. Lily only put this level of work in when it was a special occasion. So why the sudden effort?

"Wow, this looks amazing. What's the occasion?"

Lily smiled; lips pulled into a tight line. Her father slouched miserably in the head chair.

"I just think it's been far too long since the three of us really sat down together, don't you?"

The way she asked, as if baiting her, perked Alessa's interest. She supposed it had been a while since the three of them spent any time together as a unit. After Aria went missing, it felt strange to do so. They could have done this at any point, Alessa thought, so why wait until Aria was locked up?

"Sure," Alessa replied.

"I think it's long overdue," Lily added and gestured to the chair nearest Alessa. "Take a seat, dear."

She did as told without protest, shooting one last questioning look at her father, who immediately turned away, keeping his eyes on the table. Weird. Alessa squirmed, trying to get comfortable in a room that felt anything but. Everything in the room was... off. Alessa did her best to distract herself from it by busying her hands and draping the cloth napkin over her lap.

"Oh! Joshua, you forgot to grab the cider! Will you do that for me?"

He flinched when Lily spoke his name, as if struck by some unseen whip. Joshua vanished into the kitchen. Moments later, her father returned with three full glasses of sparkling apple cider, as well as the open bottle to pour from. Alessa tried to catch his eye when he placed the glass flute in front of her, but he pointedly avoided her gaze. When he returned to his chair, his head hung with the affectation of a kicked puppy. Alessa imagined he was still reeling over Aria being taken away.

They joined hands and Lily said grace, a peaceful smile on her lips. The word of God instilled a sense of tranquility in her that no one else could match. It used to make Alessa envious. Now, it just seemed sad.

Forks and knives scraped against porcelain, filling the otherwise quiet room. Alessa ate slowly, eyes bouncing back and forth between her parents. Joshua remained focused on his plate, scooping, and shoving each forkful into his mouth with the precision and speed of a drill sergeant. Lily took her time, savoring each bite with a soft hum. Alessa sipped her cider eagerly, hoping the carbonation would settle her churning stomach. She was sure if she spoke, the air itself would shatter, but she couldn't bear it any longer.

"Dinner is delicious, Mom," she muttered, stabbing her fork into another thick slice of roast.

"Yes." Alessa's heart nearly lurched out of her chest when her father finally spoke, his voice even and unexpressive. "You've outdone yourself."

It was an obviously forced compliment, and Alessa bit down on her tongue as she waited for the inevitable bomb to drop. It never came. Lily's smile widened. But Alessa couldn't tell if she really didn't understand his tone, or if she was choosing to ignore it.

"That's very kind of you to say, dear," she replied, mouth stretching to bare her teeth. "It's not often that I receive such high praise."

Alessa's heart sank. Lily's tone took on a more sinister edge. She knew then that something was wrong, looming in the distance like an approaching storm. But she couldn't put her finger on it. Alessa downed the last bit of her cider and prepped for the explosion.

"It's odd... after all I've done, and after all the effort I've put into this family, that I'm not acknowledged for it more often." Her head snapped to Alessa. "Don't you agree, Alessa?"

Alessa's body flushed hot with shame. She opened her mouth to reply, but only managed a pathetic stutter. Lily's glacial, unblinking stare made her shrink back into her chair.

"I knew becoming a mother would mean coming second. The children come first, always, and unequivocally. As parents, we put our heart, and our souls–our entire beings into ensuring our children are taken care of."

Lily shook her head with a scoff, her smile never leaving her lips even as she tore the next piece of meat from her fork and chewed. "I guess I didn't realize what a thankless job it is. Maybe I'm just naïve."

The shame fattened and expanded, taking on a life of its own. Like a serpent, it slinked into all Alessa's secret crevices, intertwining with her organs until they became indistinguishable. She swallowed down the wave of hot saliva that filled her mouth as the serpent's head prodded at her uvula. Her hand flew to her forehead. It was damp. Oh God, she was sweating. Alessa stuffed another bite of mashed potato into her mouth, not knowing what else to do.

"You know, for a long time, I wasn't sure I wanted to be a mother," Lily added. Alessa cringed in silence. "Didn't think I was cut out for it, but... things change."

She shot a pointed look at her husband, who sank even deeper into himself and his chair. Lily did not linger on him long, her sharp eyes locking back onto Alessa.

"When I became pregnant with your sister, I felt a new sense of purpose, one I never imagined possible. I felt in my soul, it's what I was truly meant for. I saw God's path laid out before me, and I was ready for the journey, ready to do whatever it took to be the best mother I could be."

Alessa slowly set down her fork, the thought of another bite making her nauseous. Her insides were hot and fuzzy, spreading warmth to her limbs and contrasting against the erratic shrieks of warning going off in her head. Alessa wanted to run, the urge making her hands shake, but she couldn't move. Why was it so hot in here? Her mother continued without missing a beat. She stabbed her fork into her roast with a particular harshness.

"I did just as my parents taught me. I raised my daughters to be honorable. Or I thought I did. And I expected to be shown the same respect I gave my own mother and father. I expected to be shown the same level of grace, to know that my sacrifices meant something."

Alessa opened her mouth, but her movements were slow and labored. The room shifted ever so slightly around her, and when she spoke, her voice sounded like it was muffled behind layers of cotton.

"Mom, what is going on?"

"Hush," Lily cut her off. Anger surged in her mother's eyes, cold and eviscerating.

"I never envisioned things turning out like this. I never wanted this. But you need to understand that I did the best I could. I accepted my role. It is... just like your sister to complicate things."

The entire world turned, and Alessa gripped the arms of her chair to keep her balance. It was like being stuck in the eye of a storm. A darker meaning lingered behind her mother's words. She knew that now, but she felt powerless to intervene. Her limbs were heavy, and her brain was like quicksand. The more she tried to fight against it, the more it sucked her down. Shadows encroached on Alessa's vision.

"Aria never did quite understand that sometimes you have to do things you might not like because it's the right thing." Lily shook her head with a scoff. "I prepared her the only way I knew how, but the girl's never been grateful for a day in her life."

She jabbed her roast yet again, even more forcefully, and the metal screeched as it slid across the plate. It stung Alessa's ears. She glanced at her father, desperate to find solace in his gaze. Joshua continued to look away from her. He'd stopped eating or drinking, his hands resting in his lap instead.

"D-Dad... please..." Alessa slurred, losing feeling in her tongue. Distantly, she knew someone had drugged her. She glanced at the food and the cider; it could have been either of them.

"It was supposed to be different with you, Alessa. But as I've discovered, life has a way of laughing in my face. So here I am, forced to swallow it down and commit to my duties all over again."

Alessa tried to stand, her feet moving only inches, even with the greatest effort. The moment her feet were flat on the floor, her ankles buckled beneath her, bones melting into slush. She hit the ground with a loud bang, the chair legs scraping as she accidentally kicked it mid-collapse. The hardwood was a cool relief against her hot skin. Her face landed near her father's feet, hand sliding and leaving a wet trail as she attempted to reach for him. She didn't quite make it; her fingers stopped just short of the hem of his pants.

Tunnel vision set in by the time they rolled Alessa onto her back. Through bleary eyes, she saw her mother standing over her, staring down at her in disgusted disappointment. Alessa's mind let go, submerging into the all-encompassing void, as tears slipped from her cheeks.

Chapter 31

Aria sat in the dimly lit corner of the holding cell; they immediately moved her after her outburst. She was partly grateful they'd escorted her in here. She didn't have the energy to answer any more questions, and at least in here she would get some privacy. It was only temporary, of course. One of them would be back to guard the cell, but they'd stepped out, no doubt to discuss what to do with her.

She was finding it difficult to care what happened to her anymore. Not that she understood why, but it all felt so pointless now. As the other inside of her grew, so did her apathy, and she knew it would soon take over.

The screams faded a while ago, but the chatter remained. They continued to whisper to her, ephemeral and indistinct, but she understood them. They were calling to her still, awaiting her return to the undergrowth. The other yearned to go to them. Aria refused to abandon Alessa and Noah again. As they warred, she stepped up on the bed to level her head with the barred window and bask her face in the blue spotlight of the moon.

Across the field behind the station, she saw its figure again, the doppelgänger. It walked toward her in slow, unhurried steps, black eyeless sockets burning the trail ahead. The other twisted inside of her excitedly, and Aria, bone-tired and desperate, found herself relieved by its approach. Maybe it was time. It was stronger, and she was so tired. So goddamn tired.

A sudden, sharp pinch in the back of her shoulder shattered the doppelgänger's hypnotic pull. Aria reached around, feeling a small, hard object sticking out of her shoulder blade, and ripped it out. It was a small dart with a feathered tip. The spot it struck was becoming warm, lava creeping slowly through her veins. Aria turned around, her movements already lagging. Roswell was standing on the other side of the bars, holding a slender, black tranquilizer gun, his left eye peering through the scope.

Aria stumbled off the bed. Whatever he used was slow working, and she still had the use of most of her limbs, even if it felt like dragging herself through ten feet of mud. His one visible eye shot open in shock when she made it halfway across the cell and slammed his finger on the trigger again. Another dart caught her in the right side of her chest. The heat spread quicker, and her vision doubled. She fumbled, ankles knocking together as she tottered in a zigzag, still making her way toward Roswell, hands lifting and ready to shred.

"Jesus Christ!" Roswell gasped, his arms trembling. One of these darts was usually enough to take out a bear, but this girl was still coming. She was drawing closer, arms outstretched, and teeth bared. They looked pointed in the light.

Aria's arms had barely reached through the bars by the time he popped off a last shot. The last dart went right into her neck. She grabbed a hold of Roswell's collar. Petrified, he threw himself backwards, slipping from her grasp as she plummeted to the floor. He watched, panting, as her eyes fluttered a few times until they closed completely, her chest rising and falling in a steady rhythm.

"Boss?"

Roswell's heart nearly gave out in that very moment. He hadn't heard Shirley enter the room. He glanced over, hand clutching his chest. Shirley was standing in the doorway, passively looking at the unconscious form on the ground. She rose a concerned brow his way.

"You good, sir?"

Roswell gathered himself and expelled a hefty sigh.

"Yeah, I'm fine." He took an eager step away from the cell, wanting to put as much distance between himself and the girl as possible. "Help me prep the car."

Chapter 32

The morning light was soft and warm as it peered through the curtains of Alessa's bedroom window. When she first opened her eyes, she was still in that heavenly, in-between space where she didn't know if she was awake or still in dreamland. The sun caught the window just right, splashing across dew drops that sprinkled the glass, and sent rainbow prisms dancing over her wall. It was so beautiful. She could have watched them for hours.

You already did. A voice whispered to her.

When she looked back at the colorful beams of light, Alessa realized it was true. She'd seen these lights before, been in this moment before.

Alessa shot out of bed, panic setting in. She couldn't find her clock anywhere, so she couldn't tell what time it was. She could be gone already. Alessa bolted out of her room, but it felt like wading through waist-deep water. Had the hallway always been this long? Finally, she reached her sister's room. The door was already open.

"Aria!" Alessa yelled, her words coming out weak and muted no matter how much she strained her vocal cords. Her bedroom was empty. Alessa went to the window. The trees seemed to loom taller than ever, breaching the clouds, their bark as black as night.

Aria was standing in the yard behind their house, her back to Alessa and facing the forest. Her skin was caked and smeared with red, but aside from that, she was naked to the elements.

CHAPTER 32

And then Alessa was standing on their back porch, winter air blasting her cheeks like daggers. She didn't recall how she got down here or having moved at all. All she knew was she had to keep going. She had to get to her sister before her sister reached the trees.

"Aria!" Alessa screamed again, her voice whisked away with the howling wind. Aria walked at a steady pace toward the trees. The yard seemed to stretch as Alessa ran, creating a larger gap. Her muscles flamed in protest, but she couldn't stop now.

No matter how fast Alessa ran, she never closed the distance between them. Aria stopped when she reached the shadow of the tree line. Alessa reached for her, a final wrenching scream bursting from her lungs, and her sister finally turned around.

Dark, eyeless sockets crusted with blood stared back at her, and she smiled with a mouthful of razor-sharp teeth.

Alessa woke blearily, feeling like someone had clobbered her over the head with a baseball bat. Her mouth was dry and fuzzy, and the sensation in her tongue was slowly coming back. A small trickle of drool spilled from the corner of her mouth. The memories came back to her in hazy flashes: sitting at the dinner table with her parents, the cider she eagerly gulped down, and the disdain in her mother's eyes as Alessa succumbed to the dark.

Alessa's entire body ached when she tried to lift her head. The more sensation returned to her tongue, the more she moved it, and in doing so, she realized someone had gagged her. A cloth was pulled tight around her mouth, cutting into her cheeks, and making it impossible to speak. When she tried, it came out as a garbled whine.

Her hands and ankles were bound as well with thick rope. She used her shoulders and head as leverage to push herself to her knees, ankles tucked uncomfortably beneath her and aching wrists resting on her lap. It sapped most of her energy, and she still felt foggy and weary from the drugs, but at least she knew where she was now.

The grand crucifix pinned with the body of a tortured Jesus Christ was the first thing she saw. It was an image she'd grown accustomed to with all the years she spent inside this church. A hole ripped open inside of Alessa, but it wasn't because of where she was—somehow, she knew this is where it would all end up. It was because she wasn't alone.

Alessa let out a quiet but agonizing sob when she looked to her left to see Maya and Noah, bound and gagged as well, leaning against the pews. Candlelight illuminated the tears glistening on Maya's face, and the blood caked in her hair around a gash that stopped just below her hairline. Noah seemed unharmed, but he, too, appeared exhausted and confused. Both of them, seeing Alessa was now awake, began to jerk and mumble under their gags.

Alessa scanned the church, fear morphing into unfettered dread. The church was dark aside from the dozens of candles placed on various surfaces. It bathed the room in a sinister red light. Cloaked figures, draped in white, stood around them, each holding lit candles of their own. Peering through the flickering shadows, she made out a few of their faces. She recognized all of them. They were people she saw every day, people she'd known her entire life—all of them longstanding members of the church. She saw the owners of the Cupcake Corner, Gloria's friend Ruth McIntyre, and Doctor Sutton. The faces that surprised Alessa the most were Maya's parents, both of them holding their heads high, gazing over their child as if she didn't exist.

"Glad to see you've finally joined us, Alessa."

Father Samuel stepped into the light, his black robes blending in with the shadows. Flanking either side of him were Lily and Joshua, wearing the same white robes as the others. Only theirs were detailed in embroidered patterns stitched in gold thread. They also held candles in front of their chests, heads bowed as they followed the priest to his podium.

"I worried we would have to continue while you slept," he said with a smile, "but that would not have been nearly as satisfying."

He lifted the ancient tome, and Alessa heard the entire room hold its breath. Without looking, she knew all of their eyes were on him as he lowered it with great care to rest on the podium. Alessa joined in their collective exhale.

Something about that book made Alessa want to purge the poison in her stomach. Perhaps it was the old leather that looked like charred, broken flesh, or the sickening yellow pages that reminded her of a puss-filled wound. There was something deeply wrong with that book. Alessa's eyes flashed to her parents for guidance—for any type of acknowledgement—but they stonewalled her. Her mother's focus centered on Father Samuel, emanating veneration, whilst her father continued to look back and forth from the priest to the lobby doors.

Outside, beyond the stained-glass portraits of their holy saints, the night was pitch black, dark clouds blotting out the stars. Beneath Alessa, the core of the earth rumbled as the wind whistled through the church's shingles, and the room grew cold. Another winter storm brewed, a big one this time. She smelled snow in the air. On a night like this, no one would be outside, no one would hear them scream. No one was coming to their rescue.

Devastated by the realization, Alessa stressed against her bindings, pulling her muscles taught until they burned, but nothing budged. Noah and Maya looked on as she grappled with their new reality with both understanding and immense pain. Maya's eyes glistened anew, and Noah clenched his fists until his nails drew blood from his palms. Father Samuel paid them no mind. His smile remained as he opened the journal to the desired page.

The white-robed members followed his movements with their eyes. They were like statues, or maybe soldiers were the better word. Alessa imagined they'd jump to do just about anything Father Samuel told them, with how they lingered on his every movement. Father Samuel placed his hand on the book and drew in a deep breath as if he was drawing upon the text's strength. Everyone in the room followed suit, exhaling only when the priest did.

"It should only be a few more minutes now, and then we can begin. We must not forget; patience is a virtue. Good fortune will rain down upon us once more, but only if we stay true to His path."

No one spoke, but there were nods of agreement from all around. Barely 60 seconds later, a loud knock on the double doors leading to the lobby echoed through the sanctuary. Alessa jumped. She tried keeping her eyes on as many people as she could, not willing to keep her back toward anyone for too long. She backed herself against the pews, across from Maya and Noah.

Father Samuel grinned, nodding to his subjects. "Perfect timing. Please, Mrs. Walker, if you would do the honors?"

Alessa watched Maya's mother step out of the circle, nodding with a pleasant smile at Father Samuel without even a second of hesitation. Alessa's heart, already mangled beyond recognition, shattered for Maya when she heard the cry of confusion and anguish behind her friend's gag. Her bound hands reached for Maya's and gripped them with the little strength she had. The rope cut into her wrists and her hands tingled from the impedance of her circulation.

Clarissa Walker opened the double doors, her candle still in hand. She stood, poised and serene after propping the doors. She awaited her father-in-law's next instructions.

From the darkness of the hallway emerged two more figures, taller than the rest, wearing robes with executioner-style hoods pulled over their faces. A shrill, creaking noise pierced the air, and behind the black robes appeared Roswell and Shirley, each maneuvering one side of a giant wooden cross that had been braced on a metal frame with wheels.

On the cross hung Aria's unconscious body, held in place by straps around her wrists and ankles, like Jesus being crucified. There was also a long leather strap around her midsection. Alessa screamed, the noise sounding pitiful even to her own ears. Noah's garbled yells mixed with her own, and the muscles in his neck throbbed with strain as he thrashed against his bindings, eyes shining white with fear.

"Bring her forth," Samuel instructed. The executioners led, and the officers followed. Aria's head dangled over her chest, hair around her face like a curtain. It bobbed and swayed with every movement. Her eyes twitched. Two more executioners filed out behind them, one holding a clear tarp, and the other carrying a metal tray with an assortment of various blades. Alessa forgot how to breathe.

The group formed a steady congregation, and their movements were calculated and practiced. They'd been preparing for this.

"Ley heh gauh!" A furious voice cut straight through her thoughts. Alessa was so enraptured in her terror that she hadn't noticed Noah scramble to his feet, leaning on the pew for support. The executioners, however, never ceased their journey to the front of the church.

"RAGH!" Unleashing a warrior's cry, Noah launched himself at the black-robed figure closest to him, pushing himself off the pew to propel his body forward, and crashed into one of them.

The executioner side-stepped him easily, and as Noah fell forward, losing his momentum, they drilled their fist into his gut. Noah doubled over, his ribs cracking as the knuckles drove in. He coughed from behind his gag, saliva and blood exploding from between his lips. Noah hit the floor and curled into a ball, favoring and protecting his stomach as he struggled to breathe. The church filled with the sounds of his wheezing; the black-robed person stood over him but didn't make another move to hurt him. Father Samuel grunted with repugnance, turning his nose up at the scene.

"Remove his gag. I have plans for him, and they do not involve him writhing on the floor and choking to death," he commanded.

The executioner merely nodded his hooded head and did as they were told, roughly loosening the knot of the gag before throwing it to the floor. Noah gasped for air, and sucked in huge, loud gulps, globs of spit and blood. He spit some out onto the clean floor and shot a withering glare at the priest.

"What the hell is going on? What are you doing with Aria?"

Father Samuel did not reply at first and waved his hand at the black-robed soldier. They lifted Noah by the back of his shirt and dragged him over to Alessa and Maya. Despite his kicking and flailing, he was harshly flung to the ground. The back of his head smacked against the wooden pew. Roswell and Shirley placed the cross with Aria at the front of the room, to the right of Samuel's podium.

"Let her GO!" Noah screamed. Father Samuel's smile grew.

"You three are very lucky. This is truly an unprecedented moment in our town's history. It is a genuine test from God. The kind of test that rarely comes along in a person's lifetime. A test of strength, a test of will, but most of all, a test of faith. Few people get to experience such an event." Samuel lifted his head to address his parishioners. "Let us begin with a prayer."

Everyone bowed their heads in unison, like they were all one organism, the firelight dancing over their features and making them look gaunt and freakish.

"To our Lord, we thank you. We thank you for your love and for your patience. We thank you for your trust and tests of faith, for they give us the opportunity to prove our worth to you. Lord, thank you for this chance to repent and express our devotion. We will not squander this second chance, and the gifts you have given us.

"Please, grant us safety and guidance through this night. Help us drain the poison from our town and cut the cancer from the source.

CHAPTER 32

We will never again give you reason to doubt us!"

A smattering of mumbled agreements came from all around Alessa, their heads nodding, expressions screwed in intense concentration. She turned to Aria. Her hair was shielding most of her face from view still. A slight movement caught Alessa's eye; Aria's fingers were flexing.

"Help us right this egregious wrong, Dear Lord. We will not disappoint you. We bind ourselves to you wholly and adoringly, and we will not take your love and benevolence for granted. Amen."

Alessa kept her eyes on Aria, hoping that by sheer force of will, she could resurrect Aria from her mental prison.

"Amen," the room responded, their voices forming a single, harmonious wave. It seemed to do the trick. Aria's head jolted upward, muscles tensing and eyelids quivering. Alessa shuddered, relieved.

"Ari!" Noah cried out.

Aria looked around, eyes widening as she took it all in. Roswell kept his gun leveled at her. She tried to move her arms and legs, but they were held tightly in place, the leather straps biting into the soft tissue of her wrists and ankles. Aria hissed in pain, throwing her head back and knocking it against the wood. She scanned the orange-lit room, the white and black robes, Father Samuel with her parents, and then finally Alessa.

When the sisters locked eyes on each other, reality clicked back into place. Aria watched Alessa with a horrifying look of resignation, like she knew they'd end up here all along.

All of Aria's fury and misery erupted in a wretched howl that silenced the room. It sounded like hundreds of voices stacked on top of one another; a chorus of anguished souls. The white robes gasped, covering their ears, and the windows trembled. The glass splintered into webs of silver fissures. Alessa wished they would break; she'd gladly watch as the shards of their precious saints rained death down upon them.

"Silence her!" Father Samuel boomed, barely audible beneath Aria's scream. The executioner, holding the tray of weapons, wordlessly grabbed a switchblade and plunged it into the center of Aria's stomach. Alessa's throat burned as she yelled. Maya threw her head back and screwed her eyes shut to block it all out, tears hot on her cheeks. It stifled Aria's scream, the voices stopping all at once. Red bubbled around the wound, staining her thin clothes as it ran down her torso and legs.

Noah cried out her name, his complexion going white, and he tried to push himself with his restrained feet across the floor.

"Please, stop! Why are you doing this?!" he begged, watching as Aria's blood puddled beneath her on the floor. Noah twisted so he could look Father Samuel in the face. The man was watching Aria in rapt curiosity but kept his distance from her. Noah spat out a wad of saliva mixed with blood.

"Hey, fucker! Answer me!"

Father Samuel glanced at him. He made a waving motion with his hand in Aria's direction and two of the executioners jumped to attention. One laid out the clear tarp beneath Aria, covering as much of the floor as possible, while the other handed various instruments of destruction to the remaining black robes. The one who'd previously beaten Noah grabbed the boy's shirt and hauled him to his knees.

"There is much you need to learn, son," the man replied.

Noah slowly lifted his head to face the person holding him in place. A gloved fist pulled the executioner's hood from their head.

"Dad?" Noah stuttered.

Alessa thought she might pass out. How many people were in on this?

"What is happening?" Noah whispered. His father's frown deepened, and he looked at the priest, awaiting his next orders. The old man smiling, his mouth reaching ear to ear. Alessa pictured it opening up wider and wider until his head split open and all that remained were pink muscles and teeth.

"You should feel honored, Noah. You're finally going to learn the true history of this town, but not the stories they teach you in class. No. Those are diluted versions of half-truths we told to keep the town functioning when more outsiders came and set down roots here."

Father Samuel had all of their attention now, and it made him beam with pride. He was in his element again, preaching his word to a loyal audience. He saw the confusion on their faces and chuckled.

"You see, for many, many years, the only inhabitants of our town were direct descendants of the original founders of Pine Hollow. They are all around you now." Maya flinched when he briefly, but pointedly rested his eyes on her. "Our lineage goes all the way back to the beginning, Maya, to when this land was originally settled. My great-great-grandfather was the first to walk his bare feet across this sacred ground. He was here when others attempted to steal our home, and when the first railroads were implemented. But most important of all, he was here when they came."

A hush settled over the room, leaving nothing but the wind batting against the side of the church and Aria's strained breathing. Many of the disciples muttered prayers to themselves, pressing their lips to the crosses held in their shaking hands.

"They?" Noah asked.

Shadows fell over Samuel's gaze, his smile fading. "We've called them by many names over the decades; the harvesters, echoes, the ravagers. Each of them is correct, in their own right. Although, I must admit I've always believed ravagers suited them best. Horrible beasts from the forest."

Maya's grip on Alessa's fingers tightened to the point of pain, but she didn't dare pull away.

"Yes," he replied as his eyes glazed over. He looked out the quivering windows at the black sky.

"True hunters. They lived in the woods, in the shadows between the trees. Creatures older and stronger than anything known. Fierce and vile things. After our ancestors broke ground and started building their life here, those who ventured too far beyond the tree line were swept away, never to be seen again. They found the remains of a few, but only bones—licked clean. Our people were terrified, their numbers were dwindling, and being unable to breach the forest made it impossible to hunt. There were rumors of voices coming from the trees, trying to lure people into the night. People were dying—they were desperate."

He cast his glower upon Aria next, hand resting on his ancient book as if to soak its strength into his skin. She was shivering, the sharp lines of her emaciated body illuminated by firelight.

"The ravagers almost succeeded. No matter what we tried to defend ourselves, they continued to best us. Until, one day, my grandfather received a message. A message from God."

The prayers stopped, and the disciples leaned in, hanging on his every word. It was hard for Alessa not to do the same, but she was dangling on his hook, and he knew it. She needed to know the truth. What did these alleged beasts have to do with her sister? Father Samuel lifted his head to the sky, basking in his Lord's imagined radiance.

"He was gifted with visions and knowledge, and through his guidance, our ancestors learned how to kill these monsters, a task previously believed to be impossible. Not long after the visions came, they slayed their first one. The town celebrated for weeks; even those who once questioned my grandfather became loyal servants to God and his teachings. Finally, our people stood a chance, and there was hope.

"Grandfather knew the fight was not over. The visions kept coming, and he told tales of more beasts lying in wait. They wouldn't stop until they reduced us to a pile of bones. The men readied their weapons,

CHAPTER 32

and the hunted became the hunters."

The executioner in charge of the tarp approached the priest and handed him an ornate, golden chalice, head bowing deeply to express respect. Samuel accepted it gratefully.

"Chaos—war—ensued. Each ravager alone contains the strength of over twenty men, but with all of our forces combined, we came to a stalemate. We proved ourselves a force to be reckoned with. Had it continued down that path, it would not have been long before everyone was dead.

"Grandfather remained steadfast in his belief that the Lord was paving the way to a better future for all of them. He just needed to look for the signs. None of his visions prepared him for what came next, but he was right again—because an opportunity presented itself. A way out of mutually assured destruction. These ravagers, even with all their viciousness and savagery, could communicate. Grandfather and his closest disciples spoke to one on a dark, winter night when things were at their worst. By his account, the creature remained shaded by the trees, but its voice carried on the wind. All they noted seeing were a pair of ruby eyes. That night, our ancestors and the beasts came to an agreement."

The closest executioner grabbed Alessa and wrenched her out of Maya's grasp. They screamed and cried, Alessa trying to wriggle out of his hold, but the man's grip tightened he dragged her to the front. He tossed her onto her stomach when they reached the sanctuary, and she landed inches from Father Samuel's feet. The executioner forced her into a kneeling position. She was closer to Aria as well. She saw the blood trails running down her sister's legs.

A gloved hand grabbed Alessa's jaw, forcing her to face ahead. Father Samuel stood in front of his podium now, book forgotten in favor of the chalice. Now that she had a closer look, she noticed it was the same chalice they used for communion every Sunday.

"To avoid an all-out slaughter, they made a compromise. They would allow us to enter and hunt the forest safely, without interference, from that day on. Only at a certain distance, but it allowed men to provide for their families again and ensure they didn't go hungry in the winter. We would no longer have to fear the forest in its entirety and stay trapped in our homes, wondering who would be next. But to provide us with safety, they would need something from us in return."

Father Samuel stepped down from the sanctuary to stand right in front of Alessa. She saw the chalice up close. Red liquid sloshed in its golden mouth. He cupped her chin. His thumb brushed her cheek, almost lovingly, as any grandfather would.

"We came and took the land they'd been using as hunting grounds for centuries. Them giving us a piece was no paltry offer. In doing so, they were giving up their primary source of food. Us. In order to keep our people alive, and to allow the chance for Pine Hollow to prosper, we needed to offer something that carried equal importance. There are few things more important to humans than their children."

The pieces were clicking into place. Aria, Dominic, and Constance, all children related to members of this church, and all of them with a lineage dating back to the beginning of Pine Hollow. Both of Alessa's parents were born and raised here, and their parents before them, and she knew the same to be true of the other two lost kids as well.

"Every generation we randomly choose a family from the original settlement to hand over their first-born child."

Alessa whimpered, shaking her head. She didn't want to listen anymore. She didn't want any of this to be true. Her stomach twisted, and she was sick with guilt. She had asked for this; she was the one that couldn't keep her nose out of things. Her obsession brought them here. Noah and Maya deserved better than this.

"It's nothing personal, Alessa. Your family was just next in line."

Alessa jerked her head out of his hand. He simply chuckled, amused by her spite.

Noah scowled at the hold man, disgust painting his every word. "So, you have kids just to kill them? Why let them live at all? Why not just give them off as soon as they're born?" he hissed.

"Babies do not provide enough sustenance. Besides, it's a great honor to be given to the ravagers, those chosen are making the ultimate sacrifice–their lives ensure our safety. Without them, the madness would never end. Giving these heroes a taste of life, a chance to be with their families, and to feel love and happiness–it is the least we can do."

Aria lifted her head, panting through the pain as she pulled at her bindings. The hilt of the knife caught on the strap across her midsection, getting a pained yelp from her and stopping her from moving.

"Aria was to fulfill her purpose, just like those who came before her. Everything went according to plan; we administered medication to help her sleep. She was never supposed to feel any pain. We left our offering, as we always have. But something went wrong."

Father Samuel pinned Aria with a glare sharp enough to cut down even the most confident of men. Aria's eyes blazed with incandescent fury, meeting his disdain with equal loathing.

"Our offering was not enough. It was returned to us. Perhaps we were too hasty. Tradition dictates the child must be eighteen, but once we discovered her plan to race out of town before her birthday, we didn't have any time to waste. Aria was not fit for sacrifice, so instead, they tainted her."

An executioner appeared at Aria's side and tore the knife from her stomach. Aria released another ragged scream.

"Jesus! Fuck! What is wrong with you people?" Noah sobbed.

Alessa's tears dampened her gag, coating her mouth in the taste of salt and shame. The knife left a hole in Aria's shirt, exposing the wet, glistening wound where her belly button once was. A small, slow stream of blood dribbled from between the flaps of torn flesh but came to an abrupt stop.

And then the skin started stitching itself back together.

Alessa went numb, her mind going blank as she watched the wound sow itself into a smooth plain of flesh. The muscles and skin moved of their own accord to bind what was broken. In less than a minute, it healed completely, leaving only blood behind. This wasn't real, Alessa immediately told herself. It was impossible–unthinkable.

She closed her eyes and saw Aria at the end of their hallway again, dark liquid running down her face, and then the mauled raccoon in the yard. Alessa pictured Aria, hunched in the snow, face buried in the viscera of the poor, dead animal, her eyes red and full of hunger. Alessa gazed up at her sister; she didn't know whether to be amazed or terrified by what she'd witnessed, by what she knew to be true even if her mind tried to reject it.

Aria disappeared from her room that day as a normal teenage girl. She came back as something else.

"They corrupted her soul and made her like them. We may never truly understand how or why. But I believe she was returned to us for a reason."

Father Samuel took Alessa's chin in his hand again. This time, she was too drained to care.

"She was sent as a test of our strength, and our willingness to contribute to the greater good. Aria's failure tipped the scales, but your success will restore them to balance."

Alessa's heart, maybe even time itself, stopped when she heard those words. She threw herself back but landed in the arms of the executioner. He quickly set her straight, hand like a vice on the back of her neck. The screams of Noah and Maya came to her from miles away, as if from the other side of a long tunnel.

"Don't do this!" Aria growled.

Noah tried to get to his feet again, but his father was on him in an instant, wrapping his arms around the boy's torso to keep the boy pinned to his chest. Another executioner moved to guard Maya when the girl tried to scoot herself closer to Alessa, and she froze when she caught the glint of a butcher knife in their hand.

"Are you ready to serve your Lord, Alessa?" Samuel asked.

She tried to lean away when he lifted his hand to her face and tugged her gag out of her mouth. A shimmering web of spit connected her bottom lip to the cloth, and she coughed, the lingering fuzziness of the drug still coating the inside of her mouth.

"Please," she choked out, shaking her head, "don't do this."

Father Samuel was unmoved. "It's time for communion, Ms. Hale. Open up."

"Please, Father! Please—you don't have to!" Alessa pleaded, pushing away from him as he lifted the chalice to her face, "you don't even know if this will work-!"

Father Samuel shoved the lip of the chalice against her mouth while she was mid-speech and tilted it to pour the red wine down her throat. Alessa sputtered, trying not to swallow, but they fisted her hair and forced her head back. There was nowhere for the alcohol to go but down. It was dry and bitter on her tongue and settled like hot sludge in her stomach. She hacked and sucked in desperate gasps for air, but he didn't stop until she'd consumed every drop. Warmth filled her body.

"Now we begin."

Alessa's body no longer felt like her own. Everything was hazy and light. When they finally let go, she collapsed onto the floor in a tangle of useless limbs, her arms and legs as weak as spaghetti noodles.

Strangely, even though she heard Noah and Maya's pleas, even though she saw Aria fighting against her bindings as Father Samuel and three executioners approached her, she felt calm. A bubble of serenity formed around her. Alessa's mind caught up quickly. They had drugged her again. She remained awake, but intensely groggy, she willed her body to move, but it did not respond.

The executioners converged on Aria, her movements becoming more erratic. Silver glinted in their hands, long and serrated. Noah's hysterical voice rose to a fever pitch.

Alessa's bubble burst when the jagged edge of the first saw cut into Aria's arm, and the church echoed with her sister's screams.

Chapter 33

There came a time as they cowered under the eyes of their crucified Lord, when Aria didn't know what screams belonged to who anymore. Noah, Maya, Alessa, and Aria. Their wails morphed into a ghastly harmony of pain. Her throat was raw, and she tasted blood.

Blood. It was everywhere, spraying out of the lacerations carved into her arms and thighs. Each executioner carried his own handheld bone saw and went to work on removing her limbs. They worked in silence even as she cried out—even as she begged for them to stop.

Lily and Joshua stood nearby. Their mother was the picture of serenity, and quietly praying. Her eyes were closed, face risen in an expression of absolute peace, and body undulating with her Aria's pleas. Joshua stood next to her, tense but unreadable. If it weren't for him blinking, she would have thought him made of stone.

Aria's right arm was the first to go, dropping to the floor with a sickening, wet thud. Her pale, thin appendage landing in a shallow pool of blood. The jagged edge of her bone pierced the ruined the flesh, shining against bits of wiry, pink muscle. The agony was sharp, relentless, and all-consuming. Aria was no longer sure if she and the pain were not one and the same. Eventually, she could no longer scream, her throat full of knives.

Another limb hit the soaked tarp, this time one of her legs. She felt light and heavy all at once; the blood gushing from her veins and leaving her cold. Voices became muddled and deep, like listening to someone underwater. Her eyelids fluttered, vision fading, but she tried to push through it. Aria pictured Alessa's smiling face, transforming from the young girl she knew now to the soft, rounder features her sister possessed as a toddler. The moment Alessa was born, she'd been perfect. God, how Aria loved her, so beautiful and innocent. She was supposed to protect that little girl, and all she brought was ruin.

Her left arm dropped next, and her body fell limp and clammy against the wooden cross, glazed eyes staring dazedly at the ceiling. Vomit spewed from Noah's lips and dribbled down his chest, coating his father's arms in bile. The sour smell burned the man's eyes, and he loosened his grip as he leaned back to avoid it. Noah saw his chance. Using the leeway, his father accidentally gave him to rear his head back, crushing his skull into the man's nose with a moist crunch. Immediately, his arms unraveled from around his son to cradle his throbbing face, blood already trailing down his lips and chin. Noah's battle cry rang out as he shoved away from his father.

Noah launched at the nearest executioner, their bodies colliding and slamming onto the blood drenched tarp. In the chaos, Noah did the only thing he could think of and bit down on the man's ear through the hood.

"Gah! Get the fuck off, you little shit!" The guy wriggled and wailed, both of them covered and slick with blood, but Noah never lost his grip.

He bit down harder and pulled until the flesh tore between his teeth. It wasn't long, unfortunately, before the remaining executioners were on him, wrangling him into submission. Noah kicked his feet furiously, blood staining his mouth. Father Samuel glided toward him. His wrinkled hand dipped smoothly beneath his vestment.

"Let me go! Fuck you guys, you fucking freaks!"

"What the hell is wrong with you?!" Noah screeched, fear bordering on mania. "Do you really think this is what God wants?! You fucking monsters! ARIA!"

Father Samuel closed the gap between them in five steps, unveiling his arm from its concealment. A flash of light reflected off his hand and into Aria's eyes. They held Noah in place with their bruising grip.

"ARI-!"

Samuel gripped Noah's shoulder with one hand, brandishing a knife in the other, and plunged the blade into Noah's soft stomach all the way to the hilt. It cut Noah's pleas short. He tried to lean away.

Noah's shattered scream caused Aria's head to perk back up, breaking through her detachment. She groggily lifted her pounding, heavy head, forcing herself to bear witness to what she knew, in her heart, might very well be the end of her. She saw Father Samuel's hand, now soaked in red, keeping the blade inside as the boy she loved sputtered and hacked up thick globs of blood. Confusion and despair glittered like diamonds in his eyes. The priest cupped Noah's cheek with a gentle palm and held the boy's gaze as he clamped his fist tighter on the hilt and dragged the knife up from gut to sternum.

Whatever remained of Aria broke when his innards came spilling out onto the floor, a growing pile of pink and red intestines spiraling at his feet. Her sanity splintered into hundreds of pieces, scattering to the furthest reaches of her psyche. It no longer mattered what remained of her when this was over. The Aria she once was had ceased to exist.

Alessa's consciousness faded just as the knife met its home in Noah's chest, his insides all over the floor. Maya wept on the floor.

Father Samuel pushed away from Noah, and the executioners let go. His body, now nothing more than a sack of skin and bones, crashed to the floor noisily. Samuel looked at Noah's father, chest puffed, and shoulders rolled back in a challenging stance, as if goading the man to question him. Mr. Harrison's eyes flickered from the priest to his son motionless on the floor, but he made no motions to defy his elder. In fact, he barely lingered on Noah for a few seconds before he was grabbing his hood and slipping it back over his head. The priest smiled as Noah's father graciously took his knife, the very weapon that brought about son's demise, and wiped the blood off on his robe.

"I feel for your loss, Mr. Harrison, but as you know, there was no other way." Samuel's hand clenched the man's forearm in a sympathetic gesture. The executioner bowed his head, a practiced move Aria could tell they'd all performed a hundred times.

Noticing Alessa's current state, the old man chuckled lightheartedly, until he set his sights once again on his own progeny. Maya's fear made her body go rigid, even as he indicated for his followers to bring her closer to the front. A mewl got caught in her throat when powerful arms hoisted her off the cold floor and dragged her to her grandfather's feet. She landed on the tarp and blood immediately soaked into her clothes.

"I know this is scary, granddaughter, but I tried to warn you. I tried to keep you away from them. You could have avoided so much pain, my dear, if you'd just stayed away," Samuel ruminated, sliding a soft finger over her cheekbone. She pulled away.

"I know you wish there was more you could have done, but I assure you, their fates were sealed long ago. It is not our job to question the teachings of our Lord. It is as it was, as it always has been, and as it always will be.

"I know you care for Alessa and for her sister. You've always had such a kind and generous heart. That is our family curse, after all, caring too much—always wanting to do what is right. But this beast... this *devil*." Samuel lifted a withering finger at Aria. "You allowed her in. You allowed her to manipulate and corrupt you into turning against your own family."

She shook her head. Maya grumbled against her gag. Unbothered by his granddaughter's snarling, and gripped her chin, Samuel pinched the skin just hard enough to show her he meant business. Maya hissed and allowed him to position her head as he pleased.

"Now it is your duty to witness the final rite."

He forced her head to turn, and she had no choice but to take it all in. An ocean of blood now covered the tarp, spilling out a little onto the wooden floor. The executioners formed a semi-circle around Aria's mangled form, her arms and legs resting in a pile nearby. Aria was still alive. Her chest was bouncing up and down convulsively, and she'd lost all color by this point, a sheen of feverish sweat coating what remained of her. Her pink lips were ghostly white, and her wild, golden eyes fixated on one point: Noah's lifeless form.

"Lily, Joshua."

The Hale couple stood at attention.

"Now is the time to say your goodbyes to Aria, if you so desire."

Joshua was the first to take the offer. Lily remained rooted to her spot as her husband approached Aria, keeping his head up to avoid the carnage at his feet.

"Stand back, allow our brother some privacy," Samuel spoke as he motioned for everyone to back away. Joshua stopped when he reached Aria's side, hovering as close as the giant cross would allow.

"Let us all bow our heads and pray for our brother, Joseph. His family is truly giving the ultimate sacrifice, and we should feel honored to share in their grief."

"Praise be!" a disciple chattered.

"Amen!" came another excited reply from the sidelines.

Samuel imbued the once quiet audience with a new sense of purpose, no doubt feeling further motivated by the sight of their long-reviled beast being bled like a stuck pig. All of them lowered their heads and closed their eyes to pray, except for Maya.

Joshua took a steadying breath, his hands moving over Aria but never touching her. Aria didn't notice him; she only saw Noah—or what was left of him.

"Aria," Joshua whispered, low enough for only her to hear, "my sweet, sweet girl. I'm so sorry. This isn't how I wanted things to be. God, I know how meaningless that sounds, but it's true. This is the only life I know, the only life my parents knew. What kind of excuse is that?"

He finally mustered the courage to place a hand on her cold cheek. "Please, Ari, look at me."

It took her a while and a great deal of effort, but she finally tilted her head to face her father. Her vision was bleary, and she registered who he was, more by his voice than his face. Her head fell against his warm palm, and when she got a whiff of his cologne, buried below layers of iron, she felt like a sick child again, being comforted and tended to by her daddy. An influx of love washed over her, but the other met it with an equal level of hatred, still writhing in her guts and in her brain. Aria both wanted to lean into him for support and sink her teeth into the pliable skin at his wrist. She couldn't decide if she wanted to embrace him or rip him apart.

"I have failed you; I know that now. How can I call myself a father and do the horrible things I've done? But even though I failed, you and your sister still came out pretty damn good. You are the strongest person I know, honey."

Joshua sniffled and wiped wearily at his wet face with the back of his hand. He leaned over Aria, one arm arching over her to bring her into some weak semblance of a hug, his face coming close to hers. Joshua slipped his hand under his robe and into the waistband of his pants.

"Don't let my failings decide your future. I've taken enough from you," Joshua spoke against her ear. Aria's mind still warred with itself.

All she needed to do was lift her head a little and her teeth would be in his neck. Instead, she bit her tongue hard enough to split it open, warm blood spurting out of it like a geyser. It reminded her she still had control over her own body.

"If I can help you take something back, well... it may not earn me your forgiveness, I'm not sure I'll ever be worthy of that."

Joshua cast a cursory glance around the room to ensure everyone's heads stayed bowed and eyes were still closed. He landed on Maya, stiffening in surprise at her harsh, unblinking glare. They froze like that, stuck in time for what seemed like eons, but was only for a few seconds. Joshua kept eye contact even as he slid an object out from within his cloak. He opened his palm to Maya, so she'd see what it was, but only briefly, before he slid the small, thin object into the pocket of Aria's blood drenched pants. Aria couldn't see it, but she could feel it. It was sharp against her hip.

"I hope at the very least... this counts for something." His words rushed over her like water, slipping in and out of her grasp. Aria teetered on the edge of delirium; she was running out of time. "I love you, sweetheart. No matter what you believe, that is the truth."

Joshua departed with one last kiss on her forehead. His footsteps signaled the end of the prayer, and Father Samuel turned to Lily with an arched brow. She immediately shook her head as Joshua rejoined her side.

"I've already said my goodbyes, Father. Quite a long time ago," Lily said. Aria almost laughed at the predictability of it all. Samuel's smile exuded pride.

"Then it is time." He turned to his executioners, voice exploding with confidence. "My brothers! Let us end this, and may God smile upon us all."

"Amen, Father," they replied in unison.

"Let's bring them down."

The cross jolted underneath Aria, her body twitching with every movement, and then she was rolling. Her head lolled to the side. There were two black-robed figures on either side of her, moving the cross back down the aisle. The other disciples slipped between the pews, stopping at the aisle to take her in with hungry eyes. Commotion erupted behind her, but someone silenced it efficiently with a loud slap. A flurry of footsteps followed them.

They brought the girls down to the basement. The executioners lifted Maya off of her feet to drag her down the stairs. Once they reached the secret door, now uncovered in its entirety from behind the organ, they removed Aria from the cross. The journey came to her in bits and pieces, the excessive blood loss making her consciousness spotty. She was glad for it, because, in the dark, the pain and the humiliation of her present situation couldn't get to her.

When she came to again, she was at the bottom of the stairs, in a room she never knew existed. It was frigid, sterile, and smelled of soil and chemicals. Once they hit the landing, they tossed Maya into the corner, her head nearly cracking against the wall. She sniffled and backed away from them until she had nowhere else to go, her body trying to make itself as small as possible. The executioners tossed Aria's limbs into a pile next to Maya. The object in Aria's pocket pinched her skin. Her eyes widened, the spark of an idea flickering to life in her mind. Maybe there was still a chance. She just had to make sure the object landed in the right hands.

Aria turned her head, opened her mouth wide, and buried her teeth in the executioner's tender neck just below the flap of his hood. The flesh gave way easily, blood filling her mouth. The man shrieked, trying to pull her off, but her jaw locked in place. They would have to pry her away. She wasn't going down without taking something with her.

"Gah! Get her off! GET HER OFF!"

The others rushed to help him. Father Samuel watched from the safety of the doorway. "Brothers, handle this."

CHAPTER 33

Aria grinned madly, biting harder. She locked eyes with Maya trembling in the corner. She only hoped the girl understood what she was trying to convey. Without her, all of this was for nothing. It took three executioners to pull her away, but part of the man went with her. When they finally wrangle her off of him, she ripped a chunk of flesh from his neck, blood spraying in every direction. He collapsed, not dead yet but barely hanging on, his body shuddering as he pressed his hands to the wound to stop the bleeding. Aria smiled at Father Samuel and spit her trophy at his feet. They threw her down; the ground knocked the wind out of her as she landed on her stomach.

The others tended to their wounded brother, and Father Samuel shouted orders. Aria's and Maya's eyes met. Aria nodded her head toward her pocket and watched understanding pass over the girl's face. Maya lowered herself into an army crawl, and pushed herself toward Aria. Aria braced for impact when Maya threw herself on top of her, dramatically wailing against her gag.

"Right pocket," Aria whispered. Maya responded by crying even louder while her restrained hands frantically patted her sides.

"There is nothing more you can do. He's beyond help," Samuel called over them, brows narrowing, when he noticed his granddaughter had moved.

"That's enough! Everyone focus!" he commanded. The executioners lingered over their fallen friend and then stepped away. The man's breathing was shallow now. It wouldn't be much longer. Maya's sweat-slicked hands continued in their secret search.

"Now get her up!"

Boots bounded toward Maya; her fingers slipped into Aria's pocket. One second Aria felt Maya's weight and then it was gone, hoisted from her by the priest's lapdog's and returned to her corner. The battering ram of Aria's heart made her sternum shake, and she searched for Maya's eyes in the sea of activity. Black cloaks blocked her view, and they raised her into the air once again, this time to place her on the cold, metal slab. She arched her neck until she glimpsed Maya amidst the insanity. Maya sat huddled in the corner, knees to her chest, and when she noticed Aria was watching, she replied with a nod of her own. Aria's head fell back in relief.

Father Samuel approached Aria and sighed in disappointment.

"Things could have turned out so differently, Aria. If you had only understood your place."

There were a million things she wanted to say to him; but she settled for, "I'll see you in, Hell, Father."

His jaw clenched in irritation, but he resisted the urge to bite back, gathering himself with a deep breath as he performed the sign of the cross. When he rose his hand to his lips, she saw it, the antique gold ring she'd kept envisioning.

"Your sister will restore balance. Her soul will right your wrongs. It is our Lord's job to judge you now, and we defer to His great wisdom. May your death bring our peace."

He turned to Maya. "You, I will deal with later. In the meantime, your punishment will be to listen." Samuel smiled at Aria again.

"Farewell, Miss Hale."

Samuel stepped away, and suddenly she was moving again. The metal grate slid beneath her, pushing her into a long cement and brick chamber. The interior was smooth, save for a large green cylinder sticking out of the ceiling. Darkness blanketed the tight space when the door of the chamber shut with a sharp clang. Claustrophobia set in. The air was hot and stale, and the smell of gas burned her nostrils. She tried to calm her breathing and remain focused. She had to trust Maya would know what to do. They'd gotten this far.

Aria wriggled uselessly and uncomfortably; it was getting warmer at an alarming rate. She wanted to kick her legs or throw her arms, none of which was possible. Light flashed, wiping out the dark, and a sharp gasp escaped her. Flames flickered to life below the grate she rested on, and dark, thick smoke filling the chamber. When Aria felt the first lick of fire along her spine, she screamed.

Chapter 34

The flames under the grate were inescapable, the entire underside of her body searing with brand new pain. And here she thought she was beyond feeling anymore. The fire danced over her back, blistering the flesh but not melting it yet, but each time the wounded skin reformed itself, her body not allowing itself to go down without a fight. However, it was useless unless the fire ceased. She knew the only reason they hadn't incinerated her yet was because the machine was still warming. It was only going to get worse.

"RAAHH!" Aria howled, the other howling with her, their distress becoming a united front.

Smoke filled her lungs, making it impossible to breathe, and the heat was climbing higher. She gasped for air. Her mind was slipping, everything was becoming hazy, her head throbbing with pressure. The flames rose, and the blisters started popping. She let out a strangled squeal, trying to arch away despite the impossibility.

"Please... please... AAAHH!"

As her head slammed back down against the grate, the chamber fell eerily quiet. No longer could she hear the whirring of the machine as it churned to life, or the crackling of the flames even though she saw they were still alight. She blinked in confusion, sniffing the air, but it wasn't smoke she smelled, it was pine. Something shuffled in the dark near where her feet were supposed to be.

Black sockets and a sharp, bloody smile stared back. Her doppelgänger. But this time Aria did not fear the copy. She welcomed it, her stomach whirling with the other's excitement. She laid back down as the doppelgänger crawled over her until they were face to face. Aria no longer felt the fire. Her copy seemed to bring the cold with it, and it wrapped them both in a cocoon. As Aria gazed into its black holes, she knew it was time. Maybe she had always known, no matter how long or how far she ran, it would always catch up to her. It was time to stop running, and she was so, so tired.

To her surprise, the doppelgänger's smile softened, its abyssal eyes exuding a softness she didn't think possible. Her stomach settled, the other knowing its relief was coming soon. When the doppelgänger lifted its hand over her face, she didn't fight it—she welcomed it. Aria let her eyes close, and the copy placed its frigid palm on her forehead.

Skin touched skin, and it all came back. Every memory she'd buried or believed lost came crashing back in a flurry, slotting themselves into her brain like puzzle pieces. Aria finally saw all of it, from beginning to end.

She remembered asking her mother for a sleeping pill, and Lily giving it to her with a mug of warm milk, sprinkled with cinnamon, just as she liked it. Within minutes of her head hitting the pillow, she drifted off into a deep and dreamless slumber.

She remembered being jostled awake, the cool night air dusting her cheeks, bleary eyes blinking up at a starry sky. Exhaustion still had its hooks in her, and the rhythmic swaying of her body was only making it more difficult to stay awake. Words fluttered around her, but she only grasped a few.

"*Just as the Son of Man did not come to be served, but to serve, and give His life as a ransom for many!*"

She remembered the wrinkled hand with the gold ring as it placed a sour smelling cloth over her face, and she descended into the blackness once more.

She remembered waking up alone in the woods, not knowing where she was or how she got there. Clad in a white dress, and head pounding, she screamed to the sky and started her journey.

Aria suddenly recalled spending days in those woods, walking in what felt like infinite circles, until her feet were raw and bloody, and she stank of sweat. Nights were growing colder; winter was fast approaching. Time became meaningless.

Aria relived herself being hungry. Hungrier than she ever thought possible, not knowing how to hunt for food and realizing that sustaining herself on water and berries would only last her so long. The ravenous clawing in her stomach was all-consuming. Every nerve and cell in her body shrieked for food. It was then that she noticed something was watching her, following her.

Aria remembered it never leaving her. She felt its eyes on her all the time, heard its breath whispering in the night, its footsteps never far behind even when she ran. It filled her fitful sleep with nightmares, images of mutilation and brutality, calling to her in the voices of people she loved. Aria never saw it, but knew it was getting closer. She stopped running when her body started eating itself.

Aria remembered her last moments of being Aria. The first snow had come and gone, and finally depleted of energy, she collapsed at a nearby stream. What she saw in her reflection was a thinly wrapped skeleton, her ribs protruding like blades, cheekbones jutting out and giving her an alien appearance. Her lips were shredded and dry. She'd taken to chewing on them days ago to fill the void. She no longer felt her toes or fingers, their tips black. A rustling from across the stream caught her attention.

Aria did not remember seeing it, even then. She knew now there was nothing to see. All the same, she knew it was there. Two small, red

CHAPTER 34

orbs peered at her from between the trees, their hypnotic pull locked her in. They held her there as a shadow skittered across the water, slithered up her torso like a snake, and buried itself in her throat as the world went dark.

She remembered staggering through the woods after, knowing nothing and feeling nothing but hunger. Always searching, constantly vigilant. Aria was little more than a meat puppet, watching from inside as this other thing hunted.

She remembered Jason, the man in the woods. He'd heard her calling for help, breaking through the bushes as the hunger finally overcame her completely. She'd become something else then, something new, and horrifying, and beautiful, and dangerous. It was agony and ecstasy as her bones, muscles, and skin warped and mutated. Hot blood hit her throat as she tore into him, popping strips of flesh into her mouth like candy, her fangs slicing through him with ease. At the end, when she saw the ruin she'd caused, her mind snapped, ripping away the memory of what she'd become before she stumbled back into town.

That wasn't all. Along with her memories came the memories of the spirit that dwelled inside of her. The one that stalked her, the one that turned her. Memories of carnage and slaughter, of humans desecrating other creatures just like it, of mourning their loss, and of seeking vengeance.

Aria came to with a gasp, back inside the incinerator. The fire now raged, heat reaching its peak. It strangled her, knotting her throat. Her heartbeat was slowing. She was out of time.

Was it truly going to end this way? She wished she had done more; she thought of Noah lying in a pile of his own mutilated innards, and Alessa, who was no doubt being dragged to the woods just as she'd been.

"I'm sorry, Squirt..." Aria uttered between brittle lips.

She no longer felt trepidation or fear. All she felt now was acceptance.

White light flooded her vision, and someone yanked her from the hellish chamber, the grate sliding out with relative ease. Spots dotted her eyes as they adjusted to the new light, and she found she was staring at the ceiling of the secret room again. To her left was Maya.

The girl was haggard, curly hair flying in every direction, expression stuck in a mask of shock, her mouth a pale line slashing through the center of her face. Sweat glistened on her face, and her wrists and ankles were now completely unbound, her gag removed. Gripped in her hand was the object her father gave her: a shard of broken mirror, cutting into her palm until it bled. They stared at one another, neither needing to say anything. A silent understanding passed over them. Tendrils of smoke twirled in the air, fire still blasting behind her.

"My arms and legs... I need them," Aria croaked, mouth and throat still dry as a dessert. Now out of the flames, her skin healed itself completely, leaving no trace of any burns of blisters. The pain was receding. Maya glanced between Aria and the limbs that were left behind. The thought of picking them up made her gag.

"Please, Maya... I'll heal faster..."

Aria didn't question where this knowledge came from. It was just there. She was the creature, and the creature was her. She knew what it knew. There was no untangling them now. She'd ride with it until the end, until the final pieces of her soul were jettisoned and nothing more remained.

Maya muscled through her hesitation, steeling herself as she picked up the first arm, biting her tongue to keep from vomiting.

"Just place it where it needs to be... that's right, you'll need to hold it for a few seconds."

Aria's voice smoothed out as her insides healed. Maya held her right arm against its corresponding shoulder and held it in place. Aria bared her teeth, sucking in a harsh breath. Muscles and tendons wiggled back into place, reattaching themselves to the lost arm, the bone slotting back into place. The skin both tickled and stung as it stitched itself. If it weren't for the situation, the look of surprise on Maya would be comical. As soon as she knew the arm wasn't going to move, she ripped her hands away. A tingling sensation returned to Aria's fingers.

"The others, hurry!"

Maya was faster now that she knew it worked. She rushed to grab the next arm and repeated the original maneuver. She watched the second arm reseal successfully. In Aria's right arm, blood was pumping again, a full feeling coming back. Smoke was filling the room and sneaking under the crack in the door. By the time Maya returned with one of her legs, Aria held it in place herself as Maya retrieved the final one. As the final limb reattached, Maya stepped back for Aria to undo the leather strap around her midsection. She stretched when she was back on her feet, bones popping and clicking. She rolled her wrists and ankles, re-familiarizing herself.

"How is this real?"

Tears filled Maya's eyes, and she was trembling. Aria met her with a solemn frown, a calm settling over her as she finally saw everything for what it was.

"It just is," she said. It wasn't enough, but it would have to do.

Aria took stock of their surroundings, the heat from the incinerator, the smoke that would soon cloak the room, and the locked door that was their only escape. Her mind was blissfully clear, and despite their situation, Aria felt no more fear, no more panic. She knew nothing but one singular goal: to get to her sister. The spirit did not rage, for their goals were now the same, because saving her sister also meant the demise of Father Samuel and all of his pathetic little disciples.

"How long have they been gone?" Aria questioned in a flat tone.

"I don't know, maybe ten minutes? Fifteen tops," Maya stammered.

Aria flexed her limbs again, ensuring full sensation and strength had returned to all, and approached the door. Maya gave her a wide breadth, throwing her arm over her mouth and nose to keep from inhaling too much smoke. She slammed her first down on the wooden door, resulting in a loud crack and a split opening in the center. Maya watched in silence as she landed another blow, splinters exploding around Aria, the door breaking further. It was the third hit that did it, the now shattered door smashing against the stairs. Aria grabbed a large shard of wood that broke off of it and turned to Maya.

"Go, now," she demanded; brushing past her to reach the incinerator.

"What are you talking about? What about you?"

"You don't have much time; you'll inhale too much smoke. Go. I'll be right behind you."

"Aria, please just come with me! Think about Alessa!" Maya pleaded.

"I am," she said, glancing over her shoulder at the girl once last time, "there's something I need to do first. Understand?"

Aria gestured to the slab of wood she was carrying, nodding to the incinerator. Maya's eyes widened when the realization dawned on her. She responded with a hesitant nod.

"Now, go," Aria repeated.

Maya didn't argue, hair whipping behind her as she darted up the stairs without a beat. Satisfied the girl was far enough away, she stuck the end of the wooden piece into the fire until it caught flame. She let the incinerator run at full heat, carrying the flaming board to the basement floor, smoke following her. Aria grabbed anything and everything from photo albums to old sheets, to broken furniture, and set it all alight. The fire latched to all it touched, and soon the entire room was flaring yellow and red. She tossed the wood into the inferno when she was done. The rest would take care of itself.

The church was dark now, save for a few lanterns, giving the brutal

CHAPTER 34

scene in the sanctuary an even more haunting feel. The blood looked black now, and even the air was still and lifeless. In her peripheral, the fire was climbing up the stairs, but she couldn't resist the urge to enter the main hall, anyway.

She stopped when she reached Noah's body, gravitating toward it like a magnet. Any mad hope she may have had about finding him alive was dashed when she finally laid eyes on him. His corpse was still and cold, rigor already beginning to set in due to the winter chill. His eyes and mouth remained open in a horrible, terrified scream, the fear imprinting on him even in death. This was not the boy she loved, not anymore.

She knew she should be crying, but she felt disconnected from the well of her emotions. All that remained of the true Aria was the tiny spark that sought to protect Alessa. It was the only thing keeping her intact. The creature was tugging at her insides, telling her to go. They had a job to do. Aria clenched her fists, shaking her head. No. He did not deserve to go out like this. She grabbed the back of his collar and dragged.

The fire had reached the first floor by the time Aria pulled Noah into the lobby. Shoving the front door open, the pair emerged into the winter night. The cold was heavenly on Aria's skin. She turned her head up to the sky, basking in the snowflakes that drizzled onto her cheeks. Angry clouds rolled overhead.

"Aria!"

Maya was standing on the sidewalk a few feet away, hand frantically rubbing at her own arms to keep warm. Her breath came out in white puffs of steam. Aria pulled Noah down the steps and into the yard, frost crunching under her bare feet. Maya rushed to meet her in the middle as she carefully placed Noah in the grass, rolling him onto his back.

"Oh my God," Maya whimpered, flinging her hands over her mouth.

Aria kneeled down to his level and traced his eyebrows with her finger, brushing stray curls out of his face. He was beautiful, even now.

"Should we close his eyes?" Maya asked.

Aria cupped his cheek with a sigh and shook her head. "No. He always loved looking up at the stars."

Eventually, Aria pulled away from him. She rose to her feet and started toward the woods; Maya rushed after her.

"Wait! Where are you going?"

Aria paused, looking over her shoulder. "You should get in your car and leave this place, Maya. Press the gas pedal, and never turn back, like I should have done years ago."

Glass shattered as the fire in the church broke through the windows on the first floor. Maya flinched with a startled squeal.

"This town breeds nothing but anguish. If I don't end it, the cycle will never stop. Pine Hollow will never be a home for us. Maybe it never was to begin with."

"Aria, what are you going to do?"

A Cheshire grin slipped onto Aria's face. "I'm going to restore balance."

Maya started backing away.

"Just promise me something," Aria added.

"What?"

Aria's smile fell. "Live a life that's truly your own, and make sure my sister does the same."

Maya hesitated, taken aback, but after taking a long look at Aria, she agreed. "I promise."

"Thank you," Aria replied. Whatever she had to do to get through this night didn't matter. All that mattered was Alessa. "Now run."

Aria didn't wait to see if she was leaving before turning her back on Maya and stalking back to the trees. As she submerged herself in the

CHAPTER 34

undergrowth, it felt like coming home.

Chapter 35

Ultimately, it was the cold that woke Alessa. Howling winds whipped at her face, and her body was shifting in a swaying motion that caused her nausea to return tenfold. She clenched her teeth and swallowed the bile back down, trying to breathe through it. Memories came to her in sporadic flashes, the church, Noah's body, her sister strung up on the cross, and being force-fed wine. She tried to open her eyes, but an intense bout of dizziness made her close them again.

"Yet it shall not be so among you; but whoever desires to be great among you, let him be your servant," Father Samuel's voice. Alessa forced herself to remain still, eyes shut. They didn't know she was awake yet, and she wanted to keep it that way.

"And whoever desires to be first among you, let him be your slave—just as the Son of Man did not come to be served, but to serve, and give His life as ransom for many," he continued.

What had they done with Aria? With Maya? Alessa wondered. Were they still alive?

The swaying stopped, as did the sermon. Alessa felt her body being lowered to the ground, the cold and wet from the snow seeping instantly through her clothes. She bit the inside of her cheek to keep from calling out. Footsteps crunched in the frost, getting further away. It was deathly silent for a long few minutes.

"Hear me!" Samuel yelled, his voice bouncing through the trees. "We humbly request your forgiveness for our previous offering! We have failed you and, in turn, have shamed ourselves. This is not who we are!"

The white robes echoed his statement with feverish excitement; Alessa's body broke out in shivers.

"We have brought a new offering, younger and pure. May she serve as our apology. We only wish to make things right, to continue in this partnership that has served us both for so many decades. Please, allow us the grace to atone for our mistakes!"

Silence followed his pleas. Alessa waited, taut and tense, as she awaited the sound of breaking branches, or rustling brush to signal an emergence from the woods. Waiting for whatever was coming for her. Seconds dragged on into minutes, but still nothing.

"Shouldn't we leave her here?" someone asked.

"After Aria's return, I do not wish to risk such a thing happening again," Samuel replied. And so, they continued to wait.

Nothing.

"Please! We wish only to express our contrition. If you express your acceptance, we will be on our way!"

Again, nothing.

Alessa opened one of her eyes just a slit to get a bearing on her surroundings. They were in a clearing; the group forming a semi-circle around her, but they kept their eyes on the trees. If she chose her moment perfectly, while they were distracted, she could make a break for it.

"Why aren't they responding?" someone else questioned, anxiety dripping from every word.

"We did everything we were supposed to!" another one whined.

"Remain calm, everyone," Samuel responded smoothly, "let us pray together, let us lay bare our souls to God so the creatures may know of our honest intent. Bow your heads!"

Now, Alessa thought, the second their eyes were closed, she would run for the trees. Once she was free from the clearing, it would be near impossible for them to catch her. She waited until a wave of mumbling and whispered prayers filled the air before opening her eyes all the way. Alessa noted their inattention, pinpointed where she needed to run, and scrambled to her feet.

Her body, however, was still catching up to her brain after being drugged. Her movements were sluggish and delayed, and her knees wobbled like noodles, but she got to her feet. Alessa broke into a jog, ankles pushing through the growing layer of snow and slowing her down, but she kept her focus on the trees. If she looked back or hesitated, it would all be over. She barely exited the semi-circle before someone yelled.

"She's running!"

"Stop her!"

Alessa made it halfway to the trees before something heavy crashed into her back, slamming her body into the ground. A broken cry escaped her, ice filling her mouth on impact. Alessa tried to get back up, but the person who tackled her was bigger than her and wrangled her flailing arms effortlessly. In seconds, someone wrenched her to her feet, wrists forced behind her back. She spit out snow and screamed.

"HELP ME!"

Pain blossomed in her jaw when a fist knocked her head to the side, shutting her up. She tasted iron when she tongued the corner of her mouth, the entire right side of her face pulsating.

"What in God's name is going on here?" Samuel howled, storming toward her. "She shouldn't be awake in the first place!"

He shot a suspicious glare at Joshua. "You poured her cup, Joshua. What do you have to say for yourself?"

Joshua threw his hands up in defense. "I am so sorry, Father. Truly,

I thought I gave her the right amount. I measured it exactly as Doctor Sutton instructed. I swear to you."

Alessa's eyes darted back and forth between the men. Father Samuel considered his explanation, but Alessa wasn't so sure he believed it.

"Do you swear in the name of our Lord?" he prodded.

"I do, Father," Joshua replied with conviction.

"I suppose it doesn't matter either way." He faced the black robe holding Alessa. "Make sure she can't go anywhere this time."

Every twitch made Alessa's jaw throb, and the black robe dragged her to the nearest tree. A white robe passed him a rope, and they coiled it around her and the trunk. Soon her back was pressed against the bark, it cut through her clothes, pressing into her shoulder blades and spine, the rope chafing her arms. After he was sure she was secure, Father Samuel returned to his beckoning.

"I implore you to hear us!" the priest bellowed to the forest. "Please, all we ask is for you to acknowledge our offering–for your acceptance–and we will leave you be! In God's glorious name, we swear, we swear to gift you only the purest of children, the best of us. We will not fail again!"

The forest, however, was persistent in its silence. Alessa saw a tinge of concern in Samuel's wide eyes. He continued to scan the woods. The disciples were becoming restless, shooting nervous glances at one another and the priest, none of them knowing how to proceed. Roswell and Shirley were among them. Roswell approached Samuel.

"Maybe it's best if we go. You know they don't like to be seen," he stated, and a few of the members mumbled in agreement. Samuel looked at the cop, aghast.

"After what has happened, you would turn your back and allow history to repeat itself? We can't let what happened to Aria happen again. If we make another mistake, you know the Hell that will reign down on us. Do you want to be held responsible for that?"

Roswell didn't look happy about it, but he acquiesced. He turned to the others, raising his hands to calm the crowd. Alessa got the impression he was Samuel's enforcer, maybe even second in command. No one else here was confident enough to approach, let alone look the priest in the eye.

"Everyone let's just relax. Let's give it a little longer. These are extenuating circumstances. We all share the same goal. Let's be patient."

It did little to soothe the crowd, but it stopped the questions for now.

"Remember, brothers and sisters, this is a test of our faith, and what is a test without hurdles to overcome?" the priest rallied his followers, but Alessa saw the way his hands trembled when he wrung them together. He was worried. "Perhaps we should try an alternative approach."

Roswell arched his brow and followed Samuel's gaze to Alessa.

"Bleed her. They'll smell it and come running. It will be impossible to resist then."

Alessa shook her head frantically. Roswell didn't take any convincing. A black robe slipped a knife into his hand, and he was coming.

"No! No, please!" Alessa begged, fighting against the pain in her jaw. Her legs kicking out but only going so far. She tried wriggling and thrashing, but she didn't budge, the ropes keeping her firmly in place. "Please, Roswell! Y-You don't have to do this! You don't!"

He didn't even break his stride, carving a path in the snow, blade reflecting moonlight.

"It will be much easier if you stay still, Alessa," Roswell stated. Alessa released a strangled cry. Father Samuel smiled at them maniacally from several feet away.

"It'll all be over soon."

Alessa came untethered, weeping openly as he drew close enough to hear his breath.

CHAPTER 35

"Please, no, no, NO!"

As Roswell rose his arm, knife in the air, a savage, guttural roar exploded all around them. Birds shot, shrieking from the safety of their nests, and everyone in the clearing froze. Even the wind stopped moving, its howling descending to a mere whisper. The roar shook the ground. They felt it in their bones. It was a horrible sound. Alessa knew it would haunt her for the rest of her days. If she ever made it out of here.

When it finally ceased, a few white robes dropped to the ground, skin going as white as their cloaks as they cried out in terror. Others huddled together, unnerved voices stumbling over top of each other. Alessa caught Roswell's eye. His expression mirrored the terror she felt.

A branch snapped. They all held their breath. The rustling drew closer.

Alessa gasped as Aria emerged from the trees, fully reformed, and healed, arms and legs caked in blood. She approached the group steadily, gliding through the shin-deep snow effortlessly. Yelps of shock and horror peppered the crowd, and the white robes tucked themselves behind their leader. Shirley pulled her gun from her holster, assuming a defensive stance.

There was something off about her, about her face. It was as if someone had created an Aria mask and slipped it over someone else's skeleton, only it didn't exactly fit. And her eyes, Alessa didn't recall them being so big. She didn't recall them being red either.

"What the hell is happening?" Alessa gaped.

Samuel's shock was written all over his face, all pretenses abandoned. He backed away from the approaching girl, nearly tripping over his own robes.

"H-How? How is this possible? You should be dead!"

Aria stopped walking within ten feet of them, a placid expression on her face. Her lack of response only fueled his irritation.

"What is going on? Why are you here?" Samuel erupted, spit flying from his lips, irises rimmed in furious red.

"You're wasting your time, priest," Aria spoke evenly, and the hysterical chatter immediately stopped.

Samuel narrowed his eyes. "What do you mean?"

"It means that they..." Aria stopped herself, tilting her head as if confused, but quickly recovered, "*we*... are no longer interested in your offerings."

The color drained from Samuel's face, a rush of alarm spreading again through his disciples like wildfire. He shook his head, uncomprehending.

"I don't understand. We have a deal, the same deal that's been in place for decades! And we have honored it to the letter!"

"Do I need to remind you what that deal was built on?" Aria countered. "Your ancestors stole our hunting ground to make a home. They invaded a space that didn't belong to them and when we reminded them of the natural order out here, they returned with violence."

Her voice lacked any emotional inflection. The more she spoke, the less it sounded like Aria. Alessa still heard her but layered on top of it was another voice entirely dark and penetrating.

"You were slaughtering our people; we had no choice," Samuel sniped.

"Because you do not belong here!" Aria scowled. "This forest was ours. It was ours long before your ancestors, and it will continue to be long after you."

Another shifting in the brush made the group clamor closer together, first to the South, and then a branch cracking, this time to the West. The white and black robes kept their backs to each other to watch the trees, never knowing where the next noise was going to come from.

"We don't want your offerings; we never really did. At least, not for the reasons you believed."

Ice crunching, dead leaves fluttering, trees creaking. The noises were coming from all around them now. Alessa swore she heard a huff of breath behind her. A rotten stench filled her nose, like decaying flesh, and it wasn't long before it swept the entire clearing. A few people covered their faces, some gagging, while others unloaded barely digested food onto the ground. Roswell abandoned Alessa's side, replacing his knife with his gun as he returned to Shirley.

"We have fulfilled our duty as servants of the Lord. It was God who brought our ancestors to this land, and who showed us how to defeat your kind. And it was God All Mighty who opened the pathway so that our ancestors might come to this agreement, so we may both live on for another day. We have only ever done what is best through His will. Would you deny that you have benefitted from His grace? Would you turn your back on His offering? After all He has provided you with? If it weren't for our Lord and Savior, we would have destroyed each other."

Aria was unmoved by his passionate plea and gave him a pitying smile. Roswell and Shirley carefully raised their weapons, moving within range to land a killing blow if necessary. Alessa noticed her father inching away from the front. He locked eyes with her over a sea of heads. He was creeping toward her.

"Is that what you truly believe? Your ancestors have failed you greatly, priest."

Samuel fumed, a vein throbbing in his temple. "We have done everything you asked! We have given you everything! You have your food, just take it!"

"Oh, little priest. The offerings were never about food," Aria mused, the sounds from the forest growing louder and closer, "they were to fill in for the lives your people took."

She had all of their attention now. A hush fell over the group.

"W-What?" Samuel stammered, barely audible. Aria's lips spread into a wide grin, the corners of her mouth stretching all the way to her ears, and exposing a mouth filled with rows upon rows of pointed teeth.

"Five. That's how many of us your ancestors carved up, burned, and buried. Five. The same number of children you cast out. I think you're smart enough to figure it out, priest."

And just like that, the dam keeping the peace broke. Chaos sent the disciples into a frenzy, some of them sobbing in anguish and regret, while others argued. Shirley briefly lost her footing, gun shaking in her hands, the revelation hitting her square in the gut. Joshua pushed his way through the insanity, shuffling toward Alessa while everyone else was preoccupied. He kept checking over his shoulder to ensure no one was following.

"You're lying," Samuel retorted, confidence waning. Aria scoffed, the whites around her irises turning impossibly black.

"Why don't you ask that God of yours whether I'm lying?"

Heavy footsteps rumbled from the forest, creeping closer. The stench burned Alessa's eyes, but she tried to keep them on her sister. Joshua was halfway to reaching Alessa, his steps hurried. Samuel's face twisted in rabid fury. Aria's mouth opened wide, too wide, her jaw cracking as it unhinged itself. Roswell and Shirley took aim.

"SHOOT HER!" Samuel commanded.

Bullets sliced the air.

Aria lunged.

Chapter 36

Gunfire exploded in the night as Roswell and Shirley unloaded their clips. They struck Aria with a spray of bullets mid-lunge, small holes bursting open all over her body, blood spewing out like confetti. All Hell broke loose, disciples screamed and hit the ground, others scattered, tripping all over each other. It was utter madness. Alessa turned away, unable to watch her sister's frail form convulse like a rag doll with each hit. Amidst the insanity, Joshua charged toward her.

Aria was still standing, even when their guns were empty, and it forced them to reload. Oozing wounds littered her arms and torso, but Aria remained upright and breathing, her lungs rattling. Roswell and Shirley paused as they fished out their extra clips, neither of them daring to move an inch. Shirley's palms were sweating as she reloaded, nearly dropping the bullets on the ground.

Aria smiled, her teeth stained red, and spit a wad of blood onto the pristine snow. She took another step forward, slower now. Roswell lifted his gun again, but Shirley hesitated. Her eyes flew to the wounds as they pulsed, blood clots sliding out as if something was pushing them, until a small, shiny object popped out and allowed the hole to seal completely. Despite the mess, Shirley saw it for what it was: a bullet. Aria's body continued to expel them, bullets sinking into frost every couple of seconds as she approached, skin smoothing itself over.

Shirley instinctively backed away even as Roswell held his stance, but she saw the sweat forming on his temples.

"Put her down," the priest commanded from behind them, their bodies serving as his shield, "KILL HER!"

"Shirley–Shirley!"

She finally snapped out of it, looking at her boss. His face was white as a sheet.

"Aim for the head."

She stared at him, dazed and uncomprehending. He shot her a frustrated glare. "Now!"

They took aim again, Aria was getting closer, almost within arm's reach. Barrels pointed at Aria's head, then fired.

The side of her skull broke open like a pinata, one of their many bullets finally sliding home. Blood and brain matter shimmered in the moonlight. Her eyes rolled back, and Aria hit the ground. Roswell and Shirley watched, ready and waiting, her fingers and toes twitching. The pool of blood around her face expanded. She was down–for now.

Alessa choked back a sob. Her sister looked so fragile from where she was. She willed her to get up, to do anything, but she wasn't moving. Was this really the end? Did Aria survive all of this only to be gunned down? It couldn't be. They'd come so far.

"Joshua? Joshua! What are you doing?!"

Her mother's voice pulled her away. Lily was pushing her way through the frantic crowd, her eyes widening when she saw where Joshua was going. He finally reached Alessa, panting from exertion, and pulled out a small kitchen knife from beneath his robes.

"Dad, what are you doing?"

He didn't reply immediately, instead, he sucked in gulps of icy air and went to work on slicing the rope that kept her bound. "What's going on?" she whimpered.

"I'm sorry," he panted, "I'm so sorry, sweetheart."

CHAPTER 36

"Joshua!" Lily screeched, shoving people out of her way. He didn't skip a beat.

"I never wanted this, I never wanted any of this," he continued to ramble. Joshua was drenched in sweat, the knife almost slipping out of his grasp from his erratic movements. When Alessa looked up again, Lily was halfway to them.

"She's coming... Dad—she's coming!"

"It's going to be okay, Alessa. It's all going to be all right, I promise."

The ropes were falling, one by one. It was becoming easier for Alessa to move. Now she could breathe without her chest aching.

"How could you? HOW DARE YOU?"

Alessa gasped as Lily launched at her husband, throwing herself onto his back as he tried to cut the last of the rope. She pounded on him with her fists wherever she could reach, yanked his hair, and clawed at his face. Joshua grunted and yelped in pain, shoving her off. She was back up without much effort, throwing her body at his, latching on like a spider monkey.

"You did this! This is ALL YOUR FAULT!"

"Mom, stop, please!" Alessa cried. Aria was now on the ground, still unmoving, and the panic had momentarily ceased. Father Samuel regarded his followers, taking notice of her parent's squabble. He mouthed something to his black robes, and they charged. Alessa tried to kick herself the rest of the way free, but it still wasn't loose enough.

Lily raked her nails over her husband's face and tore his hair from the roots. He gritted his teeth, using one arm to bat her off and the other to cut. Joshua was just about there when the black robes descended upon the family. They tackled her father and sent her mother rolling into the dirt. Alessa met Lily's eyes. She looked crazed, her hair a knotted mess, and her fingernails broken and bleeding. She imagined this was what her mother's soul must really look like: haggard, angry, and evil.

One of the executioners wrestled the knife from her father, bending his wrist until it popped. Joshua released a choked howl. They hoisted him aloft and dragged him across the clearing. Father Samuel met them halfway along with Roswell while Shirley watched Aria.

"Dad!" Alessa wailed.

"I want him on his knees," Samuel demanded, his tone sharp as ice. They responded in kind, shoving the battered man into a kneeling position before their leader. Lily scrambled to her feet, smoothing out her frazzled appearance. Alessa's heart shriveled with hatred. Even after all this, people's perception of her was still the one thing she cared about most.

"It's going to be okay, Alessa!" he called back. An executioner railed his fist into Joshua's jaw.

"No, please!"

"Please, Father," Lily sniveled, "I had nothing to do with this. I would never betray our cause. Please have mercy on me!" She fell to her knees and lifted her hands in prayer. "My husband's sins are his alone."

Samuel considered her. Lily let out a harsh sigh of relief when he placed a hand on her shoulder and said, "I believe you."

Lily shuffled away when he released her, and he turned his attention back to Joshua.

"What do you have to say for yourself?" Samuel questioned.

Joshua chuckled. "Fuck you."

Another fist slammed into the other side of his jaw, tearing another cry from Alessa as his head whipped to the side. Blood filled his mouth and was dripping down his chin, but he rose his head to face the priest anyway.

"I want to hear you say it. Why you've chosen to betray everything we stand for, everything our ancestors stood for! Everything we have done has been for the greater good, to protect our families and our town. Without us, there would be nothing left."

"It was wrong," Joshua said.

"It is God's will! As long as we walk in his footsteps, we cannot be wrong!"

Joshua shook his head, frowning with both disdain and pity at the old man. "God's will isn't worth the lives of my daughters."

Samuel held the man's eyes with a glower of disgust and sighed. "Fine. It appears you've made up your mind." Joshua remained stoic.

At the flick of Samuel's wrist, Roswell stepped forward, gun in hand. "Is there anything else you'd like to say before you face judgment, Mister Hale?"

Roswell brought the barrel of his gun to Joshua's forehead, the cold metal kissing his skin. Alessa thrashed against the last of the rope; she wriggled one of her arms out, and then the other. Joshua smiled serenely and closed his eyes.

"Dad – DAD!"

"I love you girls! And I'm sorr – !"

BANG. Alessa's scream died in her throat as Roswell pulled the trigger and sent her father's brain splattered across the snow. The back of his head cracked open like a melon and his body crumpled, leaving him facing Alessa with that smile forever frozen on his face. Alessa slumped against the tree in defeat, her body, her mind, and her soul all going numb. He was gone.

Roswell nudged Joshua with his foot, satisfied when there was no response. He nodded to the priest in confirmation.

"What should we do with her, Father?" Roswell asked, tilting his head at Alessa.

"She can't be allowed to leave knowing what she knows."

Roswell required no further explanation, and Alessa didn't fight it when he stalked toward her, readying for the kill. She had nothing left. Everything she had known and loved was gone. It didn't matter anymore. It gave her a little comfort to think of her dad waiting on the other side for her.

"HELP!"

A distant wail from beyond the trees made everyone stop short and listen. Roswell stopped within arm's reach of Alessa and, like the others, searched the forest for the source. All of the disciples were still accounted for, and the sound was from too far away to belong to any of them.

"HELP ME!" it rang out again, the same voice.

Alessa heard Roswell mutter near her, "What the fuck?"

"HELP!" an unfamiliar voice this time, and while the first sounded feminine, this one was undoubtedly male. It was impossible to tell what direction it was coming from.

"Can anyone hear me? Please, help me!" the male continued. One of the white robes that Alessa recognized as the manager of their local grocery store, Melissa Singer, jerked to attention.

"Oh my God, that's Thomas!"

Thomas Singer? Alessa's mind whirled. He was the guy who went missing with his wife while walking their dog a few days ago, the one their parents asked them about.

"HELP!" he cried desperately; his voice was all around them.

"Thomas!" Thomas' sister bellowed.

The feminine voice returned. Followed by another and then another, all different, all familiar, and all of them begging for help. Father Samuel stood in the center of it all, bewildered at not knowing which way to turn. His followers scattered, searching the woods for signs of life, signs of their loved ones who called out to them from the dark.

Ruth, the woman who always turned her nose up at the mention of Aria's name, hobbled toward the trees. "Gloria?"

"Ruth, please help me!" an old voice crooned back.

"Oh, Gloria…"

"Everyone remain calm!" Samuel said, trying to rally them together once more, but no one heard him.

"Oh God, please help us! PLEASE HELP US PLEASE HELP US PLEASE HELP!"

Their cries descended on them in an avalanche until they could hear nothing else. Disciples screamed in horror, covering their eyes, and tearing out their own hair.

"Listen! Listen to me! We mustn't panic!" Samuel yelled, words falling on deaf ears.

That was when the first person darted into the forest, one of the owners of the Cupcake Corner. Shoving his wife to the side, he abandoned the flock and plunged into the trees. She followed seconds later.

"No! Stop! It's a trick!"

They no longer heard him.

The cries for help continued, and other disciples followed the couple's lead, racing into the forest to rescue their loved ones. All at once, the screaming stopped, leaving behind only the crashing of snow and bramble under sprinting feet as the followers searched.

And then the real screaming began. Splitting shrieks of terror and agony, skin tearing, and bones snapping mixed with gnashing teeth and guttural snarls. Madness swept the remaining flock. A few collapsed, weeping, in prayer, while others took to the woods, hoping against all hope that they'd be the ones to make it through, only to have their screams of pain join the rest. Father Samuel hurriedly backed into the center of the clearing, putting as much distance between himself and the trees as possible. Roswell looked between Alessa and his gun, unsure of how to proceed.

"Father! Father?" Shirley called to no response. "Fuck—Roswell!"

Alessa traced Roswell's gaze back to Shirley. She was still standing in the same spot, gun lifted halfway. Aria's back was arching entirely off the ground, arms and legs jerking wildly, and mouth gaping open in a silent scream. Roswell took off toward them.

Shirley tried to lift her gun higher, but her arms were shaking so violently it was difficult to keep aim. Aria jolted to her feet, her movements strange and disjointed. She looked like a puppet getting used to its strings. Her head lolled to the side, eyes burning like crimson embers in black pits. The red, wet tissue of Aria's brain reformed, and the part of her skull that was blasted open curved back into place, resealing with a series of clicks.

"Dear God..." Shirley gasped.

As the skin healed over the rest of her injury, Aria lumbered forward.

"Shirley!" Roswell called, still running.

Shirley stood there, motionless as Aria drew closer, weapon still trembling in her sweaty hands. She made no move to raise it even when Aria reached her, wrapping her spindly, clawed fingers around Shirley's throat. Terror-stricken, she dropped her gun, hot urine running down her leg as Aria brought them face to face and then tossed her easily to the side.

Alessa's eyes widened, and she watched Shirley get tossed into the air, landing with a wet smack several feet away before skidding to a halt. She rolled onto her back, groaning. Roswell was gaining on them.

"Aria!" Alessa tried to warn her, but as soon as Roswell was close enough to take aim, she was on him, overcoming their distance in two great strides. She was too quick for him to get a shot off, immediately clawing at his clothes and face. Her nails sliced through his skin like tissue paper, and he smacked the side of her head with the butt of his weapon.

Alessa resumed her struggle to escape, her now free arms working at the last of the rope. Her fingers were raw when she finally pulled the last knot loose and pushed herself off the tree. She lost her balance and fell into the snow, the last bits of the drug still working through her system. Alessa paused to catch her breath.

Her heart lurched when a shadow moved in the corner of her eye, and a man stepped out from under the cover of the trees. He was nude and strikingly thin, his skeletal figure resembling her sister's, and his eyes matched Aria's as well. He walked, steady and purposeful, toward the chaos. Alessa inched forward, remaining low to the ground so as not to draw attention, when a nude woman emerged from the forest next.

Alessa recognized her immediately as Constance Peterson, miraculously looking like she hadn't aged a day since she went missing. She shared the same gaunt frame and simmering eyes as the others. Alessa stopped dead, afraid if she went any further, they would catch her in their sights.

Roswell rammed the steel toe of his boot into Aria's shin, but she barely flinched. His arm reeled back, ready to land another blow to her head, but she snatched his wrist in a crushing grip. Using her leverage, she tugged him forward with ease, their noses nearly brushing. She sliced her talons across his stomach, tearing it open and sending blood spraying, and plunged her hand wrist-deep into the wound.

His body seized up, and he lost grip of his gun. Aria wrapped her fingers around his innards and squeezed. His mouth flew open, but all that emerged was a sputtering of blood and a garbled whimper. She held his gaze and pulled. Hot bile spewed from Alessa's throat as she watched Aria yank his organs from his stomach, squishing his entrails like putty in her hand. She held his chin in place, forcing him to look at her until his eyes went hazy and the last of him came spilling out. Aria tossed him aside.

The few remaining disciples scattered, any hope of forming a unified front having abandoned their thoughts long ago. The ones who edged too close to the trees unleashed shrieks of terror as gnarled hands grabbed them and dragged them into the dark. Those who noticed their naked visitors did all they could to avoid getting too close to them. There were four of them now. Two girls and two guys, all of them looking to be close in age. One of them, a dark-skinned boy with a shaved head and a familiar face, trudged in Shirley's direction. Father Samuel stood in the center of it all, turning in constant circles and looking over his shoulder, looking completely and utterly lost.

Aria stepped over the now motionless police chief and set her sights on her next target, Lily. Their mother was still on the ground and began shuffling away when she noticed Aria walking toward her. She fumbled through the snow, tripping over her robes to get away, but she wasn't fast enough. Aria slowed when she found Joshua's body, examining it with an expression Alessa couldn't decipher. She kneeled down and, with a surprisingly tender touch, closed their father's eyes before resuming her hunt. In seconds she was standing over their mother, the woman still trying and failing to crawl her way through the snow. Aria circled her, a predator homing in on its prey. Lily made herself as small as possible, palms rising in surrender. Her body quivered, now soaking wet.

"You don't have to do this, sweetheart," Lily blubbered, "we can fix this!"

Aria continued to circle her methodically. Alessa watched from a few feet away.

"Please, Aria! I'm your mother. You know I only want what's best for you and Alessa. I always have! This was the only way to keep us safe. All of us," Lily babbled.

"Didn't you know, Mom? All I ever wanted was to make you proud," she replied in that icy, layered voice. She came to a stop in front of their mother. "I spent so many years trying, just wanting you to see me, to know I was worth something. All my life, I thought I was a mistake. A burden. A failure. But really, you were just preparing yourself for what was coming. There was no point being invested in me if I wasn't going to be here forever."

She stepped closer to Lily, forcing the woman to arch her neck to keep eye contact with her.

"I did the best that I could," Lily whined, "you don't know what it's like, the responsibility and the pressure!" She stopped short when Aria shushed her, placing an icy finger against her mother's lips.

"After all those years of trying, it finally sank in that my efforts were for nothing. You are who you are. I could have never changed that," Aria said, the jagged claw on her thumb tracing their mother's delicate jaw. "After everything that happened, after everything you did... in those last moments, the last time that I was... *me*, all I wanted was my mom."

The last bits of color seeped from Lily's face, and before she uttered another word, Aria stomped on her knee, shattering the bone with a nauseating, wet crunch. Lily's shriek of agony caused goosebumps to erupt across Alessa's flesh, but she hated to admit the satisfaction she found in watching her sister finally get the revenge she deserved. Finally, Lily would experience a fraction of the pain she'd caused her children. Even when Aria grabbed Lily's arm and snapped it over her knee, Alessa stayed silent and remained still as Aria rendered Lily's other arm and leg useless.

Lily was no longer screaming by the time Aria was done, and she'd devolved into a mess of groaning sobs. Aria silenced those next as the crack of her fist crushed Lily's windpipe. The woman wheezed, writhing on the ground, her legs and arms flopping worthlessly. Aria dragged her through the snow and propped her sitting up against a tree near Alessa.

Alessa scanned the clearing again. There were barely any white robes left, and only one black robe. Distant echoes of terror still resounded from the forest. Trails of blood streaked the snow, leading to the trees. A much closer scream brought her to Shirley, who was lying on her back, weapon long forgotten, the nude man towering over her. At this angle, Alessa had a better view of his face, and she finally realized. Dominic. She turned away just as he threw himself upon her, teeth shredding her neck.

Aria leaned Lily's head against the tree trunk. Tears slipped down the woman's cheeks.

"Starving to death is a slow process. It's not days, it drags on for weeks," Aria said, a clinical coldness in her tone. "First, you'll feel the hunger pangs. They're not so bad at first. You'll be able to ignore it for a while, but eventually, it will become... everything. It'll be excruciating, unbearable. It'll take over your mind. Time will cease to matter. Nothing will matter but the hunger. Maybe you'll be lucky, and the animals will take you first. Either way, you'll be begging for the end long before it comes."

Aria stood, surveyed the clearing, and then looked to Alessa; she sucked in a surprised breath. It was strange being examined by those eyes, the eyes that shouldn't belong to her sister, and yet somehow did. She wasn't sure if she was looking at Aria or something else. Could it be both?

"Is it you?" Alessa stuttered.

A small, barely noticeable smile rose on Aria's lips. "Everything's going to be okay, Squirt. It's almost over."

At that moment, Alessa knew her sister was still in there. The rest was background noise.

"Oh, God! Oh, my Lord, forgive me!" The girls followed the sound, finding Father Samuel mewling in the snow, eyes to the heavens. "I am your loyal servant, and I have lived my life by your word! Please, show mercy!"

Alessa pushed herself to her feet, still shaky, but she kept her balance. She wasn't quick enough to keep up with Aria, who was hustling toward the fallen priest. The four visitors lingered nearby, and none

CHAPTER 36

of them seemed to pay Alessa any mind as she staggered sluggishly along. They too were watching Aria. There were no more screams coming from the woods. The glade was deathly quiet.

"Heavenly Father, please hear me! I have trusted in you, always. I've never questioned you. Grant me safety from harm and I will never again fail you. I swear on my mortal soul, I am yours to command!"

"Tell me," Aria interrupted him, "all these years you've pleaded for your God. Has He ever responded?"

Samuel flinched away when she got closer, pressing his chin to his chest as he continued his prayers. Aria smirked.

"Lord, protect me from evil. Surround me in your divine light! Lend me your strength!"

Aria kneeled to his eye level, but he kept his head low. "Do you want to know the truth?" she asked; he cracked one eye open. "About your ancestors. The real source of their knowledge."

Samuel didn't reply, still muttering prayers under his breath, but he didn't look away either.

"They wanted you to believe it was God's plan. It was easier that way. No one would listen if they knew what really happened—that God's great and powerful visions were a hoax."

"Lying demon!" Samuel raged; Aria's smirk widened.

"In their desperation, your ancestors went searching—hunting for answers. They found others, humans who'd passed through our home long before they did, humans who knew better. They warned your ancestors to leave and insisted it was the only way. Your people didn't like that very much. So, they did what they always do—they took what they needed with force."

A wad of saliva slapped her cheek, accompanied by another growl of protest from the priest. She swiped it away with the back of her hand, unphased. He barreled on with his prayers, louder this time, trying to drown her out.

"I know you hear me, priest!" Aria goaded him. "God didn't grant them the knowledge they desired. There were no visions. The answers they sought came from the mouths of screaming humans as your ancestors bled them dry!"

"I will say of the Lord, he is my refuge and my fortress, my God in whom I trust!" Samuel was yelling now, words blending together. "My Lord, be my shield and my rampart! I choose to walk and live under the protection of you, my God!"

"GOD'S NOT HERE!" Aria screamed, pointed teeth snapping within an inch of his face. He cowered beneath her.

She leaned in close and hissed, "He never was."

As Samuel parted his lips to speak, she snatched his jaw, holding it open as her other hand plunged inside his mouth. Samuel jerked and twitched, his throat pulsing as he tried to breathe, and his eyes rolling into the back of his head. In a sharp, swift motion, Aria grabbed his tongue and pulled.

A sickening gurgle bubbled in Samuel's chest as she ripped the slick muscle from his throat. Blood and webs of pink tissue splattered across the snow. Alessa steadied herself, the universe tilting as Aria lifted the tongue above her head. Her jaw opened wide again, fangs glinting white, and she dropped the tongue into her mouth. It made a popping sound as she chewed, her teeth shredding the muscle as if it were tissue paper. Alessa tried not to hurl again. Samuel's cries became a horrible wailing that reminded Alessa of a dying animal.

The last bits of tongue slid down Aria's gullet, and she released a contented sigh. Samuel tried to stifle the flow of blood by clamping his hands over his ruined mouth. Aria licked her lips. When she looked back at Alessa, it was with a small, sad smile. There was a wrongness to her face. The muscles were shifting, like bugs were skittering underneath her skin, and her eyes seemed to take up half her face now. Alessa wasn't sure if she should move toward her sister or away.

CHAPTER 36

"You should run, Alessa. Get far away from here," she said, but Alessa didn't move. She wasn't going to abandon her, not when they'd come so far. Aria's smile faltered; the flesh of her arms rippled.

"At least... close your eyes..." she continued.

Alessa raised her hands to shield her eyes. Her stomach was in knots, a million thoughts darting in her head all at once. She couldn't help but flinch when she heard the first growl. She pressed her palms hard enough into her closed eyes to see spots of color burst against her eyelids. A drop of cold sweat slid down her spine.

It started with growling, her sister's voice becoming less like her own, and deepening into a rumbling bass that made Alessa's bones shake. Then came the cracking, like large branches being snapped in two, followed by a series of wet pops. Alessa couldn't resist her curiosity and opened her eye to peer through the gaps in her fingers.

She saw it in flashes, the way Aria's body transformed. Arms and legs stretching. Claws and teeth extending. Sharp bones that protruded from her joints like jagged, white growths. Ravenous red eyes. A skeletal, hairless beast wrapped in desiccated flesh.

Alessa broke out into a sprint when the beast roared, heading for the trees. As she reached the edge of the glade, she looked over her shoulder one last time to see the creature that was once her sister sinking her teeth into Father Samuel's neck. Clenching her fists, she turned back to the forest and took off.

Chapter 37

Alessa darted as fast as her legs would carry her, bobbing and weaving between trees, avoiding brambles and stray branches. She didn't stop; she didn't turn back. Her chest burned with every breath, cramps smarting her sides, but still she pushed forward. Every time an image of Aria's body twisting, and mutating popped into her head, it spurred her on, reminding her of what could happen if she hesitated.

She let out a sigh of relief when the trees parted, and she stumbled out of the undergrowth. Alessa landed on a long, thin stretch of road, the only one that led in and out of Pine Hollow. On either side of the street, the forest stood, waiting. Alessa spun around, unsure of which way to turn, and not knowing whether going back into town was the safest idea. A pair of blinding headlights crested the horizon; Alessa shielded her eyes. She heard a distant rumbling and the squeaking of old tires. Alessa lowered her arm as the car rolled to a gradual stop.

"Alessa?!"

A figure draped in shadow stepped out of the parked car and rushed forward into the light. It illuminated a head of dark curls; Maya. They stared at one another in disbelief.

"Oh my God, you're alive," Maya said, sniffling, "are you okay? Are you hurt?"

Alessa didn't waste another moment and ran to her. In that moment all else was forgotten. The only thing Alessa cared about right now was Maya. They met in the middle, throwing their arms around each other in a crushing embrace. Alessa cupped Maya's cheeks, adrenaline pumping in her veins, and pressed their lips together. Maya froze at first, lips going still and Alessa nearly pulled away, but when she tried, Maya grabbed her face and pulled her in for more. It was messy, and wet from their tears, but to Alessa, it was everything she'd imagined and more.

Alessa was breathless when they parted, her heart doing somersaults. Maya blinked at her eyes wide and smiling in bewilderment.

"I always thought I'd be the one to make the first move," she said, pulling a chuckle from both of them. Maya's smile fell.

"What happened? Where's Aria? Last I saw her, she was looking for you."

Alessa shuddered, the memories rushing back to her. "Th-They're all dead... Father Samuel... Roswell..." She paled as the carnage replayed in her mind.

"And Aria?"

"I saw her... she... she was..." Alessa couldn't finish the thought, didn't even know where to begin. How was she supposed to tell Maya what she'd seen tonight, what her sister had become? All she knew for certain was her life would never be the same. She shook her head helplessly; Maya took her hand.

"Okay, okay. It's all right. Come on, we need to get out of here."

Maya pulled Alessa toward her car but stopped in her tracks when a figure stepped out of the trees and into the middle of the street. A rail-thin body. A flash of red hair.

"Aria?" Alessa whispered.

As they came closer to the car, Alessa noticed how she'd changed. Aria was naked now, but she was cloaked head to toe in blood. Her irises shimmered gold. She was Aria again. Alessa's hand slipped out of Maya's as she rushed to her sister.

"You're back!" she exclaimed, eyes stinging with newly formed tears. Alessa stopped short before touching Aria. "Are you... are you okay?"

Aria held her smile, but it did not reach her eyes. Alessa's brain was scrambled. She didn't know what to do or say. Even now, knowing everything she knew, it still didn't feel completely real. But her sister was here, alive, and safe, and that was all she'd wanted. Finally, they had a real chance at putting all of this behind them.

"I'm so sorry for what they did to you. I'm sorry I said no when you asked me to leave all those months ago. I didn't see before that something was wrong," Alessa rambled, wracked with shame. If she had only listened. If she had just paid attention when Aria was struggling, maybe none of this would have happened.

"There's nothing you could have done to change it," Aria's layered voice replied.

"No! If I listened to you–if we'd just gotten in the car like you said, drove away, and never looked back - you would have been safe!"

"It's over now, Alessa. You made it out."

Alessa started at this, brows narrowing in confusion. "No, Ari, we made it out! Like you said, it's over! They're all gone now–Father Samuel is gone! We can finally leave, we can start fresh, just like you wanted!"

Alessa's heart sank when Aria said nothing, still wearing that damned smile. The tears came, unimpeded, and she swallowed a cry that was rising in her throat. Alessa grabbed Aria's wrist and tried to pull, but the girl didn't budge an inch.

"Come on, Ari, we need to go! It's okay now!"

Aria shook her head. A desperate sob escaped Alessa, and she pulled harder. Still nothing.

"Please, Ari! Please!"

"You know I can't do that, Squirt," Aria murmured.

"No!" Alessa barked. "No, I can't lose you again, Ari. I can't! Just come with us! We can figure this out!"

Aria held firm. "I'm sorry, Alessa."

"Why not?" Alessa demanded, barely tugging on Aria's arm now, her energy fading.

"Alessa, you know what I am, what I... we need to survive. I don't belong out there anymore," she calmly explained, but Alessa swore she heard a twinge of regret in her tone.

"You can't ask me to leave you here."

"There's nothing out there for me, Alessa." Aria glanced down at her stomach, placing her palm over it. "I'm not Aria, anymore. Not as you knew her to be. I feel her inside of me still, like a whisper, but just as all humans eventually do... the remnants of her will fade away. And when that day comes, nothing human will be left."

Alessa didn't want to believe the sister she loved, the one she'd fought for so long trying to bring back, was lost to her. Beneath the placid smile and the empty eyes, Alessa saw glimmers of her. Aria was still in there, but for how long? She thought back to the beast with its maw around Samuel's neck. Was Alessa condemning others to a similar fate by insisting Aria come with them?

Aria gestured to the forest. "This is where I belong now."

To her core, Alessa knew Aria was right, but she refused to admit it. "All you've ever wanted was to get out of Pine Hollow... to see the world. You're really going to give all of that up?"

"You'll just have to see it all for me, Squirt."

Reality finally sank in as Aria said these words, and Alessa understood that if she was going to leave this place, it was going to be without her sister. Alessa wept openly, an unbearable ache unfurling from the center of her chest.

"Promise me something."

Alessa paused, gazing up at her sister through bleary eyes. "O-Of course."

"When you think of me... remember me as I was before. Not like this."

Alessa stared at her sister, at the otherworldly being she'd become; a stunning monster decorated in the remains of those who created her. Icy wind chilled the tears on her cheeks. Hundreds of images of a life unlived cluttered Alessa's brain. She saw a smiling Aria with a camera around her neck and wearing a college sweater. She saw her with windswept hair, running down and beach and kicking sand into the air.

The fractured reel of Aria's imagined life played in Alessa's mind's eye like a film. In one scene, Aria was standing at her side as Alessa got married. In another, she was with Noah, stupidly and blissfully happy, neither of them knowing pain. She watched as her sister lived her life, as she aged, as she loved, and she was happy.

"Alessa."

The film reel crackled, curling at the edges until the pictures turned black and warped. A beautiful future reduced to ash. Alessa finally saw Aria, not as the beautiful and untouched figure of her dreams, but as she truly was. It was exactly as Aria said; she was no longer the girl Alessa knew. Those monsters led that girl into the cold, and the dark, to die. What came out of the woods was something else. Something the rest of the world wasn't ready for.

Aria's chance at a normal life was over the moment her head hit the pillow that night. Perhaps, Alessa thought, it was stolen from her the moment she'd been born to Joshua and Lily Hale.

Alessa felt this new reality dragging her into the core of the earth, because it was then that the truth officially settled in. She and Aria could no longer co-exist in the same world.

"Please," Aria pleaded, her voice a hair above a tremor. Alessa watched the remnants of her sister struggle against the bestial instincts that pumped like electricity in her veins. Soon, what little remained of the human Aria would be gone forever. Alessa knew Aria wouldn't want her to witness it, as the last traces of her sister's light faded from her eyes. Even if Alessa tried, she knew she'd never recover after seeing that.

"I promise," she stated.

Alessa tossed herself at Aria, her arms wrapping around her bony frame. At first, Aria did nothing, her arms dangling awkwardly at her sides. Alessa cared not for the blood that slid from Aria's skin and stained her clothes. She pressed her damp face deep into the crook of Aria's neck, and while choking down the heady stench of blood, she allowed herself to breathe her sister in. One last time. Eventually, she felt the weight of Aria's hands on her back as she finally returned to the embrace.

"I love you, Aria. I'm so sorry," she sniveled, the pain in her chest engulfing her entire being. Aria tightened her grip around Alessa.

"I love you, Squirt," Aria whispered back. "You've always been the best thing in my life. Never forget that."

Alessa trembled under the force of her sobs, never wanting to let go, wanting to live here forever so long as it meant being with Aria for a few more seconds. She resisted when Aria pulled away.

"It's time for you to go," Aria said as she took a step back. Alessa's arms fell limp as her sister's hands slipped out of hers. All of it slipping away.

Maya appeared at her side, arms going around her to keep her afloat. "Come on, Alessa."

Alessa scanned her sister's face, committing every detail to memory, from the slope of her smile to the way her hair fluttered in the breeze. Her incredible, beautiful, hilarious older sister. She and Maya began backing up to the car. Alessa thought she saw tears in Aria's eyes. Or maybe it was a trick of the light.

"Take care of each other, okay?" Aria said. Maya nodded in fervent agreement.

Alessa stopped when she felt the cold metal of the car press into her back. Maya opened the passenger side door for her. Alessa lingered until Aria's lips curled into a bright smile, a true, Aria smile. Maya gave her an encouraging nudge and she sank into the car; the door slamming behind her.

Maya piled in after her, cranking the heat as high as it would go. She put the car in drive but hesitated before pressing on the gas. Maya glanced at Alessa, who was staring straight ahead at the empty stretch of road before them. She reached over and grabbed Alessa's freezing hand. Alessa looked at her and, after a silent moment, squeezed Maya's hand in return. Maya took it as her cue, and they were off to a slow roll.

Night looming overhead, they began their long trek away from Pine Hollow, no plans on where to stop, or what to do. Only a dark road and an uncertain future ahead. Alessa took one last look in the rearview mirror and observed the tiny figure of her sister getting smaller in the distance until eventually she was gone from sight.

Alessa squeezed Maya's hand again, leaned back, and closed her eyes, readying herself for whatever came next.

Epilogue

Many Decades Later...

The road leading into Pine Hollow looked the same as it did when she was sixteen. One long winding path flanked by towering trees. It was like being in another world. It was hard to believe that she grew up here. The closer he got to her hometown, the harder her stomach clenched. She couldn't remember the last time she'd been this nervous.

Maya adjusted the rearview mirror of her minivan, catching her reflection. The years had been good to her, physically, at least in her opinion. She was definitely not the spry young ball of energy she was when she left this place; her face was carved with new wrinkles almost every day. Her once-tight body had rounded out with age, sagging here, and stretching there, not to mention the near-constant ache of her old bones, but she wore her age with pride. There was a time once when Maya thought she would never see beyond high school, when these years were almost stolen from her. She was grateful for every single minute of it.

The tires squeaked as the car came to a stop on the side of the narrow road, silently thanking whoever invented the heated seat she reached for the map sitting in her passenger seat. She unfolded it, triple checking her notes, and muttered confirmations to herself. Maya zipped up her winter coat, pulling it snug around her, and tightened the strings of her boots. Frost and mud squelched under her feet when she stepped out of the car and grabbed her backpack from the trunk, hoisting it over her weary shoulders. She paused when she reached the passenger side and took a long breath, steadying herself.

No turning back now. Maya swung the door open and smiled at the urn resting on the seat. It was simple and silver, with a design etched around the base and just below the lid. She had latched the seatbelt around the urn to keep it from moving.

"We made it, Alessa," she said and leaned over to unhook it. Maya tucked the urn into the crook of her arm like a small child and brushed a bit of dust off the top. "Shall we?"

Maya followed the notes on her map through the woods, following them with careful precision. She only needed to stop and reorient herself once, her thick scarf protecting her from the stinging breeze. After about thirty minutes of walking, she exited through a break in the trees, which opened up into a large glade. The same glade they took Aria and Alessa to all those years ago. To this day, it remained untouched. The town, Maya understood, had not been so lucky.

After that night, after the end, Pine Hollow slowly fell apart. The carnage did not stop in this clearing, and it did not end with those who occupied their church. The beasts finished what they started, slowly and methodically, until Pine Hollow turned into a ghost town. Some ran, abandoning their homes overnight, others were lost in the woods. Last she heard; it was still empty. The beasts had taken their hunting ground back, just like they always wanted.

Maya walked out into the middle of the clearing and let the wind dance over her cheeks. She breathed in the natural air, the scent of the forest. Maya missed it more than she'd realized. She watched the trees, waiting, hearing nothing but the chittering of wildlife.

"I told her this was going to be strange," Maya began, face flushing,

EPILOGUE

"it took all I had to come back here. I thought I was going to have a heart attack and crash the car on the way. I had to pull over a few times and catch my breath. But I had to, I had to see it through... for her." She gestured to the urn.

Maya felt ridiculous, talking to no one, but she made a promise. She tried to picture who she was talking to, her old mind sifting through watery memories. Maya imagined a young girl with freckled skin and red hair. Maybe she was listening, maybe she was long gone. It didn't matter. Maya wasn't turning back now; she would see this through to the end.

"I know you never wanted us to come back here, but considering all the promises Alessa made you, I figured it was okay to break one, just this one time," she continued, wearing a soft smile. "She wanted to come back as soon as we left you. She didn't say it... not at first... but I could tell. Leaving you behind was the hardest thing she ever had to do."

Maya inhaled a trembling breath, the emotions bubbling up inside of her. Every time she thought she had them under control, that there was nothing left to unleash, they came rushing back. She placed a delicate, loving hand on the top of the urn.

"We stayed together, despite what everyone else thought. We made a life outside of Pine Hollow, a real life, a wonderful life. That never would have happened without you, Aria. I should have thanked you all those years ago. So, I'm thanking you now. For all of it. For everything.

"It wasn't always easy. There were times when both of us thought we weren't going to make it, times when we pushed each other away. But we always came back. No one else could ever understand what we'd been through. Even when it felt impossible, we always made it work."

Maya startled when a twig splintered in the distance. She looked around again, searching the tree line and listening, but nothing emerged.

"I just wanted you to know that Alessa had an amazing life, filled with so much light and love. She made friends, she traveled all over the world, and she was happy. And she loved you until the very end. No matter what, when she spoke about you, it was always to sing your praises."

A feeble chuckle escaped her as she held the urn tight against her heart. Maya carefully unscrewed the top, placing it in her coat pocket.

"She wanted to be here with you... when it was all over. That's what she made me promise." Tears filled Maya's eyes, dripping onto the urn. "The rest of her is spread at the beach, in the ocean. She was always talking about how much you wanted to go to the sea."

Maya dipped her hand inside the urn and plastic packaging, her fingers brushing ash. A fist clenched around her heart. Even though she'd done this already, it still wasn't easy. She took a trembling handful of Alessa's ashes and lifted them to the sky, and as she opened her fingers, let the winter wind blow them away. She repeated the motion a few more times until she was down to the last handful. Maya held it close to her chest for a long, agonizing moment as she said her silent goodbye, and then let the wind take the rest of her.

"Thank you, Aria," Maya whispered, at last, a warm feeling of contentment washing over her. It was done.

Maya went back the way she came, wiping the tears from her cheeks. She only took a few steps past the tree line when she felt it, a ripple of energy shifting in the air. Maya turned slowly, holding her breath.

There, in the center of the clearing, she stood. Aria, looking not a day older than she had the night they left. She tilted her face toward the sky, but Maya couldn't make out her expression. She watched as the breeze lifted Alessa's ashes to dance around Aria's head. Aria raised her hand as if to touch them.

A smile curled onto Maya's lips, and she backed away without

EPILOGUE

another word, disappearing into the woods and whispering her final farewell as the Hale sisters reunited one last time.

Acknowledgement

First and foremost, I want to thank my parents, Mari Richardson, and Michael Drury. Ever since I was a child, you have both consistently encouraged me to chase my dreams and do what makes me happy. You've always supported me, whether it is when I need financial help, or when I just need to vent to someone. If I didn't have you two in my corner, I'm not sure I'd have ever finished this book. Thank you ... for everything.

I also want to thank my husband, Matt Cooley, my number one fan, and the love of my life. Thanks to your belief in me, I was able to believe in myself. You have always had my back, and even when I was at my lowest, you saw the best in me. Thank you for listening to me as I rambled about my ideas, and for talking through creative blocks with me. Thank you for celebrating all my achievements, no matter how small. And more than anything, thank you for loving me and for giving me the chance to love you.

Thank you immensely to my Author Coach Christina Kaye of Book Boss Academy. Working with you truly brought my book to the next level, and because of you, the process of bringing this book to life has gone better than I ever could have foreseen. You are an absolute wealth of information and knowledge, not to mention you are a delight to work with. Thank you for helping me prepare in ways I never knew I needed to, so I could start my author career off right. Thank you to your editing team for their weeks of diligent work, I know they had a very wordy manuscript on their hands. I deeply appreciate all your advice and will be forever grateful for all the work you have put in to help make this book happen.

A huge thank you to Marisa Wesley of Cover Me Darling for her amazing work on my cover. You brought my vision to life. Thank you for all your hard work, and for always being communicative, and genuinely lovely to work with.

I want to also acknowledge my dear friend Christina Kishpaugh. Our weekly writing nights kept me on track. Thank you for cheering me on, having creative discussions with me, and helping me work through any and all writing dilemmas. Your friendship is magic, and I will always be grateful for it.

Thank you to my friends and followers on #BookTok. Returning to the book community via TikTok during the pandemic brought me to this moment. It reignited my love of books and writing, and it exposed me to an incredible community full of talented, intelligent, and unbelievable people. If I hadn't become involved in #BookTok, I don't know that I would have ever reached this point.

About the Author

Sarah Cooley is a horror author from Norfolk, Virginia. Her fascination for the genre started as early as elementary school when she spent countless weekends perusing the aisles at Blockbuster and reading the back of every horror DVD even though she was too afraid to watch them. The only thing to rival her love for horror is her passion for writing, and as a child, she even wrote poetry books for her parents.

Sarah is an avid member of the TikTok book community. Her down time is spent curled up in her book nook, and desperately trying to catch up on her TBR list. Presently, she lives in Los Angeles with her husband; and their black cat, Lilith.

You can learn more about Sarah by visiting her website https://author sarahcooley.com/ and you can follow her on all social media platforms under the handle @authorsarahcooley.

Made in the USA
Monee, IL
29 July 2023

40089107R00223